MARKED FOR DEATH

"What if we went to the police and we didn't tell them anything about what happened with Rachel?" Brynn asks carefully. "What if we just told them what's going on now and that somebody is obviously threatening us?"

"How long do you think it's going to take them to figure out that what's going on now has something to do with something that happened in the past?" Fiona asks. "Specifically when we were in college?"

"If Cassie would just call us back . . . You did leave her a message on her cell phone voice mail, right?"

"Three. Cassie said she was going to take off, remember?" Fiona goes on. "And she told Alec the same thing."

"That doesn't mean she's safe."

"No, but we both know there's no reason for us to start panicking until we know for sure something's happened to—"

"Stop!" Brynn holds up a hand to cut her off. "Don't even say it."

Brynn hugs herself, still quaking from her latest bout with nausea, which has everything to do with what she found inside the parcel left by her front door.

There was an identical one at Fiona's door.

Both packages contained framed copies of their sorority composite picture from ten years ago.

Four smiling faces are circled in thick black marker: Brynn's, Fiona's, Cassie's and Tildy's.

And both Cassie's and Tildy's are crossed out with an ominous, blood-red X . . .

Books by Wendy Corsi Staub

Published by Kensington Publishing Corporation

Don't Scream

Wendy Corsi Staub

ZEBRA BOOKS
KENSINGTON PUBLISHING CORP.
www.kensingtonbooks.com

ZEBRA BOOKS are published by

Kensington Publishing Corp.
850 Third Avenue
New York, NY 10022

All Kensington titles, imprints, and distributed lines are available at special quantity discounts for bulk purchases for sales promotion, premiums, fund-raising, educational, or institutional use.

Special book excerpts or customized printings can also be created to fit specific needs. For details, write or phone the office of the Kensington Special Sales Manager: Attn. Special Sales Department. Kensington Publishing Corp., 850 Third Avenue, New York, NY 10022. Phone: 1-800-221-2647.

Zebra and the Z logo Reg. U.S. Pat. & TM Off.

ISBN-13: 978-0-8217-7972-9
ISBN-10: 0-8217-7972-9

First Printing: May 2007
10 9 8 7 6 5

Printed in the United States of America

Dedicated in loving memory of my grandfather,
Samuel J. Ricotta (April 1915–May 2006)
and in honor of my grandmother, Sara J. Ricotta.

And for Mark, Morgan, and Brody.

Acknowledgments

I am grateful to Carolyn MacNeil and Officer Michael Mc-Carthy of the Boston Police Department, who patiently answered countless questions about murder and mayhem. Any errors in police procedural are strictly my own. In addition, I owe a tremendous thank you to my editor, John Scognamiglio, and the staff at Kensington Books; to my agents, Laura Blake Peterson, Holly Frederick, and the staff at Curtis Brown, Ltd; to my publicists, Nancy Berland and Elizabeth Middaugh, as well as Kim Miller and the rest of the staff at Nancy Berland Public Relations.

Heartfelt thanks as well to Cathy Cadek and Laura Pennock and staff at Levy Home entertainment for their ongoing, enthusiastic support, and to Levy's Sales Promotions team— Pam Nelson, Sarah Donaldson, Janet Krey, Emily Hixon, Devar Spight, Kathleen Koelbl, Justine Willis, Renna Thomas, and George Tyrrell—for making the K-mart/Levy Sizzling Summer Author Tour such fun! Thanks to Carol Fitzgerald, Sunil Kumar, and the staff at The Book Report Network; and to Rick and Patty Donovan, Phil Pelletier, and their staff at my favorite store, The Book Nook, in Dunkirk, N.Y. Finally, Mark Staub: I could never do any of it without your feedback and support every step of the way along every literary journey.

PROLOGUE

September, ten years earlier

". . . and I do solemnly swear that I will never ever tell another living soul what happened here tonight . . ."

"And I do solemnly swear that I will never ever tell another living soul what happened here tonight," the female voices echo dutifully, none without a quaver.

Brynn's is the most tremulous of all, barely audible even to her own ears. She prays Tildy won't notice and single her out to repeat the pledge solo. If that happens . . .

What will I do?

What can *I do?*

She'll just have to go along with it, the way she's gone along with all of this, right from the start. Against her better judgment, against her conscience, and, ultimately . . .

Against the law?

Tildy says no. Adamantly. She insists that they haven't broken any laws.

"It's not like we've murdered someone," she hissed when Brynn balked at the proposed plan. "Anyone in our situation would do the exact same thing."

Brynn highly doubts that, but she can't bring herself to say it.

There was a time when Brynn Costello—apple of her daddy's eye, valedictorian of her high school class, dean's list candidate for her first four semesters at Stonebridge College, Zeta Delta Kappa pledge—would have stood up to all of them. Even Matilda Harrington.

So why didn't you?

Why are you standing here in the woods in the middle of the night being sworn to secrecy?

This can't really be happening. If anyone ever found out . . .

But nobody will find out.

They're not going to tell.

Anyway, Tildy was right when she pointed out that what happened isn't their fault.

Still . . .

I just want to get out of here, go back to the sorority house, and forget this ever happened.

Or, better yet, just go home.

Home.

Swept by a wave of nostalgia, Brynn swallows hard over a lump in her throat. She longs for worn oak floors, oval braided rugs, chintz slipcovers. The savory aroma of fresh-brewed coffee, and onions frying in olive oil. The radio in the background, sock-hop standards and sixties' anthems of the local oldies station. Clutter, and laundry, and people coming and going . . .

Home.

But the seaside blue-collar household on Cape Cod is two hundred miles and a world away from the campus nestled in the Berkshires, the mountains of western Massachusetts.

And there's no going back—not the way Brynn yearns to do.

Before her thoughts can meander down the fateful path that ultimately led to Stonebridge College, she's dragged back to the present.

Tildy, apparently deciding their oath needs something more to make it official, solemnly declares, "So help me God."

"So help me God," the others obediently intone.

Not Brynn. She just moves her lips, refusing to invoke God. Not under these circumstances.

"Now we'll sing the sorority song," Tildy commands, lifting her hand to push her blonde hair back from her face. Her sorority bracelet, a silver rope of clasped rosebuds, glints in the moonlight. They're all wearing them—including Rachel— and each is personalized with dangling silver initial charms.

Brynn manages to join the others in singing. The ingrained lyrics she secretly always considered embarrassingly hokey now seem bittersweet as she forces them past the lump in her throat.

We'll always remember
That fateful September
We'll never forget
The new sisters we met
We'll face tomorrow together
In all kinds of weather
ZDK girls, now side by side
May travel far and wide
But wherever we roam
Sweet ZDK will be our home.

The sisters' voices give way to the hushed nocturnal woodland descant: chirping crickets, a rushing creek, and the September breeze that gently rustles the maple boughs high above the clearing.

Then another sound reaches Brynn's ears . . .

The faint, yet resonant crack of a branch splintering underfoot.

She clutches her friend Fiona's arm, asking in a high-pitched whisper, "Did anyone hear that?"

"Hear what?" Tildy's tone is sharp.

"Shhh!" Standing absolutely still, afraid to breathe, Brynn listens intently.

They all do.

There is nothing.

Nothing but the crickets, the creek, a gust stirring the leaves overhead. Just like before.

After a long, tense moment, Cassie says, "I don't hear anything, Brynn."

Brynn doesn't either. Not now.

But someone is there.

She can feel it.

Someone is lurking in the shadows among the trees, listening.

Perhaps even watching . . .

And recognizing.

PART I

HAPPY BIRTHDAY,
DEAR RACHEL

CHAPTER 1

September, present day
Cedar Crest, Massachusetts

It happened ten years ago this week, just after Labor Day, and just a few miles from here.

In fact, if one knows where to look, one can pinpoint up in the greenish-golden Berkshires backdrop, beyond the row of nineteenth-century rooftops, precisely the spot where it happened.

And I know where to look . . . because I was there. I know exactly what really happened that night, and it's time that—

"Oh, excuse me!" The elderly woman is apologetic, having just rounded the corner from Second Street. "I didn't mean to bump into you . . . I'm so sorry."

She looks so familiar . . .

It takes just a split second for the memory to surface. Right, she used to be a cashier at the little deli down the block. The place that always had hazelnut decaf. Yes, and she was always so chatty.

What was her name? Mary? Molly?

What is she doing out at this hour? The sky is still dark in the west, and none of the businesses along Main Street are open yet.

Don't panic. She probably doesn't even recognize you. Just smile and say something casual . . .

"Oh, that's all right, ma'am."

Good. Now turn your back. Slowly, so that you don't draw any more attention to yourself.

Good. Now get the heck out of here, before—

"Excuse me!"

Dammit! The old lady again.

What can she possibly want now?

"You must have dropped this when I bumped you." With a gnarled, blue-veined hand, she proffers a white envelope.

"Oh . . . thank you."

Could she have glanced at the address on the front before she handed it over? If she did, could she have recognized the recipient's name?

"It's going to be a nice day today." She gestures at the glow in the eastern sky, above the mountain peaks. "We needed that rain, though, at this time of year."

"Mmm-hmm." *Just nod. Be polite.*

"Well . . . Enjoy the day."

"I will." *But not as much as I'll enjoy tomorrow.* "You, too."

With a cheerful wave, the woman turns and makes her way down the block.

The post office is just a few doors in the opposite direction. These last two envelopes—the ones to be delivered right here in town—must go out in this morning's mail.

It's important that they be mailed from here, so that the recipients will realize that the sender is nearby.

The timing is just as crucial. All four cards need to arrive at their destination tomorrow, on the anniversary.

The others went out first thing yesterday morning—one to Boston, one to Connecticut. That excursion was uneventful. It was raining, and there were no witnesses . . .

Unlike today.

Now isn't the time to start taking chances. Not after months of painstakingly laying the groundwork. Not when it's finally about to begin at last.

Millie.

That's her name.

The post office can wait. The first pickup won't be for at least another hour.

What a shame, Millie.

What a shame you weren't more careful.

"Whoa, hang on there, kiddo!" Brynn Saddler swoops toward her barefoot toddler as he dashes across the front lawn toward the street.

"Hey, good catch, Mom!" Arnie, the mail carrier, calls from the sidewalk a few doors down leafy Tamarack Lane as Brynn lifts her squirming son into her arms.

"I'm getting enough practice . . . third time he's made a run for it in the last five minutes!" Laughing, Brynn carries Jeremy back to the steps of their Craftsman bungalow, where they've been waiting for the school bus in the late summer sunshine.

This is Caleb's first day of kindergarten at Cedar Crest Elementary; she's been holding her breath and checking her watch for almost seven hours. She won't relax until the moment he's safely home again. But the whole process is bound to kick in again tomorrow morning . . .

And, she supposes, every morning until high school graduation. She can't imagine ever getting used to sending her child off each morning with a wave, a kiss, and a fervent prayer that he'll be safe until he's home again.

Never mind her friend Fiona swearing that by next August, Brynn will be counting down the days until school begins—and maybe even looking for a job.

Fee isn't exactly a doting mother. Not that she doesn't

love her only daughter. But given the option of spending her time with Ashley or at work, Fee would undoubtedly choose the latter, and always has. Her marriage ended because she couldn't give her husband the second child he wanted.

No, not "couldn't," Brynn amends. *Wouldn't.*

It isn't that she believes Fee should have had another baby she didn't want.

Just . . .

Well, lately, Brynn can identify with Fee's ex, Patrick.

She wants another baby. Garth does not.

But it's not going to destroy our marriage.

"Mommy," Jeremy croons, and plants a wet kiss on her lips before she can stop him.

"Oh, no, sweetie . . . Mommy's been sick." She does her best to wipe off his mouth with the sleeve of her T-shirt.

Chances are, he'll come down with strep throat anyway. It's surprising he didn't catch it when Caleb first became ill last week, as Brynn did. Thanks to antibiotics, they're both on the mend; she's been hoping to spare Jeremy.

"I love you." Jeremy reaches up around her neck to yank her high brown ponytail with playful, and painful, affection.

"I love you too, baby." She laughs even as she winces, knowing there will come a day when she'll once again be able to wear her naturally wavy chestnut-colored hair loose around her shoulders. She'll be able to wear earrings without worrying about tugs, or white shorts free of smudges from chubby, sticky little fingers.

But will she even want to?

She's never been prone to fussing with hair, jewelry, and clothes. Her mother, Marie, used to say it was a good thing Brynn was naturally pretty, since she refused to primp. She always had her share of boyfriends, drawn to her wide-set brown eyes, long-waisted, willowy-looking athletic figure, and a generous length of wavy brown hair becomingly streaked lighter from the sun.

When she got to college, her sorority sister Tildy dubbed

her W2, shorthand for Wash and Wear, because that was invariably the case with Brynn's hair, face, clothes.

It still is—though on rare occasions, it might be nice not to look like a domestic refugee.

Sometimes she wonders if Garth is thinking the same thing when he walks in the door to find her in tattered jeans and sweatshirts, covered in flour or glitter glue.

But Brynn is having so much fun with her boys that she isn't particularly anxious to reclaim her former unmaternal self, or the career she never got off the ground, or the hours of "me" time she sacrificed along this path.

Healthy children, a loving husband, a cozy antique house in a charming New England town . . .

She has everything she ever hoped for, everything her own mother had.

Did Brynn Costello Saddler ever really want anything more out of life?

She went to college, after all. But not necessarily with the single-minded goal of earning a degree and becoming something specific that she'd always yearned to be: a businesswoman, an artist, a doctor . . .

No, unlike her more ambitious friends, she was mainly at Stonebridge College because she couldn't bear to be at home anymore.

After four years there, on the verge of being sprung into the world to either return home or start fresh somewhere else and make something of herself, she fell in love.

Dr. Garth Saddler was older, someone with whom she could recreate the domestic stability she'd had growing up, before her mother died and that world dissolved.

And here I am.

Me, living my life . . .

My mother's life, too . . .

And it's fulfilling.

And maybe I need to see it through for both of us.

"Hi! Hi!" Jeremy calls out, clambering off Brynn's lap

and waving frantically as the postal carrier arrives at the steps.

Brynn sees old Mr. Chase look up disapprovingly from the chrysanthemums he's planting over by the driveway of his meticulous yard next door. He isn't particularly fond of kids.

"Hi, buddy. Where's your partner in crime today?" Arnie asks, sorting through a cluster of envelopes and catalogues in his hand.

"Caleb started kindergarten this morning, Arnie, can you believe it?" Brynn watches Jeremy bend over to study a big black ant parading along the sidewalk.

"Bug!" Jeremy shrieks. "Bug!"

"Jeremy, no." Brynn reaches down to stop him before he can crush the ant with his bare foot. "The outdoors is the bug's house, remember? We don't hurt him when we're visiting his house. That isn't nice."

"But if the bug visits *your* house, it's a different story, eh, Mrs. Saddler?" Arnie asks with a wink as he hands her a stack of mail. He smashes a fist into his palm to mimic some hapless insect's demise.

Brynn laughs. "Exactly."

"So kindergarten already, huh?" Arnie asks. "Time sure flies, doesn't it? Next thing you know, your kids will be all grown up and gone, like my girls are."

"By then, I'll probably be grateful for the peace and quiet."

"No," Arnie says with a sad smile, "you'll wish these years back."

And Brynn is wistful once again.

I want another baby.

Not necessarily a daughter, no matter what countless random strangers say.

"Going to try again for a girl?" people like to ask when they spot Brynn with her two boys in the supermarket, the library, the park. The worst offenders are mothers of pretty little blue-eyed blondes wearing frilly dresses and ribbons and bows—women who assume that any mother of two brown-haired, brown-eyed boys with perpetual juice mustaches and skinned knees must be secretly envious.

Not Brynn.

She grew up a tomboy with older brothers. As a ten-year-old she almost drowned trying to out-swim them in rough surf off the Cape. By high school she was a champion swimmer and beach lifeguard. She was also the only varsity cheerleader who implicitly understood football and basketball and would have preferred playing to bouncing around on the sidelines.

She's perfectly comfortable living in an all-male household. In fact, having survived the overflowing Zeta Delta Kappa house back in her college days, she won't complain if she never again shares a roof with another female.

So a third son would be just fine with her. Gender doesn't matter, she just wants—no, *longs for*—another child.

She tried to convince Garth over the summer. Her husband's initial response: *If memory serves, you were the one who begged me to convince the doctor to tie your tubes after you delivered Jeremy.*

She pointed out that she came up with that idea—which, thank God, the doctor refused to accommodate—mere moments after enduring a fourteen-hour labor, but *before* she cradled her second son in her arms.

"Bye! Bye!" Jeremy calls as Arnie heads back down the walk to continue his daily rounds.

"See you later, buddy. And don't run toward the street again, okay? People drive like maniacs around here lately. You never know when someone is going to come barreling around a corner and . . ." Arnie once again slams his fist into his palm, shakes his head sadly, and asks Brynn, "Did you hear what happened to Millie Dubinski yesterday?"

"Millie Dubinski . . . Oh, you mean the lady who used to work at the deli?"

Arnie nods. "She was out for her early-morning walk, and some crazy driver ran her down. Poor thing had just stepped into the crosswalk on Fourth Street. Died on the spot."

"Oh, no."

"Oh, yes. Hit and run. No witnesses. Probably some college kid."

Brynn says nothing to that.

Arnie, like many Cedar Crest old-timers, has little patience for the five thousand Stonebridge College students who invade the town every September.

"So you stay away from the street, buddy," Arnie warns Jeremy again with a grandfatherly pat on his head. "You hear?"

Jeremy replies, "Street! Bus!"

Arnie chuckles. "Your big brother should be along any second now."

Yes, he should . . . But there's still no sign of the bus.

Brynn waves to Arnie as he retreats down the walk toward the Chases' house.

Then, keeping one eye on Jeremy as he plucks a fuzzy white dandelion from the grass, she flips through the stack of mail in her hand. Bill, bill, something from Cedar Crest Travel . . . ?

Oh, right, that would be Garth's plane ticket to Arizona for the sociology symposium next month.

What else? Bill, credit card offer, bill . . .

Hmm.

Coming to a larger white envelope that looks like it must contain a greeting card, Brynn sees that it's for her.

But her name and address aren't handwritten in ink. The envelope bears a printed label. It's probably one of those time-share invitations, she decides, slipping her finger under the flap. Perpetually homesick for the sea, she was tempted to accept the one that came the other day—four inexpensive days at a beautiful oceanfront resort in Florida, and all they'd have had to do was listen to a sales pitch.

Garth said no way. A nervous flier, he dreads the academic conferences he has to attend, other than the nearby Boston one last June, to which he drove.

Of course he vetoed the Florida resort. But maybe—

Brynn's thought is interrupted by the unmistakable rumble of a large vehicle making the turn onto Tamarack Lane.

"The bus, Jeremy! Caleb's home!" she announces with relief, the mail tossed aside onto the step, forgotten as she hurries toward the curb to greet her son at last.

"Here's your mail, Ms. Fitzgerald."

"Thanks, Emily." Fiona doesn't look up from her computer screen or miss a beat as her manicured fingers fly along the keyboard. "Just put it down. I'll get to it in a second. And be ready to go FedEx this cover letter and the contract to James Bingham's office in Boston in about five minutes."

"James Bingham?"

"Hello? The new client? The one with the multimillion-dollar telecommunications company?"

The one who travels in the same Boston circles as Fiona's friend Tildy, who introduced them in June . . .

The one who happens to be New England's most eligible bachelor.

"Oh, right. The new client." But Emily sounds as vacant as she probably looks.

Fiona opts not to glance up, knowing the visual evidence of Emily's cluelessness will just irritate her further.

She sighs inwardly, wishing the damned building weren't nonsmoking, because she desperately needs a cigarette.

Stress. This is what she gets for hiring a college sophomore as the new part-time office assistant at her public relations firm. Emily is a pale wisp of a girl whose personality leaves much to be desired. Still, she showed up for the interview ten minutes early and appropriately dressed—neither of which she has done since she started the job.

Fiona should have gone with someone more savvy, more professional . . . and older. At least, beyond school-age.

Right . . . like whom?

There's not a large pool of applicants to choose from; Cedar Crest isn't exactly crawling with upwardly mobile types. This is a college town—a tourist town as well during the summer, foliage, and ski seasons. The year-round population—mostly upper-middle-class families and a smattering of well-off retirees—provides precious few candidates willing to consider part-time clerical employment. And those who *are* willing prefer to work for Stonebridge College, with its benefits, higher pay, and college calendar.

Fiona thinks wistfully of the lone exception: her former office manager, the folksy-yet-efficient Sharon. She moved to Albany at the end of August to be near her grandchildren and her newly divorced daughter, a choice Fiona quite vocally discouraged—and privately derided. The way Sharon went on and on about the tribulations facing her poor, poor daughter, you'd think raising a child and running a household without a man was a challenge equivalent to heading FEMA.

Expertly juggling single motherhood and a household *plus* a full-time career, Fiona has little sympathy or patience for anyone who can't seem to independently accomplish a fraction as much as she does in twice the time.

Which is precisely why the future isn't looking particularly bright for halting, clueless Emily of the granola-crunchy wardrobe and limp, flyaway hair.

But I'll worry about her later. Right now, there's too much to do.

Fiona rereads the letter she just composed, hits SAVE, then PRINT, and closes the document. There. Done.

She notes the angle of the sun falling through the tall window beside her desk and realizes that it's probably too late to eat lunch. Which is a shame, because she's hungry.

Breakfast was, as usual, black coffee chased by a sugar-free breath mint.

Oh, well, just a few more hours until dinner.

Maybe more than a few, she amends, remembering that Ashley has an after-school playdate with a friend whose mother is keeping her for dinner and bringing the girls to their gymnastics class afterward. So Fiona doesn't have to be home until eight.

"Emily!" she calls, and swivels her leather desk chair toward the adjacent antique console. "Come here, please."

Plucking the paper from the printer, she scans it briefly, signs it with a flourish, and clips it to the prepared contract.

"Emily!" she calls again, frustrated.

The girl appears, looking flustered, in the graceful doorway that once divided the pair of formal Victorian parlors that now are the reception area and Fiona's office.

"Sorry . . . I was, uh, wiping up something I spilled."

Fiona groans. "What was it? And where did it spill?"

Please let her say water . . . and on the floor by the Poland Spring cooler.

"Coffee . . . on my desk."

Terrific.

"Did you get it on any papers?"

"Just a couple of pages of the Jackson proposal . . . I'm sure they'll dry."

Fiona exhales through puffed cheeks and forces herself to count to three. Then she thrusts the Bingham contract and cover letter at her assistant. "Here, take this over to Mail Boxes Etc. for FedEx delivery first thing in the morning. Then come right back and deal with your desk. You need to toss the Jackson proposal and print it out again."

"The whole thing? But . . . Only a few pages got wet. That would be a waste of paper."

This is what you get for hiring a tree hugger, Fiona tells herself, wondering why she didn't consider membership in the campus environmentalist club as a red flag on Emily's resume.

"You need to reprint the whole thing," she snaps.

She swivels her chair to face her desk again as her assistant obediently retreats with the contract.

Today's stack of mail is a few inches high, as usual. Fiona begins sorting it efficiently into piles: trade information, client queries, bills . . . personal?

Yes, personal.

She examines the large rectangular white envelope that looks like a greeting card or invitation. The printed label is addressed not to Fiona Fitzgerald Public Relations, but to Ms. Fiona Fitzgerald. It's postmarked right here in Cedar Crest.

That's unusual. Her personal correspondence invariably goes to her home several blocks away from this converted Victorian office building on Main Street.

Then again, her home address has been unlisted, as a safety measure, ever since she got divorced and started dating again. A single woman just can't be too careful these days.

Fiona is curious about the contents of the envelope—but not curious enough to interrupt sorting the remaining mail and open it. One doesn't get as far as she has by being easily sidetracked from the task at hand.

Self-discipline. That's what it's all about.

Anyway, she's seen enough junk mail disguised as personal correspondence that she should probably just toss the card into the garbage can unopened.

But she'll probably open it. Later, when she has a chance. Just in case it really is a greeting card, or an invitation. Fiona doesn't receive many of those these days, unless they're business-related.

She was a shrewd negotiator in the divorce—she got their two-story, 2,000-square-foot Tudor home and all the furniture, plus the BMW, full custody of Ashley, and shared use of the vacation cabin up in the mountains.

Patrick got the Jeep, parental visitation rights . . .

And the friends.

She probably shouldn't have been surprised that everyone in their old social circle—both husbands and wives—chose to align themselves with Pat. Her ex is easily the most affable guy in town—when it comes to everything and everyone but Fiona, that is.

Theirs was a bitter divorce. She had hoped they could at least be civil—as much for Ashley's sake as for her own. This is a small town, she doesn't care to have their marital disaster aired for public opinion. Yet even now, two years after the papers were signed, Pat has very little to say to her—and too much to say through the local grapevine.

The lines are clearly drawn, and it's lonely on Fiona's side.

Even her own parents are once again all but estranged from her. Staunch Catholics, they were devastated by her divorce and abandoned her in a time when she really could have used their support.

Oh, well. She still has Brynn, even if they don't have a lot in common these days—or much time for each other.

That doesn't matter. They'll always be sisters—just bonded by friendship rather than by blood.

Or maybe a bit of both, Fiona thinks with a shudder, remembering that awful night.

"We'll always remember . . . That fateful September . . ."

How often in the past decade has she been haunted by the opening lines to the Zeta Delta Kappa song?

Haunted, and taunted.

Maybe Brynn is, too. But they don't talk about it.

Better to forget it ever happened and keep their friendship—their sisterhood—grounded in the present.

Yes, Fiona has Brynn. She has a flesh-and-blood sister, too: Deirdre—or Dee, as she was called before she shed the childhood nickname, along with her ties to Cedar Crest and just about everyone in it.

Deirdre might not possess Fiona's type A energy, but she is literally Fiona's other half—not just her identical twin but her mirror image. In genetic terms, that means the egg didn't split until late in the embryonic stage. Any later, Fiona learned in a college biology class, and twins would be conjoined.

For practical purposes, "mirror image" means that Fiona is left-handed while Deirdre is right-handed; Fiona's auburn hair naturally parts on the right, Deirdre's on the left. They have the same petite, waiflike figure, the same whiter-than-white, unblemished complexion, the same slanty green eyes.

So close were they throughout their childhood that Fiona and Deirdre—Fee and Dee—might just as well have been literally joined at the hip.

Not anymore.

Fiona hasn't seen her sister since she visited Deirdre at her home on St. John in the Virgin Islands to celebrate their twenty-ninth birthday almost a year ago.

"What are we going to do for our thirtieth?" Deirdre asked as they said good-bye at the airport. "How about an Alaskan cruise?"

Fiona countered with, "Why don't you come to Cedar Crest and we'll just drink a bottle of champagne, or two or three, together? I'll buy you a plane ticket."

"You know I can't plan that far ahead."

"You *can,* Dee . . . You just don't like to."

"Exactly. Anyway, Antoinette will want to be with me on my birthday."

"So bring her," Fiona suggested, as though her sister bringing her lesbian lover for a hometown visit is an everyday event.

"Yeah, Mom and Dad would love that."

"Are you kidding? You think I'm planning on celebrating my birthday—*our* birthday—with *them?* They won't even have to know you're in town. You'd stay with me."

"Well, considering they told me never to darken their doorstep again, you know I wouldn't stay with *them*."

"Does that mean I should go ahead and buy you a ticket? You and Antoinette?"

"I can't plan that now, Fee. I probably won't even know until the day before what I feel like doing for my thirtieth birthday."

Thirty!

Another looming milestone for Fiona.

One Brynn is facing as well. And within the next month, too. Even Matilda.

And Rachel . . .

Rachel would have been thirty this year, too. In fact . . .

Fiona's eyes automatically go to her desk calendar.

Today, she realizes, startled by the coincidence. *Today would have been Rachel's thirtieth birthday.*

Yes, she's positive about the date. It's indelibly imprinted on her brain.

Rachel Lorent was born on September 7th . . . the same day she died.

"What's that, baby?"

"Hmm?" Cassandra Ashford looks up to see her fiancé watching her with interest.

She quickly tucks the greeting card and its envelope into the new issue of *Essence,* which arrived in the same batch of mail she picked up on their way into the condo just now.

Alec Bennett tilts his head. "You have a secret admirer or something?"

"A secret admirer?" Cassie forces a laugh as she shoves the magazine into her brown leather tote bag, still slung over her shoulder. "Why would you say that?"

"Because you just hid that card in your magazine, that's why. And now you're trying to hide the magazine in your bag." He reaches across the breakfast bar to playfully tug at the bag. "Is there something in there that you don't want me to see?"

"No!" she says quickly—too quickly—and pulls away.

Alec raises an eyebrow and thoughtfully rubs his neatly trimmed black goatee. "Really."

"Really." Cassie kicks off her white leather shoes and walks barefoot across the beige-colored carpet toward her bedroom, still carrying her bag.

"Where are you going?"

"To take a shower."

"I thought we were going out for Italian."

"We are. I want to get cleaned up first."

"Good, then I can catch the beginning of the Red Sox game."

His secret admirer suspicions apparently forgotten, Alec heads for her living room and the portable TV that is perched almost as an afterthought on an end table.

Before Alec came along, it was barely used. When she wasn't working around the clock on her medical residency in pediatrics, Cassie was content to spend her meager free time riding her beloved horse, Marshmallow, boarded at a nearby barn.

Or, of course, catching up on much-needed sleep.

Alec, who will be bringing his 42-inch plasma screen television when he moves into her condo after their November wedding, is a televised-sports fanatic. Most of the time, that's fine with Cassie. He's a successful podiatrist who has a lot more time on his hands than she does. Television keeps him busy while she's finishing her last year of residency at the hospital in Danbury.

Almost one more year to go on that . . . and less than three months now until they walk down the aisle. If Cassie had her way, the nuptials would wait until next fall. But Alec is anxious to wed—an unusual quality in most men she's encountered.

He sounds too good to be true—for God's sake, don't let him get away, Tildy advised last spring after he proposed, when Cassie confessed her ambiguity about getting married so soon.

Tildy.

Cassie has to call her right away.

In the white-carpeted master bedroom, she closes the door behind her, and, after a moment's hesitation, presses the knob button to lock it. Not that she expects Alec to barge in; he respects her privacy.

The bedroom is shadowy. She left the blinds drawn this morning in her haste to get to the hospital for early rounds. She debates opening them now to let in some late-day sun, but decides against it. It'll be dark outside in an hour or so— and they're leaving the house anyway.

She does turn on a lamp, but oddly the splash of light does little to warm the room.

As Cassie hangs her tote bag on the white iron bedpost, she glances from the sunny yellow and white patchwork quilt to her framed art posters to the antique bookcase brimming with well-worn childhood favorites.

Why does she feel so skittish in her own room, among familiar belongings?

Because I'm scared, that's why.

Finding that card in the mail—like she needed a reminder that today is September 7th—has put all sorts of crazy thoughts into her head.

Now, as she takes the cordless phone from its cradle on the nightstand, she finds herself looking over her shoulder, almost as if . . .

As if someone might be here with her, watching her?

Yeah, right. She's alone in the bedroom, and Alec is way on the opposite end of the condo.

You're not thinking about Alec, are you? You're thinking about some nameless, faceless stranger.

Someone who knows . . .

What nobody can possibly know.

Unless one of the others told.

But we swore each other to secrecy.

Cassie refuses to consider that any one of her friends—her *sisters*—could possibly have broken that solemn vow made a decade ago tonight.

Yes, just as she refuses, absolutely *refuses,* to check under the bed and behind the slats in the louvered closet door.

Frightened little girls do things like that. Especially frightened little girls whose big brothers warn them incessantly about the lurking bogeyman.

But Cassie's a grown woman now—a doctor, for God's sake.

Shaking her head at her folly, she takes the phone into the bathroom and closes that door, too. Then, just to be safe, she turns on the shower. The sound of the water will drown out her voice, should her fiancé decide to eavesdrop.

Which he won't. Alec will be safely ensconced in front of the Red Sox game for however long she takes to get ready for dinner.

She presses the familiar series of touch-tone numbers. The phone rings once on the other end, and again. And then again.

Come on, pick up, Tildy . . . Where are you?

The machine picks up with a lengthy greeting. Not surprising. Tildy always did like to hear herself talk.

Waiting for the outgoing message to give way to a beep, Cassie gazes into the mirror above the sink. She looks the same as she always does at the end of a workday: a touch of makeup to accentuate her fine bone structure and mocha complexion, her hair in neat cornrows that hang well below her shoulders, her only jewelry a pair of simple gold post earrings, and, of course, her diamond engagement ring.

Her mahogany eyes are different tonight, though.

I look like I've just seen the bogeyman, she notes, staring at herself as the fog from the shower rolls in from the edges of the mirror.

Or maybe, I've just heard from him.

"Hey, it's Cassie . . . Listen, you need to call me, please, as soon as you get this message. I have to talk to you . . ."

Matilda Harrington quickly presses a button on the answering machine.

"Message . . . deleted . . ." a computerized voice informs her.

Tildy turns and walks briskly from the den, an alcove on one end of the living room, toward the back of the town house.

Her eyes shift briefly, as always, to the gilt-framed oil painting in the hall.

The only formal Harrington family portrait that was ever done—or ever will be. The canvas is illuminated from the arc of gallery lighting positioned directly above. It casts the four faces—father, mother, daughter, son—in a soft, almost ethereal glow.

Tildy has a vague memory of sitting for the portrait at her family's Beacon Hill mansion, where Daddy still lives.

She remembers how little baby Jonathan kept spitting up as usual, and her mother had to repeatedly hand him to the nanny to be cleaned up.

And how she got to sit on her father's knee for hours, and how the artist commented that she was such a good little girl, never fidgeting or complaining.

Tildy's mother said something like, "Oh, Daddy's Little Girl would be content to just sit there on his lap forever."

She sounded somewhat wistful about that, Tildy remembers. For a long time afterward, she thought that must have been because Mother regretted that Daddy was usually much too busy with his real estate empire to spend much time with his family.

But later—much later, years after the plane crash that killed Mother and Jonathan—Daddy mentioned that her mother was often jealous.

"She always thought you loved me more than you loved her, Matilda."

That's because I did, Tildy thought matter-of-factly, and without guilt.

Distraught as she was to lose her mother and baby brother so suddenly and violently, she remembers how relieved she was that it wasn't Jason Harrington who died that awful night.

Daddy was her favorite, the one she always worried about; the one who traveled all over the world on business, usually on his private jet.

Ironic, then, that it was Mother and Jonathan who were killed, along with Daddy's pilot, when the jet went down in a snowstorm near Baltimore. That night, Tildy was back home in Beacon Hill with Lena, her nanny; Daddy was at a business dinner with his protégé and closest friend, Tildy's godfather, Troy Allerson.

It wasn't even snowing in Boston that night. Tildy's biggest worries were that she'd lose a hand of Old Maid to Lena, and that her father wouldn't make it back home in time to tuck her in, though he'd promised he'd try.

But she wasn't worried about her mother and brother, even though she knew little Jonathan was very sick with some kind of degenerative disease. That was nothing new; he had been ailing since birth. Her mother took him to specialists all over the country; they were on their way to Johns Hopkins on that particular trip.

Tildy won Old Maid. She always did. She didn't realize back then that Lena always let her win.

But Daddy never made it home to tuck her in.

She woke, late, to find him sitting on her bed in her darkened room, sobbing. He held her close and he told her that Mother and Jonathan were gone. He promised her that he would always take care of her.

"But you're never home, Daddy," Tildy cried.

"That will change now, baby. You'll see."

And it did.

Daddy's Girl. That's Matilda Harrington, to this day.

The heels of her Dior pumps click across the hardwood floor of the hall and into the dining room, where they encounter the antique area rug that once belonged to French royalty, and then to American royalty. It had been passed down through the Kennedy family, and one of the cousins gave it to Daddy, who later agreed that it would look beautiful in Tildy's dining room.

The swinging door to the kitchen is propped open, as always, with a cast iron pineapple-shaped doorstop, also antique. Troy bought it at auction and gave it to her as a housewarming gift.

"A pineapple?" she asked dubiously.

Troy told her that in Colonial times, wealthy hostesses kept their dining room doors closed so their guests could only anticipate the luscious food being prepared in the kitchen. When the elaborate, sumptuous platters were ceremoniously presented—topped with precious, expensive pineapples— the guests were duly impressed.

Now, according to Troy, the fruit symbolizes elegant hospitality.

Tildy decided it would be ironically fitting to use the doorstop in her own dining room—where, incidentally, the door to the kitchen is always kept open. She doesn't cook, though she did just install professional-grade chef's appliances.

A few more tapping footsteps across the newly lain stone floor of the just renovated—and yet-to-be-used—kitchen, and Tildy reaches the rear French door.

As she emerges into the twilight, she notes that the night is warm, much too warm to light the living room fireplace.

She hesitates on the brick patio, gazing across the small, stockade-fenced yard toward the woodpile in the far corner neatly covered by a blue tarp. She could lay a small fire—just a couple of logs and some kindling.

But what if one of her Back Bay neighbors smells the wood smoke and asks her about it?

So what? That's not going to prove anything.

Still . . . better to avoid the slightest chance of arousing suspicion.

Tildy returns to the kitchen. This is her favorite room in the Victorian-era Commonwealth Avenue town house, which she's spent three years renovating from top to bottom. She spared no expense, and barely put a dent in her trust fund, as she pointed out to Daddy when he mentioned that she'll never get back out of the house what she's put into it.

"Who says I'm selling it?" she retorted.

"You will when you meet someone and settle down."

"I am settled," she informed him, neglecting to add that she's already met *someone*.

Pacing, she considers her next move—even as she appreciates the aesthetics of the recently completed room.

The stunning floor is made of flat stone imported from Provence; the countertops are gray granite, the sleek new appliances stainless and black. The only splash of color in the monochromatic room is the bouquet of red tulips in a vase beside the stainless steel double sink.

Tulips. Out of season, and as out of place in her cool modern decor as that loser Ray Wilmington is in her life. But he can't seem to take a hint.

"Did you get my flowers?" he asked this morning, showing up beside her desk at the nonprofit organization where they both work—Tildy, because it's something to do and the minuscule salary is inconsequential; Ray, because he fervently believes in the cause.

"Yes, I got them, thank you." She offered a brief, closed-lip smile.

"I saw those red tulips and of course I thought of you."

She couldn't help but wonder why. She's not Dutch, she never wears red, and, anyway, what business does he have thinking of her?

She *never* thinks of him.

That is, she never *thought* of him until the flowers arrived.

Well, she can fix that.

With a haughty toss of her flaxen hair, she marches over to the counter, wraps a fist around the red petals, and pulls the flowers from their vase. Turning on the faucet and the garbage disposal, she feeds the tulips down the sink drain stem by stem, satisfied by the subterranean rumbling as they're devoured.

Then she grabs the vase—stock florist-shop glass, not even crystal—and deposits it into the empty rolling garbage bin concealed behind a white cabinet door. It makes a satisfying shattering sound as it smashes against the bottom.

Perfect.

Now that all reminders of Ray Wilmington have been obliterated from her house, she can focus again on the matter at hand.

She turns the front burner of the gas stove on HIGH, producing a satisfying orange-blue flame. Then she takes wood-handled barbecue tongs from a drawer.

She reaches into the pocket of her navy blazer, which, according to dorky Ray, exactly matches her eyes. Can't argue with that.

And she didn't.

Compliments, she'll accept.

She removes from her pocket the envelope she took out of her mailbox when she got home, and, after a moment's thought, opens the flap. She wants to give the card a final once-over.

It's as generic as a greeting card can get: a cluster of primary-colored balloons against a white background beneath the words "Happy Birthday" in gold script.

Inside, letters clipped from newspaper headlines spell out the words "TO ME," and beneath that, "XOXOXOXO, R."

She signed everything that way.

It stood for *"Hugs and Kisses, Rachel."*

Oh, hell . . .

Tildy might have known this could happen—that the dark secret from her past could resurface someday.

But when year after year went by, the memory of that night fading like a photo left out in the sun, she pushed the possibility from her mind with increasing ease.

Okay, Rachel . . . So you've come back to haunt me.

Well, guess what? I don't get spooked that easily.

The tongs steady in her hand, Tildy extends the card over the open flame and thoughtfully watches it burn.

CHAPTER 2

Just minutes ago, Brynn was lamenting the fact that Thursday is Garth's late night on campus; he has a class until nine o'clock and often stays on campus for hours afterward, doing research in the library and his office there.

A sociology professor whose concentration is the study of death and dying, he's been working for a few years on a book. The den at home was littered with macabre research materials until recently. Brynn asked him to move it all to his campus office after she caught Caleb browsing through a gruesome book on the forensics of death.

The downside of having Garth move most of his research away from home is that it takes him away, too.

Too bad, Brynn was thinking just now, that her husband couldn't be here to hear Caleb's happy kindergarten chatter. As he plowed through his favorite meal of macaroni and cheese with ketchup, her older son regaled her with breathless details about snack time, potty time, lunchtime, nap time, construction-paper art time . . .

Waiting to share a more adult meal with her husband later, Brynn sat with her children at the table in her pretty blue and yellow kitchen. She was multitasking as usual: listening to Caleb's ongoing account of his first day, overseeing Jeremy in his booster seat, and opening the day's mail.

HAPPY BIRTHDAY . . . TO ME.
XOXOXOXO, R

She actually gasped aloud when she read it, dropping the card on the table like a red-hot coal. Then she snatched it up again . . . as if it mattered. Even if the boys could read cursive, they wouldn't understand the seemingly innocuous message.

Nor would Garth, if he stumbles across the card—which he won't, because she plans to hide it, just as she's hidden the dark truth about Rachel all these years.

"Mommy, what's wrong?" Caleb asks as she reaches for the phone.

She stammers some kind of reply, her thoughts reeling.

Her hands shaking so badly she can barely hit the right buttons on the dial, she can only think *thank God, thank God, thank God Garth isn't here.*

Her husband doesn't know what happened that night.

Nobody knows.

Nobody but her three sorority sisters who were there.

Or so Brynn always tried to convince herself, despite the nagging memory of that twig snapping in the forest.

Was somebody really spying on them?

Did—*does*—somebody know?

As Alec pulls into the parking lot of her condo complex after a quick dinner at Mama Rossi's, Cassie cradles on her lap the still-warm foil-wrapped package that contains her barely touched lasagna.

She'd have been content to leave it behind on the plate, but Alec insisted that she bring it back.

"I'll eat it later, baby," he told her, "as a midnight snack."

Now she debates whether or not to tell him she'd rather be alone tonight. She could just come right out and say it—that she's tired, and she has to be up early, and she'd rather he didn't stay over.

Then again, maybe she shouldn't be alone. Maybe she's too spooked by that card she got in the mail. Maybe she'd feel more comfortable with Alec there, just in case . . .

Well, in case the bogeyman shows up.

She smiles faintly, remembering how Marcus used to torment her with bogeyman tales when they were kids, still living at home.

That was before they were both enrolled in fancy Connecticut boarding schools located well over an hour from their home in the city, and more than two hours from each other.

She was eleven when her parents sent her away. After that, she saw them and her beloved big brother only on holiday breaks and the occasional long weekend.

Summers were spent at sleepaway camp, which was fine with Cassie, actually. There were lots of horses at camp, and she would always rather ride than do anything else in the world.

She still feels that way.

"Alec," she says abruptly, "I think you should sleep at your place tonight. I've got an early day tomorrow and . . . I'm just beat."

He's silent for a moment, busy steering into a spot in front of her building. Then he says, "Okay, baby, no problem."

Her momentary relief that he didn't argue is followed quickly by regret that he didn't argue.

If he did, she would relent.

Because, looking up at the dark windows of her condo— she didn't leave lights on; why didn't she leave lights on?— she doesn't want to venture inside alone.

Just in case she finds that she isn't. Alone, that is.

"Do you want me to walk you in?" Alec asks, but he doesn't shift the car into PARK.

He thinks I'm going to say no. He probably senses that I just need some solitude.

Her fiancé likes to brag that he's getting pretty good at reading her moods. "By the time we walk down the aisle, I'll be able to read your mind," he often says lately.

But he isn't reading it right now.

If he was, he'd come inside with her, and he'd turn on all the lights and look under the bed and inside all the closets.

Well, I don't need him for that. I can take care of myself.

"No, you can go," Cassie tells him. "Thanks for dinner."

"See you tomorrow?"

"What's tomorrow?"

"Friday," he says, as if that's all the answer she had in mind.

Oh. Right. He said "see you tomorrow" not because it's any special occasion, but because they see each other every day now.

That's what people do when they're getting married. And after they're married.

They see each other every day for the rest of their lives.

Till death do us part, Cassandra thinks, and suppresses an involuntary shudder as she plants a light kiss on her fiancé's cheek and walks slowly up the path toward her darkened condo.

And so it's begun.

I only wish I could be in four places at once tonight.

Yes, it would be a pleasure to personally witness their reactions to the day's mail—to see the looks on their faces now that they know the secret isn't theirs alone.

Listening to them is the next best thing.

The bugs have been in place for a long time now, in anticipation of today.

At first it was titillating to eavesdrop on even the most inane conversations: Fiona barking orders, Brynn reading to her children, Cassandra unenthusiastically planning her wedding, and Tildy . . .

Ah, Tildy's private life yielded the most interesting gem of all.

Still, even that became tiresome after awhile.

It was all just mind-numbing chatter.

But not anymore.

"Fiona Fitzgerald Public Relations."

Brynn is momentarily caught off guard by the unfamiliar voice. She was expecting Fee's longtime office manager. Then she remembers that Sharon moved away last week—thus "abandoning" Fiona, as Fee so dramatically put it.

"Is . . . Is Fiona there?" she manages to get out to whoever just answered the phone.

"May I ask who's calling, please?"

She clears her throat, but her voice still comes out sounding strangled. "Tell her it's Brynn."

"Brenda?"

"Brynn!"

"One moment."

She flashes a reassuring smile at her sons, both of whom have stopped eating and are watching her worriedly.

"It's okay, guys . . . Mommy just has to make a quick call, that's all. I'll be right with you."

"Ketchup!" Jeremy bangs the table with his fists.

She is hurriedly squirting another dollop on his already oozing-red macaroni when the voice comes back on the line. "Ms. Fitzgerald said to take a message and she'll call you back."

"The message is pick up the Godda—the gosh-darned phone right now!" Brynn says through clenched teeth.

There's a pause.

"Excuse me?"

"Look, tell her it's an extreme emergency and I need to speak to her immediately."

"All right, I'll tell her. Can I have a number where she can reach you?"

"No, you can't, because I'm not hanging up! Please tell her to pick up right now."

The girl hesitates.

Realizing Fiona has already put the fear of God in her new employee, Brynn softens her tone to say, "Listen, I will take full blame for this. Just tell her I need to talk to her. Please."

"Hang on."

Pacing the kitchen, Brynn absently glances from the sink full of dirty dishes to the steaks thawing on the white laminate countertop to the cheery blue welcome mat askew on the hardwood floor beside the door leading out to the deck.

The orange prescription bottles on the windowsill momentarily trigger her consciousness. Both she and Caleb are due for another dose of antibiotics. She'd better not forget.

Then there's a click on the line, and Fiona asks crisply, "What's going on, Brynn? I'm in the middle of—"

"Whatever it is, this is more important," she cuts in, furtively taking the phone into the dining room.

"I doubt that. I've got a really important new client on the other line, so make it snappy."

"Mommy!" Jeremy protests from the kitchen.

"I'll be right back, boys. Caleb, sing to him!"

Ever obedient, her older son obliges with a singsong, *"A-B-C-D-E-F-G . . ."*

"What's this about, Brynn? Emily said it was a life-or-death emergency. I hear the kids in the background so I'm assuming you're not calling me to dash over and save one of them."

Yeah, right. Fiona is the last person she'd call in that situation.

"Listen," she says in a whisper, "it's about Rachel."

Silence.

Brynn can hear Caleb singing "Twinkle, Twinkle, Little Star" in the kitchen.

Then . . .

"Did you say *Rachel?*"

"Yes."

"Rachel Lorent?" Fiona's voice is as hushed as Brynn's.

"Right."

"I know, today's her birthday. I was thinking about her earlier, actually, and—"

"Fee, I just got a card. In the mail. From Rachel, supposedly."

No response.

"Fee?"

"Hang on a second."

Brynn pokes her head into the kitchen, to make sure the boys are okay.

Caleb has progressed to "Mary Had A Little Lamb," obviously moving right along through his musical repertoire. Jeremy is wearing most of his macaroni and cheese, the rest scattered on the hardwood floor beside the overturned bowl.

Fiona curses softly in Brynn's ear.

"What?"

"Me, too. I got one, too."

"Got what?"

"A card. In the mail. As soon as you said it, I remembered there was an envelope—I was too busy to open it earlier, but . . . My God, Brynn, what's going on? Is this some kind of sick joke?"

"Played by who?"

Fiona takes a moment to answer. "Tildy? Or Cassie?" she asks, and exhales audibly, the way she does when she's puffing on a cigarette. Which she probably is. Sitting right beneath the NO SMOKING sign above her desk.

"You honestly believe that either of them would think this is the least bit funny?"

"No. Of course not. Anyway, it was postmarked in Cedar Crest, so . . ."

"I know. Fee, I have to ask you . . . Did you ever tell anyone?"

"Are you kidding me? No. Did you?"

Brynn's "No!" is as decisive as Fiona's, but her friend asks, "Are you sure? Not even Garth?"

"I didn't tell Garth. What about Pat?" she returns.

"Do you honestly think I would violate a sorority oath for *him?*" Fiona's tone is laced with disdain.

"One of the others must have, then."

"Right, Tildy or Cassie must have told someone, and whoever it was probably thought it would be funny to play this sick trick on us."

"I don't know . . ." Brynn examines the card again. "This looks real. This is how Rachel signed everything."

"Rachel's dead, Brynn. It can't be real."

"No, I know, but . . . If it was somebody else, somebody Tildy or Cassie told, then how would that person know about the *X*s and *O*s?"

"I don't know . . . Lucky guess? Rachel sent a message from beyond the grave? I mean, what do you want me to say here, Brynn?"

I want you to say you did it yourself . . . that you sent me the card, thinking it would be funny, and now that you know I'm all freaked out about it, you can't figure out how to get out of it.

But Fiona doesn't say any of that.

She asks, "When was the last time you talked to Tildy or Cassie?"

"Tildy, not in over a year. I spoke to Cassie when she got engaged last spring. How about you?"

"Me? I don't keep in touch with anyone lately. If you didn't live here in town I'd probably have lost you, too." She is more matter-of-fact than apologetic.

"I think we need to see them as soon as possible, Fee."

"See them? How are we going to do that? I'm too busy to go anywhere, and Tildy's in Boston and Cassie's in Rhode Island."

"Connecticut. Listen, we'll have to meet somewhere in between and discuss this. All four of us, together."

She can hear Fiona tapping keys.

"Just so you know, my schedule is crammed full for the next week," she informs Brynn, obviously having brought up her electronic calendar.

"Make room." Brynn's voice is hoarse, and not from the strep throat. "This is bad, Fee. Really bad."

"It's probably just a joke."

No, it's not.

Brynn can feel it.

The past has caught up to them at last, just as she always feared it would.

The Zeta Delta Kappa house is brightly lit on this September night. Several windows are cracked open and music spills through the screens to mingle with the spirited chatter from the group of girls hanging out on the front steps.

They're talking about courses they're taking and guys they're dating and the upcoming rush. Every trite word they've said for the past hour and a half has been clearly audible from this shadowy bench in the deserted park across the street.

The Zeta sisters have no idea that someone is eavesdropping tonight.

Watching.

Remembering.

Really, all that has changed in ten years are the names, the faces, and the voices.

Flash back ten years and a day, and Rachel could easily have been among the girls on the steps, gossiping, laughing.

Flash back just ten years, though—ten years ago this night and . . .

No more Rachel.

Across the street, the screen door creaks open.

"Come on, girls, let's call it a night."

That's the housemother's voice. Sara "Puffy" Trovato, still sounding exactly the same after all this time.

Still bantering, the girls gradually disperse into the house. Finally, the door closes behind the last pair. The porch lamps are turned off.

All is still.

It's easy to picture the girls retreating to their rooms now to finish course assignments, read magazines, watch TV, or check e-mail. Eventually, one by one, they'll change into their pajamas, turn out the lights, climb into bed.

Chances are, they've all heard of Rachel Lorent. They might be aware that this is the tenth anniversary of her disappearance.

Maybe, as they lie in the dark, the current Zeta sisters are even secretly worried that something will happen to one of them.

Maybe they should be.

CHAPTER 3

"Whoa!" Garth, dressed in khakis and a cream-colored T-shirt under a lightweight brown blazer, stops short in the doorway. "Brynn, I didn't know we were having company at breakfast this morning!"

Startled, she looks up from the pancake she's about to flip on the hot skillet.

Oh. Her husband is just teasing, of course. The only other occupants of the kitchen are their two sons.

Brynn manages a faint smile as Garth feigns confusion, asking, "Who is that big schoolboy at the table? And where's Caleb?"

"Daddy! It's me!" Caleb, dressed in a button-down and khakis, his hair neatly slicked to one side, pipes up proudly. "I'm the big schoolboy!"

Wide-eyed, Garth says, "No, you can't possibly be Caleb. He's just a little guy, like this." He ruffles Jeremy's hair.

"It is me, Daddy. Really!" Caleb shoots a glance at Brynn, one that says, *Poor Daddy is clueless!*

Normally she gets a kick out of playing along with Garth's antics, but today, she simply doesn't have the energy or inclination for anything beyond the basic requirements. It was all she could do to get the boys dressed and hurriedly go through the motions of taking a shower herself, not even bothering to blow-dry her hair. She'll regret it later when she tries to get a comb through the still-damp waves hanging loosely around her face.

She was about to dole out cold cereal when Caleb reminded her that last night she promised them pancakes this morning. Right. That was before she opened her mail and her world turned upside down.

But mommy guilt set in and here she is, dishing up a hot breakfast when all she wants to do is crawl back into bed and hide.

"No way," Garth is persisting as he takes down a mug and pours himself a cup of coffee. "You can't be Caleb."

"Yes way! I go to school now, remember?" Caleb asks earnestly.

Brynn flips another pancake and sees that the bottom is scorched. She turns down the burner, then looks over her shoulder and sighs in dismay.

In his booster seat, Jeremy is finger painting the table with maple syrup.

Oblivious to the mess, Garth scratches his head, studying his older son. "Hmm . . . can it be?"

"Mommy! Tell him!"

"It really is Caleb, Daddy," Brynn obliges as she grabs a sponge from the sink and descends on Jeremy's sticky masterpiece. "He's in kindergarten now, remember? He rides the bus and everything."

Yes, and thanks to his mom, he's got exactly five minutes to finish his breakfast before he has to be down at the bus stop.

Brynn, who wakes with the sun daily and never bothers to set an alarm, overslept. She's been scrambling to catch up for the last forty-five minutes.

What a way to start the second day of school . . .

And Caleb's imminent departure is the least of her worries today.

"Did you want pancakes?" she asks Garth, realizing she's scorched three of the four on the skillet.

"Do you *have* pancakes?"

"I was making these for you, but . . ." She shrugs and indicates the smoking pan. "Sorry."

"It's okay. I'll just stick with coffee. I've got to take off a few pounds anyway."

No, he doesn't.

Tall and lean, with hair and eyes the warm shade of a well-loved baseball mitt, Garth Saddler looks the same as he did the first time Brynn laid eyes on him.

Not that she recalls much about their first official connection. It wasn't love at first sight, or even remote interest at first sight. She walked into the lecture hall on the first day of her final semester at Stonebridge, and there he was, standing quite unremarkably down in front, passing out copies of the syllabus.

He had a professorial beard back then, obscuring enough of his handsome face that it took awhile for Brynn to notice him. *Really* notice him.

It was Tildy who pointed out his masculine appeal one brisk day as they were crossing the campus and spotted him jogging past. "Look, there's Dr. Saddler. Wow, how hot is he?"

Brynn checked him out and saw that her sorority sister had a point. He looked a lot different with his muscular legs bared in running shorts, his sweat-dampened hair standing on end, than he did buttoned-up and intellectual in front of the class.

"I have him for that morbid Soc course I'm taking," she told Tildy.

"'Death and Dying'? I took it last semester. It was awesome. And so is he."

It wasn't long afterward that Brynn realized Garth Saddler was, indeed, pretty awesome. She even got the feeling the attraction was mutual.

But he didn't ask her out until the semester was over and she had her diploma in hand.

That, he told her, would have violated the rules.

"College rules?" she asked.

"No, mine."

She didn't expect to fall in love with him that first night. Nor did she plan to stay on in Cedar Crest that summer instead of returning home to the Cape.

But she did stay.

Not just for the summer. For . . .

Ever.

Things just fell into place for them, and she never looked back.

She worked nights as a desk clerk at the Amble On Inn nearby. So much for her newly minted bachelor's degree in English. And so much for returning home to the Cape.

Any potential postgraduation plans she had in mind— and she didn't have many—evaporated the moment Garth told her he loved her and wanted her to stay. By the time the fall semester began, she had moved into his apartment just off campus.

"Do you think things are happening too fast between us?" she asked him, more than once. Just to be sure this was all as much his idea as it was hers.

"No," he said, but she wondered if he meant it.

Sometimes, he seemed taken aback at the way their lives had melded so swiftly and completely. But she never doubted that he loved her, or that she loved him. They belonged together.

They were married in July, a little over a year into their relationship.

When the Amble On Inn abruptly shut down that fall, Garth found her a secretarial job in the registrar's office.

She quit that when Caleb came along eighteen months later, followed by Jeremy.

And the years have flown by, and here I am.

Here we *are.*

Living happily ever after . . .

Until now.

No, don't start thinking that way, she warns herself, watching Garth stir Splenda into his coffee, and Caleb munching his pancakes, and Jeremy licking maple syrup from his fingers. *Everything is going to be fine.*

Which is precisely the same thing she assured herself fifteen years ago, when a routine X-ray showed a suspicious shadow on her mother's lung.

Mom didn't even smoke and Dad gave it up years ago, so it couldn't be cancer . . .

But it *was* cancer.

Well, Brynn wasn't going to let it rob her of her mother . . .

But it did, in the space of a few months.

It robbed her as well of the jovial, loving family man who loved chocolate with nuts, the Red Sox, doo-wop music, and his wife and children. Not in that order.

Her father's heart and soul died with her mother, leaving in his outer shell a brooding, often-angry stranger. The house was silent and dusty, the fridge filled with expired condiments, no dairy or fresh vegetables.

That stage lasted only a few months, and was replaced with one that was, in Brynn's opinion, far more disturbing.

At first, though, she was grateful whenever Sue Learner, her mother's longtime friend from her women's bowling league, came around with the proverbial casseroles and condolences. Sue was a former nurse practitioner; she had a nurturing, maternal air that Brynn welcomed. She poured out her grief to Sue, along with a flood of adolescent angst.

She finally figured out that Sue was hanging around the house not to comfort her late friend's motherless children, but to seduce their widowed father.

Mom could never convince Daddy to go bowling, but somehow, Sue did. One of Brynn's friends spotted them together late one night at Lucky Lanes. Brynn didn't believe it, but she questioned her father—and he confessed.

That bombshell struck Brynn about twenty-four hours before he threw a far more explosive one: he was getting remarried. To Sue.

"It's what your mother would want," he said—so often that Brynn wondered if he was trying to convince himself.

Personally, she doubted her mother had drawn her last breath fervently hoping that her good friend would move into her house, and her bed, before the granite slab was even laid over her grave.

Brynn, who, until that tumultuous loss, had wondered how she would ever go away to college without becoming terribly homesick, lived for the day when she could leave.

Once she did, she rarely looked back.

"Are you okay, Brynn?" Garth asks, and she looks up to see him watching her over the rim of his coffee cup.

"Fine. Just tired." For emphasis, she tacks on a yawn that starts out forced, but winds up the real thing.

"You didn't sleep well?"

She shakes her head at the understatement. But then, Garth wouldn't know she tossed and turned all night behind their closed master bedroom door.

A lifelong insomniac, he rarely joins her in bed before dawn. Some nights—like last night—he stays on campus working on his book until the wee hours. Others, he doesn't reach the bedroom at all, presumably sitting up in the den either writing or watching television, occasionally snoozing in his easy chair there when she emerges in the morning.

Early in their marriage, Brynn got up often to check on Garth or coax him to bed. Whenever he obliged, she felt like she was trying to sleep alongside a restless animal desperate to escape its cage. She gave up, years ago, the notion of climbing into bed beside her husband every night.

"I guess it's not surprising that you couldn't get much

sleep last night. After all, yesterday was a major milestone." Garth tilts his head toward Caleb.

"Definitely a milestone," she agrees. *And not just in the way you think.*

Last night, she should have climbed into bed warmed by the afterglow of her son's big, successful day.

Instead, she was tormented by visions that jabbed like icy fingers into her consciousness, keeping sleep at bay, forcing her to relive in horrifying detail the unthinkable events that unfolded exactly a decade before . . .

> *It was Brynn who unwittingly set things in motion.*
>
> *"Did you notice how bummed Rachel was at dinner tonight?" she asked Fee as they left the library at dusk after a scant ninety minutes of studying.*
>
> *"Not really," Fiona returned predictably, her thoughts most likely on her boyfriend—or herself. "Why?"*
>
> *"She just seemed down, even when Puffy brought out the cake and we were all singing 'Happy Birthday' to her."*
>
> *Puffy Trovato was the sorority housemother, a warm, maternal woman whose nickname came from her round physique. Nobody knew her real name, and she didn't seem to mind.*
>
> *Her specialty was triple-layer Devil's Food Cake topped with whipped-cream frosting and a spray of fresh red roses—the sorority flower. She made it for every one of the sisters' birthdays, serving it up with a scoop of vanilla bean ice cream and a maternal bear hug.*
>
> *Then everyone would serenade the guest of honor, first with the birthday song, then with the official sorority song.*
>
> *Tonight, watching Rachel pick at her cake before pushing the plate away and leaving the table, Brynn*

wanted to ask if everything was okay. Petite Rachel, with her free-spirited gypsy style and easy smile, was usually the most upbeat, laid-back sister in the house. Last year on her birthday, she stood on her chair and laughingly conducted the Happy Birthday *chorus, then followed that up with a hammy, operatic solo of her own.*

Rachel, pursuing a bachelor of fine arts degree, had been taking voice lessons since childhood. She had a vague ambition to one day have a career on a concert stage; she just hadn't decided whether it should be at the Met, backed by a full orchestra, or at the Garden, backed by electric guitars.

"Maybe Rach is just feeling old, leaving her teens behind," Brynn decided, and Fiona rolled her eyes.

"Oh, as if. Who wants to be stuck in their teens? I can't wait to turn legal so I can officially hang out at the Rat with Pat."

The Rat, of course, was short for The Rathskeller, the off-campus pub where Fiona's older boyfriend tended bar. Her fake ID was useless here in town, where the locals had known her since she was born.

"I hate to break it to you, but legal's going to take awhile," Brynn informed her friend. "You've got to turn twenty before you can turn twenty-one, remember?"

"When I do, though, I'm throwing myself one hell of a birthday party at the Rat. And I know just who I'm inviting, too."

"Already?"

"Yup, because by that time, graduation will be right around the corner and I'm going to be networking every chance I get."

Accustomed to retrieving conversations that had been commandeered and steered off course by the self-centered Fiona, Brynn prodded, "In the meantime,

*what are we going to do about Rachel? Her birthday
is today, and so far it seems to suck."*

*"Well . . . I've got a bottle of decent champagne Pat
gave me last weekend to celebrate the new semester."*

"You didn't drink it with him?"

*"Nah, he only drinks beer and bourbon. Come on,
let's go find Tildy and Cassie and surprise Rach with a
little party."*

"At the sorority house?"

"Uh-uh, then we'd have to invite everyone else."
Fiona was currently feuding with more than one of
their fellow sisters, as usual.

Anyway, the five of them were the closest, ironically
because of how their birthdays fell. For some reason,
the college systematically grouped incoming freshmen
into dorms based on when they were born. Brynn, Fiona,
Tildy, and Cassie all had October birthdays. Living in
close quarters on the same hall, they formed a quick,
intimate bond long before they pledged the same sorority.

Rachel, whose birthday was a month earlier, lived
at the opposite end of the hall, but latched on to their
foursome because, as she put it, "All those September
Virgos down at my end are too conservative and un-
emotional. You Libras are much more easy-going and
social."

Brynn often popped up to point out that she was actually a Scorpio, born on the twenty-ninth. But Rachel,
who was into astrology, told her she had more Libra
traits—and that strong-willed control-freak Fiona had
more Scorpio ones.

"We'll do this party for Rachel up at the Prom,"
Fiona said in her usual case-closed way.

The Prom was local shorthand for promontory, and
referred to an enormous, flat rock outcropping high in

the woods above the campus. Secluded despite relatively easy access via a winding trail, the sweeping vista plus a cluster of makeshift log benches made the Prom a favorite Stonebridge party spot.

"Just so you know, I'm going to invite my sister, too, if she's around when we get back to the house," Fiona added.

Brynn said nothing to that. She knew that Tildy was getting annoyed about Deirdre's continued presence in the sorority house, and she wouldn't be welcome tonight. She had been staying with Fee for over a week now, trying to get her life together after being thrown out of their parents' house.

Luckily, Dee wasn't hanging around that night to join the party and further complicate matters.

Only the five sorority sisters slipped out of the house and headed up the trail, armed with flashlights, the champagne, a portable CD player, and jackets or sweaters to ward off the autumn chill.

They gossiped and giggled as they ascended, four of them unaware that the fifth had concealed something lethal beneath her silver-gray and cardinal-red sorority sweater—and that when the night drew to its grim conclusion, only four Zeta Delta Kappa sisters would descend.

"Matilda Harrington," Tildy says crisply into the telephone receiver.

"Good morning, gorgeous," a low voice croons.

She quickly looks around to see if anyone is in earshot of her cubicle, lamenting as always the fact that her position as special events manager at the nonprofit doesn't even warrant walls that reach all the way to the ceiling.

At least the coast is relatively clear this morning. It's just past nine; most people aren't at their desks yet. No sign of the perpetually lurking Ray Wilmington, even.

"Hey, there, gorgeous yourself," she says, low, into the receiver. She pushes aside the yellow legal pad containing the guest list and RSVPs for her thirtieth birthday party in a few weeks. Plenty of time to go through those later. "When did you leave?"

"Oh, around three or so. I kissed you good-bye but you were snoring blissfully."

That would be thanks to the tranquilizer Tildy had popped shortly before he showed up unexpectedly on her doorstep. Had she known he was coming, she'd have foregone the pill and relied on him instead to provide a distraction from . . .

From *Happy Birthday . . . to me.*

Tildy didn't tell him about it, of course. That, or the drugs that were necessary when she grasped the full, horrifying implication of the greeting card.

Renewed uneasiness threads its way through her even as she protests lightly into the phone, "Hey, I don't snore!"

"Oh, but you do. Delicate little snores, like a kitten taking a nap in the sun."

If Ray said something like that, Tildy would immediately roll her blue eyes.

Funny how the difference in whether a flirtatious line comes across as hopelessly sappy or infinitely sexy lies in the speaker himself.

"So listen . . . What are you doing for lunch?" Tildy asks throatily, after casting another furtive glance around the office.

"You," is his satisfying reply.

Smiling, she hangs up a moment later, then belatedly opens her date book to make sure today's noon slot is free.

It isn't.

She simply erases her lunch tasting meeting with the caterer who's doing her birthday party. That can wait until tomorrow or the day after, she thinks, bending over the page to blow away the shreds of pink eraser.

Life has been so much easier ever since Tildy took to

writing her appointments in pencil—a necessity when you're living an active love life strictly on short notice.

She's flipping through her Rolodex in search of the caterer's phone number to cancel their lunch when a long shadow falls over her desk.

Ray Wilmington.

She knows it must be him before she even looks up to find his gaunt, black-bearded Abe Lincolnesque presence looming above her.

"What up?" he asks.

She snorts—aloud—at the ludicrous gangsta greeting spilling from the wimpiest, most white-bread human in all of Boston.

"God bless you," he says politely.

She doesn't bother to inform him that it wasn't a sneeze, but a snort. Of laughter. At him.

"How are the tulips holding up, Matilda?"

Ah, the tulips.

She debates telling him that they wilted and she had to throw them away.

No, he might then decide to send her another bouquet.

Her desire to avoid that scenario is based less on the futile expense to his limited budget than it is on the inconvenience to her.

She'd have to go through the motions of thanking him again, and risk clogging the disposal with all those stems, or cutting herself on the shards of another useless glass vase.

Much less complicated to simply say, "The tulips are fine," and resume her Rolodex perusal.

"Did your lunch meeting cancel on you?" Ray asks, and she sees that he's peering over her shoulder at the newly erased twelve o'clock slot in her date book. "Because if you're suddenly free, I know a great little place—"

"I'm not free," she interrupts curtly, wishing he would just get lost.

"Then how about tomorrow?"

Presumptuous is the perfect adjective for Ray Wilmington, from his investigative interest in the details of her life to his assumption that she might be willing to share a precious free moment of it with the likes of him.

It isn't just his looks that are off-putting—although Tildy's certainly not the least bit drawn to him. He's tall and dark, yes . . . though the *handsome* is conspicuously missing. Put a stovepipe hat on top of his prematurely thinning hair, and he really would be a dead ringer for old Honest Abe.

Abe Lincoln would hardly be Tildy's type.

Especially if Abe was making a pitiful salary and living at home with his mother in Dedham.

But it's more that Ray's blatant interest in her, which began right from the day he started at work here in July, gives her the creeps. Her well-honed inner radar interprets him more as a potential stalker than potential suitor.

Ignoring his query about tomorrow, she tells him pointedly, "I've got some phone calls to make," as she lifts the phone receiver again.

"All right, Waltzing Matilda." Ray emits a self-satisfied chuckle at his own cleverness, apparently assuming he's the first person ever to call her that. "I guess I'll see you later, then."

God, I hope not, she thinks grimly, dialing the caterer.

CHAPTER 4

Cedar Crest is divided into neighborhoods, each with its own distinct character.

On the outskirts of town, closest to the highway exit, is the ubiquitous commercial strip lined with fast food restaurants, chain hotels, supermarkets, discount stores like Wal-Mart and Target.

Then there's Stonebridge campus itself, a forested, self-contained enclave connected by a series of winding paths that meander past brick dormitories and academic buildings, a new sports facility, sprawling athletic fields.

Adjacent to the campus is a grid of old streets with two- and three-story homes. Once, they were upper-middle-class family residences; today, most are student housing with bikes and furniture on porches, doors and windows perpetually ajar. Most could use a fresh coat of paint, a handyman, and some yard work. Those in best repair display Greek letters beneath the eaves.

Today's middle class resides on the opposite end of town, where winding streets like Tamarack Lane reflect architecture from the first half of the twentieth century: primarily Tudor and Arts and Crafts. Here, yards are well kept. Late summer perennials are in bloom, local election signs are already springing up on lawns sprinkled with the season's first fallen leaves. SUVs and station wagons sit in driveways. There are wooden backyard swing sets and domed curbside mailboxes.

Both residential areas are dotted with churches, parks, and playgrounds; they're bridged by the central business district, with Main Street running its length. Stores and restaurants spill onto the perpendicular numbered streets along the way.

There are no chains here, but plenty of locally owned bars, sub and pizza shops, and coffeehouses that cater to the college crowd. Those—along with a Laundromat, a coffee shop, and shops that sell books and postcards, T-shirts and Stonebridge memorabilia—are clustered on the north end, closest to campus.

The southern end is home to banks and realtors, cafés and pharmacies, a children's clothing store, a couple of small markets, a yoga studio.

Fiona Fitzgerald Public Relations is here, on the ground floor of a turreted mustard-yellow Victorian mansion that's been converted to office space.

Brynn makes the fifteen-minute walk over from the bus stop, pushing Jeremy's collapsible canvas umbrella stroller in the cool September sunshine.

"Come on, little guy, let's go visit Auntie Fee," she says with false cheer, and unstraps Jeremy from his stroller.

"No!"

"Yes."

"No!" Jeremy squirms in her arms.

She's forced to haul him up the wooden front steps, leaving the stroller behind. Well, if anyone wants to steal it, they're welcome to it. It's definitely the worse for wear after carting first Caleb, then Jeremy, around town.

Brynn really should pick up another one at Target before this one gives out altogether. But money is tight this month.

This month?

When isn't it tight?

Well, it was less tight when they were a two-person household living on two incomes as opposed to a four-person household trying to make it on one.

She supposes she could always put Jeremy in day care and get some kind of job . . .

But she doesn't want to do that. She wants to stay at home, fully available, the kind of mother *she* had.

Except that I'll live to see my children graduate high school, and college, and get married, and have children of their own . . .

She wants to witness the big milestones just as she's been able to witness the little ones: first steps, first words, first teeth . . .

I just want to be their mom. And Garth's wife. That's all I really need to be.

Which is good, because that's all I am. And I love my life just the way it is . . .

There's just something about being in Fiona's presence that makes her a little self-conscious about the decidedly domestic path she's chosen.

She crosses the porch with a still-protesting Jeremy on her hip, wondering if maybe she should have called first, instead of just barging in here.

Glancing at her watch, she notes that Fee will most certainly be in the office at this hour. She's in the office at just about any waking hour—including some hours that the rest of the world may not necessarily count as *waking*.

"Shh, Jeremy."

Opening one of the tall double entrance doors, Brynn steps into the dim hall that was once a grand foyer. High ceilings, ornate moldings, and a sweeping staircase bear testimony to the building's past; several closed, placard-bearing doors to its present.

"It's dark," Jeremy informs her in a small voice.

"I know, it's okay. See? Here we are." Opening the door fronted by Fiona's name, she steps into one-half of the former double parlor. It's easy to picture the tall, double-hung windows, hardwood floors, and marble fireplace looking exactly the same in the late-1800s. The reception area, like Fee's adjacent office, is tastefully decorated with nineteenth-century reproduction wallpaper and fabrics, and antique furnishings.

A skinny blonde looks up from the tall potted fern she's watering beside one of the two windows.

"Hi, I'm Brynn, a friend of Fiona's."

"Oh . . . hi." The girl looks so uncertain that Brynn knows immediately that her days here are numbered.

Fee has absolutely no patience for indecision.

That's why Sharon, who, during their college years had been the private secretary for the dean at Stonebridge, was the perfect office manager for her. The older woman doesn't have a wishy-washy bone in her body. If she likes you, you know it on sight. Same thing if she doesn't like you. Brynn, she always liked, and the feeling is mutual.

Toying with the watering can, the new girl asks, "You don't have an appointment . . . do you?"

Brynn shakes her head, feeling almost sorry for the girl. She's painfully skinny and inappropriately dressed in a gauze skirt and thick, flat sandals. Her long forehead and plain, egg-shaped face are unnecessarily accentuated by straight, wispy, straw-colored hair parted in the middle.

"I need a cup," Jeremy announces, eyeing the Poland Spring cooler.

"Is it all right if I get him a drink of water?" Brynn asks.

Again, the girl is riddled with incertitude.

Brynn shifts Jeremy to her other hip and fills a paper cup anyway.

He takes a big gulp, squirms, and demands, "I want to get down."

"No, Mommy's going to hold you," she tells him firmly,

acutely aware of the stained glass lamp and porcelain bowl of potpourri on a nearby table.

I shouldn't have brought him, she realizes, and on the heels of that thought, *but I had no choice.*

What she wouldn't give to have a doting grandma nearby, as most of her friends do. But her father and stepmother are a world away in every sense, and Garth's parents are retired in Florida. For Brynn, getting out of the house without one or both the kids is an impossible weekday challenge.

She hands her son the empty paper cup to play with and decides she'd better get down to business before Jeremy's limited patience runs its course.

"You must be Fiona's new assistant," she tells the girl.

"That's right."

"What was your name again?" Brynn prods, fully aware that she never said.

She isn't rude . . . just young. And clueless.

You poor thing, she thinks sadly. *Fiona's going to eat you alive.*

"Oh, I'm Emily." Of that, at least, she seems certain.

"Nice to meet you. So is Fiona here?"

"I'm not supposed to disturb her unless it's an emergency."

"Is she alone in there?"

Emily nods. "But—"

Brynn starts for Fee's closed door.

"No, wait—"

"It's okay," Brynn tells her, as she reaches for the knob with the hand that isn't wrapped around Jeremy. "You're not disturbing her. I am."

Settling into a booth in the Cedar Crest Coffee Shop on the northern end of Main Street, Isaac Halpern accepts the laminated menu from a pretty student waitress. She blatantly checks him out.

With his traditional good looks—clean-cut dark hair and

blue eyes, a strong, but not too strong, nose, and a tall frame that's both lean and muscular—he does get his share of attention from women.

Especially back home in Manhattan, where straight, single, successful men are as valuable a commodity as rent-controlled real estate.

"Know what you want?" the waitress asks with a toss of her long black hair.

"I haven't even looked at the menu yet."

She shrugs. "Most people already know."

"Just give me a minute, okay?" he asks, and she drifts away.

The menu is stained with brownish splashes and there is a grain of dried rice plastered to the laminate. Terrific.

Holding it gingerly, Isaac scans the lengthy list of offerings beneath the heading:

Breakfast Served 24 Hours

Eggs, omelets, French Toast, pancakes, bagels, cereal, fruit, sides of anything you can imagine . . .

Pretty much the same menu as in any diner back in New York, but at less than half the price for everything. Pretty much the same setup, too—long counter along one wall, a row of booths along the other. Most of those are empty, and only a few of the stools at the counter are occupied.

But this is a college town; this place is ten times busier at two in the morning after the bars close than it is now.

Just a stone's throw from here is the Zeta Delta Kappa house, its gray shingles freshly painted this semester with red trim. Those are the official sorority colors, the red representing the sorority mascot, which is the cardinal.

Why a cardinal? Isaac asked Rachel once, when she was poring over her secret sorority notebook, cramming for the pledge quiz. *Why not something more exotic, like a pink flamingo, or a peacock?*

Because cardinals stand out more than anything else, and they're cheerful, and they're everywhere, she replied with her usual Rachel decisiveness. *When was the last time you looked out the window and saw a pink flamingo? There's nothing better than spotting a beautiful, cheerful splotch of red in the trees on a gray winter morning.*

There hasn't been a gray winter morning since she said it that Isaac hasn't searched—to no avail—for a cardinal.

"Did you decide?"

He looks up. The waitress is back already, pad poised, hair still hanging around her face. Shouldn't she be wearing a hairnet, or a ponytail, or something? That she isn't doesn't bode well for the cuisine.

Yeah, he should tell her he changed his mind and get out of here.

Instead, he hears himself say, "I'll just have a Western Omelet and whole-grain toast. And coffee."

He isn't the least bit hungry, but he's here; he should eat.

And why are *you here?*

Not here in the coffee shop; here in Cedar Crest.

I'm here because . . .

Because . . .

God, I shouldn't be here. What the hell is wrong with me? Why do I keep coming back here every September?

This was a bad, impulsive idea.

Not the first in his life, though, and it surely won't be his last.

All because of her.

Rachel.

The waitress departs. As if on cue, his cell phone begins to vibrate in the back pocket of his jeans; he hurriedly grabs it and flips it open. The number displayed in the caller ID box is a familiar one.

"Hey," a female voice says. "It's me."

"Hey. How's San Francisco?"

"Foggy. How's New York?"

He hesitates.

"Sunny," he says, because it was supposed to be; he caught the local weather forecast on Z100 before leaving for Massachusetts.

"Did you remember to feed Smoochy this morning?"

The cat. Damn.

"Yes," he lies.

That tabby is so fat he can probably survive off his own body fat for weeks. Still, Isaac should have remembered to feed him. If anything happens to the cat, Kylah will be heartbroken. And furious with him. Particularly when she finds out her pet's well-being was sacrificed for this little annual expedition to New England.

No, not *when*.

Not even *if*.

She won't find out. She's safely on the West Coast, he'll be home in New York before she is, and the world's fattest feline will be fine.

"I miss you," she says with a sigh.

"I miss you, too. How's the conference going?"

"You know. Same as they always go. It's all a big blur of name tags and handouts and bad food and watered-down drinks. I can't wait to get home tomorrow. Don't forget—my flight gets in at six and I'm coming straight home, so . . ."

"I'll be there."

And he will. Because he can't stay here in Cedar Crest indefinitely.

But he'll be back again.

And again, and again . . .

For as long as it takes.

About to protest the abrupt intrusion, Fiona looks up from her desk to see not the hapless Emily, but Brynn, framed in the open doorway.

Her heart sinks.

She isn't in the mood. True, she was just sitting here, craving a cigarette and brooding about the very thing Brynn is undoubtedly here to discuss, but . . .

But I don't want to talk about it. Not yet. Not until I've decided how I'm going to approach this whole mess.

Looks like she doesn't have a choice, though.

"Hey." Fiona stands and feigns an affectionate smile at Jeremy, whose lower face appears to be covered in some kind of sticky sludge. Lovely. "What are you guys doing here?"

Brynn just sends her a level look and closes the door behind herself just as Emily pops up, hovering nervously and looking apologetic.

I've got to get rid of her, Fiona thinks wearily. *I'll fire her first chance I get . . .*

And replace her with whom?

"Listen, we need to talk about this thing," Brynn is saying in a low voice.

"Did you get ahold of them?" Fiona asks.

Of course Brynn knows who she's talking about. Cassie and Tildy.

"No, I couldn't." She sinks onto the visitor's chair beside the desk with Jeremy on her lap.

"Did you try?"

Brynn shakes her head.

"Brynn, you said you'd call them last night."

"I know I did, but by the time I got the kids ready for bed, Garth was home, and—"

"You didn't tell *him,* did you?"

"Are you *kidding* me?"

"Shh." Fiona frowns and nods at the closed door, beyond which Emily could presumably be eavesdropping, though she sincerely doubts it.

That would take initiative and, as far as she can tell, her assistant doesn't possess a blessed ounce of it.

Nor, apparently, does Brynn. She said she would call the others.

Figures. Well, you learned long ago that if you want something done right . . . You do it yourself.

"I'm just making sure you weren't tempted to tell Garth," Fiona says in a low voice. "I mean, he had Rachel in class, and he was in that faculty search party, so I thought maybe you figured—"

"Well, I didn't say anything. *You* didn't tell anyone, did you?" Brynn whispers.

"No." Fiona ignores the slightest twinge in the vicinity of her conscience. "Who am I going to tell?"

"Jeremy, no!" Brynn unpries her son's fingers from the fringed lampshade beside the chair.

He protests loudly as she removes several strands of maroon thread that are plastered to his sticky hands.

"Sorry, Fee."

She nods, not about to say that it's okay. Because it isn't.

Brynn should know better than to come barging into her office first thing in the morning—or anytime, for that matter—particularly with a toddler in tow.

Anyway, this isn't the time or place to discuss what happened in the past . . . ten years ago, or yesterday.

Then her friend looks up at her with those big puppy dog eyes of hers and says, "I'm scared, Fee."

Fiona's irritation dribbles away.

So am I, she wants to admit.

"The more I think about it, the more I'm sure it's just Tildy or Cassie playing a stupid and totally unfunny joke," she assures Brynn instead.

"Really?"

No.

"I mean, who else can it possibly be?" she asks Brynn,

but her attention is focused on Jeremy, reaching for the tall Lladro figurine on her desk.

It depicts a mother and child; Deirdre sent it from Spain as a gift for Fee's first Mother's Day.

Fiona was stuck at home with a newborn at the time. For her, the beautiful porcelain figure was less a testament to new motherhood than it was a symbol of her lost freedom.

She had never been to Europe then. Saddled with a baby and a husband whose salary barely covered the rent, she probably never would get there . . . or so she believed at the time.

She pulls the Lladro slightly closer to herself, out of Jeremy's grasp.

Brynn doesn't seem to notice.

"I can think of someone else it can be," she says, and Fiona's heart skips a beat.

"Who?"

"Think about it, Fee."

"I *am* thinking about it. Who are you talking about, Brynn?"

"Rachel," comes the unanticipated reply, just as Jeremy grasps the figurine and drops it onto the hardwood floor, where it shatters deafeningly.

The Dave Matthews Band was on the portable CD player, drowning out the night sounds.

"Go for it, Fee!" Tildy commanded and Fiona, standing on the crest of The Prom, facing the lights of Cedar Crest in dazzling array below, popped the champagne bottle with two thumbs. The cork shot out into oblivion; then they heard the faint rustle of its landing in the thicket far below.

"Woo-hoo!" Tildy reached to take the bottle from her.

"Um, shouldn't Rachel have the first sip?" Brynn spoke up. "Since she's the birthday girl?"

"Oh, that's okay." Rachel reached into her sweater. "I've got something better."

She produced a pint-sized mason jar.

"What's that?"

"Grain alcohol." Unscrewing the lid, Rachel took a swig, made a face, and offered the jar to the others. "Who wants some?"

"Are you kidding?" Tildy wrinkled her cosmetically perfected nose. "Where'd you get that? Somebody's disgusting bathtub?"

"No, from my stepbrother, over the summer."

"Which stepbrother?" Fiona asked. Rachel's family was a blend of full-, half-, and step-siblings as well as former and present stepfathers and stepmothers.

"Which one do you think? I've only got two steps, and Joshua is only in fourth grade."

That would leave the older stepbrother, whose father had married her mother briefly a few years ago. Their parents had long since gone their separate ways, but Rachel was still close to him. He had graduated last May from Morgantown University in West Virginia; now he was living and working in New York. The sorority sisters were planning a road trip to Manhattan later in the fall, and Rachel said they could stay with him.

"So where did your brother get grain alcohol?" Cassie asked, after a delicate sip from the champagne bottle.

"Where else? This came straight from the mountains of West Virginny."

"Hey, Rach, that hillbilly twang is about as believable as your fake English accent," Fiona told her.

"Yeah, but at least it's a lot better than her fake Southern drawl," Brynn put in teasingly.

"Hey, my drawl was pretty good," Rachel protested. "That guy I met in the Rat the other night believed me when I said I was from Mississippi."

"Yeah, up until you told him your name was Scarlett," Tildy said with a snort.

"You guys were in the Rat the other night?" Fiona asked.

They exchanged guilty glances.

"Sorry, Fee," Brynn said. "You were working that night anyway."

"Whatever. Just because I can't set foot in there until I'm twenty-one doesn't mean you all have to stay away."

But she didn't sound as though she meant it.

And she added a bit sharply, "Just don't go in there when Pat's tending bar. He knows you're underage. He can get busted if he lets you stay."

Somebody changed the subject to the upcoming Rush Week before anyone could point out that Pat had seen them there and looked the other way, plenty of times.

Fiona had some funny hang-ups about being the lone townie among them. It wasn't easy for her to watch the rest of them hit the popular local bars with their fake IDs.

"Sure you guys don't want any? It's homemade." Rachel brandished the jar of grain alcohol as though she was proudly referring to a tray of decadent brownies.

Still no takers.

Rachel shrugged and swigged, going about it almost grimly when she thought nobody was paying much attention.

But they were—each of the four, in her own way.

They all noticed there was something off about Rachel that night. As the night wore on, her voice vacillated between somber and shrill, but she didn't really say much of anything.

Nothing that would strike any of them, later, as having shed light on her strange mood.

"You'd better go easy on that stuff," advised Cassie, who took her pre-med studies seriously. "You're so petite, Rach—you can't handle that much. It can make you sick."

"It's my party, and I'll barf if I want to," Rachel sang to the tune of the old Leslie Gore song.

They all laughed . . . at first.

But their amusement faded as the four of them passed around the bottle of champagne while Rachel guzzled the contents of the mason jar, clearly hell-bent on getting trashed.

There was no joy in it; it was clear to them even then that this was no celebration.

Something was troubling their friend.

Brynn even pulled her aside and asked her, at one point, what was wrong.

"If I could tell you, I would, Brynnie. But I can't."

And sweet, pretty Rachel Lorent carried her secret to her death that night . . . or so they all believed.

Cassie's cell phone rings a few minutes after she turns it on, just as she slips behind the wheel of her car in the hospital parking lot.

It's probably Alec. She left him a message earlier saying that he shouldn't come over tonight; that she feels as though she's coming down with something.

He'll probably insist on coming anyway, with chicken soup or ginger ale or flowers. That's the kind of guy he is.

A great guy.

And I don't deserve him, Cassie tells herself, not for the first time.

Why is she consumed by a familiar urge to drive straight to the barn, climb on her horse, and gallop off as fast as she dares . . . ?

Where? Where would you go?

Anyplace other than here, in my life.

Because it doesn't feel *like my life.*

She reluctantly presses the SEND button on her ringing phone.

"Cassie?"

It's a female voice. Unfamiliar . . .

But only in that first instant.

"Hello? Are you there?" the caller asks, and Cassie realizes, with a quickening pulse, just who it is.

"Brynn?"

"Oh, you *are* there. I heard a click a second ago and I thought you'd hung up."

"No, I'm here."

"Can you talk? I mean . . . you know . . . Is anyone around?"

At her furtive words and hushed tone, Cassie understands why she must be calling.

"Yes," she says reluctantly. "I can talk."

"Did you get one, too?"

Cassie's heart erupts in a wild pounding.

"Yes," she says simply.

So it wasn't just me.

"So did Fiona."

Then what about Tildy?

Maybe I have a voice mail from her, Cassie thinks—though there wasn't one the last time she checked, on her lunch break.

"Listen, we're meeting at one tomorrow afternoon, near Springfield, to talk about it. Can you be there?"

"Who's meeting?"

"Me, Fee, Tildy . . . and you."

"You talked to Tildy?"

"Fiona did. She tracked her down at work."

"So she got one, too? Tildy?"

And why didn't she call me back last night?

"All four of us did. Can you be there tomorrow?"

"Tomorrow? No, I can't—"

"You're working?"

At her hesitation, Brynn says firmly, "Cassie, you have to come."

"But—"

"You have to."

Brynn is right.

Cassie dutifully writes down the directions to the meeting place.

"You haven't told anyone about . . ." Brynn hesitates.

"Come on, do you really have to ask that? We took an oath, remember?"

"I remember. But that was ten years ago."

"An oath is an oath, Brynn."

There's a pause.

"I know. I'll see you tomorrow at one."

Tomorrow.

At one.

That's going to take some juggling to arrange, but it has to be done.

There's no way I'm going to miss this.

Four so-called sisters, together again at last.

The precious bond of trust, stretched thin across the span of years, is on the verge of snapping.

They're wondering, now, who among them might have violated the sacred vow.

They're wondering whether carefully sealed closet doors are about to be thrown open, brittle, decade-old bones tumbling out.

Ah, ladies . . . if you only knew.

One moment, Rachel was there, clutching the almost-empty mason jar.

*The next, she was precariously close to the brink of
The Prom, laughing hysterically about something.*

Or maybe she was crying.

It was hard to tell; she was incoherent.

*All four of them warned her to get away from the
edge.*

*And all four watched as she lost her footing and
fell.*

*Unlike the champagne cork, she didn't sail out over
the edge of the cliff. No, she rolled off, grasping helplessly, her terrified screams punctuated by a horrible
thrashing descent, curtailed abruptly with a sickening
thud far below.*

Fiona lives still in the house she and Pat bought during
their marriage: a vintage 1920s Tudor tucked into a quiet,
winding side street in Cedar Crest.

"Don't you want to sell it and start fresh in a place where
there are no memories?" Brynn asked, after the divorce.

"Trust me, there are no real memories here."

No meaningful ones, anyway—good, bad, or even trivial,
day-to-day stuff. As far as she's concerned, everything about
her marriage was behind her the moment they signed the
separation papers. The house itself was always just a roof
over their heads and a façade behind which they could carry
on the charade of marriage and family life.

The mountain cabin is even less meaningful. They bought
it just a few months before the split—Fiona more as an in-
vestment, and Pat because he wanted to actually use the
place. As far as she knows, he rarely goes up there—and she
never does. They keep the key under the doormat, and Fiona
has more than once urged Brynn and Garth to use it as an escape. Mostly because she doesn't want Pat to think he has
sole dibs.

"Leave the kids and take a second honeymoon," she tells

the Saddlers every so often. God knows they could stand a break.

But they keep protesting that they don't have anyplace where they can leave their kids, and Fiona isn't about to offer to watch them for a weekend.

"Why don't you ever go up, Fee?" Brynn wanted to know once.

"Because I like my creature comforts. I'm not the rough-it type."

Brynn laughed. "No, you're definitely not."

Now, as Fiona stands in the master bedroom taking off the suit she wore to the office, she admires the Waverly floral wallpaper, coordinating draperies and area rug; the white iron bed she bought at an estate sale in Lenox, along with an antique dressing table, bureau, and wardrobe.

The first thing she did after Pat left was strip off all the old striped wallpaper, rip up the carpeting, and get rid of the bedroom suite they had bought with their wedding money.

She gave that to Sharon, who was thrilled with all those polished cherry Ethan Allen pieces.

Of course, they didn't fit in the small rectangular bedroom of her ranch house, so she put the armoire in the living room to hold her television and all those Hummel figurines she collected, and used one of the nightstands as an end table. Fiona privately thought it looked out of place beneath a stack of paperback romance novels and a ten-dollar Wal-Mart lamp, positioned beside the sagging orange and brown plaid couch.

When Sharon moved in with her daughter last month, she offered the furniture back to Fiona, who told her to go ahead and sell it at her tag sale. In the end, Sharon reported, it was hauled away by a young family in a battered pickup truck, who had paid for it mainly in ones and fives.

Fiona found some satisfaction in knowing that those people, who could never afford new furniture, were enjoying her luxurious bedroom suite.

She found much more satisfaction in mentioning that to Patrick and watching him turn purple with fury.

"There was nothing in the divorce agreement that specified what I had to do with the furniture I got in the settlement," she pointed out. "If you thought there should have been, you should have spoken up to your attorney. Oh, wait, I forgot . . . Legal issues aren't exactly your strong suit."

That, of course, alluded to the fact that he flunked out of law school not long after they were married. She had no idea he was even struggling, though she should probably have guessed.

When he came home and told her, she walked right out the door, with no intention of ever going back.

Fate intervened by way of a positive pregnancy test.

Oh, well. At least she wasn't stuck with Patrick Hagan forever.

She divorced him the moment her business was comfortably established, and immediately reclaimed her maiden name.

It isn't that she's particularly eager to be associated with her estranged parents in any way, but it was better than keeping Hagan. Besides, she likes the alliteration. *Fiona Fitzgerald Public Relations* . . . It really flows quite nicely.

Things have a way of falling into place.

These days, Pat takes Ashley to dinner at least once a week and she spends every other weekend with him, from after school on Friday afternoons until eleven on Sunday mornings. Fiona insisted he have her back that early so that she can take Ashley to noon mass with her. Pat was raised Catholic, too, but he hasn't gone to church in years.

Fiona stopped going, too, for awhile, after they got married. She stayed away from the church until—

She stops the jarring wisp of thought before it can balloon into a full-fledged recollection.

No, she doesn't like to think about *that*.

The sins of the past belong in the past. You can't change them.

All you can do is go to mass every Sunday, and pray for forgiveness.

She still attends Saint Vincent's Church, the parish where she and Deirdre made their First Communions. But she diligently avoids the ten o'clock mass her parents have attended for thirty-some years. She doesn't like to see them unless absolutely necessary; nor does she want Ashley to spend time with them, knowing they're apt to fill her ears with self-righteous garbage—most likely about the sins of her mother and aunt.

Back in her college days, Fee all but wrote off her parents when they disowned her twin sister.

She softened a bit after Ashley was born, though—in part because she was desperately lonely, but mostly because she needed someone to watch Ashley so she could begin working as a freelance PR consultant for a small local agency. She and Pat couldn't afford childcare and her mother was willing to acquiesce, free of charge.

That worked out for awhile. Then Fiona got divorced—in her parents' eyes, a crime as serious as Deirdre's homosexuality—and it was all over. Just as well. She certainly doesn't need anyone looking over her shoulder these days.

Hearing a car's tires crunching on the gravel driveway below her bedroom window, Fiona quickly pulls on a pair of yoga pants and a T-shirt from the hook behind the closet door. She hurries down the stairs just as Ashley, giggling about something her father is saying, is opening the door.

With her dark hair and eyes, porcelain skin, and lanky figure, Fiona's daughter looks so much like her father. Acts like him, too, with her increasingly lackadaisical attitude. Sometimes, Fiona just can't relate to her daughter—and sometimes, she secretly, ashamedly, even resents her.

"Hi, Mom! Guess what? We went to Applebee's! I love Applebee's! So does Dad!"

Fiona hates Applebee's.

"That's great, Ash." She musters a thin smile for her daughter, conscious of Pat looming on the other side of the threshold. He hasn't been invited to cross it since the divorce.

Fiona flicks a lighter over a cigarette—both because she wants one and because Pat is a militant antismoker. She turns her head to blow a stream of smoke well away from her daughter's face and asks, "Listen, did you feed your goldfish this morning?"

"I forgot."

"Again?" Fiona's jaw tightens. She's so much like her father. "You really need to learn how to be more responsible. Can you please go down and feed it?"

"Right this second?"

"Right this second."

"Okay."

Ashley won the goldfish at a carnival Pat took her to last spring. She brought it home, sickly looking, in a plastic sandwich baggy, and informed Fiona that she had already named it Bubbles La Rue.

She then begged to keep it here, rather than at Pat's place, saying her father might forget to feed it. Fiona agreed, on the condition that she keep the bowl in the basement playroom, and secretly assuming the fish would last all of a day or two. A week at most.

Somehow, like a philodendron that mysteriously thrives without regular watering, the stubborn creature has hung in there ever since, despite Ashley's sporadic care.

"See you tomorrow morning, Daddy." Ashley stretches on her tiptoes to kiss her father.

"See you tomorrow morning, Princess."

Only when Ashley is skipping away does Fiona look at Pat. He's already turned on his heel, about to leave.

"Wait a second." She doesn't say his name. She hasn't, in conversation, since their marriage ended. There's something too intimate, too cordial, about addressing someone by name.

He turns back. "Yeah?" He casts a disdainful look at the lit cigarette in her hand.

"Cynthia Reynolds called right after I got home about fifteen minutes ago."

Pat waits silently for her to go on, standing on the brick doorstep, his black eyes expressionless and fixed on hers. Clearly, he knows who Cynthia Reynolds is.

Fiona didn't, when she called. Not right away. It took her a moment to realize that she's the mother of one of Ashley's friends.

For some reason, it bothers her that Pat knows that detail. Then again, he has plenty of time and attention for Ashley and her friends and their parents. What else does he have to do?

"She's taking Meg to the mall tomorrow for lunch at the new Rainforest Cafe," Fiona tells him in the brisk tone she uses with Emily at work, "then to see some new Disney movie. She invited Ashley to join them."

In the next room, an eavesdropping Ashley squeals with joy.

"Ashley! Go feed your fish," Fiona commands.

"But I can go, right?" she calls. "With Meg and her mom?"

Fiona looks at Pat.

"Saturdays are my days with her," he growls in a low voice.

"You can go with Meg," Fiona calls back to her daughter. "Go feed your fish."

She hears the basement door open, and Ashley's footsteps skipping down the stairs.

Fiona looks her glaring ex in the eye and exhales a stream of smoke in his direction. "She really wants to go."

Pat curses and waves away the smoke. "Don't you think it should have been my decision? Especially since she was supposed to be spending the day with *me?*"

"You're the one who always wants her to make lots of friends and be social. You know how much she likes Meg. And anyway, if you don't want her to go shopping with her friend tomorrow, *you* can go ahead and be the one to tell her and break her heart, and then call the mom back and break Meg's heart, too."

Pat scowls.

She can tell there's a lot he wants to say.

But he calls, "Good night, Ashley, honey! I'll pick you up in the morning!" in the sweet Daddy voice he uses with their daughter.

So different from the deadly cold tone he uses with Fiona.

He turns and storms away without a good-bye.

Good riddance to you, too.

She kicks the door closed with a resounding slam.

Life would be so much simpler, she thinks as she moves through the living room, smoking, straightening throw pillows that don't need it, if she and Pat didn't have a child together.

Then she could have made a clean break, picked up and moved out of town after the divorce.

Yes, Fiona Fitzgerald Public Relations would be in the heart of Manhattan if not for the relocation clause in the divorce settlement, which states that neither she nor Pat can move beyond a fifty-mile radius of Cedar Crest without reopening their case.

She isn't about to do that, especially now that she's worked so hard to become a success. Why should Pat reap the benefits in any way?

So, she's stuck here for at least another ten years. At least they have only one child, thank goodness. *Thanks to me.*

By the time Ashley is in college, she'll be pushing forty.

Another milestone.

But the pivotal one is right around the corner: she'll turn thirty next month.

And Rachel . . .

Rachel would have turned thirty yesterday.

Would have?

Brynn wasn't so sure those two words were accurate.

Now Fiona tries the phrase without them—*Rachel turned thirty yesterday*—and a chill slithers down her spine.

She watched Rachel Lorent fall to her death ten years ago last night . . .

Or did she?

> It was Tildy who immediately made her way down to the spot where Rachel had fallen, clutching a flashlight whose beam bobbed eerily in the night. The rest of them clung to each other above, sobbing helplessly and hopelessly.
>
> It was Tildy who felt their friend's—their sister's— neck for a pulse, and found none.
>
> And it was Tildy who tearfully left Rachel at the base of the cliff exactly where she had fallen, on a thick bed of pine needles a few feet away from a stone marker at the edge of the hiking trail.
>
> Back at the top, Tildy was visibly shaken, trembling violently.
>
> They all were.
>
> But after they had cried hysterically, and pulled themselves together—the others considerably more quickly than Brynn—Tildy declared that they couldn't tell anyone what had happened.
>
> "Are you crazy?" Brynn protested. "We can't just leave her there. We have to go call the police."
>
> "And tell them what?"
>
> "That it was an accident," Brynn choked out in her grief, "that Rachel was drunk out of her mind, and we warned her. We tried to stop her."
>
> "But we didn't stop her," Tildy pointed out. "And now she's dead. And we're involved. Look what happened to the Sigs, and nobody even died."
>
> Sigma Tau was a fraternity whose chapter at a neighboring college was investigated for hazing last fall

after a sophomore pledge landed in the hospital with severe alcohol poisoning. In the end, he suffered permanent brain damage, the Sigs had their charter revoked, and several of their officers were still facing charges in a lawsuit.

"That could happen to the four of us in a heartbeat," Tildy warned them. "Cassie, can you imagine what your parents would say if you were arrested?"

Cassie, the daughter of a high-powered New York politician mother and a neurosurgeon father, looked as though she was going to faint.

They all knew about her notoriously perfectionist parents. The Ashfords were let down enough when a learning disability, undiagnosed until her senior year at a prestigious Connecticut boarding school, prevented Cassie from earning Ivy League grades and attending their alma mater as her brother did.

Trouble with the law would put them over the edge.

"What about you, Brynn?" Tildy went on. "You're here on a full academic scholarship. Do you actually think the college will let you stay if you're involved in something this scandalous?"

Brynn was silent. The answer was obvious.

"What about you, Fee? You're a local. You know everyone in town. And what about your parents? Look what they did to your sister last year when she came out and the whole town was gossiping about it. What do you think they'll do if your name is dragged through the local press in connection with something like this?"

"I don't want to think about that," Fiona said grimly. "None of us can afford to get involved. This would ruin our lives."

"Not to mention destroy the sorority," declared its loyal president. "We owe it to our sisters to keep this quiet."

"But we didn't do anything wrong, Tildy. We didn't

force Rachel to drink, like the Sigs forced that pledge," Brynn protested.

"Says who?" Tildy asked.

"What do you mean? Of course the four of us will stand up for ourselves and say we're innocent."

"Those Sig guys claimed the same thing. Who believed them?"

"That was different. They were hazing."

"Do you think anyone will really care about the details, Brynn?" Cassie spoke up at last, sounding almost frantic. *"All they'll see is a bunch of underage sorority girls drinking in the woods."*

"My God, Rachel is dead!" Brynn cried. *"We can't just leave her here in the woods. Isn't that against the law?"*

"No," Tildy said firmly. *"It isn't."*

"How do you know?"

"Because it's not like we've murdered someone."

"But leaving her here is wrong," Brynn said in desperation. *"Maybe it's not against the law—which it might actually be—but it's wrong."*

"Brynn, there's nothing we can do for her now," Fiona said gently.

"Rachel would never want us to incriminate ourselves," Tildy added. *"We have to leave her. Anyone in our situation would do the exact same thing."*

Brynn shook her head miserably, unconvinced.

"Look, somebody will find her as soon as the sun comes up, which is"—Tildy checked her watch with almost preternatural calm—*"a few hours from now. We all know that hikers are out on that trail every single morning, right? And she's lying right there on the path. Nobody could possibly miss her. She'll be found, and the police will assume that she wandered up here alone, drunk . . . and fell."*

"I don't know . . ." Even Cassie looked uncertain. "Why would she come up into the woods alone?"

"She was acting strangely all day yesterday," Tildy said. "Brynn noticed it, and so did I, and I bet other people did, too."

"I did," Cassie said.

"So did I, definitely," Fiona agreed, and Brynn shot her a look.

Fiona shrugged.

Clearly, it was three against one.

"Look, nobody knows we were up here with her tonight, right?" Tildy asked. "You guys didn't tell anyone where you were going?"

All three shook their heads.

And swore each other to secrecy.

And the next morning waited uneasily for the news that Rachel's body had been found in the woods below The Prom.

It never came.

As far as the rest of the world was concerned, Rachel Lorent had vanished into thin air. On the morning after her twentieth birthday, her bed in her room at the sorority house hadn't been slept in, she never showed up for classes . . . in short, she was never heard from again.

The campus was in a turmoil. Faculty and students formed search teams that walked shoulder to shoulder over acres of ground, searching.

They found nothing.

A few days after Rachel's mother had filed a Missing Person's Report and fliers bearing her smiling face had gone up all over campus, Brynn, Fiona, Cassie, and Tildy walked silently up the trail to the spot where she had landed, dead.

It was empty. Not even a sign that Rachel had ever been there.

How was that possible?

As Tildy had said, there was no way anyone passing along could have missed her body on the path . . . and there was no way, with the beautiful late-summer weather, that the trail hadn't been traveled in all that time. Anyway, the searchers had repeatedly covered this ground in the past few days.

Maybe wild animals dragged her away that first night and devoured her remains, a fate too horrible for any of them to envision.

For months afterward, they held their collective breath, expecting some sign of their lost sister to turn up . . . perhaps a disembodied limb found deep in the woods, or a shred of clothing, or even the mason jar . . .

But nothing ever did.

Rachel Lorent had never been heard from again.

Or had she?

CHAPTER 5

It was Fiona who selected the meeting place: Glenview Springhouse, an elegant eighteenth-century country inn not far from where the Mass Pike and Interstate 91 converge. It's centrally located for all of them: a little over an hour west of Boston, ninety minutes north of Danbury, and almost an hour east of Cedar Crest.

It makes sense for Brynn and Fiona to go together. Fee insists on driving, though Brynn offered.

"I can't leave the office until noon, and I've got to get back for a three forty-five appointment," was her reasoning.

Brynn pointed out that they would get there and back in the same amount of time regardless of who drove.

Fee didn't dispute that, but Brynn could tell she wanted to . . . And she would have been right.

The speedometer of Fiona's silver BMW quickly rises to eighty as they leave Cedar Crest, and never falls until they pull off the exit.

"You drive like the car was just catapulted out of a cannon. You know that, don't you?" Brynn pulls her cell phone out of her purse as Fiona stops at a light and quickly snaps down the visor mirror to check her reflection.

"Of course I know that. I can't afford to tool along taking in the sights. Who are you calling?"

"Garth." She pauses, about to hit SEND. "Why?"

"Why are you calling him?"

"To see how the boys are doing."

"Already?" Fiona's tone smoothly melds amusement with disapproval.

Brynn shrugs and dials anyway, needing the connection to her life back home. Especially now, when she's about to come face-to-face with the past.

She told her husband the truth about today's getaway, in a sense, saying she and Fiona are meeting two old sorority sisters for lunch near Springfield.

She just didn't tell him why.

Nor did he ask.

He merely told her he was glad she was taking some weekend time to do something for herself for a change.

She felt guilty that he was so sweet about it, and about the money she'll be spending on a fancy lunch they can't really afford.

"Hey, it's me. How are the boys?" she asks when Garth cheerfully answers the phone.

"They're good. Where are you?"

"Just about to get to the restaurant."

"That was fast."

"You have no idea," she says wryly. "What are the boys doing? Did you remember to give Caleb his antibiotics? Did they eat lunch?"

She glances at Fiona, who is looking in the mirror. Her lips are pursed to apply more lipstick, but probably would be anyway.

"I'm making lunch now, yes on the medicine, and they're on the couch watching *Dora the Explorer*."

"That's what I was afraid of."

She made Garth promise he wouldn't stick the kids in front of the television all day.

"It's just to keep them out from underfoot while I make lunch."

She wonders what he can possibly be making that's so involved it might take longer than a minute or two, but doesn't ask. She would if Fiona wasn't sitting beside her in silent disapproval.

"You know the boys like the crusts cut off their bread if you're making sandwiches, don't you?"

He pauses just long enough for her to realize that, somehow, he doesn't know that.

"I know."

She smiles faintly. "Just making sure."

"Listen, have fun," Garth says before they hang up, as the light changes and Fiona guns the engine to hurtle them on toward the inn.

"I will."

No, she won't.

"Tell the girls I said hello."

"I will."

No, she won't.

He knows Tildy and Cassie, of course, just as he knew Rachel. He had them in class during their days at Stonebridge. Both Tildy and Cassie popped in and out of Brynn's life in the early years of her marriage, before the boys came along and everyone drifted.

But today isn't about catching up on each other's families, jobs, lives.

It's about something Brynn isn't yet prepared to dredge from the murky depths of her memory.

But it's too late to back out now, even if she dared suggest that to Fiona.

She and Fee haven't spoken much during the drive—and not at all about the birthday cards, or Rachel, or the past. Or, thank goodness, the expensive Lladro figurine Jeremy demolished in Fiona's office yesterday, which Brynn offered to pay for, and was grateful when Fiona refused. She knew it would probably cost more than a mortgage payment, and she and Garth are having a hard enough time making those lately.

Fee spent much of the last hour on her cell phone with clients, in as blatant disregard of the mandatory hands-free headset tossed carelessly on the backseat as she is the posted speed limit.

At least she didn't smoke.

Well, not after the first cigarette she was already puffing on when she pulled into the Saddlers' driveway.

Brynn asked her not to smoke in the car.

"I can roll down the window."

"It still bothers me. I get nauseous, and you don't want me to vomit all over your car, do you?"

Obviously, Fiona did not.

Glenview Springhouse is a sprawling, white clapboard house. Judging by the rambling architectural style, Brynn concludes it's probably been added on to repeatedly over the years. The restaurant entrance is off to one side, in a wing that consists mainly of a glassed-in atrium.

Here we go, Brynn thinks, still clenching her cell phone in a hand that remains white-knuckled even now that her speed-demon friend has stopped the car.

She can't help but wonder what she's doing here.

She should be home in Cedar Crest, eating peanut butter sandwiches—no crusts—with the boys, and nagging Garth about fixing the plastic towel bar in the bathroom that dropped off the tile wall again this morning.

That's her life, not this . . . this . . .

This nightmare.

"Do you think they're here?" she asks as Fiona pulls into an empty spot and turns off the engine.

"Tildy definitely is." Fee indicates a gleaming red Ferrari 612 Scaglietti parked nearby.

"That's her car? How do you know?" Brynn asks uneasily, remembering Fiona claimed earlier that she hasn't seen Matilda in years, either.

Claimed?

So you think she was lying about that?

Why would she?

Her thoughts awhirl with paranoia and suspicion, Brynn can't seem to look her friend in the eye.

No matter. Fee is too busy looking herself in the eye, focused again on the visor mirror as she says matter-of-factly, "I don't know it's Tildy's for sure. But that's a quarter-of-a-million-dollar car, and I'm willing to bet it's hers. It's her style."

Brynn, noting that she herself failed to discern said quarter-of-a-million-dollar car from the red Hyundai parked next to it, is mired in a familiar sense of being well out of her league.

When she first met the infinitely astute Fiona, Brynn marveled that a girl who grew up in a blue-collar Cedar Crest household could possibly be so worldly.

Brynn has long since accepted that it's no accident. Driven by ambition long before she was voted Most Likely to Succeed at Saint Vincent's High, Fee shed her local roots like a worn housecoat.

She'd have gone away to college if her parents could have afforded it; instead, she used local connections and worked her way through Stonebridge. By the time she was asked to pledge Zeta Delta Kappa, no one outside her closest circle of friends even realized she was a townie.

She seemed to have everything, even back then: brains, ambition, friends, a great wardrobe—and one of the hottest boyfriends around.

Four years older than Fee when she began her freshman year, Pat was a law student at Stonebridge by day and a bartender by night. Plenty of girls were drawn to his affable personality and striking good looks. Black Irish, Fiona used to say, with his shock of dark hair and sooty lashes that fringed coal-colored eyes.

Pat was from New York—Brooklyn. He was going to be a big-shot lawyer. Fiona often spoke of how they would move to Manhattan, where she would work for some top PR firm.

But Pat never made it to the Bar, thanks in large part to the bar: the Rat, where he worked.

It was obvious that Pat preferred doling out drinks and socializing to studying law. Obvious, that is, to all but single-minded Fiona, so in love with Pat that she saw only what she wanted to see.

Brynn supposes their relationship boiled down to plain-old chemistry: a wild, mutual attraction that struck at first sight, lingered for a few years, and wore off soon after the wedding.

They had been married a few months when Pat flunked out of law school.

Stunned, Fiona turned up on Brynn's doorstep late that blustery night, saying she had left him.

"I don't belong with some loser dropout. I deserve a lot better than that."

The next morning she woke up, ran straight to the bathroom to vomit, and miserably asked Brynn to run over to CVS to pick up a pregnancy test.

Ashley was born eight months later.

To appease his wife—and support her and his new daughter—Pat landed a job with a couple of sleazy divorce attorneys up in Pittsfield, working as a paralegal. He continued to tend bar at the Rat at night and on weekends, but spent every spare moment with Ashley.

He still does. He's a devoted daddy—even Fiona will give him that.

Pat longed for a second child.

Fiona Fitzgerald Public Relations was born the September Ashley entered preschool, and there was no looking back.

Fee might not be working in a fancy, high-profile New York PR firm, but she was running a thriving business. One that unfortunately propelled her spiraling marriage right into the ground.

Brynn often wonders whether her friend ever has regrets—and whether she occasionally she envies the Saddlers' stable lives.

Probably not.

Now, watching her friend check her teeth for lipstick, then snap the visor mirror back into place, she asks, "What do you think they're going to say about all of this?"

They, of course, are the two sorority sisters presumably waiting inside.

"Only one way to find out. Come on."

Reluctantly, Brynn climbs out of the car and follows Fiona on wobbly legs.

It's too late in the season for summer vacationers and too early for foliage spectators, yet the inn's large dining room is fairly crowded this first weekend after Labor Day. The round tables, draped in rich amber linen and centered with flickering candles and fresh autumn-hued flowers, are occupied mainly by couples and retirees.

Matilda Harrington is the lone occupant of a round table for four. She had asked the hostess to move her twice before deciding this was as private a location as possible, in a relatively secluded corner beside a tall, lace-curtained window.

Tildy sips her chilled white wine and takes in the Colonial ambience: the low-beamed ceiling, white-painted woodwork, gleaming, dark hardwood floors. Windows on three walls open onto profuse perennial gardens in brilliant, late-summer bloom and, beyond, a verdant woodland backdrop sure to be ablaze with color in another couple of weeks.

Glenview Springhouse would be the perfect place to spend

a romantic birthday weekend, considering that she can't appear in public with the man in her life. Not as a couple, anyway.

Just last night, she made the mistake of saying, *"I'm so sick of sneaking around that I'm starting to think I don't care who finds out."*

His eyes darkened so swiftly at that remark that she wished she could take it back. He grew quiet and left soon afterward, saying he had to get home.

He *always* has to get home.

What Tildy wouldn't give to spend just one night—the entire night—in his arms.

I deserve that, she concludes. *And this would be the perfect place.*

She'll have to pick up an inn brochure on the way out, so she can show it to him. With enough advance notice, maybe he'll be able to swing it.

"After all," she'll tell him, "I'm only turning thirty once in my life. I want to celebrate it privately, with you."

She's beginning to wish she had never planned the big party. She booked the date—the night before her birthday—at the Imperial Ballroom at the Park Plaza Hotel a few months ago.

Spotting her sorority sisters approaching the table with the hostess, Tildy lowers her wineglass. Maybe she should have invited them to the party, she thinks—but only for a split second.

No, she shouldn't have. They're not a part of her life now. They wouldn't fit in.

Brynn, she hasn't seen in years. Tildy notes, reluctantly, that her former sorority sister hasn't lost her fresh-faced, wholesome prettiness, nor her willowy figure.

But the cut of her dark blazer is all wrong, and she's wearing it over a pair of Gap khakis, with flat brown loafers of all things.

Tildy herself is appropriately dressed in Ralph Lauren Black Label, perfect for a Saturday luncheon in the country. Fresh from the salon, her hair is newly cut in sophisticated layers that fall to her shoulders.

Brynn's is still long, pulled back in a simple ponytail, and she's got on precious little makeup.

With some eyeliner, a flattering haircut, and stylish clothes, Tildy thinks, she'd be a knockout.

As it is, she just looks so . . . small-town New England. Like someone's wife, someone's mom. All of which, Tildy reminds herself, she is.

But she doesn't have to look the part, for God's sake.

Jealous, are you? an annoying little voice pipes up.

Certainly not. Not of Brynn's looks, anyway.

And not of anything else. Not anymore.

Ah, there's Fiona. She hasn't changed much since she was in Boston in June, when Tildy introduced her to her old boarding-school friend James Bingham over an elegant seafood dinner at Aura.

Her well-cut trim charcoal designer suit is a little businesslike for Tildy's taste. Still, it's expensive, fashionable, and becoming, and her legs look fabulous in the above-the-knee pencil-slim skirt and tall-heeled pumps. Her jewelry is gold and tastefully expensive.

Her painstaking assessment sliding north, Tildy notes that Fee's hair is twisted from its sleek right part into its usual smooth auburn chignon, her porcelain skin is flawless as ever, and her green eyes are expertly highlighted with a smoky shadow.

She looks good, she thinks grudgingly. *But not better than I do.*

Standing, Tildy takes turns air-kissing both their cheeks and notices that Brynn's eyes are suspiciously bright.

"You're not going to cry, for God's sake, are you?" she asks lightly as they pull out chairs.

Rather, she intends it to come out lightly, a quip among old friends.

Instead, she sounds bitchy, even to her own ears.

"I'm trying not to." Brynn studies her cloth napkin as she spreads it in her lap. "I'm just a little emotional about . . . everything."

"You always were," Fiona comments with a hint of affection, and gives her shoulder a pat. But, looking at Tildy across Brynn's bowed head, she smirks, just a little.

"And *you* never were," Tildy can't help but comment, as she lifts her glass again in a silent, and not necessarily approving, toast to Fiona.

"I never was what? Emotional?" Fiona shrugs and picks up the leather-bound wine list. "To my credit, no, I wasn't. I wasn't a lot of things Brynn was. Is that Chardonnay you're drinking?"

"Pinot Grigio."

Fiona flags a passing waiter; not theirs. "I'd like a glass of the Bouchard Père & Fils Puligny-Montrachet. Brynn?"

She looks up. "Oh . . . Just an iced tea, please. With lemon."

"Oh, come on, Brynn, live a little," Tildy urges. "At least have a glass of wine with us."

Brynn shakes her head. "I'm just getting over strep throat and I'm still on antibiotics. I'll be the designated driver."

"I don't think so," Fiona says briskly, and turns to Tildy. "Have you heard from Cassandra?"

"She left me a message this morning." And one last night, as well. Tildy screened both calls.

"What did she say?"

"Just that she'll be here. She must have hit traffic. Did you know she's getting married to some guy in November?"

"She e-mailed us both when she got engaged," Brynn says. "I called her to say congratulations and catch up. She told me about her fiancé . . . She said they met at the hospital where she's doing her residency. He's a doctor, right? A podiatrist or something?"

"I think so." Tildy idly inspects her manicure.

"She said you met him when they came to Boston for a Red Sox game this summer. What's he like?"

Tildy wonders if Brynn really cares, or is just trying to keep the conversation afloat until Cassie arrives and they can get down to business.

Fiona is busy pulling her Blackberry from her pocket and flipping it open under the table, checking for e-mail.

"Alex? He's nice enough," Tildy says briefly. She can think of nothing to add other than, "Good-looking, too."

"Oh, it's *Alex?*" Brynn asks. "I thought it was Alec."

Hmm. Maybe it is. Tildy makes a mental note to pay more attention next time Cassie mentions him.

Fiona tucks her phone back into her pocket and casts a glance over each shoulder before asking Tildy in a low voice, "So, what did you think when you got that birthday card in the mail?"

"To be honest? I thought one of you had a sick sense of humor."

"It wasn't us," Brynn tells her definitively. "And Cassie swears it wasn't her. So unless it was you—"

"It wasn't me. Please!" Tildy rolls her eyes.

"Well, then, who the heck do you think it could have been?"

Hmm, Brynn seems to have a bit more spunk than she ever did back in college, Tildy notes with some satisfaction. Good for her.

"I don't know what to think," she replies evenly, and fights the urge to pick up her wineglass again. She doesn't want them to think she's drinking to calm herself.

And anyway, she'd better keep her wits about her, or this could go very badly.

Fifteen minutes after watching Brynn and Fiona climb out of the BMW and walk into the restaurant, Cassie is still sitting in her Toyota parked at the far end of the parking lot.

She's got to go in.

Either that, or just drive away.

But she can't just sit here indefinitely, mulling things over. *I shouldn't have come at all.*

Really, there's so much she could be—*should be*—doing instead, with every free moment she's not working at the hospital. She has to finalize the reception menu. Meet again with the seamstress who's doing the final alterations on her wedding gown. Give Alec's sister the final guest list for next month's shower, which she was supposed to have completed weeks ago.

"Go ahead and invite anyone you want," Tammy urged her. "Neighbors, distant relatives, old college pals . . . I'm serious, I've got plenty of room."

Cassie suspects that her future sister-in-law is as eager to be graciously accommodating as she is to show off her newly built 7,000-square-foot brick Colonial facing the Long Island Sound.

"Someday, we'll have a spread like this, baby," Alec said when they walked through it for the first time last month. "You and me and our five beautiful kids. They can each have their own room."

"*Five* kids?" Cassie laughed nervously.

"You're right, let's go for six. I don't like odd numbers. And we'll put up a big stable for Marshmallow, and you can ride him whenever you want, every day if you want."

"Ride him where?"

"On our beautiful property. We'll have a few acres, lots of trees, a water view, white picket fence, the whole nine yards."

White picket might as well be barbed wire, she found herself thinking illogically, as her fiancé pulled her in for a kiss.

She tried to relax and let him kiss her, but she couldn't.

"What's wrong?" he asked.

She shook her head. "Nothing."

He gave her a long look and was about to question her further when his sister stuck her head in and told them dinner was ready.

How much longer can I go on pretending everything is fine? Cassie asks herself now, resting her head against the steering wheel.

She had enough to worry about before this whole Rachel thing reared its ugly head the other day. Between her medical residency and her wedding plans, she's barely had time to digest what that birthday card might signify.

All she knows is that her life is finally thrashing out of control like a wild stallion.

And she has two choices.

She can either tightly take hold of the reins while there's still time . . .

Or she can close her eyes, allow fate to toss her wherever it may, and pray for a safe landing.

There she goes at last, heading tentatively up the wide brick steps and disappearing into Glenview Springhouse.

For God's sake, it took Cassandra Ashford long enough to get out of the damned car.

In contrast, it takes no time at all to furtively dart from the silver BMW to the red Ferrari to the blue Toyota and slip a white envelope beneath the driver's side windshield wiper on each.

There you go, ladies. A nice little surprise for all of you . . . Especially Matilda.

She'll look at it with confusion, and certainly with disdain, and, perhaps, ultimately, with dread.

That's the point.

At the very least, she and the others will come to realize that they aren't alone here at this secluded inn in the woods.

That, in fact, after this they can never really be sure they're alone anywhere.

CHAPTER 6

"Daddy!"

About to settle into his desk chair at the computer, Garth bolts back to the living room at the blood-curdling shriek.

"What is it? What's wrong?" He skids to a stop in the doorway. Both the boys are sitting calmly on their little wooden stools pulled up to the cluttered coffee table, where he left them just a moment ago.

"There's crust on his bread!" Caleb explains, one eye trained on the television, where SpongeBob Squarepants is doing a little dance.

Oops. Brynn did say he was supposed to cut off the crust.

"Crust!" Jeremy bellows like someone in the throes of physical torture. "Yucky!"

"Cut that out, Jeremy. Crust is good for you."

"No crust!"

"Okay, okay, stop shouting." Garth reaches past a tall stack of magazines and a taller one of unpaid bills to retrieve the paper plate containing the peanut butter sandwich he just made.

"There's crust on mine, too, Daddy."

"Yeah, yeah, I'll cut it off." Picking up Caleb's sandwich

as well, he retreats back to the kitchen, where this morning's cereal boxes still litter the white countertop, along with plentiful toast crumbs.

He promised Brynn he'd clean up everything and load the dishwasher with the cereal bowls, milk-soggy and still in the sink.

"Just go get ready for your lunch," he urged her, as she surveyed the messy kitchen.

She protested, but only for a moment. When she emerged from the bedroom a half hour later, she looked like her old self again—in khakis and a nice blazer rather than the T-shirts and raggy-hemmed faded jeans she favored most days.

Her old self, as in the person she used to be, before the boys came along.

She smiled when he complimented her. Then he caught her looking at the mess he hadn't yet touched.

"Don't worry, I'm on it," he promised. "You just go have fun."

"I will. But . . ." She shook her head.

"What's wrong?"

"That superglue didn't hold. The towel bar just dropped off the bathroom wall again. Can you fix it?"

He sighed. "Yeah, I'll fix it."

"Soon? Because I don't want one of the boys to get hurt."

How, exactly, she thought one of the boys could get hurt by a missing towel bar was, and still is, beyond him.

Yet Garth knows better than to argue with illogical maternal logic. He never wins.

"You go have fun with the girls, and forget about everything here. I'll hold down the fort."

"I hate to leave."

"It's only for a few hours, and you never go anywhere. Enjoy it."

"I am kind of looking forward to a change of scenery," she admitted. "In fact, I was thinking maybe one weekend in October, we could take a ride to the Cape to see my father."

"I don't know . . . It's such a long drive for just two days, between Friday-night traffic and Sunday-night traffic."

"We could go on Columbus Day weekend."

"Isn't that when I'm in Arizona?"

"Oh, right. I forgot."

"Why don't you go anyway," he suggested, "with the boys?"

He expected her to accuse him of not wanting to see her family, as she has before. But, surprisingly, all she said was, "Maybe I will."

Good. She should. Her father and stepmother will want to see her and the boys . . . And Garth is well aware that they'd just as soon do it without him around.

There's never been much love lost between him and his father-in-law. Joe Costello is an old-fashioned, blue-collar guy who wasn't thrilled when his only daughter shacked up with her professor the summer after graduation. That she went on to marry him and settle down on the opposite end of the state didn't help matters as much as one might expect.

Joe and his wife are civil enough these days, but Garth is never entirely comfortable in their presence—nor are they in his.

Brynn's father frequently likes to point out that he's just "a regular guy"—as opposed to Garth, who ostensibly is not.

"I don't get all that professor talk," he remarks pointedly whenever Garth uses a word containing more than three syllables. "Can you say that again in plain English?"

No, Garth isn't anxious to visit the Cape anytime soon. Let Brynn go with the boys, and explain that he's off somewhere indulging in "professor talk."

"Daddy?"

Right, the sandwiches.

"Coming, guys."

He opens the silverware drawer and roots around. Butter knife, steak knife, paring knife, meat cleaver . . . Don't they have a regular old bread knife?

"I'm hungry!" Jeremy whines from the next room.

"You'll have to be patient," Garth calls back, and decides his youngest child is spoiled rotten.

Maybe that's what happens when you're the baby of the family. He wouldn't know. He's an only child, and his parents were older, and far from doting.

Brynn dotes.

Nothing wrong with that; she adores the boys. So does Garth, for that matter.

But . . . Motherhood is Brynn's life. To the extent that she's actually suggested—more than once—that they have another baby.

Garth laughed . . . until he realized she was dead serious.

Brynn cried when he ruled it out.

He often relents when she cries, but not about this. Their little house is already overflowing, they can't afford to move; they can't afford another child, period. Money is too tight.

She didn't see it that way.

"Daddy!"

"I've got it!" Garth swiftly hacks through eight slabs of Wonder Bread crust with a butter knife, drops it among the dirty dishes in the sink, and returns the sandwiches to the boys.

Caleb, still glued to the television, doesn't acknowledge him, just reaches for a sandwich and chews, robotic, fixated on SpongeBob.

Jeremy, however, breaks into a baby-toothed grin and announces, "No crust! Yay! I love Daddy!"

Garth's heart melts. Maybe he's not spoiled rotten after all.

But they definitely are not having another child. No way.

The phone rings before he can return to his work. It's Maggie, a mom down the street, wanting to set up a playdate with Jeremy and her son, Zack.

"That's Brynn's department," Garth tells her. "I'll have her get back to you."

"Where is she?"

"Out to lunch with some old friends."

"Lucky her," Maggie says. "If you have trouble holding down the fort, feel free to drop the boys here to play with mine."

Garth, who resents the implication that he's incapable of holding down the fort, tells her that won't be necessary.

At last he returns to the den, a former sunroom with tall windows on three walls, adjacent to the living room.

It's warm in here, the midday sun causing a greenhouse effect through the row of southern-exposure windows. Garth uses the old-fashioned hand cranks to open all of them, as well as the tree-shaded north-facing ones on the opposite wall. Instantly, a cross-breeze wafts into the room.

There. Much better.

He settles once again at his large desk, the broad wooden top entirely obscured by research books—though no more "gruesome" ones, in keeping with his promise to Brynn— along with stacks upon stacks of papers and notes, plus his desktop computer components.

The computer is on its last legs, but of course they can't afford a new one. It takes a few full minutes for the anti-quated system to boot up.

As he waits, Garth stares at a framed photo of himself with Brynn, snapped just before their wedding. She framed it for him as a gift that first Christmas together, when their newlywed budget was too strained for extravagances.

Which it has been ever since. Last Christmas they didn't even exchange gifts with each other, opting instead to ensure that Santa could bring the boys most of what they asked for.

Garth tilts the frame to reduce the glare of the sun stream-ing through the windows, gazing at his wife's image.

Look at her. She's so different now.

It isn't that she's aged, exactly. The picture was taken just eight years ago when she was in her early twenties; she still hasn't chronologically, or physically, left that youthful decade behind.

But the Brynn in the picture exudes carefree joy, and her attention is focused solely on her husband-to-be. That's how it always was back then—so different from now.

When was the last time she looked at him like that? As though she was really noticing him?

It's been a long, long time.

Definitely not since Jeremy came along.

She looks at the boys that way, though.

Garth often catches her staring at one or the other of their sons, utterly captivated by their most mundane actions . . . or, sometimes, it seems, by their mere existence.

But in this long-ago moment captured on film, she's looking only at Garth.

And Garth is looking at the camera.

More specifically, at the woman holding the camera.

How well he remembers that day spent wandering around the autumn arts-and-crafts festival in town, one that was attended by the locals as well as by college students and alumni.

How well he remembers the irony that *she,* of all people, would offer to take a picture of him with Brynn that day.

"Okay, smile," she said casually, aiming the lens.

Does she still remember that day? Does she remember what happened the night before, when Brynn was working the overnight shift at the Amble On Inn?

And if she remembers . . . Will she keep her promise never to tell Brynn their secret?

You'd better not tell, he warns her silently.

Not about what happened years ago . . . or about the sordid past revisited not so long ago at all.

Fiona immediately spies a familiar figure at the table as she reenters the dining room. Lithe, exotic Cassandra Ashford, wearing a coral sweater that's striking against her mocha complexion, now occupies the fourth chair.

"Cassie! Good, you're here." Fiona pauses to give her old friend a quick hug before sliding back into her seat. "Where have you been?"

"I . . . I had a little trouble finding this place."

"And where the heck have *you* been?"

Fiona looks up to find Tildy gazing intently at her from across the table, chin resting in her propped hand.

"In the ladies' room," she lies smoothly.

"No, you weren't. You were outside sneaking a smoke and checking your cell phone."

Fiona shrugs. "Guilty as charged . . . since that apparently is a crime?"

"Cassie, I almost forgot, let's see your engagement ring!" Brynn cuts in brightly.

"Oh, that's right, congratulations on that," Fiona tells her.

She can't help but notice that Cassie isn't exactly a gushing bride-to-be as she obligingly extends her left hand. Her smile is stiff, and she's having trouble answering basic questions about the wedding.

Either she's been utterly derailed by this impromptu sorority reunion and the strange birthday card that triggered it, or she isn't thrilled about getting married.

Maybe it's both, Fiona concludes.

The waiter arrives to take Cassie's drink order—club soda with lime—and to recite the daily specials.

"Are you ready to order?"

They look at each other.

Typically, Tildy decides, without asking, that they are. "I'd like the escargot to start," she says promptly, "and then the warm duck club sandwich."

"Shouldn't we at least let Cassie look at the menu?" Brynn protests.

"Oh, I'm fine. Do you have a chicken Caesar salad?" Cassie asks the waiter, who nods. "I'll have that."

That's probably not what she wanted, Fiona concludes, watching Cassie as Brynn is ordering a burger.

She's as low-maintenance as ever; she didn't want to make us wait while she looked at the menu.

Unlike high-maintenance me.

When it's her turn, Fiona quizzes the waiter at length about the ceviche and the sorrel salad before deciding on the wild mushroom tart.

"What?" she asks, catching Tildy giving her another look.

"Some things never change," Tildy comments with a smug shake of her head.

"Like . . . ?"

"Like being in a restaurant with you. Have you ever just walked into a place and ordered something off the cuff?"

"No, because when I do get a chance to eat, I like to make sure things are going to turn out to be exactly the way I want them. Otherwise it's all just a big waste of time."

Ostensibly, Fiona is talking about food. But she could be discussing life in general. Or her failed marriage.

She waits for the waiter to retreat before clearing her throat as a prelude to her announcement: "So, Brynn thinks Rachel is still alive."

Three jaws drop simultaneously.

"Why do *you* look so stunned?" Fiona asks Brynn. "You're the one who said it in the first place."

"Yeah, but . . . I didn't think you were just going to throw it out there like that."

"How can Rachel still be alive?"

Fiona shrugs at Cassie's bewildered question and asks pointedly, "What do *you* think, Tildy?"

Matilda Harrington seems to have no qualms about looking her in the eye as she responds, "She isn't alive. I checked her myself that night."

Which, of course, means nothing.

It wouldn't be the first time Tildy carried on a lying charade right under their noses.

But when it comes to *that* illicit situation, Fiona concludes that it's better for everyone involved to let some bygones be bygones, rather than go dredging up every last secret from the sisters' shared past.

Because what Brynn doesn't know can't hurt her.

At least, I hope not, Fiona thinks uneasily.

To Tildy, she says, "All we have is your word that Rachel didn't have a pulse when you climbed down there."

"'*All*' you have?" Tildy echoes. "What else do you need? You know my word is worth more than . . . well, more than . . ."

"More than you are?" Cassie supplies. "I mean financially."

Tildy responds with a tight little smile.

"So . . . the oath," Fiona says thoughtfully. "I guess that's what this is all about in the first place, isn't it? We gave each other our word that we wouldn't tell a soul what happened that night. But obviously, somebody did."

Silence as that sinks in.

Then Tildy commandeers the conversation. "So then, of the three of you sitting at this table, whose word is completely worthless?"

"There are *four* of us at this table, Tildy," Brynn points out.

"Do you really think *I* told? You're forgetting that I was the one who had to convince the rest of you to do what was best for our sisters."

"Rachel was our sister." Brynn's jaw is set firmly. "Was leaving her there in the woods best for her?"

"You mean leaving her *body* there," Tildy clarifies. "We had nothing to do with her death itself. We didn't cause it or even contribute to the cause. She drank her own disgusting grain alcohol; it's not like we gave it to her, or pushed her off that rock."

Tildy pauses to let that sink in.

Then she continues, "Look, we all know Rachel was responsible for her own actions that night. We tried to stop her, for God's sake. But who would have believed we were entirely innocent after what happened to the Sigmas? That night, we did what was best for *all* of the sisters, not just the four of us. That was my biggest priority. I was the sorority president, remember? I took my oath more seriously than anyone else. I wouldn't break it."

"I honestly don't think any of us would," Cassie speaks up. She looks from Fiona to Brynn. "Look, I'm a doctor. That was a hell of a fall. Do you honestly think . . . what? That Rachel was really alive down there, and Tildy lied about it? You believe that Rachel got up after that fall and walked away—and now she's back to torment the rest of us?"

Her words hang in the air, punctuated by ambient restaurant sounds: silver clinking against china, murmured conversations, classical music.

"It's either that," Brynn says quietly after a long moment, "or one of us told somebody what happened."

Fiona looks around the table. "Anyone want to come clean on that?"

More silence.

"I didn't think so," she mutters, reaching for her purse, and her cigarettes, before remembering that she can't smoke here.

"This is ridiculous." Tildy pushes back her chair. "I'm not sitting here while the three of you accuse me of something so heinous, after all I've done for all of you."

"I'm not accusing you of anything," Cassie protests.

"No, *you're* not," Tildy concedes, taking her leather Hermes bag from the back of her chair and slinging the strap over her shoulder. "*They* are."

"We're not accusing you, either." Brynn touches Tildy's arm, and looks to Fiona for agreement.

As irked by Brynn's benevolent attitude as she is by Tildy's self-righteous outrage, Fiona merely shrugs.

"We're just trying to figure out who could have sent those cards, and why," Brynn goes on, turning back to Tildy, "and how they could have known what happened."

"Maybe they *didn't* know," Cassie suggests, and is promptly on the receiving end of three blank stares.

"What do you mean?" Fee asks.

"Maybe whoever sent the cards just knew that Rachel disappeared on her birthday ten years ago, and that she was our friend. It was all over the news at the time, remember?"

"Remember?" Fiona echoes, thinking back to the media blitz that followed that terrible night. "Is there anything about any of it that we can possibly ever forget?"

Rachel's pretty face was plastered everywhere, from *The Today Show* to the evening news, from the front page of all the New York tabloids to *People* magazine.

Impressive coverage. The case held certain elements of mass appeal: a beautiful coed from a privileged family had vanished without a trace, and on her birthday, no less. People ate that stuff up.

Always have, always will.

In the past decade, other beautiful young women have mysteriously disappeared, just as Rachel did.

Chandra Levy, Elizabeth Smart, Natalie Holloway . . .

Sometimes, their stories have happy endings. Others conclude tragically. But even recovered remains bring closure.

There was no closure for the Lorent family. There were no remains to bury in the family plot on Long Island.

Eventually, rumblings began to surface in the media, just as there were rumors on campus, that Rachel had simply run off somewhere on her own. Gradually, her story faded from the public eye.

Of course, she was resurrected in the local press on the first few anniversaries of her disappearance, and when her father died of cancer a couple of years ago, and whenever a similarly high-profile case came along. But for the most part, it was over.

For everyone but Rachel's family . . .

And the four of us . . .

And whoever sent the cards.

"So, if that's the case—if the cards came from someone who knew about Rachel from the news, and not what really happened," Brynn says slowly, absorbing Cassie's theory, "then maybe it's just some sicko who remembers reading about it in the press, and the four of us aren't the only ones who got them."

"What do you mean?" Fiona asks impatiently.

"Maybe some of her other friends got the cards, too," Cassie says.

Brynn nods. "We need to find out."

"How are we going to do that?"

"We aren't," Fiona firmly informs both Cassie and Brynn, noticing that Tildy has remained conspicuously silent through their speculation, though she's made no further move to leave.

"Don't you think we should know whether this is strictly about the four of us, and somebody possibly knowing what happened that night?" Brynn asks.

"I'd love to find out, but we can't go around looking up the Zetas and asking questions without making ourselves look suspicious."

"I disagree."

Fiona shakes her head at Brynn's stubborn expression. "You want to start calling people and saying we all got cards from Rachel, and did they get them, too?"

"Not flat out, but—"

"No, Fee is right," Tildy pipes up at last. "We don't need anyone thinking we might know something about Rachel. Not even now, after all these years. The best thing we can do about all this is keep quiet."

"But—"

Brynn's protest is interrupted by the waiter returning with a loaded tray.

They wait in silence as he places their meals before them. As soon as he departs, Fiona says, "Let's assume that whoever sent those cards knows what we did that night. What do you think she—or he—is going to do about it?"

"Blackmail us." Tildy's answer is immediate.

Fiona had been thinking the same thing.

"What if it's Rachel?" Brynn asks, her meal still untouched, like the others'. "You think she'd want to blackmail us?"

"It can't be Rachel, Brynn," Cassie insists. "How did she survive? Where has she been all these years? Why did she disappear?"

"I don't know!" Brynn squeezes her fingertips against her temples. "It doesn't make sense, but I can't think of anything else that does, either."

"Blackmail makes sense," Fiona admits.

"So should we go to the police, then?"

"No," the other three answer Brynn's question in decisive unison.

"So we should just . . . what, then? Sit around waiting for something else to happen? Wait for someone to blackmail us? Or . . . worse?"

Nobody answers that.

You would expect Fiona to be the first to emerge from the inn, with Brynn dogging her heels, but that's not how it happens.

No, it's Matilda Harrington who steps out onto the porch less than an hour after Cassie's arrival, unaware that she's being watched from the stand of trees alongside the parking lot.

She looks straight ahead through huge designer sunglasses as she strides toward her Ferrari as though she can't wait to get in and drive away.

Already clutching her keys, she unlocks the door with the remote when she's still a few yards away. She slips behind the wheel, closes the door, starts the engine . . .

Is she going to drive off without even spotting the white rectangle on the windshield?

No.

The door opens and a hand snakes out to pluck away the envelope.

Seconds later, the car shifts into REVERSE and rolls backward, tires crunching on the gravel lot.

Did she even look at it?

There wasn't much time for that.

No, she most likely tossed it recklessly onto the seat next to her, probably thinking it's some kind of advertising flier.

Matilda's face is visible through the windshield for a moment as the Ferrari rolls past the hiding spot en route to the exit.

She appears to be utterly poised, as always.

She wouldn't be if she'd read what was in the envelope.

No, not at all.

Oh, Matilda. You, of everyone, should have bothered to look at it.

Well, don't say I didn't warn you . . .

Because, in my own clever way, I tried.

In the small ladies' room with its antiquated fixtures, Cassie leans toward her reflection to reapply her coral-shaded lipstick with a shaky hand as Brynn comes out of the lone stall.

She washes her hands at the sink. Her eyes meet Cassie's in the mirror.

"I didn't even ask you anything else about your wedding."

"That's . . . understandable." Cassie gives a choked little laugh and puts the cap back on her lipstick. "It's the last thing on my mind right now."

"It shouldn't be, though. You can't let this get to you, Cassie. This should be the best time in your life."

Yes. It should be.

"Did you . . . um, pick out your flowers yet?" Brynn asks, sounding as though she genuinely cares.

That's the thing about Brynn—she really does care.

Maybe more than I do, Cassie thinks wryly.

"I'm meeting with the florist soon," she says aloud, trying to remember the correct answer to the question, "and I was thinking of doing all roses."

"In red? That was our sorority flower, remember?"

"Maybe red, but not really because of the sorority. Maybe I won't do roses at all."

"I had pink and white roses with baby's breath at my wedding," Brynn volunteers as she dries her hands thoroughly on the roller towel.

"I guess I'd go with deeper colors. I wouldn't want pastels since the wedding is in November."

"When is it again?"

"The weekend after Thanksgiving." Cassie guiltily avoids meeting her friend's gaze again in the mirror above the sink.

Maybe she should invite Brynn and Fee after all. She opted to include only Tildy on the guest list, reasoning that she's been in more regular contact with her than anyone else these past few years.

And why is that?

Because she's always been closer to Tildy, even back in their college days.

And why is that, *Cassie?* her inner voice demands.

Because the Boston Harringtons hobnob with the equally wealthy and similarly tragedy-ridden Boston Kennedys. They even have a friendly political rivalry, kindred folk who happen to belong to opposing parties. Of course, the Harringtons are actually involved in politics only through their close association with Troy Allerson.

Yes, the Boston Harringtons are, according to Cassie's parents, the kind of people it's good to know in this life.

As opposed to the Cape Cod Costellos and the Cedar Crest Fitzgeralds.

It isn't that Cassie herself subscribes to that brand of snobbery. It's just that she has precious little time to stay in touch with anyone from her past, so when she does have an opportunity to catch up with someone, it might as well be Tildy.

That way, whenever her parents invariably ask how Matilda is and when she last spoke to her, Cassie at least has a satisfactory reply.

Fiona sticks her head in the door. "Brynn, come on. We could have been halfway home by now!"

"I'm coming."

"Well, hurry up!" The door bangs closed.

Brynn and Cassie look at each other.

"Listen," Brynn says, "about all this—"

"I know," Cassie cuts in. "It's bad. I'm scared. But, Brynn, you can't tell anyone. Please swear to me that you're not going to do something crazy, like—"

"Go to the police."

"Please don't."

"You know I won't. Not behind your backs."

Cassie doesn't know that. She doesn't know Brynn. Not anymore. She was part of another life, one she left behind—or so she hoped.

"Just . . ." Brynn reaches out and gives her a quick hug. "Have a beautiful wedding, okay? I'm happy for you."

Cassie nods, suddenly unable to speak, and watches her walk out the door.

Stepping out onto the porch of the inn, Fiona lights up and takes a deep, satisfying drag.

There. She feels better already.

Peace and quiet, fresh air—okay, and smoke.

After all the tension inside the restaurant, Fiona savors the momentary solitude.

The only sound is the stream of smoke exiting her lungs and the faint hum of a car passing out onto the highway.

She should check her messages on her office voice mail

again. She did just a few minutes ago, while they were waiting for the check, but the call she's expecting from James
Bingham hasn't come in yet.

He should be at his weekend house: once the Gilded-Age
"cottage" of a New York financial magnate, the place has
forty rooms and sits on a hundred wooded acres high above
Cedar Crest.

Fiona is aching to visit it—and she's sure she will, if she
plays her cards right.

Patience is the key. Patience and professional decorum,
with just a slight hint of flirtation. And restraint. Definitely
restraint.

Surely James has called and left her a voice mail by now.
And maybe her sister has finally called back, too. Fee has
been trying to reach her, needing to talk . . .

About the card. Just in case—

A large winged creature flutters on a branch overhead before swooping toward the dense thicket surrounding the parking lot. Fiona's eye follows it as she inhales her cigarette,
and she sees a bulky shadow of movement amid the trees.

She blinks, startled.

What *is* that?

Nothing. No big deal.

But the shadow is moving; someone is definitely there.

Or maybe just *something*. Can it be a large animal?

It could be . . . except a glint of some shiny object just
caught the sunlight out there, a few feet off the ground and
animals in the wild don't reflect light. Nothing like . . .

There it is again.

Jewelry? Eyeglasses? What the heck *is* that?

Is somebody out there, watching her?

Peering into the trees through narrowed eyes, Fiona feels
her heart begin to race.

The door to the inn opens suddenly and she jumps at the
abrupt sound.

Brynn.

"What's wrong?" she asks Fiona.

"Nothing. It's about time," she mutters, stubbing out her cigarette beneath her pointy-toed shoe. "Let's go."

As they cross the wide porch toward the steps at the far end, closest to the woods, Fiona's heart is pounding painfully.

You have to calm down. It was nothing.

But she stares into the trees, certain someone is lurking there.

Isaac can hear the music coming from behind the apartment door as he approaches.

Did he leave the radio on before he left?

No, it can't be. He was listening to Z100 that morning. They play popular music.

This is John Coltrane.

Kylah loves jazz.

"I love it almost as much as I love you," she said before dragging him off to the Newport Jazz Festival last month.

That bothered him. He couldn't tell her he loved her, too.

He does like her. A lot. Much more than he likes jazz.

But nowhere near as much as he likes—*loves*—Rachel.

He shifts his overnight bag to his right hand and checks his watch on his left.

What is Kylah doing here?

Right now, she should be at least 35,000 feet above the Ohio Valley, flipping through a magazine and sipping a tiny paper cup of bad airline coffee.

She shouldn't be in New York, in her Ninth Street apartment—*no, our apartment, now*—listening to jazz.

His heart sinking, Isaac stands in the corridor outside the door, wondering what he's supposed to do now.

He can turn around, walk away, and . . .

What? Never come back?

Just leave her?

No. He can't do that. Not yet, anyway.

There's only one option.

Lie.

Watching Fiona aim the remote at the BMW to unlock it, Brynn notices that Fiona's hand is trembling.

She catches her once again looking nervously toward the woods on the far side of the parking lot as she gets into the car.

Following Fiona's gaze, she sees nothing unusual.

"Fee?" she asks uneasily. "Is something out there?"

"What?" Startled, Fiona swivels her head toward Brynn, then shakes her head. "No, sorry, I'm just . . . distracted. I've got a lot of stress right now with work, and . . . you know."

Yeah. I know.

It isn't just about work.

Brynn fastens her seat belt as Fiona turns her neck to back out of the parking lot, dialing her phone with one hand as she steers with the other.

Something white on the windshield catches Brynn's eye.

"What's that?" she asks.

"Wait, hang on a second." Fiona presses a key on her phone, then props it against her ear with her shoulder so that she can shift into DRIVE.

"There's a flier or something stuck under the wiper," Brynn says in a stage whisper as Fee steers toward the entrance, apparently not noticing the white rectangle on the windshield.

"Shh!" Fiona is still listening to the phone, though not talking into it. She must be playing her messages; Brynn can hear the uninterrupted rumble of a male voice on the other end.

Shaking her head, Brynn turns away, gazing out the passenger's side window at the passing greenery. The car picks up speed quickly, heading onto the highway.

Something white flies past the window, interrupting Brynn's train of thought. She swivels her head to see that it was apparently the white paper that was stuck beneath the wiper.

"That thing just flew off the windshield," she informs Fiona, who is just snapping her cell phone closed.

Fee shrugs, looking distracted by the call. "Oh, well. It was probably just some advertisement. You'd think a nice place like that would make sure people don't go around sticking fliers on cars in their parking lot."

Right. And you'd think people who find fliers on their cars would take them off before driving, rather than leaving them there to blow away in the wind.

Shaking her head, still feeling unsettled, Brynn folds her arms and leans back. It's going to be a long ride home no matter how fast Fiona drives.

Cassie notices the white rectangle on the windshield just as she's opening the driver's side door. Curious, she lifts the wiper blade to remove it and realizes it's an envelope.

Just like the other day.

Only that one arrived in the mail, addressed to her.

This one is blank.

It's probably just some kind of menu or maybe a promotion the inn is doing, she tries to reassure herself.

Still, as she slips behind the wheel, she finds herself looking nervously around the parking lot, almost as if . . .

Well, as if she expects to see somebody lurking nearby, watching her.

Her hand shakes slightly as she opens the envelope flap.

Calm down. You're starting to get all freaky again, over nothing.

She pulls out what looks like a card . . .

No, it's an invitation.

On the front is a cartoonish guy holding a finger to his

lips. A dialogue bubble extending from his head reads, "SHHH!"

Inside is the line "IT'S A SURPRISE PARTY!" Below that, a series of preprinted headings have been filled out in what looks like old-fashioned typewriter type.

```
FOR: Matilda Harrington's Thirtieth
     Birthday
WHEN: October 4
WHERE: Matilda's House
GIVEN BY: A Friend
```

Relieved, Cassie smiles. A surprise party. Fiona must be throwing it. Or Brynn.

She wonders why they opted to leave the invitation on her car rather than hand it to her after Tildy left. They probably put it here earlier, not realizing Tildy would be the first to leave.

Cassie tucks the invitation into the glove compartment and starts the engine.

Too bad she won't be able to make it. October 4 is the day of her wedding shower—to which Tildy was going to be invited.

Well, she'd better not send her an invitation and risk throwing a wrench into the surprise party plans.

Uh-oh. Cassie's mother will be disappointed. She has long known that Tildy's godfather, "Uncle Troy," is also known as former Massachusetts governor Troy Allerson. His handsome face is everywhere lately, along with the requisite beautiful, two-decades-younger blonde wife, Lisa, and their beautiful blonde school-age triplets.

The quintessential Boston Brahmin, Allerson, like Tildy's father, is Harvard-educated, immensely wealthy, has New England roots dating back centuries, and is politically connected. In fact, he's rumored to be a future presidential candidate—which is, of course, right up Regina Ashford's networking alley.

But the shower is supposed to be about the bride-to-be, not about the mother-of-the-bride-to-be rubbing shoulders with the politically connected Matilda Harrington.

Cassie's thoughts are so preoccupied with all she still has to do before her wedding that she's almost at the Danbury exit before she realizes the invitation lacked a specific time for the party . . . and RSVP information.

Probably an oversight.

Whatever.

She'll have to remember to send Tildy something nice for her milestone birthday. What do you get the woman who has everything?

A bottle of champagne? A bouquet of roses?

Roses . . .

That reminds her, she really has to set up a meeting with the florist.

And get the shower guest list to Tammy.

And speak to the caterer.

And do a million other things, none of which she has time to do. None of which she *wants* to do.

I'm sure I'll feel more excited about it when some of the planning stress is behind me, she tells herself, trying to ignore the increasingly familiar hollow feeling inside.

Lying should come easily now. Isaac has been doing it long enough. Not just with Kylah, but with Lindsey before she left, and, for that matter, with just about everyone else in his life.

But it doesn't come easily at all to unlock the door, paste on a smile, and casually call, "Babe? Is that you?"

Smoochy the cat, alive and well and napping on the couch, opens one eye, then closes it again.

"It's me." Kylah steps out of the bedroom, hanger in hand.

Blonde, blue-eyed, slender, pretty. The kind of girl who never had a problem finding a boyfriend, even in Manhattan.

If we broke up, she wouldn't be alone for long, Isaac finds himself thinking.

He says, casually, "I thought you weren't coming back till tonight."

"I caught an earlier flight. I left you a couple of messages this morning to tell you."

"On my cell? Because I didn't—"

"No, not on your cell. You're always home on Saturday mornings."

Emphasis on the word *always,* which buzzes his ears like a cloying mosquito. Has she really known him long enough to apply *always* to anything about him?

"I called here," she goes on. "I wanted to let you know I was coming early, just in case you might be planning to surprise me at the airport."

"I was planning to," he says as smoothly as the saxophone gliding along in the background. "In fact, I was just stopping home before heading over there."

"Stopping home to drop off your bag?" she asks, eyeing his duffel.

"Right." *Here we go . . .*

"Where have you been? Because, obviously, you haven't been here the last few days. Your toothbrush and shaving stuff aren't in the bathroom. Smoochy's water dish was empty, and so was his dry food. His milk bowl was sour, and there were no empty Purina cans in the garbage." She pauses for effect, then bookends that detective work with, "Where have you been?"

Kylah has every right to investigate and ask questions, he reminds himself, after coming home to an empty apartment. She has every right to stand there looking at him with that disillusioned look on her face.

Lindsey wore that same expression, perpetually, when she began to suspect there was another woman.

"I'm sorry, babe." He drops the duffel and crosses the room to hug her.

She's stiff in his arms, but she lets him do it.

Still, she persists, "Where were you?"

He can't tell her the truth. Kylah doesn't know about Rachel. If he has his way, she never will. Look what happened when he told Lindsey.

"One of our clients up in Boston had a system crash yesterday and I had to drop everything and go." She knows as little about his business—computers—as he does about hers: pharmaceuticals.

"Why didn't you tell me you were leaving?"

"I couldn't reach you," he says simply.

She shrugs, looking thoughtful. Looking as though she thinks it could actually be true . . .

After all, she spends little time in her room during conferences, and she always turns off her cell phone when she's giving seminars.

Of course, he *could* have left her a voice mail . . .

But she doesn't even bring that up.

Maybe because she desperately wants to believe him, regardless of how credible she actually finds his story.

"I'm going to go finish unpacking," she says, slipping from his grasp and heading back toward the bedroom. "Why don't you do the same thing, and then we'll go over to Dojo and get some dinner?"

Dojo. Her favorite. She's a vegetarian.

Not Isaac. He'll take a steak—cold-bloody-rare, Rachel's preference as well—over hummus, sprouts, and tofu any day.

But Rachel isn't here with him now.

Kylah is, and she's waiting for him to respond.

"That sounds good." He forces a smile.

"Good." She returns an equally strained version.

"I'll be right there." He waits until she's disappeared into the next room before quietly unzipping his duffel bag and feeling around inside.

Locating the packet of photos, he quickly crosses to the desk in the far corner. They both use it, but she won't look inside the file drawer anytime soon.

The moment he has a chance, he'll return the photos to their usual spot: safely tucked into his own locked drawer in his own apartment near Gramercy Park.

She doesn't know about that, either.

The apartment. She *knew* about it, of course—past tense. She thinks he let it go when he moved in with her. She believes he gave all the furniture to a new entry-level guy at work, and she assumes that Isaac stopped paying rent on that supposedly vacated apartment the month he started paying half of hers.

Kylah doesn't know he has no intention of letting the apartment go—that he can't possibly let it go.

Kylah doesn't know about a lot of things.

And what she doesn't know, Isaac reminds himself, ignoring the guilty twist in his gut, can't possibly hurt her.

Isaac ignores the mocking voice in his head.

You know, sometimes, things turn out quite differently from what you had in mind.

Sometimes, you wind up hurting people.

People you hate.

And, yes, even people you love.

PART II

HAPPY BIRTHDAY, DEAR TILDY

CHAPTER 7

"Do we go trick-or-treating tonight, Mommy?" Caleb asks over breakfast, same as he has every morning this week, thanks to the wide world of kindergarten and his new Halloween-obsessed friend, Tyler Carmichael.

"Not tonight, sweetie."

"Tomorrow?"

"No, not tomorrow." Brynn sets a bowl of dry Cheerios in front of Jeremy, sitting in his plastic booster seat, and returns to the cupboard for a sippy cup.

"Then when?" Caleb dips his spoon into his bowl, shoves some milky Frosted Flakes into his mouth, and continues around a still-crunchy mouthful, "The day after tomorrow? Or . . . Wednesday?"

"Today *is* Wednesday."

He mutters under his breath, "Monday, Thursday, Wednesday . . ." Then he announces, "You're right, Mommy! Today is Wednesday. And tomorrow is Tuesday!"

Her back to him as she pours milk into the sippy cup, Brynn smiles and opts not to correct him again. He's so pleased with himself, learning the days of the week. He just hasn't mastered the order yet.

There's a lot for a first-time elementary school student to absorb, and Caleb has had his eyes opened to all sorts of new concepts in the past month.

He's definitely developed a growing awareness of organized time, even beyond a daily classroom schedule that includes his favorite, "snack time," and "quiet time," the probable favorite of his teacher, Mrs. Shimp.

And he talked so often about the classroom's monthly wall calendar adorned with seasonal icons that Brynn created a duplicate here at home. To Caleb's delight, it now hangs on the wall in the kitchen, decorated with stickers she bought at the crafts store.

For *"Oct-oh-boh,"* as Caleb calls it, there are autumn leaves and pumpkins, Christopher Columbus and his three ships, candy corn, and costumed children carrying plastic jack-o'-lantern buckets.

"We still haven't even figured out what you're going to be for Halloween yet," Brynn reminds her son.

He thinks about it. "Can I be Gary?"

"Who's Gary?"

"He's SpongeBob's pet snail."

"Oh . . . Well, isn't there somebody else you can be?" *As in, somebody who comes in a package at Target with a vinyl jumpsuit and plastic mask?*

"No, I want to be Gary. Tyler is going to be SpongeBob's friend Squidward."

"Well then, why don't you be SpongeBob?"

"Tyler says that's boring."

"I think SpongeBob is anything but boring." *I also think we need to limit your time with Tyler,* Brynn decides as she hands Jeremy the cup.

"Well, I want to be Gary. You can make me a Gary costume, right, Mommy?"

She sighs. "Sure, why not?"

"Good. I'll go get some tape. You need tape, right?" He pushes back his chair.

Brynn pushes it back in promptly with a hip check. "Whoa, hang on there, Gar', we've got plenty of time before Halloween. Eat your breakfast."

"How many days do I have?"

"Till Halloween?" She does quick mental math as she sets the sippy cup on Jeremy's plastic placemat. "About twenty five." Which means only twenty-three days until her thirtieth birthday. Yikes.

"Cool beans."

Cool beans?

She suppresses a smile. That's a new one, and yet another reminder that her firstborn is now living a whole life that doesn't involve her.

Lately, Caleb's vocabulary has been sprinkled with unfamiliar phrases like "crisscross-applesauce," "Line Leader," and "morning message." He takes as much pleasure in his parents' exaggerated confusion whenever he drops one of those phrases into conversation as he does in patiently defining them.

"How many days," he asks now, munching Frosted Flakes, "till we get to go visit Grandpa and Grandma?"

Now there's a word she doesn't like to hear. *Grandma.* She tries not to cringe when her boys use it, though. Her father insists that they refer to his wife that way, just as the other grandkids—Brynn's brothers' children—do.

For some reason, it doesn't seem to bother anyone but Brynn.

Sue shouldn't get to be Grandma.

Brynn's mother should be *Grandma* . . . even if she never got to see any of her grandchildren. *Angel Grandma in heaven,* Brynn calls her with the kids, to differentiate—and she makes sure that she talks to them about her mother a whole lot more than she does about Sue.

Or about her mother-in-law, for that matter.

Garth's mother is a good person—not as warm as Brynn's family, but she does love the boys. She's seen them an average of once a year, though . . . and she's old. Really old. Snow-white-hair, deep-wrinkles, and-a-walker old.

"Mommy? How many days till we go?" Caleb prods.

"To see Grandpa? That's next weekend."

"Grandma, too?"

"Grandma, too," she says reluctantly, and tries to smile cheerfully.

Caleb and Jeremy adore Sue. According to Caleb, she's "laughy"—meaning, she tells the boys silly jokes that crack them up. She always has a purse full of Hershey's Kisses and Bazooka Bubblegum. She takes them bowling whenever they visit, and she lets them beat her.

Mom, on the other hand, never let anyone win a game in her life. Always competitive—not to mention realistic—she thought kids should learn from an early age that loss was a part of life.

Maybe she was subconsciously trying to prepare her own children to face the world without her someday.

Or consciously, even. Sue told Brynn right after the funeral—and right before she got her claws into Brynn's father—that Mom had a feeling, long before her diagnosis, that something was going to happen to her.

"She had this thing where sometimes, she just knew things," Sue said. "It was a sixth sense kind of thing. She didn't like to talk about it, though. Especially not this past year, when she started thinking she might not be around forever."

Gazing at her two young sons over the rim of her coffee mug, Brynn can't imagine ever having to say good-bye to them forever.

What if . . . ?

Stop thinking about that right now! she chides herself as a chill creeps over her. *You're not going to kick the bucket anytime soon, so why worry about it?*

Well, maybe that's what she gets for being married to someone obsessed by death.

All right, "obsessed" isn't the right word.

The sociology of dying just happens to be Garth's chosen field of study.

Is it any wonder morbid thoughts sometimes creep into his wife's consciousness?

These days, she has no qualms about telling him to change the subject whenever he steers a conversation to a particularly ghoulish topic, particularly when others—particularly their sons—are in earshot.

But back when they were first married and she was still a little in awe of him, she feigned fascination whenever he went off on a tangent about Iroquois burial customs or ritual suicide. She dutifully read nonfiction books he recommended, with titles like *Violent Death* and *Point of No Return*. And she regularly wore the first piece of jewelry he ever bought for her—even after she discovered what it really was.

He did tell her, when he presented her with the unusual garnet-encrusted gold brooch, that it was "Victorian hair jewelry."

She thought he meant that it was antique, and that women used to wear it in their hair.

It never occurred to her that the woven brown patch encased beneath an oval of glass was actually made of hair. Human hair. As her husband explained, it was a nineteenth-century custom to memorialize the dead by making their hair into jewelry.

"Doesn't it give you chills, realizing that it was once on the head of someone who's been dead for over a century?" Garth asked with a delicious shiver.

It gave Brynn chills, all right.

But she didn't want to hurt his feelings, so she went on wearing it. For awhile, anyway.

She stopped after Caleb was born. Then she tucked it away in her jewelry box, alongside her similarly abandoned sorority bracelet of intertwined silver rosebuds with her old initials—B.C.—dangling in two small silver letter charms.

Garth never asked why she wasn't wearing the brooch.

By that time, she had stopped wearing any jewelry other than her wedding ring, along with makeup, and stockings, and heels . . .

I've really turned into a housewife drudge, she tells herself as she stands at the sink in droopy, ancient flannel pajamas, pouring soggy cereal into the garbage disposal.

On the heels of that thought, for some reason, she thinks of Tildy.

Well, actually, she's been thinking of her quite often in the month since they last saw each other.

When she first walked up to the table that day at the inn, she didn't miss Tildy looking her over from head to toe.

An hour earlier, Brynn had been so happy to get out of the house looking human for a change. But under her old friend's scrutiny, she might as well have been wearing her dingy white T-shirt with the orange SpaghettiOs stain over the right breast.

That day, Brynn was painfully aware that she alone, of the four of them, lacked the right clothes, a manicure, a real hairstyle—a *life.*

Then she came home to slobbery kisses from little boys, and a husband who told her she looked beautiful, and a message from Maggie, a fellow stay-at-home mom who understands what Fee and the others don't.

And Brynn managed to convince herself that she alone, of her four sorority sisters, *has* a life. The whole package: a stable marriage, healthy children, a real home.

Which she wouldn't trade for anything.

But sometimes, it just might be nice to feel a little less . . . domestic, she can't help but think wistfully as she leaves the boys eating cereal and dashes off to splash hot water on her face and throw on her clothes.

Less domestic, more . . . attractive.

Like Tildy. And Fiona. And Cassie.

Oh, well. She has a feeling it's going to be a long, long time before she's faced with their triple threat again—if ever.

Of the trio, she's spoken only to Fiona since that day—and even more sporadically than usual, as Fee has been wrapped up with some important new client. She still hasn't even bothered to return Brynn's phone call from last week when she left a message to see if Fee wanted to meet for coffee someday.

Well, at least the unnerving incident that sparked the sorority reunion has all but faded away. Nobody has surfaced with accusations or blackmail.

Brynn has come to realize that she'll probably never know who sent that card.

Yet she can't entirely shake the suspicion that Rachel is alive. That she got up that night and walked away from everything. From her life.

And she just wanted us to know that she's out there somewhere.

Either that, or somebody was watching.

Somebody who wants us to know we weren't alone out there that night.

But is that all they want?

The possibilities give her chills.

Thank God nothing out of the ordinary has turned up in the Saddlers' mailbox since September 7.

Nothing more to do with Rachel . . .

Not, for that matter, even a wedding invitation from Cassie.

"Do you think we'll be invited?" Brynn asked Fiona as they drove home along the Mass Pike after lunch that day.

Predictably, "God, I hope not—I've got enough on my calendar as it is," was Fiona's response.

Unpredictably, Garth said almost the same thing when she posed the question to him back at home.

"Why do you hope not? I think it would be fun to go to a wedding for a change," Brynn told him. "Considering that all we get invited to these days are kids' birthday parties. I swear, if I have to tote one more screaming, sticky, sugar-wired kid out of Chuck E. Cheese . . ."

"I'd rather do that than drive for hours to a wedding where we won't know anyone."

"Manhattan isn't hours away, and we'll know plenty of people."

"The bride."

"And Fee and Tildy."

"That's three people. You can see Fee any time you want, Brynn. And Tildy . . . Well, do you really *want* to see her? You just told me that she gave you dirty looks at lunch."

"Not dirty looks. Just . . . she looked me over. You know, my clothes, my hair . . . I'm insecure whenever people do that. But I still love Tildy anyway and of course I want to see her. She's my sorority sister," Brynn tacked on automatically.

Now, however, she realizes it's just as well that she probably isn't going to be invited to the wedding and won't be seeing Tildy again anytime soon.

Some people change for the better over the years, and some for the worse.

But some never change at all.

Tildy hasn't.

I have, Brynn thinks as she stares into the mirror above the bathroom sink. *What do I possibly have in common with Matilda Harrington these days?*

"More than you think," Tildy says with a sigh.

"Oh, come on . . . how much?" Carrot-headed Katie Donovan, one of her coworkers, protests. She's still clinging to Tildy's wrist, examining the new silver-and-Swarovski crystal beaded bracelet that caught her eye just now as Tildy handed her a memo.

"Guess."

"I don't know . . . a hundred?"

Tildy shakes her head.

"You mean it was *more* than a hundred? Forget it." Katie drops her wrist glumly. "I'm broke this week and I can't charge another thing on my Neiman Marcus card. Too bad, because that would have looked great with the black cocktail dress I'm wearing to your party tomorrow night."

Tildy opts not to tell her that the bracelet cost four hundred. On sale.

She does opt, generously and on a whim, to unfasten the silver toggle and hand it over to Katie. "Here."

"What are you doing?"

"Take it."

"You're letting me borrow it?"

"You can have it."

"What?"

"It's yours."

Katie squeals and throws her freckled arms around Tildy's neck. "Are you serious?"

"Totally. Take it."

"But . . . It's so expensive. I can't do that."

"Sure you can. I don't really like it that much anyway."

Katie's sparkly green eyes dim at that, but only slightly.

She fastens the bracelet around her wrist and admires it. "Well, thank you, Tildy. This is so sweet of you."

"No problem. See you tomorrow night."

Tildy stops in the break room for a coffee refill and heads back to her desk, pleased to have done a good deed for the day. She really didn't like the bracelet much—it was an impulse buy, made when she was browsing the jewelry counter at Neiman Marcus the other day. She figured she'd wear it once and toss it into her jewelry box with her old rosebud sorority bracelet.

But this is much better. Katie loves it. Tildy feels good about that . . .

And maybe a little better about herself.

Too bad you don't accumulate points for good deeds that you can trade in to appease the bad that you've done.

Stop thinking about that.

But she can't.

Tildy went all these years, ten years, a whole decade, without so much as a twinge from her conscience.

Why did it have to surface now?

Why, indeed.

The birthday card.

> HAPPY BIRTHDAY . . . TO ME.
> XOXOXOXO, R

And seeing them all again last month, Fiona, Brynn, and—

"So I hear tomorrow is a special day for you."

Tildy gasps at the sudden voice behind her, nearly spilling the hot coffee that sits precariously close to the edge of her desk.

"Oh, sorry . . . Did I scare you?" Ray Wilmington looms above her, wearing a short-sleeved dress shirt with a tie— one of her ultimate pet peeves—and an apologetic expression.

"Scare me? No, not at all," she says sarcastically, scowling as she moves the mug, which is imprinted with the name of a catering company, to a cheap coaster etched with the name of the nonprofit. "I never get scared when somebody creeps up behind me."

"I wasn't exactly *creeping*."

Not only were you creeping, she wants to tell him, *but you are a creep.*

She doesn't say it, though, unnerved by the way his black eyes are fixated so intently on her as he thoughtfully strokes his beard. Whenever he looks at her that way, she feels like he's trying to see something that isn't there. Or, perhaps, that he's seeing something she doesn't want him to see.

He perches on the edge of her desk in an unwelcome intimate posture. "I didn't know your birthday was tomorrow."

Oh, yes, you did.

He knew, because she overheard him talking about it the other day . . .

On her way to the break room, she had just seen him stroll in ahead of her, and was thinking twice about continuing on in herself. She wanted to grab her yogurt from the fridge, not find herself cornered by Mr. Cheesy Small Talk.

About to turn on her heel and head back to her desk until the coast was clear, she heard her name mentioned and stopped short. Ray had apparently come upon Katie discussing the birthday party tomorrow night with another of their coworkers, Allison.

Eavesdropping just outside the doorway, Tildy could hear Ray grilling them about the party, trying to sound casual, obviously hurt that he wasn't invited.

He's kept some distance from her ever since: a welcome reprieve from his typically undaunted presence in her daily life.

But he's continued to watch her from afar, same as always. She often feels his gaze on her even before she looks up to find him gawking. But at least he hasn't been popping up constantly to flirt awkwardly with her and ask incessant, annoying questions.

Until now.

"So, what are you doing to celebrate?" he asks.

"Nothing much."

"Really? But . . . You should really celebrate. Go all out. I mean, after all, it's a milestone birthday."

"How do you know that?"

"A little bird told me."

A little bird told him? Oh, for God's sake. Must he always spew antiquated clichés? He's worse than her Great Aunt Katherine, who, at least, being a relic herself, has an excuse.

Tildy flashes Ray a tight-lipped nonsmile. "I really should get back to work."

She gestures at the pile of paperwork on her desk, which she hasn't touched in a couple of days. It can wait, but he doesn't have to know that.

At this point, she's using every free moment—at home

and at the office—trying to make the final arrangements for tomorrow's party, which now feels almost anticlimactic in light of next weekend's trip.

Tildy still can't quite grasp the fact that it's actually going to happen. They're actually going to go away together for an entire weekend. She'll be able to wake up in his arms at last, two glorious mornings in a row. Eat with him in a restaurant without worrying that somebody might see them, recognize him, say something to *her*.

Yes, it's really going to happen . . . unless something goes wrong.

Why can't she shake the feeling that something might?

A nagging trepidation took hold soon after he gave her the green light to make the reservation at the inn, and it's grown steadily these past few days. It's as though she's looking out over a deceivingly calm sea and clear blue sky, armed with a near-certain forecast for an oncoming nor'easter.

"What are you working on?" Ray peers nosily over her shoulder.

"You know. The usual." She shuffles one stack of papers on top of another and then back to the bottom again in a minimal effort to seem busy.

"I'd love to take you to lunch tomorrow to celebrate your birthday."

"Sorry, can't."

"Dinner, then, tomorrow night? I'm free," he adds, followed by a significant pause.

She refuses to take the bait, and looks him squarely in the eye as she replies, "I'm not. But thanks anyway."

"No problem, Waltzing Matilda."

But it is a problem, obviously.

Ray stares at her for a long moment, as though he wants to say something else.

Is he going to come right out and ask her about the party? Does he want to know why he's one of the few people in the office who isn't invited?

If he asks, she'll just tell him the truth in as straightforward a way as she can. So much for the newly anointed Good-Deed-Doer. Sometimes, you have to be brutally blunt with a guy like this.

But Ray doesn't ask.

He just turns and walks away, head bent, leaving her inexplicably disturbed.

Oh, come on. Who cares if his feelings are hurt?

Well, maybe Tildy does . . . just a little.

She can't help it. After all, she's only human . . . and so is he. She doesn't necessarily want to hurt him any more than she'd want to kick a dog nipping at her heels . . .

But you do what you have to do.

Ray disappears around a tall filing cabinet.

So, in a matter of seconds, do Tildy's thoughts of him.

She flips her date book to the second weekend in October: *next* weekend. The date boxes are empty, of course.

Two nights and almost three days alone with him. Maybe marking them on the calendar will make it seem more real.

She doesn't dare write his name there. She never does.

She takes a pencil, and then, thinking better of it, exchanges it for a pen.

Then she marks Friday, Saturday, and Sunday with a *G.S.*

There. That's better.

Smiling smugly, she closes the date book.

"Mr. Bingham is here."

Fiona doesn't look up from the trade report she's reading, having seen quite enough of Emily—and her oversized burnt-orange nubby wool pullover—for one day.

"Send him right in."

"Okay." Emily departs with a jangling of jewelry.

Many times in the past month, Fiona's spoken to her assistant about dressing in a more professional manner. Emily is always contrite, promises to do better—and does, for a few days. She'll come in looking relatively sedate in a dark skirt, white blouse, and leather flats—basically the same outfit every day.

Then, she presumably has to launder everything and lapses right back into her gauzy Indian print skirts, dangly earrings, sandals, or, now that autumn is setting in, thick-soled boots.

"She dresses a lot like you do, actually," Fee laughingly said to her sister Deirdre a few weeks ago, during one of their long-distance gripe sessions. Fiona was griping, rather; Deirdre was mostly listening and offering advice.

Advice like: "I don't know . . . Why don't you try and look past the clothes, Fee?"

"I tried. There's nothing there, either. I have to fire her, Deirdre . . . and not just because she dresses like you."

And she will, just as soon as she finds a spare minute to look for a replacement. Business is booming; all the more reason she desperately needs someone she can count on. She's even toying with the idea of hiring an associate to take on some of the actual client contact.

But for right now, the firm remains a gloriously epony-mous one-woman show playing to glowing reviews.

The latest came from James Bingham himself, who yes-terday complimented not just Fiona's business savvy but the color of her eyes.

"Back so soon?" she asks now, looking up to see him in the doorway.

"So soon?" he echoes, crossing the carpet to take her ex-tended hand. "I don't know, it seems like ages since I saw you."

He's flirting blatantly. Good. Flirting never hurt business.

"It's been less than twenty-four hours," she says, shaking his hand, allowing her fingers to linger in his warm grasp an extra moment and her eyes to appreciate his rugged good looks.

A younger Harrison Ford?

No, that's not it. He reminds her of someone, and, for the life of her, she can't seem to put her finger on who it is.

"Twenty-four hours? Is that all?" He relinquishes her hand and sits in the guest chair.

"That's all. I thought you were going back to Boston last night."

He's based there, but also has an office at his weekend home in the mountains near Cedar Crest.

"This time of year, I like to spend more time here. But I'm headed back east just as soon as I take care of a little business with you."

"Really? What can I do for you?"

"I came to give you this." He hands her an envelope.

"What is it?"

"The payment for the first month's retainer. I got your invoice."

"You handle your own bills?"

"Not usually. But I wanted to get this here promptly."

"You could have mailed it," she says lightly.

"I know. But I didn't want to mail these."

She finds herself holding two glossy cardstock rectangles. Tickets . . .

"Behind home plate, the Red Sox playoff game tomorrow night at Fenway," he informs her. "Do you like baseball?"

Not particularly, but . . .

"Doesn't everyone?" she asks with a coquettish tilt of her head.

"So are you free to meet me in Boston tomorrow night?"

"Sure." She isn't free, not with a nine-year-old daughter in her care, but isn't about to turn down James Bingham.

Why not? she asks herself. *Because he's a client? Or because he's rich, sexy, and eligible?*

Both.

"Unfortunately, I have to work out of my Boston office tomorrow, and I've got an early meeting Friday so I have to stay put there, but if you have no problem driving in and out by yourself . . ."

"I have no problem with that at all."

No, the problem lies with Ashley.

She'll just have to ask Pat if he wants to take her over-night. He won't be particularly eager to help her out, but if she asks in Ashley's presence, he isn't likely to say no.

Dirty pool—that's invariably the name of the game when she's dealing with her ex.

"I'll make reservations for a late dinner at my favorite restaurant over on Newbury Street after the game. Do you like sushi?"

Not particularly, but . . .

"Doesn't everyone?" she asks again, and he smiles.

He leaves with a promise to call her tomorrow morning.

What are you doing? she asks herself, leaning back in her desk chair and folding her arms across her ivory silk blouse.

You don't like baseball, and you don't like raw fish, and you don't particularly like driving in and out of Boston at night . . .

No, but she likes *him*.

James Bingham isn't the first man to pay attention to her since the divorce. But he's the first who just might be worth her precious time.

Glancing at her desk calendar, she notes that tomorrow is crammed with appointments from morning to night. She'll have to rearrange the last two if she's going to escape the office early enough for the two-hour drive to Boston. Now, if she can just find two free time slots where she can put them . . .

As she glances over the next day's agenda, she's struck by the date.

That's Tildy's thirtieth birthday.

Cassie isn't ready when the doorbell rings at six thirty. She's half-dressed, and she still has to brush her teeth, put on makeup . . .

But even if she was pulled together cosmetically, she'd

still have a long way to go before she could possibly feel prepared for any of this.

Seeing her mother, who's just driven up from the city to spend the weekend . . .

Being the guest of honor at a wedding shower tomorrow night . . .

That's what this weekend is all about. Cassie's official transition into *bride-to-be,* which will imminently and fleetingly lead to *bride* before giving way permanently to *wife.*

No, she isn't ready. For any of it.

Well, you'd better get ready in a hurry, because it's full speed ahead from here on in, she tells herself as she hastily pulls a tailored navy sweater over her head.

The doorbell rings again as she's about to answer it. Twice, actually: a pair of staccato jabs at the button.

Patience never was a prominent character trait in Regina Ashford's personal repertoire. Ambitious, sophisticated, industrious, brilliant . . . yes.

Patient, never.

Cassie opens the door and comes face-to-face with the formidable Deputy Mayor for Legal Affairs of New York City.

"Hi, Mom."

"There you are, Cassandra. I thought you might not be home." Regina hugs her briefly, enveloping her in a cloud of expensive perfume. She, of course, is fully made up and impeccably dressed in a trim tweed suit, her black hair straightened and worn low at her neck in an elegant twist.

"Come in, Mom." Cassie reaches for the large black Coach satchel at her feet; a matching clutch is tucked under her mother's arm.

"Why don't you let Alec get that, honey? It's heavy."

"Alec isn't here." As she hoists the bag over the threshold, she glimpses the disappointment on her mother's face.

"Where is he?" Regina asks, stepping into the condo and giving it a sweeping visual inspection.

Accustomed to her mother's critical eye, Cassie glances around for cobwebs as she replies, "He's still at his office. He had to take care of an emergency procedure."

Alec did use the word *emergency* loosely when he called to tell Cassie about the delay. It seemed one of his regular patients was demanding a last-minute collagen injection before her daughter's wedding this coming Saturday.

"She's the mother-of-the-bride from hell," Alec confided into the phone, and Cassie pictured him rolling his eyes and shaking his head. "This isn't going to be fun."

"Tell me about it. I've got a mother-of-the-bride from hell of my own to deal with on this end," she replied wryly, and he laughed.

"Don't tell me this means he's not going to dinner with us?" Regina is looking around Cassie's living room as though she's hoping to spot Alec lurking behind a potted palm.

"He'll try to meet us there."

Cassie fervently hopes he will.

Otherwise, it will be just the two of them.

She's never been very good, one-on-one, with her mother. She still remembers the awkward solo visits Regina made to boarding school and college on weekends when Cassie's father was otherwise occupied.

Ironic that a woman who built an entire political career based on charisma has never learned to carry on a reciprocal conversation with her own daughter.

"Before I forget to tell you, Lavinia Byers can't make it tomorrow after all, but she's still coming to the wedding." Regina walks to the kitchen and takes a glass from the cupboard.

"That's too bad—that she can't make it to the shower, I mean."

"She sends her regrets and her best wishes, and she said she had something sent from Tiffany's. Probably place settings."

"That's nice." Cassie knows her mother's colleague Lavinia Byers about as well as she knows the formal china pattern on her Tiffany Bridal Registry.

She vaguely remembers picking it out one day last summer—gold and white Limoges, perhaps?—just as she vaguely remembers crossing paths with the equally sophisticated Lavinia at some political event.

She never fully anticipated the impact of encountering either of them again.

But the china is accumulating in telltale turquoise blue gift boxes at her future sister-in-law's new house in anticipation of the upcoming shower, and the wedding is really happening, a formal affair with three hundred guests including Lavinia Byers.

Of course it's really happening . . . Did you honestly think it wasn't going to?

No, it isn't that.

It's that she hasn't allowed herself to *think* at all, managing amid the bustling preparation to remain insulated from the full impact of her upcoming marriage.

Whenever a potentially explosive manifestation zinged her way—visiting the bridal registry, being fitted for a gown, hearing Alec's comment about five children—she somehow deflected it all.

Until the last few days.

Pelted by one prenuptial bombshell after another—the arrival of the boxed wedding invitations yesterday, vividly printed in undeniable black and white nearly did her in—her protective shield is beginning to crack, allowing the true implications to seep in.

She, Cassandra Ashford, is about to pledge to share every day for the rest of her life with another human being.

Not just *any* human being.

Alec.

Alec is wonderful. He loves her. She loves him.

Yet is she really prepared to relinquish her independence before she's ever had a chance to live her life on her own terms?

Three decades of following the rules, meeting other people's expectations, and now she's on the verge of breaking free at last. She'll be finished with her residency in a matter of months, after years of nonstop hard work.

Free . . .

"Free to start a family," is what Alec said just the other day. "Who knows? Maybe next year at this time, we'll be having our first child."

Cassie smiled.

But she wanted to scream.

She said, calmly, "I don't know if I want to get pregnant that quickly."

Which was a lie, because she *did* know that she didn't want to get pregnant that quickly—she was a hundred percent certain of it.

Alec protested, "You're turning thirty this month. Your biological clock is ticking. Who knows how long it might take us to conceive? We should start trying right away."

At every turn, somebody is waiting to tell her what to do: Alec. Her mother. Her father. Dr. Prevatt, her attending physician at the hospital.

When does she get to do what she wants to do?

What is it that you want to do?

She keeps asking herself that question, to no avail.

The only honest answer she can conjure is: *I want to get on my horse and ride away.*

That's about as realistic as . . .

Well, as her mother suddenly turning over a kinder, gentler leaf.

"Mom," Cassie says, realizing she's filling a glass from the tap, "I've got bottled water in the fridge."

"This isn't for me. It's for your poor philodendron." Regina marches back to the living room and dumps the glass into the wilted plant. "These things are almost impossible to kill, yet you're managing. Do you ever water this?"

No, she never does.

Once in awhile, Alec will sprinkle it with the remains of his squirt bottle of Poland Spring, but that's about it.

Cassie thinks of her parents' apartment on East Sixty-Second Street, with abundant healthy house plants clustered in each sunny window.

Regina prides herself on knowing the botanical name of each and cares for them single-handedly. When she's not busy overseeing the legal affairs for the City of New York or planning her upcoming congressional campaign, that is.

Cassie sighs inwardly.

Even if she marries Alec, lands in a thriving pediatric practice, has a waterfront mansion and a brood of beautiful children . . .

She'll still somehow feel inadequate.

She'll never live up to her mother's perfectionist expectations; why bother trying?

Why bother with any of this?

The wedding, the medical career, the stupid, half-dead philodendron . . .

Right now, she wants to shed every last burden.

But what about Alec?

He loves her.

And she does love him.

She just wishes he would give her more time. And space.

Cassie closes her eyes and pictures herself on her horse's glossy light brown back, precisely the color of a perfectly toasted marshmallow. She's surrounded by a vast green meadow, the wind in her face . . .

Then she opens her eyes, and there's her mother, shaking her head as she pinches several withered yellow-brown leaves from the twining philodendron.

* * *

"Looks like somebody's having a birthday party," comments the gray-haired, heavyset woman behind the cash register at Party City.

What is there to do but nod in agreement and watch her painstakingly ring up the purchases?

Pointy bubblegum-pink paper party hats, matching plates and cups, a bag of pink and white balloons, another of little horns that unfurl tissue tubes when you blow on their plastic mouthpieces. Plus a big, shiny pink "HAPPY BIRTHDAY" banner, wrapping paper, a package of candles.

"Only ten?" asks the woman, whose plastic name tag reads *Marge*.

"That's just how many I need." Smile pleasantly. Look her in the eye. Be casual.

"My granddaughter is ten years old, too, next week," Marge comments. "I can't believe it's been ten years already. They sure have flown by."

For you, maybe, Marge.

They haven't flown by for me at all.

"Did you want to get some goody bags, too? We have some on the shelf that match this pattern."

"No, no goody bags."

"Are you sure? My daughter says you can't have a party without goody bags."

"I've already got them."

"Then you're ahead of the game."

Very observant of you, Marge. I'm way ahead of the game.

"I hope the birthday girl enjoys her special day."

"Oh, I'm sure she will."

Marge hands over the white plastic bag filled with party supplies. "You have a nice night, now."

"I will, thanks."

And tomorrow night is sure to be even nicer.

CHAPTER 8

"I'm in a bind, I need a huge favor. Can you help me?"

Holding the phone to her ear, Brynn sits back on the rumpled bed and exhales heavily through puffed cheeks.

Leave it to Fee to barge right back into her life—at six forty AM, no less—after a week-long absence, with an immediate and brazen request for a favor.

And not just any favor . . . a *huge* favor.

"I don't know, Fee . . . What is it?" Brynn asks reluctantly, watching a towel-clad, damp-haired Garth pad back into the bedroom.

"I swear Pat is a first-class jerk."

"So what's the favor? Do you need me to find him and beat him up for you?" Brynn cracks.

"Believe me, if I thought you were serious, I'd take you up on that. He won't take Ashley for me tonight, and I have an important thing to go to in Boston."

"A meeting?"

A moment's hesitation, then Fiona clarifies, "It's a date, actually. With a client."

"Is that good for business?" Brynn asks, and wonders

why she bothered. As if Fiona would ever do anything that isn't good for business.

"Trust me, it's very good for business. Anyway, I won't be back until really late, so . . ."

"Why won't Pat take Ashley?"

"Why do you think? Spite. I asked him right in front of her last night, and he said he'd have to check his schedule and let me know. I just woke up to a text message from him saying he's busy."

"Maybe he really is."

"Doing what? Watching *Law & Order* reruns?"

Brynn yawns, checking the clock. Almost time to go wake the boys. She wishes Fiona would just get to the point . . . And she's pretty sure she knows what it is.

"I even tried calling Sharon in Albany to see if she'd come down, but her daughter said she's away on some casino trip with a busload of old farts from the senior center."

"Her daughter said that?"

"More or less. So can you, Brynn?"

She decides to feign ignorance. "Can I what?"

"Take Ashley for me tonight? She's really no problem—"

"I know she isn't—"

"And she'd help you with the boys, and the dishes, and she could clean up around your house a little."

"For God's sake, Fee, you don't have to sell her domestic skills to me. Of course I'll take her. I love Ashley."

And I know you do, too. I just wish you'd figure out how to show it more often.

"Thanks, Brynn."

"Mmm-hmm." Brynn watches as, facing the mirror, Garth drops the towel. She can't help but admire her husband's muscular shoulders, buttocks, legs. Experiencing a wanton stirring in the pit of her stomach, she casts another glance at the clock.

No, she has to get the boys moving.

Then she looks back at Garth, still standing there naked, and his reflection grins and bobs a suggestive eyebrow at her.

"Can you keep her overnight?" Fiona is asking.

"Sure, she can have my bed and I'll sleep on the couch."

"Oh, you don't have to do that, Brynn. I don't want to put you and Garth out of your room. Ashley can sleep on the couch."

Brynn shrugs, not bothering to tell Fiona that Garth probably won't even make it to their bed. It's a Thursday. He won't be home until late.

"Listen, it'll be fine. I'll take all the kids out for pizza or something," she says distractedly, as Garth turns away from the mirror with a lascivious grin.

"Great. I owe you a huge favor, Brynn."

"No problem. See you later."

She hangs up as her husband descends on the bed. She wishes she had time to quickly brush her teeth and comb her bed-head. And she's wearing one of his old thermal long-sleeved shirts and a pair of Old Navy flannel pajama bottoms circa 2000.

"I've got to get the boys up," she protests, giggling, as Garth wraps his arms around her and kisses her neck.

"They can wait a few minutes."

"A few minutes? Is that really all I get?"

"Hey, it's all about the quality, not the quantity."

Sinking back against the pillows in her husband's embrace, Brynn puts all thoughts of the boys—and Fiona, and Ashley—right out of her head for the time being.

Resting up for her bash tonight, Matilda Harrington is sipping Splenda-laced espresso and lazily flipping through *Vogue* in her sun-splashed living room when the florist truck arrives.

She sits up in her chair and leans forward to look through the tall bay window.

There's her next-door neighbor, Mrs. Stallsman, tapping her way along the block with her white cane and guide dog. Tildy wonders, as always, why she doesn't just hire somebody to do her errands for her. Not that she herself has ever offered to help. But you'd think that someone who can afford to live in this neighborhood would be able to afford a gofer.

The deliveryman emerges onto Commonwealth Avenue carrying a tall bouquet.

Uh-oh. It isn't tulips, is it?

No, thank goodness.

Even from half a story above the street, she can see that it's roses. Red ones. And only a dozen.

"Lena! Somebody's coming to the door," she calls.

The housekeeper's footsteps dutifully venture from the kitchen to the front hall.

Tildy turns her attention back to her magazine. There's a darling Marc Jacobs cashmere twinset that would be perfect for her trip next weekend with—

"Ms. Harrington? These are for you."

She looks up to see Lena standing in the doorway with a tall, cut glass—perhaps crystal?—vase.

Yes, a dozen red roses.

He gets ten points for sentimentality; none for creativity or expenditure.

Unless they aren't from him.

"You can put them right here, Lena." She indicates the polished cherry end table beside her chair.

The housekeeper sets the vase on a coaster and exits, leaving Tildy to examine the card propped amid the blossoms on a tall plastic prong.

It's plain white, preimprinted with "Happy Birthday" scrolled in gold type.

Below, in unfamiliar script, is the message:

See you tonight!

Nothing more. Not even a name.

He isn't even supposed to be at her party tonight.

She told him that if he couldn't come alone, she didn't want him to come at all.

"You know I can't come alone, Mattie." Only he calls her that. He has from the start.

"Well, I don't want to watch you dancing with *her* all night," Tildy said, knowing she sounded petulant, and not caring. It's *her* party.

So what does this note mean? Has he changed his mind? Is he possibly going to surprise her there—without his wife on his arm?

It wouldn't exactly be a surprise now that he's tipped his hand with the flowers, but . . .

Can these flowers be from somebody other than him?

Could be. A dozen red roses? He's sent her flowers often enough for her to realize these aren't his style.

But then who . . . ?

Not Ray Wilmington.

God knows he's sent her flowers before, but not roses, and, anyway, he knows he isn't invited to the party.

Unless this is his way of letting her know he's planning to crash? Would he really be that bold?

Somehow, she doesn't think so.

God, she hopes not.

But if the flowers didn't come from either of the two men who come most readily to mind, she's got a mystery on her hands. She can't think of a single person who would anonymously send her birthday flowers . . .

Nobody she's expecting to see tonight, anyway.

This would be so much easier to pull off if Kylah was traveling out of town this weekend, but she isn't.

Which means Isaac had to make up something about why he won't be home until late tonight. After midnight, probably.

He told her he was invited to a bachelor party for one of the guys from work. She didn't ask which guy, or where the party is being held, or why anyone would have a bachelor party on a weeknight.

That she trusts him and respects his privacy makes him feel even guiltier for lying.

But, as usual, he has no choice.

He can't tell her where he's really going . . . again.

Nor can he tell her, when she calls his cell phone just past four o'clock, that he's sitting not in his office, but in a rental car, in a traffic jam well north of midtown Manhattan.

"What are you doing?" she asks.

Without missing a beat he replies, "I'm in a cab going to a meeting. What are *you* doing?"

"Same exact thing. Where's your meeting?"

"Uptown. Yours?"

"Downtown. And never the twain shall meet," she says with a sigh, and he emits the obligatory laugh.

"I wish you were coming home after work tonight, Isaac. I feel like getting pizza and seeing a movie."

"Well, why don't you do that? With one of your friends?"

"Maybe I will. But I'd rather do it with you."

"Tomorrow night," he promises her, inching forward beneath the green road sign that reads NORTHBOUND NEW ENGLAND THRUWAY.

"Okay, sounds good."

He glances at the clock, then at the map on the seat beside him, wondering if there's an alternate route.

Rachel's face smiles up at him from an 8 × 10 photo lying next to the map.

"What don't you want me to see?"

So startled is he by Kylah's question that he swivels to look over his shoulder, almost expecting to see her peering through the window somehow, watching him.

What don't you want me to see?

Rachel. I don't want you to see Rachel . . . not even her picture.

But, of course, Kylah isn't here, spying on him. There's no one behind him, other than the frustrated occupants of a string of other cars at a complete standstill.

What don't you want me to see? she asked. And Isaac comes swiftly to his senses as he realizes Kylah is talking about movies. Movies are *their* thing, together.

What don't you want me to see?

He asked her the same thing just last Saturday afternoon, when he was headed to Loews Multiplex to kill a few hours while she had lunch with her sister.

Her answer was immediate: "Nothing with a meet-cute, a good love scene, or John Cusack. Save those kinds of movies to see with me."

Now, trying to muster the same light-hearted tone, he instructs her, "Don't see anything with a car chase, anything rated *R* for violence, anything with subtitles, or anything with a roman numeral after the title."

"I've never met anyone with taste as eclectic as yours," Rachel said admiringly, having discovered bookmarked copies of both Albert Camus' The Stranger *and Howard Stern's* Private Parts *on his bedside table.*

"Don't worry, I won't see any of those movies," Kylah promises him now.

Isaac attempts to switch off the vivid scene replaying in his head, but it persists, like an old movie that pops up on every channel.

"In fact," Kylah chatters on, as Rachel flashes a brilliant smile in his mental screening room, "I'm not even tempted to see anything like that. Especially the ones with roman numerals; you know I hate sequels."

"I know."

The old movie plays on in his head . . .

Rachel (looking up from the newspaper): "Hey, let's go see Free Willy 2 *tonight.*"

Isaac (incredulous): "Free Willy 2? *You're kidding, right?*"

Rachel (laughing): "Wrong. *You know how much I love whales.*"

Isaac (not aloud): You don't know how much I love you.

"Listen, you don't have to worry—I'll choose a nice chick flick to see without you. Okay?" Kylah, intruding again.

Doesn't she realize his thoughts are a million miles and a dozen years away? Doesn't she realize he's thinking about someone else?

No. She won't know unless you tell her.

And he won't make that mistake twice.

"Okay," he mutters, and lifts his foot off the gas pedal to travel another six inches of pavement before stopping again.

Dammit. This couple-hundred-mile trip could take all day . . . and for what?

So don't go.

It's not too late to back out.

Turn around, go back home, and . . .

What? Forget about Rachel?

"I need you, Isaac," she said that day. "I'm scared, and I don't know what to do. Please . . . Can you come up here tomorrow?"

"Sure," he said promptly, no additional questions asked, still reeling from what she'd just revealed and forgetting all the reasons why he couldn't—or, at least, shouldn't—drop everything and race to her side the next day.

After all, it was her birthday. And she was in trouble, facing something so unexpectedly huge that he couldn't even bring himself to ask the question whose answer would change everything.

Not over the phone, anyway.

He would wait until he saw her.

And regardless of the answer, he would do anything for her.

Anything . . .

So he can't turn around and go home now, and he can't forget about Rachel.

No way.

"I should go," he says abruptly into the cell phone.

"Me, too." Kylah sounds reluctant, though. "Do you want me to wait up for you, or are you going to be home *really* late?"

His jaw clenches so hard the tension radiates painfully into his neck. "Don't wait up."

On Thursday evening, Cassie finds herself driving along Interstate 95 to her bridal shower, *alone*—which is absolutely fine with her.

Her brother Marcus's wife, Reenie, is taking the train up from the city with Cassie's aunt Kitty. Regina will pick them up at the station in New Haven, armed with concise directions to Tammy's house.

"Are you sure you won't just ride along with us?" her mother asked earlier, as she jangled her car keys impatiently and kept looking at the clock.

"No, I've got a big day at the hospital tomorrow. If I leave a little later it will give me a chance to go over some research materials my attending gave me yesterday."

And it will give her a much-needed reprieve from her mother.

Spending almost twelve straight waking hours in the company of Regina Ashford has been enough to make Cassie wish she hadn't opted to take off today after all.

They went from breakfast to shopping to lunch to an early movie—an art-house screening of a foreign documentary Cassie wouldn't have been interested in seeing even if it was in English. Which it wasn't.

Or even if it had subtitles . . .

Which it didn't.

"What's the problem? You took several years of French in school, Cassandra," her mother reminded her.

That's true. She *took* it. She just didn't necessarily *retain* it.

She tried to doze through the movie, but her thoughts kept wandering to the shower tonight.

And to the wedding next month.

And to the rest of her life.

Her life?

Hah.

She turns up the volume on the radio—Bono wailing about something profound, not love—and looks at the green EXIT sign ahead. Is it this one? Or the next?

She hopes it's the next.

It isn't.

So, here goes. She can do this. She has to do this. What else is there?

Just take it one day at a time, she tells herself, and ignores the burgeoning seedling of an idea that was somehow planted in her mind weeks ago.

She flicks on her turn signal to get over to the right lane, glances in the rearview mirror, and starts to merge.

A deafening blast from a mighty horn startles her.

She just nearly cut off a double semi.

Swerving back into the middle lane, Cassie is shaken as the semi barrels past on the right, the trucker in the cab shaking his head.

She could have been killed.

Her hands tremble on the wheel.

Her life pretty much flashed before her eyes in that instant.

Not merely the life she's already lived, but the life she's got left to live.

In one terrifying moment, she saw it all.

Terrifying.

Because of the truck.

Yes, of course.

Thank God she's all right. Shaken, but all right.

There's another EXIT sign; only a half mile now.

She has to get over to the right.

This time, Cassie cautiously turns her head to see if there's room.

There isn't.

Rush hour. A steady line of cars blocks the right lane.

The exit is coming up.

In the rearview mirror she sees an SUV driver right on her bumper, flashing his lights impatiently. Oh. She's going only 55. Much too slowly for this busy stretch of the northeast corridor, where the wealthy and important—and sometimes merely self-important—drive fast, fancy cars in blatant disregard for the posted speed limit.

Cassie picks up her speed a little, signal still on, but she can't seem to merge right.

Dammit. She's going to miss the exit.

And then what?

Then you'll turn around at the next one and go back. That's what.

Or . . .

Or what? she asks herself impatiently. *You'll turn around and go back at the next exit. What else is there to do?*

A sedan to her right flashes its lights. Oh, for Pete's sake. Now she's going too slow for people driving alongside her?

The driver waves at her.

Oh . . . He's letting her into the lane ahead of him.

You're not going to miss the exit after all.

Go.

GO!

And she does.

But not to the right lane, and the exit.

The seedling has taken hold, its burgeoning tendrils winding their way into her soul.

Her foot pressing down on the gas pedal as if of its own accord, Cassandra Ashford speeds on ahead in the middle lane.

Heading toward Boston.

CHAPTER 9

As she steers the BMW sharply around the corner onto Tamarack Lane, Fiona is harried.

So what else is new?

Her mind is on the half dozen phone calls she needs to return before she runs home to change before leaving to meet James Bingham in Boston.

First, of course, she has to stop at the Saddlers' to drop off Ashley, who's sitting beside her in the passenger's seat.

Ashley protested when Fiona told her to climb into the front; the backseat was crowded with client files and her laptop.

"Daddy said I'm not allowed in front until I'm twelve. He said it's against the law." Ashley's dark eyes, so like her father's, flashed with accusation.

"Yeah, well, Daddy also claims you're still supposed to be riding around in a booster seat," Fiona muttered.

"I am. Till I'm bigger and taller."

"That's ridiculous. You're not a baby. You don't need a booster seat."

"Daddy makes me use one."

Daddy's an ass, Fiona wanted to retort.

She's been saying precisely that—if only to herself—all day, flying from meeting to conference call to meeting in her usual mad whirlwind. Damn Patrick for refusing to take their daughter tonight.

She hates the fact that she has to rely on Brynn. Of course Brynn doesn't mind, and Ashley squealed with delight when Fiona told her she was spending the night there. She loves to play with Brynn's boys.

Still . . .

Fee has done her best to avoid Brynn these last few weeks. Ever since the lunch they shared with Cassie and Tildy.

She has no interest in living in the past . . . And Brynn, she's starting to realize, is a part of the past.

Fiona is moving on.

Moving on, and up. She wants to forget where she's come from—all of it.

James Bingham can help her accomplish that.

Brynn cannot.

But Brynn can help me with Ashley tonight. Right now, that's what I need.

"Uh-oh."

"What is it, Ashley?" she asks, slowing before the Saddlers' driveway.

"I forgot my toothbrush."

"How could you forget? I reminded you right before we left."

"I know, but I just forgot."

"You're not going to get far in this world if you don't learn to be more organized, Ashley." Fiona sighs. "I'll have to tell Brynn to take you out to the drugstore or something and get you one."

"Can't we just go back for mine?"

Fiona shakes her head. "No time."

"But I don't want to make Brynn go out."

"She won't mind."

"What if she does?"

"She doesn't." *What else has she got to do?*

"But—"

"Trust me, Ashley. Okay?"

"Okay," Ashley tells her mother. But she doesn't.

Trust her, that is.

Sometimes, she thinks Mom just makes stuff up to make things easier for herself. Daddy says it's what she does.

Actually, Daddy mostly thinks Mom makes stuff up just to make things harder for him. Which might be true, because Mom hates Daddy.

"Here we are," she says briskly as she pulls into the Saddlers' driveway. She tilts the rearview mirror slightly, toward her face, and checks her teeth for lipstick as she says, "Have fun tonight, Ash."

"Aren't you coming inside?"

"No time, sweetie. I'll watch you from here and make sure you get in okay. Oh, look, Brynn is already there waiting for you, see?"

Ashley turns her head. Yes, there's Brynn, waving from the doorway, with Jeremy on her hip. She's smiling and saying something to him and pointing at the car.

Mom leans across the seat and gives Ashley a quick, tight hug. "Have a good time, okay? And don't forget to pick up after yourself, and help around the house. And make sure Brynn drops you at school on time in the morning. Tell her she can bring your overnight bag by the office afterward so you don't have to carry it around. I won't have time to come back here and pick it up."

Ashley says nothing to that. She'd rather carry her stuff to school than make Brynn go out of her way to drop it at Mom's office.

She opens the car door and disentangles her legs from the straps of her backpack and her green floral Vera Bradley duffel, both on the floor.

Mom taught her long ago that whenever she's going some-place with a bag, she should keep it on the mat below her feet, with the straps looped around her ankle. That way, she'll never forget it.

"If you just toss it in the backseat, Ashley, you'll leave it behind. Out of sight, out of mind."

Ashley swings her legs around and climbs out of the car, lugging her bags. "Bye, Mom."

"Bye, honey." She shifts gears and calls out the window, "Thanks again, Brynn." She's already in REVERSE, backing away.

Ashley hoists the heavy duffel onto her shoulder. Aunt Deirdre gave it to her last Christmas. She had it sent from some store. She never comes back to Cedar Crest for Christmas—or ever, for that matter.

Mom visited Aunt Deirdre on St. John last fall while Ashley was up at the cabin with Daddy. She herself hasn't seen Aunt Deirdre since she and her mother met her in Miami for a weekend almost two years ago. That was a business trip for Mom; Ashley spent most of her time at the pool getting to know her aunt.

Mom and Aunt Deirdre aren't identical, but rather, "mirror image" twins. As far as Ashley can tell, that pretty much just means Mom is left-handed and Aunt Deirdre is right, yet really, they're opposites in every way.

By the time that South Beach weekend drew to a close, she fervently wished Aunt Deirdre lived closer—and that her mother was more like her twin.

Now, walking up the sidewalk toward Brynn's welcoming smile, she thinks the same thing about her: why can't Mom be more like Brynn, who always has time? Time for her own kids, and time for Ashley.

Brynn remembers little details, too—things like Ashley's fondness for strawberries, and her newest best friend's name: Meg.

Mom forgets sometimes and thinks her name is Michelle.

Daddy keeps her friends straight, though, and he always makes sure he has strawberries in the fridge for her weekends with him. Sometimes Ashley wishes she could go live with him full time—which she once overheard her mom telling him would only happen "over my dead body," in a tone that gave Ashley chills.

Anyway, if she lived with her father she wouldn't even have her own room. Daddy just has a studio apartment with a bed in one corner, plus a pullout couch where he sleeps whenever Ashley spends the night.

She doesn't like to make him give up his bed, but Mom told Daddy she isn't allowed to visit if she has to sleep on his couch. She said it's bad for Ashley's back, even though Ashley's back has always been perfectly fine.

Hearing a horn honk, Ashley turns to see her mother driving away—much faster, she bets, than the posted 15-mile-an-hour Tamarack Lane speed limit.

"Ashley! We're so excited that you're here."

"Hi, Brynn."

"I swear, you grow another inch every time I see you!" Brynn gives her a quick hug as Jeremy grabs hold of her dark hair and gives it a tug.

"Oh, Jeremy, no, don't hurt Ashley! Let go!"

"It's okay." Ashley hides a wince behind a smile as Jeremy pulls again, hard. "He's just a little guy, aren't you, Jeremy? You don't know any better."

"He loves long hair," Brynn says, gently untangling her son's fingers. "That's why I've always got mine in a ponytail."

"I like to wear mine in a ponytail, too." But she rarely does. Mom says she needs hair around her face—"a softer look suits you better," is how she puts it.

What she means, Ashley figured out, is that Ashley isn't pretty enough to go around with all her hair pulled back— she looks much better when she can hide behind it.

So she does. She wears it loose and has developed a habit

of tilting her head when she's talking to people, so that a shadowy screen of hair falls partially across her face. It gets in her way a lot, especially when she's eating or chewing gum.

But maybe someday, when she's prettier, she can pull her hair back to keep it out of the way, like Brynn does.

"Um, where should I put my bag?" Ashley asks, just inside the door. Today, Brynn's house smells like chocolate and potpourri, and the floor is cluttered, as always, with Lego and Matchbox cars.

"You can just throw it anywhere for now," Brynn tells her, "and come into the kitchen. The boys and I were about to have brownies and milk. Then we'll go out for pizza in a little while."

"Brownies, then pizza?"

"Sure, why not? I just made them, and they taste the best when they're gooey and hot."

"I know, but . . . dessert before dinner?"

"Oh, this isn't dessert. It's a late-afternoon snack, really. Pizza will be dinner, and then the boys and I were thinking that we might have to stop at that new Cold Stone Creamery for dessert. What do you think?"

I think you're the best mom ever.

The thought catches Ashley off guard, and she almost cringes guiltily.

It isn't that she doesn't love her own mom. She does. More—she can't help but think sometimes—than her mom loves her.

"Do you want some milk?" Brynn asks her in the cheerful blue and yellow kitchen, where the fridge is covered in crayon drawings and the air is heavy with a melted cocoa scent.

"Sure."

"Chocolate or white?"

"White," Ashley decides reluctantly. Mom is always

warning her that too much chocolate isn't good for her skin or her teeth. Which reminds her . . .

"Um, Brynn? I forgot my toothbrush. Do you think we could stop off somewhere on the way out for pizza and I could buy one? I have some leftover lunch money in my bag, so—"

"Save your lunch money, sweetie. I have a couple of new toothbrushes in the medicine cabinet. I bought a bunch of extras last month so that we'll have them when we need them. I like to be organized."

That's funny, because Mom says Brynn is the least organized person she ever knew.

Ashley is starting to notice that Mom is wrong about some things—especially when she criticizes other people.

But she would never dare to point that out. Mom definitely doesn't like to be criticized herself.

"Yay! Ashley's here!" Caleb darts into the kitchen and throws his arms around her waist. "Hi! Did you hear I'm in kindergarten now?"

"I heard. Congratulations."

"How old are you, Ashley?"

"Third grade."

"Wow. My friend Tyler has a big sister in third grade," Caleb says solemnly, and turns to his mother. "Can Ashley come and live with us? I want a big sister, too. Then I can be the little brother, and Jeremy can be the pet snail, and you can be the Mommy, and—"

"Except that Ashley already has a mommy," Brynn informs him as she pours milk into plastic cups.

"She does? Who?"

"Auntie Fee."

"Auntie Fee is a mommy?" Caleb asks in disbelief.

"Of course. What did you think?"

"I thought she was a lady."

Brynn laughs at that, but Ashley doesn't.

"What about the daddy? Can Daddy be Ashley's daddy? She doesn't have one . . . does she?"

"Sure I do." Ashley manages to smile.

"Who? Do I know him?"

"I bet you don't, because he doesn't live here," Ashley tells Caleb.

Brynn is so busy cutting brownies that she can't look up. Either that, or she's pretending to be busy cutting brownies so she won't have to look up.

"He doesn't live here? Why not?"

"Because my mom and dad have a divorce. So they don't live together."

"When are you and Daddy going to get a divorce?" Caleb asks fearfully, turning to Brynn.

"Oh, honey, don't worry about that. We aren't."

Ashley watches with envy as she holds him close in a re-assuring hug, remembering that her father once did the same thing, made the same promise to her.

The next day, Mom kicked him out of the house.

But she can't imagine Brynn doing something like that.

What about Garth, though? He's different from Brynn; different from her own dad, too. He acts nice and everything, but there's something kind of creepy about him.

Mostly because he's got all those books about dead people. She knows, because once when she was here, she found a whole stack of them and snuck a peek at some of the creepy pictures until she got spooked.

Maybe, Ashley thinks hopefully, if Garth kicks Brynn out, she can marry Daddy and become Ashley's stepmother, and the boys will be her stepbrothers . . .

And what about Mom? she wonders belatedly. Where does she fit into any of that?

She doesn't, and Ashley is swept by a bad feeling.

"Brynn?" she asks in a small voice. "Do you think my mom is going to be okay?"

Still stroking Caleb's hair, Brynn looks up, startled. "What do you mean?"

"What if something bad happens to her?"

"You mean tonight, while she's in Boston?"

Ashley nods, though she's not at all sure that's what she means. Her mother's "over my dead body" is ringing in her ears for some reason, and she can't help but picture the grotesque corpse pictures she saw in Garth's books that time.

"Of course she'll be okay," Brynn says with a smile. "She'll go on her date, and then she'll come home, and tomorrow you'll—"

"Date? I thought it was a meeting."

"A meeting? Oh! Right. It is! It is a meeting, Ashley. Your mom is at a meeting. In Boston. You're absolutely right."

Brynn is good at a lot of things, Ashley notes, but lying isn't one of them.

It's long past midnight when the uniformed driver opens the back door.

A giddy, giggling Tildy, wearing an iridescent white dress with a swirling skirt, steps out of the double-parked limousine on Commonwealth Avenue.

"Are you all right, Miss Harrington?" the driver asks as she sways a bit when her feet hit the sidewalk in front of her town house.

"I'm fine! It's just these stilettos. They're hard to walk in, but I love stilettos! Don't you?"

"Absolutely."

Hmm, she notices that he seems to be awfully blurry for someone responsible for driving a car. "Hey, are you all right to get home from here?"

"Absolutely," he says again. "But I'm not so sure about you, Miss Harrington. Come on, I'll walk you up to the door."

"Oh, no, no, I'm fine."

"I promised your father that I would see you safely home."

Oh, right . . . He's Daddy's new driver, Ed. Is it Ed?

Must be. That name rings a bell.

Oh, well, whatever . . .

"I had *sssssuch* a great time tonight," she tells him. "Did you have a great time?"

"I had a very nice time," he assures her.

"Wait! You weren't at the party, Ed! You were waiting outside, weren't you? You shoulda come in! You coulda come in! Everyone shoulda come in. There was champagne, and there were mojitos, and Tapas, and . . . wait, was there a chocolate fountain? There was ssss'posed to be a chocolate fountain, but I don't remember if it was there . . ."

"I'm sure it was. Let me walk you up to your door, Miss Harrington." The driver firmly takes her arm and propels her up the brick steps. "Do you have your keys?"

She jangles them in his face and giggles.

"Good, okay, I'll open the door for you."

"You will? Well, you're a gentleman . . . What was your name? Ed? Dave?"

He just shakes his head.

Tildy grasps the black wrought iron railing to steady herself and wonders what his name is, then wonders whether she should have had that last mojito.

Of course she should have. She's the birthday girl! And it was a great party.

But it would have been even more fun if . . .

Darn! The tail end of that thought has flitted right out of her head.

Hmm . . .

What was the reason she didn't have as much fun tonight as she expected?

Did something happen at the party?

Hey, don't forget to tell what's-his-name the code so the alarm won't go off, she reminds herself briefly as Daddy's new driver sorts through the keys on her Tiffany key ring.

Then she resumes wracking her champagne and rum-soaked brain about the party again. Hmm . . . She can't seem to come up with anything negative about it.

All she remembers is a wonderful night: dancing, friends, family, food, plenty of toasts in her honor . . .

Daddy was so proud. He waltzed with her, and he told her how beautiful she is and how much he loves her, and he said . . .

Wait, what did he say?

Oh. Right. He said he's looking forward to her wedding someday; that it will be an even bigger extravaganza than tonight's birthday party.

"Someday," she told him agreeably.

"With all these eligible men under one roof," Daddy swept a hand around the ballroom, "there must be someone close to being worthy of my baby girl."

"There is someone, Daddy—"

Right! That's it. *That's* why the party wasn't as much fun as she expected.

Because *he* didn't show up.

She thought he might, after all.

He said all along that he wouldn't. So why did she think he might?

Oh! Because of the roses. And the card that said he'd see her tonight.

She really thought he'd be there. But he wasn't.

Well, maybe the roses weren't from him.

Maybe they were from . . .

"What do you think?" she asks Ed, or Dave, who is fitting the key into the lock.

"Pardon me, Miss Harrington?"

"Who sent me the roses? Were they from you?" She laughs, hard and shrill, at the thought that he might have a crush on her.

And . . .

Oh, wait, this is good: what if it was mutual? What if she

was to march right up to Daddy and report that she's finally found the man she wants to marry, and it's his new chauffeur?

God, I'm killing myself, Tildy thinks, doubled over in glee.

Oblivious that he's the source of her hysterical laughter, Ed/Dave clears his throat as he opens the door. "Here we are, home sweet home."

She straightens, sniffles, wipes her eyes. "Thank you, Dave." She attempts a curtsy but almost pitches headfirst down the steps.

"It's Albert," he says, after steadying her arm.

"Excuse me?"

"My name is Albert, Miss Harrington."

"Oh! Well then, who is Ed?"

"I have no idea."

"And you're not Dave, either?"

"I'm Albert." He tips his cap before turning and heading down the steps with a polite, "Good night."

"Good night . . . Albert." She shakes her head, closing and locking the door after him.

She feels dizzy. And a little nauseated.

A lot nauseated, all of a sudden.

No, she probably shouldn't have had that last mojito. How many did she have altogether? One before the champagne toast, and at least one after . . . and that final one . . .

Tildy's stilettos wobble a bit as she steps farther into the entry hall, her hand fumbling for a light switch along the wall.

At precisely the same second she locates the switch and flips it, she realizes something strange: the alarm never went off.

But she never told Ed the code.

Albert.

She never told Albert the code.

Why didn't it go off?

And why . . .

Why isn't the light going on?

The bulb must be burned out.

Tildy feels her way forward unsteadily, then realizes that it's getting easier to see.

That's because of the candles.

Candles?

Yes, that's definitely flickering candlelight coming from the dining room.

"Hello?" she calls, realizing she's not alone.

Only one person could have let himself into the town house. He has the key; he knows the code.

So the roses were from him after all, she realizes. This is what he meant by "See You Tonight."

He's waiting for her with candlelight and, undoubtedly, champagne and gifts, to celebrate her birthday privately.

"You are too much," she calls, giggling, pausing to prop herself against the wall with one hand and pull off her shoes with the other.

Still nauseated, she dangles the shoes from one hand by their straps and proceeds, barefoot, into the dining room.

The first thing she notices is that the swinging door that leads to the kitchen is closed, for some reason . . .

Then she stops short.

"What the . . . ?"

Tildy looks around in wonder at the pink streamers, balloons, party favors, the large cake in the center of the table. Thirty candles flicker amid the icing roses and Happy Birthday elegantly scrolled in pastel pink. Beneath those words, somebody has awkwardly written DEAR TILDY in gooey block letters using a gaudy shade of red.

Red? Why not pink? The red looks almost like fresh blood oozing over the cake . . .

No, don't think that. Not when you feel so queasy.

Why didn't he just have the bakery write in the *Dear Tildy?* she finds herself wondering as her stomach churns.

And where the heck is he, anyway?

"Honey? I'm home!" Oops, she's slurring.

She concentrates, trying hard to keep her words coherent as she calls, "Are you there?"

"I'm here," a voice answers softly from directly behind her, just inches from her ear.

The house is quiet.

Too quiet, Brynn thinks, lying on the couch and wondering whether she should turn on the television again.

She just clicked it off a few minutes ago in the midst of a cable movie's opening credits, realizing she was starting to doze at last.

Now that the living room is dark and silent, she's suddenly wide-awake again . . . and a little spooked.

Is it any wonder? Earlier, she channel-surfed until she found a Johnny Depp movie she'd never seen—a scary, bloody thriller. But, of course, she couldn't stop watching until the whopping final twist, which she never saw coming.

With a creaking of old springs beneath her weight, she turns onto her side so that her back is pressed against the lumpy couch pillows.

There. Now sleep.

Startled, Matilda Harrington opens her mouth, but a firm open palm clamps down over it before she can make a sound.

"Don't scream. Don't move. Just listen, okay? *Okay?*"

Tildy nods, her momentary panic subsiding as she realizes that this must be some kind of birthday surprise. The voice is vaguely familiar, but in her inebriated confusion, she's unable to place it.

For a moment, the only sound is her muffled breathing behind the stifling hand pressed over her lips. She wants to protest that this is uncomfortable, but, suddenly, an eerily singsong voice fills the room.

"Happy Birthday to you . . ."

I was right. Somebody's planned a party for me. A post-party party! Any second now, everyone will jump out and shout, "Surprise!"

She wriggles, trying to turn to see who's there, but she's held fast. She tries to speak, but the hand presses harder, the thumb jamming against her nostrils, cutting off her air.

Panic begins to steal over her again. She struggles to breathe in as her unexpected guest continues to sing to her.

Why isn't anyone yelling "Surprise" yet?

Where are all the other guests?

Why aren't they singing along with whoever is holding her?

And why is that damn hand covering her mouth so damn tightly that she can't inhale?

Somewhere in her drunken daze, Tildy is struck by the irony that somebody went to all this trouble to surprise her on her birthday, and she's going to pass out right here, right now, because they don't realize she can't breathe.

Hysterical, bibulous laughter bubbles up inside her to commingle with irrational fear as her body reflexively fights for oxygen, squirming, trying to break free.

Surely the other guests see what's happening here.

Surely someone will put a stop to this.

But nobody comes forward, and the singing continues, and her alcohol-induced haze is beginning to lift.

Is this a surprise party?

Or some kind of prank?

Or . . .

Dear God, I'm not actually in danger . . . am I?

Between the uncomfortable couch, her nerves, and the eerie silence, Brynn's entire body is tense.

Just go to sleep.

She has to be up extra early to get both Caleb and Ashley to school.

Ashley.

She was a tremendous help with the boys, reading them countless bedtime stories and promising she'd play with them in the morning. After Brynn gave the boys a final tuck-in and closed their doors, she found Ashley with a wistful look on her face.

"I wish I wasn't an only child," she confided.

Brynn wasn't sure what to say to that. So, of course, she said the wrong thing.

"Maybe your mom or dad will get remarried someday and have more children."

As soon as the words were out of her mouth, she wished she could take them back.

Her own father remarried. Look how she herself still felt about that, and Dad and Sue didn't even have more children together, thank God.

Ashley's smile was sad. "I don't think they will. And anyway, my mom doesn't really like kids."

"Oh, Ashley, of course she does," Brynn assured her, but it sounded, and felt, like a lie. "You know she loves you, don't you?"

"Yeah, I know she does, but . . . She's not really into being a mom, you know?"

What could Brynn say to *that?*

She opted for silence and just let Ashley talk, sensing she needed an ear. She talked for a long time, mostly about her mother and how busy she was, and how she wished Fiona didn't have to work so hard all the time.

"It takes a lot of energy to run a successful business, and I bet you're proud that your mom has done very well for herself," Brynn heard herself point out, though what she really wanted to say to Ashley was, *"You poor thing, let me hug you."*

"I'm really proud of her. I just wish she was around more. And I wish I didn't have to go home by myself some days."

"You're home by yourself?"

Ashley backpedaled furiously, seeing the look on Brynn's face. "Only for a few minutes, until my babysitter gets there. It's fine."

No, it wasn't. And Brynn made a mental note to talk to Fiona about it.

If Fiona can't get her sitter there earlier, Brynn decided, she'd just offer to have Ashley come here instead.

Finally, catching Ashley trying to stifle a tremendous yawn, Brynn told her it was time for bed. Ashley protested her offer of the master bedroom, but finally relented when Brynn said she was going to wait up late for Garth.

"Where will you guys sleep, though?" Ashley wanted to know.

"I'll sleep on the couch, and Garth will sleep in his recliner when he gets home. He does that most nights anyway."

The thing is . . .

He isn't home yet.

The whole time she was watching the movie, she kept lowering the television volume, thinking she heard him coming in. It must have been her imagination.

Where is he?

But, of course, she knows the answer to that question.

He's on campus, in the library, working on his book.

But it's getting really late, and . . .

And I'm getting really freaked out for no reason, Brynn realizes, rolling onto her back once again.

Everything is fine. There's nothing to worry about.

Right, you can think that's true from now until next year, but you aren't going to get rid of this feeling that something is just . . . wrong.

She doesn't even know what it is.

She only knows that she'd feel a whole lot better if Garth was here with her . . .

And if she had never gotten that damn birthday card for Rachel—*from Rachel?*—last month.

". . . dear Tildy, Happy Birthday to yoooooouuuuuuu."

Matilda Harrington is really struggling now. It's becoming more difficult to hold on to her.

"Stop squirming around, would you?"

She reacts with a monumental spasm teamed with an excruciating abdominal kick.

"Owwww . . . you little bitch!"

In that doubling-over, pain-blinding instant, she has broken free.

"Get back here!"

She scrambles out of reach, hurtling herself toward the dining room. Dancing candlelight grotesquely distorts her shadow as it darts along the wall toward the closed kitchen door.

Moments later, another shadow looms, and begins to furtively creep after her.

Lying on sagging cushions with a stray couch spring poking into her ribs, Brynn is increasingly uneasy.

She pulls the blanket more snugly over her shoulders and tries again to relax.

It's long past midnight. She should be sleeping.

Right, and Garth should be home.

She turns onto her left side, the way she usually sleeps, pulling the blanket with her. It's an old one, with squeaky layers of acrylic that send chills down her back. She should throw it away after tonight. Go shopping at Bed, Bath & Beyond, buy some new blankets, new pillows. Maybe a new slipcover for this worn old couch . . .

She doesn't like having her face just inches from the back cushion this way. It makes her feel uneasy, as though she's going to tip forward in her sleep and smother.

Smother? That's a crazy thought.

Her head has been filled with crazy thoughts all night, though. Troubling thoughts.

She flips onto her back again and stares into the darkness, listens for the crunch of tires in the driveway or a key turning in the lock, and she worries.

About Garth. About her boys. About Ashley. Even about Fiona.

"Do you think my mom is going to be okay? Ashley asked after Fee left—and again a little while ago, just before bed.*"What if something bad happens to her?"*

Outwardly, Brynn reassured her. Inwardly, she cringed.

Fiona drives much too fast, much too recklessly. She works too hard. She doesn't eat well, when she bothers to eat at all. She smokes too much.

She does all the things maternal instinct should guard against . . .

If she possessed a blessed ounce of it.

Yet, so far, Fee has always managed to land on her feet. It seems unfair.

Especially when Brynn's mother did everything right.

Marie swam at the Y five mornings a week. She never ate red meat; she bought organic produce back when it was next-to-impossible to find. She didn't smoke, she rarely drank caffeine or liquor, she took vitamins every day . . .

She should have lived to be ninety.

It isn't fair.

Even after all these years, an ache rises in Brynn's throat: heavy, hard, and hollow as Sue's damn bowling ball.

But she's starting to realize that it isn't just grief. Not tonight.

Tonight, it's something more, a nagging feeling that's settled over her more snugly than this horrible squeaky blanket that smells vaguely of mildew.

Something bad is going to happen.

Yes, that's it, she realizes. *That's what's been bothering me all night.*

She takes a deep breath, telling herself she's being ridiculous.

But she can't seem to shake the inexplicable feeling of trepidation.

Matilda Harrington is on her hands and knees, crawling like an animal across the cold slate floor of her beautifully remodeled kitchen.

She's alone in here for the moment, having allowed the door to swing closed after her, but she knows it won't stay that way for long. Any second now, it's going to open and—

No, don't think about it.

She pushes away the shocking image of the face she glimpsed back there—or thought she glimpsed, in the instant before she bolted.

It can't be . . . can it?

And if it is . . . why?

Why are you here?

Why are you doing this to me?

Even now, remembering the weird party setup in her dining room, she wants to believe it's some kind of warped birthday joke.

But it isn't, her gut tells her. *You have to get out of here.*

She hugs the darkness against the wall, glancing longingly at the back door across the room.

The liquor's numbing effects have been obliterated by adrenalin, making way for full-blown panic. Yes, maybe the numbness was preferable to this constricting ache of terror in her chest, but at least Tildy now has the presence of mind to stop herself from making a run for the back door.

That escape path is well illuminated in a pool of light that spills from beneath the massive stove hood; if the kitchen door opens before she gets out, she'll be in plain sight, and easily caught.

Anyway, even if she made it out the door to the backyard, she'd be trapped there by the tall privacy fence. Impossible to climb, the installer assured her not so long ago; neighborhood kids and would-be burglars wouldn't be trespassing in her backyard. There's no way anyone can get in . . .

Or out.

No, desperate as she is to flee, she's better off going full circle through the pantry to the back hall that leads through a windowed alcove into the foyer again. From there, she can run out the front door onto the street. Even at this time of night, there has to be somebody around to see her, help her. If by chance there isn't, there are still plenty of people within earshot; all she has to do is run screaming down the avenue and somebody will call the cops.

Fire, she thinks somewhere in the back of her frenzied mind as she crawls across the newly refinished wooden floor of the pantry, which still smells faintly of polyurethane.

If you're in trouble, you're supposed to yell fire, *not* help.

Isn't that true? That people don't respond to strangers screaming *help* anymore?

She thought she heard that somewhere. Never in her wildest imagination did she think she, Matilda Harrington, might find herself in that kind of trouble.

This kind of trouble.

God, please help me.

Fighting to keep from erupting into a scream, she rounds the corner into the pitch-black hall.

Don't scream.

If you scream, you're giving off a *Here I Am* signal.

Don't make a sound.

She feels her way into the alcove, where faint light spills through the bare windowpanes. She glances up, sees tree branches silhouetted against the night sky.

Maybe I can use something to break the window and climb right out from here.

Yes, and that would trigger the alarm system—

No, she remembers. Somehow, the alarm system isn't working.

And her attacker would be upon her at the sound of breaking glass, before she could get out through the window.

Her only escape is the front door.

She's almost there, and still not a sound behind her.

She makes it to the threshold of the foyer, where she struggled so fiercely, frantically, just moments ago . . .

Why? Why are you doing this to me?

What did I ever do to deserve this?

Fragmented thoughts flicker in her brain; okay, so she's no saint.

Hot tears slide from her eyes, landing on her hands splayed on the floor.

She's no saint, but she doesn't deserve to die for her sins.

Die? Oh, my God, is she about to die? Is that what's actually going to—

No! Stop it!

She isn't going to die. Not like this, crawling like an animal. Not here, now, on her birthday.

She'll be fine; she just has to stay calm.

And, look, there's the front door. Less than three yards away. Salvation.

The front hall is silent, dark, aside from the faint flickering from the next room, and seemingly deserted.

She inches her way forward, forcing herself to stay low, quiet, calm.

Still no sign of her tormentor.

Tildy is just a couple of inches from the door now.

Almost free.

Almost safe.

She stealthily kneels, reaching up, feeling around blindly.

There.

Thank God.

Thank God.

Her hand closes around the knob and turns . . .

Just as she hears a rustling whisper of sound behind her and feels the air stir with movement.

No.

Please, no–

Shattering pain explodes in the back of her head.

No!

She topples forward, her face landing on the nubby rug in front of the door.

Rough hands grab her and roll her over. Her eyes are open, but she can't see.

Oh, God.

Oh, no.

Her eyes . . .

She's been blinded.

What am I going to do? How am I going to live my life if I can't see?

A bizarre image strikes her: she sees herself, Matilda Harrington, tapping along Commonwealth Avenue with a white cane and dark glasses, like Mrs. Stallsman next door.

I can't do that. I can't live that way.

"Did you actually think you were going to walk right out the front door?" The voice is eerily close to her, and she still can't see the face. She can't see anything.

Somewhere in the back of her mind, she's aware that her vision was snuffed out in that horrible blow to her head. She's going to come out of this sightless.

Come out of this?

I'm not going to come out of this at all if I don't do something.

Oh, please. Somebody help me. Help!

No. Not help . . .

She opens her mouth, lips twitching, throat rasping.

"What? Speak up, Matilda. I can't hear you."

"Fire," she whimpers faintly.

An explosion of maniacal laughter, not her own, echoes through her brain . . . just before the next blow smashes her skull into it, obliterating her remaining four senses, and Matilda Harrington ceases to exist.

CHAPTER 10

Cassie awakens abruptly at the sound of a ringing telephone, takes one look at the unfamiliar surroundings, and manages to remember instantly where she is: at a Marriott Residence Inn somewhere in the Boston suburbs.

And her skull is throbbing.

And the phone is ringing.

Oh, God, they've found me.

Or, maybe not. Maybe it's just her cell phone. It rang a lot last evening, before she turned it off somewhere north of Providence . . .

And she never turned it back on, so it can't be ringing now.

She turns her head, painfully, to look at the room phone on the bedside table just as it rings again.

Oh, God, they really have found me.

Then she realizes that nobody on earth can possibly know where she is, unless someone was following her every move from the time she blew past her exit.

When she stopped for gas at the Rhode Island state line, she checked the glove compartment and immediately found what she was looking for. The surprise party invitation was still there, right where she stashed it after it turned up on her windshield.

But the details were sketchy. There was just a date—October 4—and a place: Tildy's house, which is on Commonwealth Avenue in Boston. Oddly, there was no time, and no phone number for an RSVP.

Figuring it must be an oversight, Cassie decided to just show up and hope for the best. With luck, she would arrive well before, or well after, the guest of honor.

But when she reached Tildy's address, she found only Lena Schicke, the housekeeper. She answered the door wearing her coat, a scarf tied over her whitish-gray bun, obviously on her way out.

"I'm here for the surprise party," Cassie whispered to her, wondering if everyone was hiding inside, waiting for Tildy.

Confusion settled in Lena's slate-gray eyes. "Surprise party?"

"For Matilda."

"Oh, that's not a surprise. She's the one who's throwing it." The housekeeper's firmly set mouth told Cassie precisely what she thought of women who threw parties for themselves.

Not to mention what she thought of women who impulsively turned up on Back Bay doorsteps looking for surprise parties where there were none.

Now it was Cassie's turn to be confused. "But . . . I mean . . . Is the party tonight?"

Lena nodded.

"Is it . . . here?"

"No, at some big fancy hotel. I can't remember which one," she added, as if sensing Cassie's next question.

Maybe she was telling the truth about that, maybe she wasn't. But her all-business demeanor made it obvious that she wasn't interested in elaborating.

There was nothing for Cassie to do but leave.

So she did, promptly.

She never gave the housekeeper her name, and, anyway, her name alone couldn't give away her current location.

Meaning, it's safe to assume that whoever might be calling this hotel room, it isn't Alec, or, God forbid, her mother.

Still, she holds her breath as she lifts the receiver with a hoarse, "Hello?"

"This is your seven AM wakeup call," a computerized voice announces.

Relieved, Cassie vaguely remembers that she called for one just before falling asleep.

"Have a pleasant day," the recorded operator advises her from the telephone pressed hard against her ear.

A pleasant day. Yeah, right.

She opens her eyes abruptly and plunks the receiver back into its cradle.

Okay. She'd better get up, get on the road . . .

Wait a minute.

Why?

So she can return to her life, and the utter shambles she's made of it?

How could you have done this to yourself? What were you thinking?

She *wasn't* thinking. If she had been, she wouldn't have done it.

Any of it.

Oh, God.

Oh, God.

She should have just gone to her bridal shower and smiled and thanked everyone and told them she'll see them all at the wedding.

Instead, for the first time in her life, she acted on sheer impulse.

And now look at you. Pounding headache, upset stomach, waking up in a strange hotel room, in Boston, of all places.

But she supposes Boston is as good a place as any, if you're going to run away from home.

Wow.

She finally, actually did it.

After a good twenty years of daydreaming about it, she finally ran away.

Actually, in her fantasies, she always galloped away, on Marshmallow.

Still, driving away felt pretty good, too.

While it lasted.

Now it's time to drive back and face the consequences.

Isn't it?

Cassie's gaze falls on the television remote lying on the table beside the phone.

She can either get up, get dressed, drive back to Connecticut, and pick up the pieces of her life . . .

Or she can stall it by lying here watching morning television, pleasantly anonymous for a little longer.

What to do, what to do . . .

As if there's any choice.

She snatches up the remote and aims it at the open armoire across from the bed. The television clicks on.

The sound is on MUTE, she realizes, as the picture fades in: Matt Lauer silently laughing with a woman who isn't Katie Couric. Oh, that's right, she left *The Today Show* awhile back, Cassie recalls—not that she ever watched it anyway, other than catching the occasional fleeting snippet of morning news in the hospital lounge.

Unaccustomed to lying around in bed, staring at the tube, she tells herself to relax, reminding herself that this is what regular people do.

Really? Do regular people also run out on their wedding showers?

Not to mention abandoning a fiancé, parents, assorted family members and friends . . .

And my job, she remembers guiltily, glancing at the digital clock next to the bed.

She was supposed to be at the hospital two hours ago.

Well, it's too late for that, isn't it? It's too late to salvage anything.

You're here, in Boston, with no one to answer to but yourself, for once in your life.

So relax and watch TV, dammit!

She idly stares at the screen for a moment, where a weather map shows a tropical depression forming in the Caribbean. As she idly presses random buttons on the remote, trying to find the volume, she accidentally hits the POWER button.

The screen sparks and goes dark.

Cassie sighs.

I can't do this, anyway. I can't just lie here and ignore my life.

She gets up, winces at the ache in her skull and the rising tide of nausea, and looks around for her purse.

It's tossed on a nearby chair, unzipped, the contents spilling over the cushion and the floor.

Relieved that her wallet, keys, and phone are accounted for, she turns on her cell phone.

Over a dozen new messages.

Cassie sinks heavily into the chair and reluctantly goes through them.

Most are from her mother, speaking above chattering female voices in the background, clearly calling from the bridal shower. At first she sounds irritated, then angry, and, finally, in calls that are interspersed with Alec's, worried.

Her fiancé's recorded voice, too, is laced with concern.

"Please call me, baby, and let me know that you're all right. Nobody knows where you are. If we don't hear from you soon we're going to call the police."

Which they did, at two AM, according to her mother's final message.

"Cassandra, I have a gut feeling that you're all right." Regina Ashford's tone has almost regained its crisp control, but with an undercurrent of distress. "Alec suspects that you might have cold feet. He says you've been less enthusiastic about the wedding than he had hoped. If that's the case, you really need to get over it and remember that a lot of people have gone out of their way to attend your shower, and it's . . . *inappropriate,* and *impolite* . . . not to show up at all."

Inappropriate.

Impolite.

That it is, Cassie thinks, fighting back the strange urge to laugh at her mother's understated choice of words.

One more message.

She braces herself to hear once again from her mother, or Alec.

Instead, she hears a chorus of female voices. Singing.

What the . . . ?

We'll always remember
That fateful September
We'll never forget
The new sisters we met
We'll face tomorrow together
In all kinds of weather
ZDK girls, now side by side
May travel far and wide
But wherever we roam
Sweet ZDK will be our home.

A chill slithers down Cassie's back as she recognizes the lyrics . . . and the voices, including her own.

Rachel's distinct soprano soars highest and sweetest on the last note.

Brushing her teeth at the sink in the hall bathroom, Brynn spots a shadowy figure looming in the doorway.

She screams.

"Shhh! You'll wake up the kids."

"You scared me!" she hisses at Garth.

"I'm sorry. I called you but you didn't hear me."

She turns off the tap with a jerk of her hand; the rush of running water gives way to the hush of the still-slumbering household.

"Listen," Garth whispers, "I just walked into our room to change. Somebody's in our bed . . . And it isn't Goldilocks. What's going on?"

"That's Ashley. Remember I told you she'd be spending the night here?" She plunges the toothbrush back into her mouth and resumes scrubbing. The minty toothpaste, usually so refreshing, seems vaguely distasteful this morning.

"No, I don't remember anything about it, but I've been so crazed lately I'm lucky if I manage to remember what time my next lecture starts. Which I can, and it's in exactly an hour and twenty minutes, and Papa Bear's got to get showered and dressed, so . . ."

Brynn leans over the sink to spit out an unpleasant mouthful of foamy Colgate. "I'll wake up Ashley in a minute."

"Thanks." Garth's gaze meets hers in the mirror. "What's wrong? You seem upset."

She *is* upset . . . And she isn't even entirely sure why. Something is still just . . . *off* with her this morning.

It might have something to do with Ashley being here last night, confiding just how absent a parent Fee has been lately.

It might also have something to do with Garth *not* being here last night.

Yes, she's aware that Thursday is his late night on campus. And that he's been working on his book every chance he gets in preparation for the symposium.

Still . . .

"You never came home," she hears herself telling him in an accusatory tone.

He raises his eyebrows. "I was working on the book . . . which you forbade me to do in the house, remember?" His tone is as accusatory as hers. "I need to have this chapter wrapped up."

"Well, you should call me if you're not coming home at all."

"When? At three-thirty in the morning? Because that's when I realized I needed to download at least another hour's worth of research before I could even finish the page I was writing."

"No . . ." Deflated, she turns to look him in the eye, face-to-face. "I'm sorry, I was just worried about you."

"Why?"

"I don't know . . . I couldn't sleep."

"I saw your pillow and that old blanket on the couch. Take it from me, it isn't the most comfortable piece of furniture we own."

"Sadly, it *is* the most comfortable piece of furniture we own," she tells him, turning on the water to rinse out the sink.

"Then let's get new furniture." He rests his hands on her shoulders and tilts her back to lean against his chest, setting his chin on her head as they stare at each other in the mirror.

"Are you kidding? We can't afford that."

"Let's get it anyway. We need something good, Brynn."

"Debt isn't good."

"Maybe I'll sell this book. I have a gut feeling that something great is right around the corner."

Why does Brynn have the very opposite gut feeling?

She leans forward, away from Garth, and abruptly opens the medicine cabinet.

"Let's go furniture shopping this weekend," he suggests as she takes out the plastic case containing her birth control pills.

"Can't. I'm working Caleb's school's booth at the arts and crafts festival Saturday, and Zack's birthday party is Sunday. Remember?"

Clearly, he doesn't.

Nor does he know who Zack is.

"Maggie's son," Brynn explains, wondering how he can be so out of touch with the daily life she lives with the kids.

"Oh. Right. Next weekend, then?"

"Can't," she says again, poking a pill from the packet into her hand. "I'm taking the boys to the Cape and you're going to that symposium in Arizona. Don't tell me you actually forgot that, too?"

"I told you, my memory isn't functioning well these days." He presses a thumb and forefinger against his forehead, looking exhausted.

"Well, a total lack of sleep will do that to a person."

"Sleep? Who has time for sleep? When did our lives become so scheduled?"

"My life isn't all that scheduled," Brynn points out, shaking her head and staring down at the little white pill in her hand. "I'm always here."

You're the one who's been overscheduled, overworked, overtired. Even more so than usual lately.

"As I recall, that's how *you* wanted it," Garth tells her. "You said you wanted to stay home with the boys while they're young."

"What are you saying? That you want me to go to work?"

She plucks that out of oblivion and flings it at him, stupidly.

And she regrets it the moment it's out there, because that isn't what he was saying at all, and she knows it.

Then again . . .

That might have been what he was thinking.

Not that he would ever admit it.

He doesn't. He rubs his temple for a minute, looking tired, before saying levelly, "Brynn, you know I support your choice to be a full-time mom, so don't put words into my mouth, okay?"

"Okay," she says quietly.

Then . . .

"If we can afford new furniture, why not a new baby?"

Oh, no. Did she actually say *that* aloud?

She must have, because a parade of expressions is marching across Garth's face like a news crawl: from weary to confused to incredulous to fuming.

"You can't be serious."

"I am serious."

"I thought we resolved this months ago."

"Well, we didn't."

Glaring at her, he reaches for the knob and jerks the bathroom door shut.

She knows it's because he doesn't want to wake the boys and Ashley, but suddenly, she's frightened. She doesn't want to be alone in this tiny room with him.

Not when he's looking at her as though . . .

No, that's crazy.

Garth is angry, yes . . . angrier than she's seen him in a long time. But she's not afraid of him. He's her husband. They love each other.

Just not so much, at this particular moment.

So drop it, she warns herself. *Drop the subject.*

"Never mind," she tells Garth. "Forget I said anything."

"There are some things even I can't forget," he shoots back as she puts the tiny pill on her tongue and bends over the sink. "You know damned well that affording a new couch and a new baby are two entirely different things."

"Not just a couch." She runs cold water into her cupped hand and tilts it into her mouth to get the pill down, then straightens to look him in the eye. "You said new *furniture.* That costs thousands of dollars. What does a baby cost? The first year, I mean. Not thousands."

"You know this isn't just about money. And what about the second year, and the third? And the sixteenth, when the baby wants to drive, and the eighteenth, when it wants to go to college?"

"You're being ridiculous."

"No, *you're* being ridiculous."

He's right. She is. He already told her in no uncertain terms that he doesn't want a third child.

Why did she even bring it up again?

Maybe because the prospect of a third child has been simmering in her mind ever since, refusing to be snuffed out by Garth's adamant refusal.

Yes, the whole thing got back-burnered in the flurry of strep throat and Caleb starting school and . . .

And Rachel.

But now all of that has faded, and life has settled back into a routine, and Brynn wants another baby.

And it isn't fair that Garth is taking that away from her.

Feeling like a kid whose PlayStation privileges have been permanently revoked, Brynn folds her arms and lifts her chin. "Why do *you* get to decide? What about what *I* want?"

"What about what I *don't?*"

They stare at each other for a long moment.

Then a terrified scream erupts from down the hall.

Caleb.

Both Brynn and Garth bolt in that direction.

Their oldest son is standing barefoot in the kitchen doorway, wearing his favorite white Skivvy Doodle pajamas with the blue puppy print.

"There's something yucky there, Mommy!" He turns and buries his head in Brynn's hip, cowering.

Relieved, she strokes his head. "What is it, baby?"

"Oh, God, I see it . . ." Garth walks gingerly toward an object on the countertop.

"What is it?" All Brynn can make out is a bright splash of red against the white laminate.

"It's a bird."

"What?"

"Is it dead?" At his father's grim nod, Caleb slips from Brynn's grasp and backs away.

She steps closer, wondering how on earth it could have gotten into the house.

Then she sees that it's lying in a pool of red blood—much more blood than one small bird's body could possibly spill—and that the pile of limp feathers and bones unmistakably belong to a cardinal.

Hearing a movement in the next room, Isaac abruptly minimizes the screen on the laptop balanced on his thighs.

None too soon.

Kylah appears in the doorway with a classic case of bed head, stretching on her tiptoes so that her T-shirt parts with the waistband of her flannel pajama bottoms to reveal her taut stomach.

"Hey," she says in her croaky morning voice. "What time did you get home? I tried to wait up for you."

"I told you not to. It was late."

"How late?"

"I have no idea, but late."

"What are you doing?" She yawns and pads toward the couch.

"Just checking my e-mail."

"Aren't you going in today?"

"To work?" He realizes that by this time, he's usually out the door. "Oh . . . Yeah, I'm going, but I'm moving a little slower than usual."

"Hungover?"

No, but . . .

Should he claim to be?

What difference would that make, in the end? He doesn't have a credible alibi, when you come down to it. He can't produce a group of guys who can vouch for his whereabouts at a bachelor party last night, so . . .

So, what?

You're being paranoid.

Just relax and stick with the story.

Balancing his open computer on his lap, he presses his forefingers into his temples and frowns as though he's got a pounding headache. "I guess I did drink a few too many."

"Beers?"

"Beers . . . and shots . . ."

Kylah sits beside him on the couch and leans toward his computer screen. "You did shots?"

"Yes . . . What are you doing?"

She looks at him in surprise, and he realizes he sounds almost frantic.

"I was going to ask you to go on weather.com to see what coat I should wear to work," she says mildly. "Why?"

"Wear your trench. It's supposed to rain."

"Really?"

He can't remember. Dammit. That just popped out. He was desperate to keep her from seeing his screen.

Not that the heading on the minimized screen bar would mean anything to her at a glance: *www.zetadeltakappa.com/ alumni.*

Still . . . She might ask questions.

"Why don't you just watch the news?" he asks Kylah, leaning forward to block the screen from her view as he reaches for the TV remote and hands it to her. "You always say it's a lot more reliable than the Internet."

"Huh? I never say that."

"Oh. Sorry. I thought you did."

Avoiding her confused expression, he snaps his laptop closed, stands, and carries it toward the next room.

"Where are you going?"

"I've got to take a shower and get out of here."

"You make it sound like you have to escape."

He emits a short burst of sound he hopes passes for a laugh. "My office isn't exactly an escape, babe."

But that's where he's headed, regardless of how tempting it is to zoom back up the New England Thruway.

No, he'll go to work, and he'll come home, same as any other day.

And the entire time, he'll be thinking about Rachel.

Same as any other day.

Ordinarily, Fiona would be livid if she arrived at Fiona Fitzgerald Public Relations at 8:37 AM and found the doors locked. Emily is supposed to be here bright and early to open up.

Of course, that hasn't been necessary any other day. Fiona usually gets here just before eight, which is when she drops Ashley at Saint Vincent's School. But Emily, who is supposed to show up at 8:30 sharp, has the keys *and* explicit instructions for getting the office up and running first thing, should Fiona ever be delayed.

She never has been, until now.

In the alcove off the reception area, Fiona opens a packet of coffee and dumps it into a filter basket. Her hands are unsteady; a light rain of black grounds scatters over the pale blue speckled Corian.

"Dammit." She grabs the sponge beside the sink and finds that it's bone dry.

It shouldn't be. Emily is supposed to wipe everything down at the close of each business day; it would still be damp if she'd done so last night.

I've got to get rid of her. This is asinine.

Fiona runs the sponge under the tap, rubs the countertop clean, and runs water into the coffee carafe.

Yes, Emily has to be fired. But not today. Not until Fiona can focus on finding the right candidate to fill her place.

With the coffeemaker beginning to sputter into action, she moves toward her shadowy office, turning on copiers, computers, and lights in her path.

It's a gray, misty morning out there today, mountain fog hanging low over Main Street. Beyond the tall windows, even the legendary autumn foliage seems more brown and tan than red and gold, as muted as Fiona's mood.

Reaching beneath the maroon fringed shade, she flicks on the tabletop lamp near her desk, spilling a pool of light across its surface.

Immediately, she spots something that wasn't there last night.

Something that dispatches an icy river of dread through her veins.

Between a neat pile of manilla folders and another of precisely stacked documents, lies a single red rose . . . in a pool of something that looks like blood.

In the end, in some ways, at least, it was easier than expected.

Burglary 101. These days, you can learn to build a nuclear bomb on the Internet. Disabling a fancy alarm system and getting into a locked house is a cakewalk compared to that.

At first, Tildy seemed far too inebriated to put up a fight. That delightfully fortuitous fact was instantly apparent in her unsteady gait and the potent liquor fumes on her breath.

How highly unusual to see the sophisticated, controlled Matilda Harrington incapacitated in any way.

That it happened last night, of all nights, is clearly a sign that it was meant to be.

True, she did eventually recover her senses enough to resist . . .

And she caught you off guard when she almost escaped, didn't she?

Yes. Live and learn.

Now you know you can't let that happen again, with the others. You have to be prepared for anything, anything at all. You can't linger, savoring the moment, no matter how much you'd like to do that. The birthday girl will always have to be incapacitated as quickly as possible.

Too bad. It would be fun to see the guest of honor go from surprised to frightened to full-blown hysterical.

Of course, there will be plenty of opportunity, when laying the groundwork, to tease and taunt the others.

But when the big day arrives and you finally come face-to-face with each of them, you just can't afford to prolong the interaction. It's too risky.

Oh, well. In the end, Matilda Harrington didn't escape, did she?

No, she was meant to pay for her terrible sin with her life.

And it was meant to happen just when it did, on her milestone birthday.

The second blow to her head killed her—that much was obvious—but the party had to go on as planned. And there was supreme satisfaction in obliterating her beautiful, typically smug features until she was unrecognizable as the esteemed Matilda Harrington . . .

As a human face, even.

But that part is over, for now . . .

Until next weekend, anyway.

Next weekend, when the next birthday girl in line will find herself the guest of honor at a unique party indeed.

CHAPTER 11

Sergeant Quincy Hiles Jr. grew up in a low-income housing complex over in Roxbury, where he witnessed more than his share of violent crime in the first two decades of his life.

That trend continued for the next three, but by then he was behind the wheel of the dark sedan with flashing red lights, rather than watching it pull up in front of the latest crime scene as he huddled with a somber, jaded cluster of sidewalk onlookers.

Single mother Devorah Hiles had been elated when Quincy, the oldest of her five children, got into a local community college on a baseball scholarship. An agile six-two with a mighty swing, he was destined to be the next Ted Williams—or so she bragged to everyone in the 'hood.

Then Quincy's kid brother, DeQuann, became a neighborhood statistic, the ultimate cliché: gunned down a block from home in a drug deal gone bad.

When Quincy dropped out of college the following semester to begin law enforcement training, his mother reacted with the same wailing, inconsolable grief she had over DeQuann's death. Devorah didn't understand why her eldest son would exchange a potential ticket out of their violent hell for a holster and, as she saw it, a target on his back.

He wasn't sure he understood it, either—or does even now. It was just something he had to do, without ever looking over his shoulder at what might have been.

He took the same approach when his thirteen-year marriage to Bev became a casualty of his occupational hazards: long hours, rotating shifts, emotional detachment—so necessary on the job, but detrimental on the home front. Bev remarried in time for her new husband, a banker, to send both of Quincy's daughters to private colleges.

Forget what might have been. Now, with his law enforcement career winding down, about to put a down payment on a Clearwater Beach condo, Sergeant Quincy Hiles doesn't look back. Ever.

He's coasting out the remainder of his career as a detective with the Boston Police Department Homicide Unit. His work takes him all over the city, often into less-than-desirable neighborhoods.

Today, however, he finds himself in Area D, District D-4, encompassing Boston's wealthy to upper-middle-class Back Bay and South End.

Never here—never *anywhere*—has the strapping detective seen anything like *this*.

In the elegant dining room of the Commonwealth Avenue town house, the mistress of the house sits at the table.

Slaughtered.

Everything in the vicinity is spattered with blood. The silk wallpaper, the oriental area rug, the furniture. Even the 14-foot tray ceiling is marred with droplets, indicating a series of violent, arcing blows.

The corpse is propped in a chair at the head of the long oval cherry table, which is decorated as if for a little girl's birthday party. Pink paper goods, noisemakers.

A pointy party hat is garishly tilted on the woman's blood-soaked flaxen hair above a skull that was brutally bashed with a heavy object.

Quincy would bet it was the antique pineapple-shaped cast iron doorstop that props open the swinging door to the kitchen.

At a glance, there's no blood on it, but he's pretty sure forensic tests will reveal traces there.

"What makes you say that?" asks Detective Deb Jackson, new on the job, as young and as blonde as the victim herself—but far less privileged.

Then again, who isn't? The Harringtons are worth tens of millions—a possible motive for the crime?

"For one thing," Quincy tells Deb, rubbing his close-cropped, gray-flecked black beard, "that doorstop just looks as though it's out of place. It seems like it should be closer to the hinge, and maybe pushing the door up against the wall."

Right now, the door is caught a few feet out, in midswing, at an angle. In a house this meticulously kept, that feels wrong; a potential red flag to a seasoned detective.

To a newbie like Deb, not so much.

"It's partly my own gut instinct," Quincy tells her with a shrug. "I could be wrong. I bet I'm not, though."

"But how do you—"

He cuts her off with a brusque, "You'll learn. Takes awhile."

He turns his attention back to the macabre scene.

Uniformed investigators—cops, forensics, the medical examiner—bustle around him, snapping pictures, dusting for prints, filling out paperwork.

The table is set for five, with paper party plates and cups, and pink plastic cutlery. In the center of the table is an untouched rectangular cake. Pink wax candles have melted into white frosting and pale pink icing that reads Happy Birthday. In darker icing, which isn't icing at all, are the words DEAR TILDY.

"Blood," Quincy declares, noting the letters' dark, congealed, maroon appearance.

"Hers?"

"Probably. We won't know until we test it."

Deb nods. To her credit, she doesn't look the least bit squeamish. Good. This is one hell of a career kickoff case. If she can handle this, she can handle anything.

She's a pretty little thing, the type of woman you'd expect to be more at home wearing a pageant banner than a police badge. At least, Quincy would—based solely on looks and first impressions.

But so far, she's proven him wrong. She's gutsy, and smart, and he almost wishes she had come along sooner, for both their sakes. Not just because she's infinitely more charming than that brute Don Kopacynski, his last rookie partner, but because she has a lot to learn—from Quincy. And with three months to go until retirement, he's not exactly in a patient, passionate-about-his-work phase of life.

No, I'm more in the Get Me the Hell Out of Here *phase,* he thinks wryly. But he's not shirking. He'll work this case the way he's worked every other homicide, with dogged determination to get the killer off the street.

Deb points at the box clutched in the body's outstretched hands that rest on the table, helping to prop her upright. "What do you think that is?"

Quincy notes the pink wrapping paper and coordinating bow.

"It's anyone's guess," he replies. "But I'd be willing to bet it's not something you'd want as a gift on *your* birthday."

Deb barely cracks a smile. "I'd be willing to bet you're right. Too bad we won't know for awhile," she adds, well aware that they can't touch the evidence until the initial investigation is complete, and forensics and the medical examiner have done their thing.

Time now to speak to the lone witness.

"Hey, McGraw, where's the housekeeper who found the body?" he asks one of the uniformed officers.

"Connelly took her out back to get some air. She kept fainting."

"Let's go," Quincy tells Deb.

As they make their way through the kitchen, he notes the stark, elegant, monochromatic décor.

"I bet that fancy stove hood costs more than you and I put together make in a month," he comments to Deb.

"Yeah, but I'll take my cozy little apartment over this place any day. There's no warmth or personality here. This kitchen looks like a magazine picture."

She's right.

And the dining room looks like a horror show.

The staged scene suggests a serial killer, but Quincy doubts the victim was chosen randomly.

It really is her birthday.

The initial attack probably took place in the blood-spattered hallway opening into the dining room.

The blow to her head would have left her . . . if not dead, then at least unconscious and very close to it. Her hands and arms are free of any self-defensive wounds that would indicate she fought back.

But the killer didn't stop there.

The blood smears on the polished hardwood and area rug mark the trail where the mortally wounded woman was dragged to the table.

There, her face was brutally hacked with some sort of cleaver or ax, obliterating any recognizable features.

A classic case of overkill.

And it, combined with the birthday timing, suggests one thing to a seasoned homicide detective like Quincy Hiles: In all probability, whoever murdered Matilda Harrington knew her—and hated her.

* * *

A squad car is parked out front of Brynn's house on Tamarack Lane when she arrives home after dropping both Caleb and Ashley at their respective schools.

Both children seemed initially unsettled about the dead bird on the kitchen counter, while little Jeremy was oblivious, of course.

A shaken Brynn and Garth passed it off as a freak accident.

"It must have gotten into the house somehow," Garth told them, "and it was flying around and it crashed into the cupboards and died."

"But there's so much blood," Caleb said.

Yes. And it didn't come from the bird.

But Brynn wasn't about to tell him that. Instead she said, "Remember how much Jeremy's forehead bled when he knocked it on the corner of the coffee table that time?"

That seemed to appease Caleb.

Ashley said very little about the dead bird. She didn't even scream when she saw it, just stopped short in the doorway and stared.

She did ask, "Are you going to just leave it there?"

"For now," Garth told her somewhat tersely, and she dropped the subject.

They were planning to call the police as soon as the kids were safely out of the house. Brynn broke a school-day rule and served them cereal in the living room, in front of the television. She was relieved when it was time to hustle them out the door.

"Call now," she whispered urgently to Garth, who was on the phone, still trying to arrange for someone else to cover his morning lecture.

He just scowled.

He must have called right away, though, because Brynn has been gone only about fifteen minutes.

Clearly, the Cedar Crest force didn't send out their most hardened detective to solve this particular case.

The lone officer—probably a rookie—is blond, handsome and clean-shaven—if he's old enough to shave, Brynn thinks, as wryly as she can under the circumstances.

She finds him standing in the kitchen with Garth, surveying the heap of red feathers and darkened, congealed blood. Jeremy is back in his booster seat, an array of dry Cheerios scattered before him and on the floor.

"This is my wife, Brynn," Garth informs the young cop as she comes into the room. "Brynn, this is Officer Demuth."

They shake hands. Hers, she knows, is ice cold, and not just because of the raw, damp autumn chill outdoors.

With Caleb and Ashley gone, she's free at last to express the anxiety she's kept bottled up all morning, threatening to explode at any given moment.

First the sleepless night, then the explosive argument with Garth, then the dead cardinal . . .

A cardinal. It can't be a coincidence . . . can it?

No.

Especially not today.

Her eyes go to the homemade construction-paper calendar on the wall. Today is Tildy's thirtieth birthday. Brynn realized it first thing this morning and planned, in the back of her mind, to give her a call.

Now she definitely will . . . and not just to say Happy Birthday.

"I was telling your husband that birds do find their way into homes, Mrs. Saddler," Officer Demuth says, "but—"

"I just want you to know this was no accident," she cuts in, turning away from the calendar. Her stomach lurches as her gaze falls on the sickening site on the counter, and she swallows hard. "Somebody broke into the house sometime in the night and left that here."

"Brynn, that's obvious," Garth speaks up before Demuth can respond. "That's what he was about to say. Why don't you just let him do the talking?"

All right, so she stated the obvious. Still, Garth doesn't

have to make her look like a blabbering fool. Embarrassed, she flashes a scowl at her husband.

Demuth says, "Again, birds do get into homes, but it looks like this one has a broken neck . . . not an injury that would bleed. Anyway, I think we're all aware that the amount of blood makes it obvious that someone planted this here, correct? And that the blood didn't come from the bird?"

Brynn nods.

"Mrs. Saddler, you were home here all night, correct?"

She nods again, wondering if Garth has already mentioned that *he* wasn't.

"Did you see or hear anything unusual?"

She thinks back to her restless hours on the couch. She thought she heard something a few times, but she figured that was just Garth coming home.

Now, she shivers at the thought that someone could have been prowling around the next room as she lay on the couch.

Oh, God. She folds her arms and tucks her fists into her armpits, and sinks into a chair, shoulders hunched with tension.

"Mrs. Saddler?"

"I don't know," she murmurs to Demuth. "I mean, I didn't hear anything *unusual,* really. But I could have heard someone . . . I just don't know."

"Do either of you have any idea who might have played a prank like this? Do you think it could have been one of your students, Dr. Saddler?"

"It could have been," he says doubtfully.

"Is there anyone you can think of who's shown any kind of animosity lately? Maybe over a bad grade?"

Garth shakes his head.

"Have either of you had run-ins with any neighbors? Teenagers, especially?"

"Only with Mr. Chase next door," Garth says. "But he's always cranky and he's no teenager."

"What was the problem?"

"He said somebody plucked the blooms off of his mums, and he thought it was one of our boys."

"He was upset about it?"

"He gets upset about everything, and he accuses everyone on the block," Brynn puts in. "Nothing unusual."

"So, other than that, neither of you can think of anything that might have triggered someone to do something like this?"

Brynn can.

Her head is spinning.

Of course she never told Garth about the birthday card.

Does she dare mention it now?

No. No, you can't!

Doing so would open the door to questions about Rachel Lorent, whose unsolved, decade-old missing persons case was handled by the Cedar Crest police.

If she doesn't bring that up, though, the cops will have no way of knowing that this is no harmless neighborhood prank.

There isn't a doubt in Brynn's mind: that bird wasn't chosen randomly.

No, there is sinister symbolism in the cardinal—the Zeta Delta Kappa mascot—and the blood.

And the date: Tildy's thirtieth birthday.

It's meant to warn her—perhaps all of them—that someone is out there, watching.

Someone who *knows*.

Fiona is sitting at her desk—where there is no longer any trace of the rose or the blood—fighting the overwhelming urge to chain smoke, when Emily informs her that Patrick is on the phone.

She didn't even realize it had rung.

At the mention of her ex's name, however, she springs to life.

"Thanks, Emily," she snaps. "And can you please close the door? Thanks."

The receptionist's obedient response is immediate. Good, maybe she's learning.

When she showed up at 8:43, Fiona let her know, in no uncertain terms, that she's on thin ice.

"If you're ever late again, you'll be fired on the spot," Fiona informed her.

Never mind that if Emily hadn't been late this morning, she would have been here to witness the gory sight in Fiona's office.

And nobody needs to know about that.

The evidence—the rose, and a wad of bleach-soaked, bloody paper towels—is sealed into a black garbage bag she tossed into a Dumpster out back moments before Emily walked through the door.

She had the gall to blame her delay on the weather, as if she had to drive a hundred miles over rain-slicked and fog-shrouded roads to get here.

Disgusted, Fiona laid into her, then retreated to her office to brood.

Now, she looks at the phone, where a lit button indicates Pat holding on Line 1.

Scowling, she jabs it as she picks up the receiver with a brusque, "Fiona Fitzgerald."

"I'm just letting you know that I'm getting Ashley today after school," her ex informs her without a greeting, same as always.

He calls her every other Friday morning to confirm his prescheduled weekends with their daughter.

"After what you did?" she retorts with a brittle laugh. "I don't think so."

There's a pause on the line.

Then Pat asks, "What the hell are you talking about?"

"You know," she says, and holds her breath.

Does he know?

Please let the rose have been from him.

Yes, some kind of sick, twisted joke meant to signify that he somehow figured out she was on a date last night.

Because if he didn't leave it here . . .

"I have no idea what you think I did," he replies so cluelessly that her heart sinks, "but if it's spending the last forty-eight hours building a partition in my apartment and redecorating so that Ash will have her own room when she visits from now on, you're right. Lucky guess."

Dammit. Who could have left the rose?

The same person who sent the card.

It makes sense that the two are related.

The sorority flower was a red rose. That this one was lying in a sticky, congealed pool of blood might have something to do with Rachel . . .

"Fiona?" Pat prods in her ear.

Jarred back to the conversation at hand, she says only, "You built a room for Ashley?"

"She's getting older. She needs privacy when she's here."

"So that's what was so important you couldn't watch her for me last night, and I had to pawn her off on Brynn?"

"You didn't *have* to do anything," he shoots back. "And if our daughter is putting such a cramp in your style, maybe we should talk about my getting full-time custody."

And the generous child support that would go along with it, no doubt.

"No." The word is curt. "She isn't cramping my style at all. But, to answer your question, you can pick her up after school and take her for the weekend."

That will give me a chance to figure out what in God's name is going on here, she thinks uneasily.

Stepping through the French door onto a brick patio, Quincy sees Detective Mike Connelly. Deceptively young-looking—though a father of three college-aged kids—jovial, red-headed Mike has a nurturing air that tends to soothe even the most shaken witness.

He's standing over a woman seated at a wrought iron table. Her gray head is buried in her hands.

Catching Mike's eye, Quincy raises his eyebrows questioningly. Mike shrugs and throws up his hands, indicating he hasn't gotten anything out of her.

Quincy glances at the notes in his hand before approaching.

"Miss Schicke?" These old-world types aren't big on "Ms."

She looks up. Her plain face is etched in tear-dampened crow's-feet.

"I'm Detective Hiles, and this is Detective Jackson." He flashes his badge, as does Deb. "We need to ask you some questions."

She nods wearily and sits up straighter in the chair. He notes that she's wearing a uniform that consists of light blue pants and a light blue top with white cuffs.

Mike and Deb hover nearby as Quincy sits across from the witness.

"Can you describe what happened this morning? Take your time."

She takes a deep breath to steady herself. "I walked in and found—"

"Wait, back up. What time was this? And how did you get in?"

"With my key. The alarm wasn't set. I knew right away something was wrong."

"And when was this?" Mike prods.

"About five to eight, I think. That's when I come every day." She falls into an emotional silence.

Quincy prompts, "So you let yourself in and . . ."

"And I found poor Matilda." Her voice breaks and she sobs.

Her grief seems authentic. Perhaps even, Quincy notes, a

bit deeper than one would expect in an employee-employer relationship.

"How long have you been working for Miss Harrington?" Deb asks.

"All her life." The woman wipes her streaming eyes with a tissue. "I was her nanny from the time she was born. Then she lost her mother, and all these years, I've taken care of her. She was like a daughter to me. I can't believe somebody could do this to her. Poor Matilda. Oh, her poor father is going to be devastated."

She's sobbing again.

Quincy waits patiently for the tears to subside.

When she pulls herself together he asks, "What did you see when you walked into the house, Miss Schicke? Step-by-step."

"There was a stain in the hall, on the floor, and some on the baseboard. But I didn't realize what it was at first. I thought it might be paint. But it wasn't." She shudders. "Then I looked in the dining room, and I saw—"

"Excuse me . . . Hiles? Can I speak to you for a second?"

Quincy looks up to see Hal Tambert, a uniformed deputy, beckoning from the back doorway.

He strides over. "What is it?"

"We've got a neighbor who says she saw someone sitting in a car parked out front late last night, for a few hours. She said it looked like he was waiting for someone . . . or maybe keeping an eye on the place."

"Do we have a description?"

"Yeah, and it's a pretty distinct one." Tambert glances at the pad in his hand. "The neighbor said he was a white male, very thin, and that"—Tambert snorts—"he bore a close resemblance to Abraham Lincoln."

As Cassandra turns down Commonwealth Avenue, she spots a commotion in the block ahead . . .

Tildy's block, she realizes. Of all the luck.

Is it a fire?

No, no fire trucks or rescue vehicles.

Just police cars.

And lots of them.

Someone must have been mugged, or something.

Then again, Cassie thinks, that's an awful lot of chaos for a mugging. Well, there can't be much crime in this neighborhood, so maybe the authorities go overboard with the response whenever something happens.

When she reaches the intersection, she sees that the next block is barricaded from traffic. A uniformed officer waves her on around the corner.

As Cassie follows his direction, she notices a couple of satellite news vans parked near the police cars, and a lot of people milling around on the sidewalk. Maybe it's a protest of some kind. The college isn't far from here, right?

Tildy can't be too thrilled with all the turmoil right on her doorstep. If she's home.

She isn't at work. Cassie had already called her office a few times and kept getting her voice mail. Finally she called the nonprofit's direct line and the receptionist said she wasn't in today.

That doesn't mean she's home, though.

Heading down Gloucester Street, Cassie spots a MASS PIKE sign and wonders if she should just get on it. Just forget about trying to talk to Tildy and leave Boston, and everything that happened here, behind . . .

For what? To go home to something even more complicated?

No, she's come this far. She might as well see if Tildy's around. She has to tell her what she heard on her voice mail.

Just thinking about it raises the hair on her arms.

Who would call her, leave that creepy recording of the sorority song, and hang up?

Her phone's electronic incoming call log revealed nothing. That call was listed as Private Name, Private Number.

Each year, every ZDK sister in the house receives a copy of the annually videotaped pledge ceremony, which concludes with the girls singing the sorority song.

That means, theoretically, suspects would be limited to Cassie's fellow ZDK sisters. In which case . . .

It has to be a stupid prank, she tells herself. Just like the birthday card.

But what if it wasn't? What if someone knows about Rachel and somehow got their hands on a copy? Are they setting up an elaborate blackmail plot now?

Or . . . What if it *is* Rachel?

But it doesn't make sense. Even if she survived the fall somehow, and lived, why would she just disappear? And why would she come back now?

She was upset about something that night. So upset she drank herself into oblivion. What was bothering her? And could it possibly have been devastating enough to make her willingly vanish for ten years, putting her family and friends, and, yes, her sorority sisters—*including the four of us*—through hell?

Maybe.

Cassie is starting to believe that anything is possible. And if that's the case . . .

Making an aimless right turn onto Newbury Street, she shudders, wondering if Rachel realized that the four of them abandoned her in the woods.

Does she want . . . revenge of some sort? Is that why she's trying to scare them?

If it's even her. And that's pretty damned far-fetched, Cassie concludes, spotting a parking garage with a VACANCY sign just ahead.

She decides to put the Rachel incident, and the voice mail message, out of her head. She's got enough going on right now.

Maybe Tildy will let me stay for awhile, till I get my act together.

Oh, who is she kidding? She doesn't have the luxury of camping out at her friend's house indefinitely . . . or even for one night.

She has to get home to her fiancé, her family, her job.

And tell them . . . ?

Well, she still has no idea what she's going to tell them.

She'll figure that out later. Maybe Tildy will have a suggestion.

Back in their sorority days, Cassie fell into the habit of consulting Tildy whenever she came to a crossroads. She still does. Her old friend always seems to offer a decisive reply when Cassie needs it most, even if it's not necessarily the advice she wants to hear.

It was Tildy who urged her to marry Alec when she was feeling wishy-washy about their engagement.

Maybe you should have listened to yourself for a change, she can't help but realize belatedly.

Then again, she never said—even to herself—that she's going to back out of her wedding. She didn't leave Alec at the altar; she just chose not to attend her shower. That's all.

So far.

She locks the car and walks briskly away from the parking garage, headed toward Tildy's house.

All you have to do is get there, she tells herself irrationally, *and everything will be okay.*

Then she rounds the corner onto Commonwealth Avenue, with a straight-shot view of the brick town house, its perimeter wrapped in yellow crime scene tape.

Quincy, Connelly, and Deb have to shoulder their way through the crowd gathered on the sidewalk—not just curious onlookers, but the media.

This, after all, is big news. The Harringtons are one of

Boston's premier families. Dashing Jason Harrington famously doted on his only child, especially after tragically losing his wife and son in a plane crash years ago. The tragedy, combined with movie-star good looks and vast wealth, enhanced the family's Kennedyesque mystique.

The beautiful, elegant Matilda Harrington has been a fixture on her father's arm since her debutante days, frequently pictured in the society pages.

Now she'll be undoubtedly on the front page:

BACK BAY SOCIALITE SLAIN

Of course, the most sensational details won't emerge in the papers. No one outside the immediate homicide investigation knows about the creepy, staged birthday party. That's a detail the detectives are keeping from the press and the public.

Quincy, Connelly, and Deb ignore the reporters' frenzied questions as they make their way to their waiting car, but their expert eyes skim the faces in the crowd.

It wouldn't be the first time Quincy spotted a suspicious onlooker who later turned out to be the culprit. Some sickos get off on showing up at the crime scene or funeral to witness the fallout from their diabolical handiwork.

Nothing here, though, at a glance.

Just a throng of curious bystanders, most of them well-heeled locals, sprinkled with press and law enforcement.

Then, out of the corner of his eye, he spots a face that draws his attention for some reason.

The young, attractive African-American woman on the fringes of the crowd is staring up at Matilda Harrington's home.

And she's wearing an expression that seems far more vested than those around her.

Turning his head to get a better look, Quincy observes that she's unmistakably grief-stricken—and something more.

She's deathly afraid, he notes, watching her from across the sea of heads.

Yes, and there's something furtive about the way she's starting to slip back from the crowd.

Quincy abruptly begins to move toward her, but there are too many people in his way. By the time he reaches the spot where she was standing, it's empty. He looks around just in time to see her disappear around the corner at the end of the block.

He heads immediately in that direction, but she's gone.

He won't forget her face, though—or the way she fled the scene as if she feared for her own life.

Hearing Brynn cry out, Garth, shirtless and shaving, turns off the tap. With his razor poised in his hand and one cheek covered in a white layer of Gillette, he opens the bathroom door and peers down the hall.

Silence.

Maybe he imagined the scream. He can hear water running in the kitchen. She's probably still disinfecting the counter where the dead bird lay until Officer Demuth took it away as evidence.

He said he'd see if they could run some tests on it. Garth could tell he was mostly humoring them, though. He was inclined to chalk it up to a prank, most likely pulled by one of Garth's students.

"It's a college town," the officer said as he left. "Things like this happen all the time."

"He's right," Garth told Brynn after Officer Demuth had driven away. "It was probably just kids. Nothing to worry about."

But she was—*is*—worried. He can tell.

But now all is quiet down the hall, aside from the running water and the faint sound of Jeremy's happy chatter.

Garth is about to close the bathroom door, his mind on

the shave he has to finish quickly if he's going to make it to campus in time for his next class, when he hears it again.

This time, it's more of a sob.

"Brynn?" He sets aside his razor and hurries down the hall.

In the kitchen, Jeremy is kneeling on the floor in front of an open cabinet, cheerfully stacking plastic Tupperware containers.

Brynn is by the sink where the tap is running for no apparent reason. Her back is to him and she's clutching the cordless phone to her ear, crying.

She must be telling someone about the dead bird, he decides. And she's definitely overreacting.

Then she turns around and he sees her stricken face.

"My God, what happened?" Garth sidesteps the Tupperware, going immediately to her side. He turns off the faucet before taking her trembling arm. "Who are you talking to?"

"It's Cassie . . ."

"Who?"

"My friend Cassandra," she clarifies impatiently, tearfully. "Garth, Tildy is dead."

"What!"

"Somebody killed her . . . Tildy. My sorority sister," she adds.

As if he doesn't know.

Garth, who knows Matilda Harrington far better than his wife would ever imagine, pulls Brynn close and buries his head in her hair, not daring, in this moment, to let her glimpse his face.

CHAPTER 12

Brynn can't seem to wrap her mind around the fact that Matilda Harrington is actually dead.

Not just dead . . .

Murdered.

Cassie didn't provide Brynn with any other details; she was too shaken. She just kept crying and repeating, "I can't believe it," and "Oh, God, poor Tildy."

With Garth at her side, Brynn couldn't even bring up the possibility of Tildy's death having anything to do with the three of them . . . and their secret . . .

And the dead cardinal she found on her countertop this morning.

But Cassie is on her way here. She said she'd leave right away, and drive straight to Cedar Crest. Brynn didn't question her, or argue.

She knows Cassie is thinking the same thing she is. And Fiona will, as well.

"Here." Garth tries to hand her a glass of cold water as she stands with the phone still clutched in her fist. "Drink this."

She waves it away, dialing with a trembling finger. "I have to call Fee."

"Do you want me to do it for you?"

"No!"

She wants him to go away, that's what she wants.

She can't think straight with him here, and Jeremy rhythmically tapping a plastic Tupperware lid on the linoleum, babbling incessantly.

"Fiona Fitzgerald's office, Emily speaking."

"Emily, this is her friend Brynn," she says in a rush, turning her back on Garth and the glass of water he's still holding out to her. "I need to speak to her right away, please."

"Ms. Fitzgerald is unavailable."

"Is she *there?*"

Emily hesitates, then repeats, "She's unavailable."

"Tell her I need to speak to her, please, right away. It's an emergency."

"She's unavail—"

"Look, someone *died,* okay?" she bites out, fed up with Fiona and her professional blockade. Who does she think she is, the president? "Get her on the damned phone!"

She realizes Jeremy has stopped tapping the lid and is watching her with interest. She flashes him a tight smile.

"Damned!" he says cheerfully. "Damned, damned, damned phone!"

"Terrific. Come here, kiddo." Garth scoops him into his arms and looks at Brynn. "Are you okay?"

"No, I'm not okay." She exhales shakily. "I feel sick."

"Sit down." Garth pulls out a chair.

But before she can move there's a click in her ear, and Fiona's voice says crisply, "Brynn? I swear, for your sake and Emily's someone had *better* be dead because I gave her explicit instructions not to—"

"It's Tildy, Fee. Tildy's dead." Her voice breaks and she's crying all over again.

Dead silence.

Then, *"What?"*

"Tildy's dead. Someone killed her."

Brynn sinks into the chair, conscious of her husband's hands on her shoulder, coaxing her down.

He hovers beside her with Jeremy in his arms as, still feeling dazed, she gives Fiona what little information she has.

"How did Cassie find out about this?"

"I don't know, Tildy's father must have called her or something. She didn't say. She was a mess."

And so am I.

She wants to tell Fee about the dead cardinal, but she can't. Not with her husband right here, listening, wanting to help.

Well, you can't get rid of him fast enough, Brynn tells herself. *You have to speak to Fee and Cassie alone.*

"She's coming right over," she tells Garth when she hangs up the phone.

"Was she upset?"

"Fiona? Of course."

She *has* to be upset. She just lost a friend.

Yet she wasn't openly distraught or emotional, like Brynn. No, when she initially realized Brynn was serious about Tildy's death, Fiona reacted with an expletive. She repeated it over and over, under her breath.

And she didn't cry.

But then, tears never were her style. Happy tears, or sad tears. She didn't cry on her wedding day, and she didn't cry over her divorce.

Unlike Brynn, who, according to Fiona, sheds tears at the slightest provocation.

But this isn't slight, and it's all she can do to pull herself together now, under Garth's watchful gaze.

"Here, Jeremy, come on, let's get you dressed." Brynn reaches for her son.

He happily stretches his arms toward her, but Garth doesn't hand him over.

"It's okay," he says. "You try to calm down a little. I'll take care of him."

"I'm calm. You have to go to campus."

And I have to talk to Fiona and Cassie in private.

"I can't go now."

"Garth, come on. You already missed your first class. What time is the next?"

"It doesn't matter. I'll stay here with you. You need me."

No, I don't.

In fact, it's the opposite, so please just go.

Brynn takes deep breaths, steels her nerves. She can't let him see how upset she is.

"I want Mommy!" Jeremy announces, and squirms toward her.

"Come here." She takes him from Garth and cuddles him close. "Want some milk?"

"Yes!"

She fills a sippy cup, balancing Jeremy on her hip. He's getting heavy. It isn't easy, especially not when she's an emotional, quivering mess on the inside.

But, outwardly, she's determined to prove to Garth that she's okay.

After a few minutes, she succeeds. He agrees to go to work.

"But only after your friends get here."

"It's fine, they're on their way. Don't be late for your class."

Brynn dresses Jeremy in his room as her husband finishes getting ready in the bathroom. Conscious that the walls are thin, she keeps up her usual singsong chatter to her son.

"Do you want to wear a red shirt today, Jeremy, or blue?"

Oh, my God. Tildy.

"Blue!"

Just hold it together, Brynn. Don't fall apart now.

"Should we wear sneakers today, or just Padders?" She waves the rubber-soled corduroy booties at him.

"Just toes! Sing, Mommy." He thrusts his bare foot onto her lap as she sits beside him on his bed. "Sing the toe song!"

Someone got into this house somehow and left that gruesome calling card.

"This little piggy went to market . . ."

Was it the same someone who killed Tildy, in Boston?

She breaks off, swallows over a fierce lump, continues, "This little piggy stayed home . . ."

Oh, God. Oh, Tildy.

"Mommy! You're sad again!" Jeremy reaches out to touch her tear-dampened cheek.

She wipes at it blindly.

"I'm ready." Garth sticks his head into the open doorway. "Are you sure you're okay with me leaving?"

"I'm fine." Her back to him, she dries her eyes on the hem of her sleeve, then turns around and forces a smile.

"Really? Because you don't look fine."

"It's just upsetting to find out that someone you know has been killed."

Even more so when you're thinking you could be next.

Her breath catches in her throat as she pushes on, "But it's not like I was that close to her these days. You know . . . It's just that we had a history . . ."

One hell of a history.

And it might very well have had something to do with Tildy's death.

Might have?

You know it does, Brynn. You know it in your gut.

"I hate to leave you here alone."

Please don't go, Garth. I'm scared out of my mind. Someone was here last night. Someone left that cardinal, and the blood . . .

"If Fiona and Cassie weren't coming, you know I wouldn't leave," Garth says, keys in hand.

"I know. But they're coming. So go ahead."

He does.

She's free, now, to privately discuss the situation with Fee and Cassie.

Free? Ha.

When Fiona arrives ten minutes later, Brynn is barricaded in the house. The front and back doors are double-locked with chairs wedged beneath the knobs, the shades drawn.

"I'm scared," she tells Fee simply.

Fee says nothing, just hugs her, hard.

And she doesn't comment when Brynn relocks the door with the dead bolt and slides the chair back into place.

A steady rain and bleak weekend forecast haven't put a dent in the population of foliage-seekers headed across the Massachusetts Turnpike toward the Berkshires this Friday morning.

Cassie stays in the right lane, able to focus on only the most rudimentary driving skills. It's a wonder, really, that she's managing to keep pace with the traffic at all. She has little memory of actually getting into the car, out of the parking garage, onto the highway.

All she has been able to focus on, from the moment she arrived in front of Tildy's house and asked a teenaged bystander what was going on, is that Tildy's gone.

The kid relayed the news so casually, even shrugged. "The girl who lives there was killed last night."

"Girl? You mean a child?" she asked in confusion.

"No, and I guess you're not a girl anymore when you hit thirty, so—my bad. Sorry."

Was he talking about Tildy?

He couldn't be.

Then another nearby stranger, a college-aged kid eavesdropping on their conversation commented, "Yeah, and I heard it was her birthday, too. Turning thirty sucks bad enough, dude, without getting murdered."

That was when the full implications began to strike Cassie like shrapnel.

Tildy's birthday.

Rachel's birthday.

The *Happy Birthday to Me* card.

The surprise-party invitation devoid of any contact information.

The sorority song mysteriously left on Cassie's voice mail sometime in the night . . .

It was all too much. Somehow, in her daze of shock and grief, it registered on Cassie that she had to get out of there.

And that she had to call Brynn and Fiona.

She literally ran the few blocks back to her car.

When she turned on her cell phone, it immediately beeped, indicating new messages.

She didn't listen to them.

She dialed Fee first, simply because she's more take-charge, and less emotional, than Brynn. Her assistant said she wasn't available, and Cassie hung up without leaving a message.

Brynn was at home, though.

Cassie didn't tell her she herself was in Boston—well, *escaping* Boston at that precise moment. Something made her instinctively keep her location to herself.

Now—her cell phone turned off again, new messages still ignored—she's headed for Cedar Crest.

In part, because she has no place else to go. She can't face the mess back home, especially now, with all that's happened since she left.

Maybe I won't ever go back, she thinks as she methodically follows the red taillights in front of her.

The wipers are beating a relentless rhythm against the windshield in time with the relentless refrain in Cassie's brain: *Tildy's . . . dead . . . Tildy's . . . dead . . . Tildy's . . . dead . . .*

The truth is sinking in gradually, and with it, another echo takes up the cadence in Cassie's head: *You're . . . next . . . you're . . . next . . . you're . . . next . . .*

* * *

The man seated across the table in the windowless inter-rogation room does bear a strong resemblance to Abraham Lincoln—Quincy will admit that.

But he suspects Ray Wilmington has little else in com-mon with good old Honest Abe.

Specifically, honesty—or a lack thereof. Ray Wilming-ton's body language—constant fidgeting, lack of eye con-tact—is a clear signal that he's lying about something.

Not about everything, however.

He did admit that he was lurking in his parked car on Commonwealth Avenue last night, waiting for Matilda Har-rington to come home from her party.

A party to which he hadn't been invited.

"Were you upset that you weren't invited, Ray?" Mike asks sympathetically.

"No."

Of course he's lying.

It's classic. This poor unattractive sap, still living at home in Dedham with his widowed mother, is nursing an infatua-tion for a woman who's way out of his league and wouldn't give him the time of day.

"So then why were you waiting for her last night?" Quincy demands.

"Because I wanted to give her a gift for her birthday."

Right. And what do you give the gal who has everything? A smashed skull and butchered face.

This, Quincy is certain, is a simple case of unrequited passion flaring out of control. With any luck, they'll have a confession out of Ray Wilmington by suppertime and Quincy will be home in time to catch most of the Red Sox playoff game on television.

"What was your gift for Matilda?" Deb is asking.

She's seated at Quincy's side, ready to become Good Cop, with Mike, to Quincy's Bad Cop when, *if*, necessary.

"It was just a bouquet of flowers," he mumbles.

"What kind of flowers?"

"Just red roses."

Red roses. A dime a dozen in Matilda Harrington's world. There was a bouquet of them on a table in her living room, Quincy recalls. Along with an unsigned card that reads, "See You Tonight."

Quincy already has someone trying to track the sender through the local florist shop.

"So, did she like your gift, then, Ray?" Mike manages to sound like he's a pal, as though they're standing around the water cooler discussing their weekends.

"I didn't give it to her."

"Why not?"

"Because when I saw her come home, I realized right away that she was completely drunk. Her driver had to help her up the steps and in the door."

"So what did you do then?" Quincy asks, with a graphically clear picture in his head.

"I left."

"With the roses?"

"No, I threw them away."

"Where did you throw them?"

"I don't know."

"You'd better figure it out pretty quickly," Quincy advises with a lethal look.

"I guess I tossed them in a garbage can by my car."

"On the street?" Wilmington nods. "Why did you throw them away?"

"Red roses are expensive," Deb puts in. "That seems like such a waste. Why not just give them to her the next day?"

"Because they wouldn't last. They were already wilting."

"So you sat in the car waiting for her for a pretty long time, then?" Deb's tone is almost compassionate. "Hours?"

"Probably."

"You do realize," Quincy leans across the table and catches Ray's shifty gaze, "that I'm about to make a couple of phone calls that will tell us whether or not there's a bouquet of red roses in a garbage can across the street from Matilda Harrington's house."

Wilmington shrugs.

Quincy leans closer. "We're not going to find any bouquet of roses in the garbage can, are we, Ray?"

No reply. But there's a telltale staccato rapping sound from beneath the table, courtesy of Ray's increasingly jittery legs.

"Why don't you spare us the trouble, Ray, and just admit you weren't at Matilda Harrington's to give her a bouquet of flowers?"

"All right, this is getting ridiculous. Where the hell is Cassie?" Seated at the Saddlers' cluttered kitchen table before a still-brimming, now-cold cup of coffee, and the dwindling pack of cigarettes she keeps going outside to smoke, Fiona checks her watch for the tenth time in as many minutes.

"She can't just beam herself here from Danbury, you know," Brynn points out as she shakily dumps boxed pasta into the boiling water on the stove.

"I know, but it shouldn't take two hours to drive here."

"It can. Especially in bad weather."

"It's not as if it's snowing or icy."

"No, but wet mountain roads and fog are no fun."

And sitting here waiting with the silent, brooding Fiona is even less fun. Silent, that is, when she's not grumbling about having to move a chair and unfasten three locks every time she goes outside for a smoke.

Brynn steps on the foot pedal of the garbage can to throw away the empty box, conscious of Fiona's eyes on her.

She's probably just noticing that the macaroni and cheese isn't even Kraft, but a store brand, Brynn thinks inconsequentially. It's almost a relief to focus, if only for a moment, on her friend's habitual assessment of her downscale lifestyle.

Anything is better than thinking about Tildy.

Dead on her birthday . . .

Just like Rachel.

Every time Brynn allows herself to piece together the big picture, she's terrified.

All four of them—she, Fiona, Cassie, Tildy—got those birthday cards last month.

What if whoever sent the cards, and most likely also left the dead bird, is responsible for Tildy's death?

And what if it isn't going to stop there?

It won't be long now before Matilda Harrington's death hits the media. It's going to be big news—and not just in Boston.

But the story hasn't exploded yet.

And you have to stop checking every five minutes to see if it has, or someone is going to get suspicious. Just go about your daily business and stay away from the Internet, the television, the radio.

No, just try to go about your daily business, same as always.

But, of course, that's not easy. Pure euphoria is difficult to keep under wraps.

It's especially hard to keep from smiling at the satisfying memory of all that blood spilling from the deep gashes in Matilda Harrington's face and neck, soaking her fancy white party dress.

The best part was that, despite her inebriated state, she realized who had finally taken her flimsy excuse for a life into capable hands, putting an end to it at last.

Yes, it was a pleasure to see Matilda twitching and struggling, looking up warily, just as that frightened, flapping cardinal did in the final second before its neck was broken with a quick, vicious twist of these same capable hands.

Hands that are, at the moment, handing over a couple of ones and accepting a cup of hot coffee from an unwitting, smiling cashier.

"There you go. Have a nice day."

"Oh, I absolutely will."

Still no Cassie.

Brynn checks the stove clock as she turns off the flame under the boiling kettle.

Jeremy has been parked in front of the television all morning. Now he needs lunch, and a nap.

Draining the macaroni into the sink, she realizes she should probably eat something, too. Her stomach has been queasy all morning.

"Do you want some of this?" she asks Fiona, who makes a face and shakes her head. No surprise there.

"How about more coffee?" Brynn offers.

Fiona shakes her head again, taps her cigarette pack against the table in a rapid staccato, and mutters, "God, where *is* she?"

"She's on her way."

"Maybe she's not coming after all."

"She would have called to tell us."

Fiona just shrugs.

Removing milk and butter from the fridge, Brynn wonders, again, if she should tell Fee about the dead cardinal. She hasn't yet, because it makes more sense to wait for Cassie.

But she can't go much longer without blurting it out.

"Oh, God," she murmurs, stirring a rapidly melting wedge of butter into the steaming pasta.

She doesn't realize she spoke out loud until Fiona asks, "What did you say?"

"Nothing."

They fall restlessly silent again.

The phone rings as Brynn dumps the powdered orange cheese sauce into the pot.

"Get it," Fee commands, as if Brynn had no intention of answering it. "Maybe it's Cassie."

It isn't.

It's Garth, wanting to know if she's okay.

"I'm trying to be," she says, walking into the hall with the phone.

"I'll come home," Garth offers promptly.

"No, don't. I'm fine, I'm not alone, Fiona is here."

"Still? I've never seen her stay put for this long anywhere other than her office."

"Come on, Garth, someone *died*."

"I know. I'm sorry."

Brynn peeks around the doorway into the living room. There's Jeremy, glued to yet another episode of *Dora*.

Pushing aside her maternal guilt, she tells Garth, "Cassie is on her way and I'm sure the two of them will stick around for awhile. If they leave and I need you, I'll call you. Okay?"

He hesitates. "Okay. Just . . . Be careful, Brynn. I don't like this. First that dead bird, and now Tildy."

Her heart races. "Who says one has anything to do with the other?"

"Maybe they don't. It didn't even occur to me, actually, until I was in the car driving over here. I wanted to turn around and come back home, but I told myself I was being ridiculous. Now I'm not so sure."

I am sure . . . And they definitely have something to do with each other.

She bites her lip, fighting the urge to spill the whole story to her husband.

She can't do that. Not with Fiona in earshot, anyway.

Ten years ago, she swore to keep their secret.

But now her own life might be in danger if she doesn't tell someone.

Garth, and the police.

They need to know. I have to tell.

But she shouldn't just blurt it out without discussing it with Fiona and Cassie first. Surely they'll agree that telling is absolutely necessary now, and damn the consequences. They have to tell for Tildy's sake.

No. For Rachel's.

How would I feel if I thought they abandoned my body alone in the woods?

You wouldn't feel anything, a reasonable voice points out, *because you'd be dead.*

But what if I wasn't? What if they only thought I was? Or claimed I was?

Was Rachel really still alive as she lay there? Did Tildy knowingly abandon her at the bottom of that ravine? Did she lie to the others about Rachel being dead?

And if the answer to all of those questions is *yes* . . .

Did Rachel return to kill Tildy for what she did?

"Listen, I'll be home as soon as I can," Garth says, still on the phone.

She forgot him; he's been silent and so has she.

"Promise me you'll call me if you need me, okay?"

I do. I need you.

Aloud she manages only, "Okay."

"I love you."

"You, too."

She disconnects the call and returns to the kitchen.

"I can't sit here all day," Fiona announces. "I've got appointments."

"Can't you cancel them? It's not like you're playing hooky." Brynn returns to the stove and sees that the orange cheese powder has clumped over the surface of the macaroni.

"Me? Play hooky? I've never done that in my life."

Attempting to stir the mixture into a more palatable concoction, Brynn points out, "I seem to remember you cutting classes to hang out with Pat."

Fiona's eyes darken at the mere mention of her ex-husband. "That was school. This is work. I can't just not show up."

"Someone died, Fiona."

"Yeah, I know that, Brynn." Her tone is sharp. She slaps her hands on the table and pushes back her chair abruptly. "I've got to get back to—"

A blast from the doorbell cuts her off.

"There's Cassie," Brynn says, and hurries to open the door.

Emerging from his office building onto Lexington Avenue, Isaac sees the drenching downpour and groans inwardly.

He should have looked out the window before heading out to get lunch.

Should he go back up and grab an umbrella, or just make a run to the deli around the corner on Forty-Sixth?

He's debating when his cell phone suddenly vibrates in his pocket.

He flips it open, checks the caller ID window, and immediately recognizes the area code and exchange.

Cedar Crest.

His heart starts to pound.

Heart racing, he steps away from the group of chatty smokers standing beneath the overhang above the entrance, keeping dry as they puff away.

"Hello?"

"Isaac? Oh, my goodness . . . I'm so glad I got you. I thought you should know . . ."

"What's wrong?"

"It's Matilda Harrington. She's just been killed," Puffy Trovato, the Zeta Delta Kappa housemother, announces breathlessly in his ear.

* * *

"We've got to tell the police," Brynn announces, again.

She's been saying it for an hour, at least, since the moment Cassie arrived.

And every time Brynn says it, Fiona vehemently disagrees.

She does again now, so loudly that Brynn shushes her with yet another, "Shh! Jeremy's sleeping."

Fiona would like nothing better than to get the hell out of here, but she can't just walk away from this intense powwow at the Saddlers' kitchen table.

The moment she does, Brynn will probably call the cops and tell them everything.

She *already* called them, actually, after she found the dead cardinal in her kitchen this morning. They apparently believe it was some kind of prank.

It wasn't, of course.

And when Brynn spoke up about the bird, and the cops, Fiona's blood ran cold.

Still, she said nothing about the rose.

She probably wouldn't have, regardless of whether Cassie immediately spoke up to announce that someone had left a recording of the sorority song on her voice mail.

"Did you tell anyone about it?" Fiona asked sharply, and was relieved when Cassie shook her head.

"What about you, Fee? Did anything strange happen to you?" Brynn asked, but still, Fiona didn't mention the rose.

And the more time that goes by, the more difficult it will be to bring it up.

So she should do it now . . .

Or she shouldn't do it at all.

She isn't entirely sure why she's unwilling . . . other than because it might push Brynn over the edge if she thinks all three of them have been targeted by the same person who murdered Tildy.

"I just don't get it. How can you believe we shouldn't report this, Fiona?" Brynn asks now, her voice almost shrill.

Fiona takes perverse pleasure in saying, "Shh! Jeremy's sleeping."

"This isn't like the birthday cards," Cassie speaks up quietly after a pause. "It's different now. Somebody's *dead*."

Fiona can tell that Brynn's paranoia is really starting to sway Cassie.

When Cassie walked in here, haggard and emotional, she kept looking over her shoulder as if she thought she was being followed. Now, she seems weary as well; she keeps yawning, and the bags beneath her eyes indicate she hasn't had a good night's sleep in awhile.

"Maybe what happened to Tildy has nothing to do with this—with us," Fiona points out stubbornly, and, all right, perhaps foolishly. Still, she goes on, "Maybe it was some random thing, a serial killer, a robbery—"

"It was her *birthday,* Fiona." Brynn's tone is contained now, but she looks as though she's on the verge of hysteria. "It has everything to do with us. And Rachel."

"Do you think Rachel did it? Is that what you're saying?"

There's a moment of silence.

Then Brynn replies, "Yes, I do, all right? I think Rachel did it."

"Because . . . ?"

Cassie answers the question. "Because we left her in the woods to die."

"Not the three of us," Fiona says. "*We* thought she was already dead. We were *told* she was already dead. If she wasn't, and Tildy lied, well, then, maybe Tildy got what was coming to her—" Wow, that's harsh, even to her own ears. "But the rest of us didn't do anything wrong."

"We still left her there, Fee." Brynn is adamant. "That was wrong."

"Not as wrong as if she were alive. I'm so damned sick of going around and around about this!"

"So am I," Cassie agrees.

"Then let's just drop it. We all know that we *thought* we were leaving a body, and that someone would find it."

"Well, *we* know, but how would Rachel know that?" Brynn asks. "How would she know Tildy lied to us—if she did lie?"

"Maybe she was listening." Fiona can't quite keep the sarcasm from her voice.

"I doubt that." Cassie shakes her head. "The chances of her even being alive after a fall like that, let alone conscious, with all she had to drink—"

"So you're saying that for all Rachel knows, we were as responsible as Tildy was."

"I'm not saying Rachel knows anything because I truly think Rachel died that night." Fiona's words are far more decisive than she feels inside, but someone has to be in charge now that Tildy's gone.

And gone forever.

Whatever happens from here on in is up to the three of them.

It can be up to me alone, if I play this right, Fiona thinks.

"The police are probably never going to connect Tildy's death with what happened to Rachel," Cassie says slowly, "or with us, unless we tell them."

"Which we can't do," Fiona responds firmly. "Something like that will destroy all our lives."

Including yours, Brynn. You just have no idea to what extent.

"We have to do it anyway," Brynn says, just as firmly, oblivious to the fact that Tildy had other secrets. Secrets that had nothing to do with Rachel and the sorority.

"We don't 'have to' do anything," Fiona tells her, longing to get off this frustrating carousel.

"We have to tell the police about this, if for no other reason than that whoever killed Tildy might be coming after us."

"Maybe not after Fiona," Cassie points out. "I mean,

nothing strange turned up on her voice mail or in her house last night."

Brynn turns to Fiona. "Are you sure? You *did* sleep at home last night, right?"

"What's that supposed to mean?"

"I know you had a date . . . in Boston," Brynn adds suddenly. Thoughtfully. "You know . . . I completely forgot that you were in Boston last night, Fee."

Wide-eyed, Cassie is looking from Brynn to Fiona. "You were in Boston? So you really were throwing Tildy a surprise party after all? Because Lena acted like—"

"Surprise party? What are you talking about? I was at the Red Sox game with one of my clients."

"You didn't give Tildy a surprise party?"

"If I did, don't you think I'd have said something to you by now?"

Cassie falls into a troubled silence again, but she's furiously chewing her bottom lip.

"So you went straight home after the game, right?"

Fiona forces herself to maintain eye contact with Brynn. "Right. After the game—and dinner at a Japanese restaurant."

And really, what happened after that is none of your business.

"What about your mail?" Brynn persists. "Did you check it when you got home?"

"Yes, I checked it."

And she did. When she stopped home this morning to shower and change just before heading to the office . . . which is where she found the bloody rose and her nice, orderly world turned upside down and inside out.

"Look." She glances from Brynn to Cassie and back again. "I know you're both shaken up by this. So am I. But I honestly don't think we're in any kind of actual danger. And I think the best thing we can do right now is just sit tight."

"That's easy for you to say." Cassie leans back in her

chair, arms folded across her chest, expression gaunt as she looks at her friends. "Your birthdays aren't coming up next weekend."

According to the municipal department, the garbage cans on and around Matilda Harrington's block haven't been emptied in the last twenty-four hours.

About to pull out of the Dunkin' Donuts parking lot long after dusk, Quincy answers his phone and is promptly informed that none of the trash receptacles in the area has yielded a discarded bouquet of red roses.

So, unless someone walked off with them . . .

"Which could have happened," Deb protests, seated in the passenger's seat of the sedan, tearing a sip hole in the plastic lid of yet another cup of black coffee.

"You're saying you believe he was telling the truth?" Quincy closes his cell phone and tucks it back into his pocket, then takes a quick, soothing swig from his own his own take-out cup.

Herbal tea. He made the permanent switch from coffee awhile back.

Predictably, his last partner, Don Kopacynski, gave him a hell of a time about it. Quincy didn't bother to tell him that coffee aggravates his irritable bowel syndrome. He figured Kopacynski would have had a field day with that added information.

Deb, to her credit, has so far refrained from commenting on Quincy's food-and-beverage choices.

"Sure," she says with a shrug, "Wilmington could be telling the truth. He might have tossed the bouquet like he said, and then someone could have walked by the garbage can, seen a beautiful bouquet of red roses, and taken it."

"Not beautiful. Wilted. And, theoretically, sure, that could have happened. But it didn't. This guy is hiding something."

"Your gut instinct again?"

"Exactly."

At least now he has something a little more solid to go on, though not enough to make an arrest.

They've just spent the last few hours interviewing Matilda Harrington's—and Ray Wilmington's—coworkers at the non-profit headquarters where they worked. Mike is still over there, wrapping things up.

The descriptions of Ray Wilmington were almost cliché, at least in Quincy's line of work. The guy is "quiet," "a loner," "keeps to himself."

He is also, everyone agreed, infatuated with Matilda Harrington, much to her coworkers' amusement—and her own ill-concealed dismay.

That she didn't welcome Ray's awkward advances was common knowledge around the office. Yet nobody seemed to know any details about her love life, and she didn't bring a date to her party.

Her date book, confiscated from her home, reveals little information that might shed any light on her dating habits.

The daily notations, all made in pencil from last June on, are pretty straightforward: work-related appointments, arrangements she was making for her birthday party, personal errands and reminders.

There is only one cryptic entry . . .

And it's for next weekend.

The initials *G.S.* are jotted on all three pages in Tildy's unmistakable handwriting.

In ink.

That alone sets the entry apart.

Why not in pencil, like the other entries?

Who is G.S.?

And who sent those roses that were found inside her house? They were ordered from a busy Back Bay florist shop weeks ago, paid for in cash. The clerk thought a woman had ordered them, but couldn't be sure.

Still pondering that, Quincy shifts into DRIVE and pulls

out of the parking lot, heading back toward headquarters. They've got a ton of paperwork to do before they can call it a night. So much for the Red Sox game.

"So we'll keep Wilmington for further questioning, right?" Deb asks from behind a cloud of steam as she blows on her coffee.

"For as long as we can. In the meantime—"

Quincy is interrupted by his ringing cell phone again.

He pulls it out and flips it open with a glance at the caller ID window. Crime Scene Investigation Unit.

"Yeah?"

Without preamble, the efficient voice on the line informs him, "We opened that gift-wrapped box, Hiles. Are you ready for this?"

Cassie called a security company from her cell phone on her way back to Danbury from Brynn's, and they promised to send someone over to her condo within a few hours.

True to their word, they sent a locksmith and an alarm installer, who are now both hard at work as Cassie sits on the couch and sips a cup of hot tea Alec forced on her.

Of course he and Cassie's parents were here when she got home, along with Marcus and Reenie.

Their momentary relief at seeing her immediately gave way to a barrage of questions, but Cassie headed them off with the news about Tildy.

They were instantly somber. Her mother cried.

Somewhere in her own anguished fog, Cassie found herself wondering, mean-spiritedly, if Regina Ashford's tears were for Cassie's—and Tildy's family's—loss, or for her own. Now she won't be able to introduce Matilda Harrington to her constituents at the wedding.

Regina pulled herself together while Marcus and Reenie stepped out to use their cell phones, and Alec and Cassie's father were in the next room notifying the police that Cassie had turned up safe and sound. Sniffling, wiping her eyes, Regina promptly started to ask questions again.

"Mother, please, not now. I can't talk about anything right now." Cassie's emotional exhaustion was genuine.

For once, Regina listened.

So Tildy's death is, for Cassandra . . . well, certainly not a *blessing*. But it has offered her a temporary reprieve from explaining why she really disappeared for twenty-four hours.

Her brother and his wife departed for their jobs in the city almost immediately, but her parents lingered, along with Alec.

"Is there anything you need, honey?" Cassie's father wanted to know. "Anything we can do to make this easier for you?"

Yes, Cassie thought, *you can leave and take Mom with you, because I just can't deal with having you here.*

Unable to say it, and still riddled with guilt over what she's put them through, Cassie sent her parents on a series of errands designed to keep them away for a little while. Actually, she suggested that Alec go, too, but they wouldn't hear of leaving her alone.

"Mrs. Ashford?" the locksmith asks from the doorway of the living room, apparently assuming Alec is her husband. "The locks are all set. How many sets of keys do you want?"

"Two is fine."

"Are you sure?"

She nods.

"We need three, actually," Alec speaks up. "We should keep a spare set here in case one of us loses ours."

Oh. He assumed one of the two she mentioned would be for him.

Of course he did. He's her fiancé. He's going to be living here full time in a matter of weeks.

"Three," Cassie confirms with a reluctant nod, wishing she didn't feel so . . . violated. She should *want* Alec to be here with her, shouldn't she?

Especially after what happened to Tildy.

For some reason, though, she wants only to be left alone, in a fortress no outsider can possibly penetrate.

But Alec isn't an outsider, she reminds herself sternly.

She stands abruptly, and he looks up questioningly at her. "Where are you going?"

"I need to go call Dr. Prevatt at the hospital."

"Do you want me to call?"

"No." The word comes out bitchier than she'd intended. She opens her mouth to apologize . . . for what?

I don't need him to make my phone calls for me. I don't need him here at all.

She closes her mouth and retreats to the phone in the bedroom, closing the door after her.

Dr. Prevatt takes the call.

Cassie apologizes for not showing up this morning, attributing the lapse to the sudden death of her best friend.

He is immediately sympathetic. "Take as much time as you need, Cassandra. I'm so sorry about your loss."

She hangs up.

Sitting on the bed, she looks around at her familiar belongings.

Those are my things, she tells herself, gazing from the books to the clothes draped over the doorknob to the framed photos on the bedside table. *This is my life.*

But it isn't sinking in. She's been gone only twenty-four hours, but she feels like she's trespassing on unfamiliar turf.

She buries her head in her hands, her breaths coming fast and shallow.

Hold it together . . . You've got to hold it together.

Alec is knocking. "The alarm guy needs to talk to you, Cassie."

"Just . . . handle it."

A pause.

"Please, Alec." Her voice comes out in something close to a wail.

"Okay."

She emerges a short time later, temporarily lucid again, to find Alec alone in the condo.

"Where did they go?" she asks him.

"They finished. They left the keys and instructions for using the alarm. I chose the code word for you."

"What?"

"You said to handle it, so I used *Marshmallow*. That's your usual password for everything anyway, right?"

Right, but . . .

"And I paid them. So you're all set."

He chose the code word.

He paid them.

This is my life . . .

But she had told him to handle it.

And he did.

Now he has the keys, the alarm code . . .

Of course he does. He should. Because this isn't my life. This is our life. This is what I signed up for when he proposed and I said yes.

And now . . .

Now you have to tell him you just can't go through with the wedding, she realizes with startling clarity.

With it comes a tide of relief.

She will. She'll break it off. She can't get married in a few weeks, on the heels of all this.

As soon as the dust settles, she'll tell Alec.

What will you say?

Just that I can't marry him yet.

Yet? nudges a persistent voice. *Or ever?*

But Cassie, consumed by the monumental task of simply keeping herself upright and breathing, can't answer that question now.

"Okay, thanks. We'll come right down and take a look." Quincy disconnects the call and looks at Deb.

"What was it?" she asks, watching him over her coffee cup.

"A piece of gray wool."

"Wool?"

"You know . . . knitted. They said it looks like it was cut from a scarf or a sweater or something."

"Was that all?"

"That was all."

"What do you think it means?"

"Who the hell can tell?" Quincy clicks on the turn signal, approaching an intersection.

"No hunches? No gut instinct?"

"Not until I know more."

"Did they say anything else at all?"

Quincy rounds the corner, heading toward the lab, his brows furrowed.

"Just that the forensic botanist ran some preliminary tests on it," he tells Deb, "and found embedded particles of soil and pine needle fragments."

PART III

HAPPY BIRTHDAY,
DEAR CASSIE

CHAPTER 13

First thing on the Wednesday morning after Tildy's death, Brynn opens her eyes and bolts for the bathroom.

Crouched over the toilet, vomiting miserably, she thinks back over last night's dinner, wondering if it's food poisoning or a stomach bug.

She's been too stressed to cook so Garth picked up KFC on the way home, but the greasy chicken didn't appeal to her. She ate only plain mashed potatoes, which couldn't have made her this—

Oh.

Oh, God.

Oh, no.

Brynn stands on shaky legs, flushes, and rinses her mouth with cold water. Then she flips on the light switch to look at herself in the mirror over the sink.

Her face is pale and puffy, her eyes sunken into purplish trenches.

Good Lord, you haven't looked this awful since . . .

Has she *ever* looked this awful?

Yes. After she lost her mother, there was a long stretch of sleepless nights and nightmarish days, just like this past week.

She remembers her high school friends—and, yes, Sue—gently helping her to pull herself together, not just emotionally but physically.

This time, though, it isn't just about emotional trauma and physical *appearance*. It's about constantly *feeling* sick. Nauseous, achy, weak, exhausted . . .

She's been so distracted by the dramatic circumstances surrounding Tildy's death—and the rumors that one of her coworkers is about to be charged in the murder—that she never stopped to consider whether her general malaise might be attributed to more than just that stress.

Never until now.

She's felt this way before, she realizes. This same distinctive blend of cloying nausea mixed with sheer exhaustion . . .

She's felt it twice before. And both times, it wasn't related to death.

It was, in fact, quite the contrary.

Tightly gripping the edge of the sink to keep from swaying, she does a quick mental calculation.

With mounting trepidation, she does it again.

And again.

You're late.

She should have had her period well over a week ago.

Brynn's reflection registers the utter shock coursing through her at the stunning, but indisputable, truth.

You're pregnant.

"Hello?"

Startled when the ringing phone gives way to a voice on the other end of the line, Fiona sits up straight in her desk chair. "Deirdre! I've been trying to call you forever!"

"Well, we had a little problem down here called Hurricane Gregory and I had to evacuate. But—don't tell me, I know you never have time to watch the news or read the papers, so you're probably clueless about that."

Actually, Fiona has been watching the news and reading the papers. But not because of the violent storm that devastated parts of the Caribbean last weekend; rather, because of the tempest that raged through her own world to a similar effect.

Reports that the Boston police have an official suspect have done little to ease Fiona's concern.

They've got the wrong person; she knows it will be only a matter of time before they figure that out. Meanwhile, for all anyone knows, the real killer is preparing to strike again.

And again . . .

And I'd give anything if I could evacuate from my life, she finds herself thinking wistfully. *If not forever, than just for the next few days, at least.*

It's been the week from hell, with no signs of letting up.

There's a memorial service for Tildy this weekend in Boston, and she knows her attendance is mandatory. A delegation of ZDK sisters, past and present, is going.

James Bingham is not. He said he and Tildy weren't really friends, and, anyway, he's having some weekend work done on his Cedar Crest house that he wants to oversee.

Fiona was mildly surprised, and immensely relieved. She doesn't want him entangled with her past in any way.

"So, are you okay down there, then?" she asks her sister, pushing unpleasant thoughts of Tildy from her head for the time being.

"We had some wind damage to the roof and we lost a shutter. We also lost a big, beautiful hibiscus Antoinette just planted out back."

Fiona toys with her Montblanc, tapping it on the stack of client folders lying untouched in her in-box.

"And the cell service and power had been down since last weekend," Deirdre continues, "but today we're back up and running—obviously, because I'm talking to you. We were lucky."

"Thank goodness. And why don't you get a regular land

line?" she asks her sister, not for the first time. "Your cell goes down all the time."

"That's fine with me. I like being incommunicado. So what's up? You didn't call just to check on me."

Fiona knows better than to pretend she did.

She and her twin have always shared some level of what Fiona has come to realize is telepathic communication. It's how she knew, without having to be told, that her sister weathered this recent hurricane without injury.

And it's how she's known in the past that Deirdre was in some kind of trouble, and vice versa.

She still clearly remembers the September morning a decade ago when Puffy summoned her to the house phone, and she unexpectedly heard her sister's voice on the other end of the line. That was a few months after Deirdre left home for good; they hadn't spoken since.

"What's going on, Fee?" Deirdre asked from somewhere in Europe.

"What do you mean?" Fiona told herself Deirdre couldn't possibly know what had happened with Rachel.

No, but Deirdre could sense that Fiona was in the midst of an ordeal.

"Something's up with you, Fee," she said that morning. "I know something's wrong. I dreamed about you last night, and you were running in the woods and something was chasing you."

Fiona forced a laugh. "Don't worry. That didn't happen."

She didn't run in the woods, and nothing chased her. Not literally, anyway.

Figuratively, Deirdre had hit the nail on the head.

"I can't explain it now," she said, conscious of the lack of privacy in the sorority house. "I will when I see you."

"Just tell me if you're okay."

"I'm okay, yes."

Now, ten years later, without a soul in earshot, Fiona can talk freely.

"Listen, where's Antoinette?"

"Outside pulling shingles out of the pool. Why?"

"She's not right there?"

"No. What's going on, Fee?"

"I just need to know . . . Did you ever tell anyone about what I told you about Rachel back when I was in college?"

There's a pause.

Slight, but long enough for Fiona to know the answer before Deirdre gives it.

"Only Antoinette. Why?"

"You swore you wouldn't tell a soul. You gave me your word, Deirdre."

"That was ten years ago. I didn't even know Antoinette back then. She and I share everything."

"Yeah, well, you and I used to share everything, and I wish we hadn't," Fiona lashes out bitterly. "How could you tell her something like that?"

"Because it was bothering me. And because I trusted her. I still trust her."

"Well, I don't. And it was my secret, not yours."

"It became mine when you told it to me. And she and I don't keep things from each other. That's how mature relationships work. You just don't realize it because you and Pat never—"

"Please don't bring Pat into this." Fiona closes her eyes, tilting her head against the back of the chair.

"All I mean," Deirdre says more gently, "is that if you'd had the kind of marriage where you share everything with each other—"

"Well, we didn't, okay?" Fiona snaps, sitting upright again, eyes wide-open. "And this isn't about my trusting Pat, which I don't, it's about my trusting you. Which I should never have done."

"You can trust me, Fee, and Antoinette, too. What's going on? Did Rachel's body turn up or something?"

"No," Fiona says curtly.

But it looks like Rachel did.

"Cassie, I'm checking to see how you are this morning. Please call me as soon as you get this message."

"Press 1 to hear this message again. Press 2 to delete this message."

Cassie presses 2.

"Cassie, it's Alec. I hope today is a better day. How about if I bring dinner over later? I need to talk to—"

Cassie presses 2.

That's it. No more new messages in the last hour since she took the phone off the hook. She disconnects from her voice mail and debates leaving it off the hook again, but decides against it.

She can't avoid human contact forever.

It's been five days since the world as she knew it came to an end.

When she left Brynn's house last Friday afternoon, she came straight home.

She didn't know what else to do. At that point, she was utterly numb with shock, grief . . . *fear*.

The first two have worn off in the days since; the last has only escalated with every passing hour.

She hasn't been back to work yet. Yesterday and today were regularly scheduled days off, but she was supposed to be there this morning. She called in sick first thing.

"Will you be in tomorrow?" asked the desk attendant who took the call.

"I'm not sure."

Well, she can't keep doing this: spending every day lying in bed, staring at the ceiling, reflecting on the past . . . and terrified about what the future might hold for her.

The Boston homicide team has reportedly detained an unnamed suspect for questioning; he's a coworker of Tildy's.

That news should probably be comforting to Cassie, but she isn't taking any chances. They could be way off the mark. They don't know about Rachel.

So Cassie's been holed up here for days, and the only saving grace is that her mother had to go back to New York on Sunday.

"I'm just glad that your name hasn't been dragged into the papers," she told Cassie before she left. "The last thing we need is for you to be in the media, associated with something like this."

How ironic, considering that just days ago, her mother would have killed to have Cassie's name linked to Matilda Harrington's in the press.

Both Alec and her mother assume she knew about Tildy's death before she took off. In fact, they think that's *why* she couldn't face going to the shower.

If they ever realize that Tildy was still alive and well when Cassie fled . . .

Well, it's really a miracle they haven't figured it out yet. The coverage has been nonstop, all over the papers and the regional television news.

It even made the network news the first night, in a story that compared the latest Harrington tragedy to the tragic losses suffered by the Kennedys. They showed footage of Jason Harrington's Beacon Hill mansion, where reportedly he was in seclusion. The cameras caught his closest friends showing up to console him, looking elegantly somber: Former Governor Allerson and his striking wife, Lisa, along with assorted Kennedy family members who have been there, done that too many times in the past.

The front page of the *Boston Herald* asked:

IS THERE A HARRINGTON CURSE?

The article inside gave a blow-by-blow timeline account of Tildy's movements on the night in question, speculating that she was killed in the wee hours.

But then, Regina Ashford doesn't read the *Boston Herald*. If she had occasion to read a Boston paper, it would be the *Globe*.

Mainly, she reads the *New York Times*. And the *Times* carried only an obituary, free of the gory details—or even details that might incriminate Cassie, such as the exact time of death.

So, for all her mother knows—along with Alec, and everyone else who had waited in vain for the guest of honor that night—Cassie was blindsided by news of her friend's death en route to the shower.

She was vague when they later asked where she went when she disappeared; they didn't press her. Nor did they press the issue that she hadn't thought to call, or check her messages.

A temporary lapse in consideration is understandable when you're in shock over your friend's murder.

Temporary.

But she's running out of excuses. Sooner or later, she's going to have to face them all. And then what will she say?

What about her birthday, just a few days away?

You aren't just running out of excuses, Cassie reminds herself as dread, now coldly familiar, ushers a death march of goose bumps over her skin.

You're running out of time.

"Here, kitty, kitty, kitty."

There's the neighbor again, calling for her lost cat, same as she's been doing for days now.

"Here, kitty. Mama has some nice cream waiting for you here. Come on, Agatha. Where are you?"

I'm in a Dumpster behind the supermarket, Mama, with my throat slit.

Ha, ha. That's rich.

Imagining what that stupid cat would say is almost as amusing as thinking about what Matilda Harrington would have said if she'd had the chance.

If there was ever any doubt that this plan could actually come to fruition—and, all right, there *was* doubt, serious doubt—it's been all but erased.

That the Boston police already have a suspect is yet another fortuitous turn of events.

The gods certainly are smiling on this ambitious venture of mine.

Of course, the investigation is ongoing. Matilda Harrington's hapless coworker will eventually be cleared . . .

Eventually?

Sooner than anyone can know.

This weekend, actually.

If they've got Ray Wilmington under surveillance when another Zeta Delta Kappa sister is murdered, he'll have to be cleared.

Then again, the way things are going in my favor . . .

Wouldn't it be ironic if the police continue to suspect Ray in Tildy's case, and merely attribute Cassandra Ashford's imminent death to a copycat killer?

Ironic, and highly unlikely.

Still, one can hope, right up until the end.

And the end will come soon enough.

For now, might as well just enjoy this little game, which has been a long time in coming.

Ten years, to be exact.

"Tell me you're not getting sick of my face," Quincy says as he leans forward on his elbows and eyes Ray Wilmington across the interrogation room table. "I know I'm getting sick of yours."

Wilmington shrugs.

But there's something different about him today.

He's wearing down, Quincy realizes. Endless hours in the claustrophobic interrogation room with the dauntless, in-your-face Quincy Hiles have a way of doing that to a person.

Maybe today, Wilmington will talk.

Confess, even.

Then again . . .

Quincy is starting to have his doubts about that.

Ray Wilmington is hiding something, but Quincy isn't sure that guilt as a murderer is it.

No, but there's *something*.

Deb and Mike, seated on either side of him, aren't even so sure of that anymore.

"Maybe he's totally innocent," Deb had said last night as they were making yet another pit stop at the ubiquitous Dunkin' Donuts: black coffee for Deb, chamomile tea for Quincy.

"Yeah, maybe he's totally innocent," Quincy had shot back, "and maybe I'm thinking of calling off my retirement and working another ten years. Without pay."

"I don't know . . . Do you think he'd have confessed by now if he were guilty?"

"Do you think he'd have made up that mythical bouquet of roses if he were innocent?"

Deb shrugged and sighed. She's been doing a lot of that these past few days.

So has Quincy. And it isn't his style.

His IBS has been acting up lately, though he's been eating all the right things and taking his medication. It's stress. Cumulative, probably. Retirement is so close he can taste it, and this case will drag on without him, but it would be pretty damned satisfying to nail Matilda Harrington's killer as his swan song.

Now—his stomach clenching painfully as he faces Ray Wilmington—Quincy says, "We're running more DNA tests from the crime scene. If you were in there, you're toast. You know that, don't you?"

"I wasn't in there."

"You said you were," Mike points out.

"Outside, not in."

Quincy shakes his head. "We have evidence to the contrary."

They don't. Yet. It's a classic interrogation ploy.

They aren't necessarily banking on DNA to connect him to the scene, but Wilmington doesn't have to know that.

There was no evidence of semen or sexual assault; no blood droplets that were likely to have belonged to anyone other than the victim. The lettering on the cake was done in blood, but it was determined to have come from a cat. The crime lab is testing a stray gray hair found near the body; Quincy figures it will turn out to be the housekeeper's. There were no foreign skin cells under the victim's fingernails the way there would be if she had clawed at her killer to fight off the brutal attack.

The forensics evidence so far has backed up Quincy's initial hypothesis that Matilda Harrington was killed almost instantly by a single blow to the head, and her face was disfigured afterward in a violent rage.

The weapon that ravaged her beautiful features has yet to turn up, but Quincy was right about the cast iron doorstop. Lab tests revealed minuscule particles of blood, skin, hair, bone, and brain . . . but no fingerprints.

There were none at the scene.

Meaning the killer had the presence of mind to wear gloves, and clean up after himself—or herself.

He—or she—did leave behind a single, strange calling card, but it raised more questions than it answered.

Quincy still doesn't know what to make of that small piece of knitted gray wool . . . ragged and raveling at the edges where it had been cut from a larger piece. Microscopic crimson fibers were found on it, suggesting that the original garment might also have contained red yarn. It apparently had spent some time in the great outdoors as well. The lab is running further tests to see if they can pinpoint a geographic region for the soil and pine needles.

For now, it's the only real link to the killer.

"What's your mother going to do, Ray, if you spend the rest of your life in prison?" Deb is asking sadly. "You're her only child. Your father's dead. She's on Social Security. She needs you, Ray. You're all she's got."

"And we know she was about to lose the house," Quincy puts in. Again. They've used this information repeatedly. Futilely. "We know she had the place mortgaged up to the hilt and all her credit cards were maxed out. Yours, too."

Mike takes it up. "You must have been upset that the bank was going to foreclose on the house where you grew up, where your mother and father were so happy together for all those years. We know she couldn't keep up the mortgage payments, even with you helping her. You both must have been feeling pretty out of sorts lately."

"Angry, even," Quincy agrees. "Furious. Keeping it all bottled up, though. Right?"

They've also gone this route before, repeatedly, to no avail.

But this time, Quincy senses a subtle change in Ray's stoic demeanor.

"How will your mother survive without the house, and without you if you go to prison, Ray? Where will she even live?"

"She won't have to worry about surviving without me because I didn't kill Matilda and I'm not going to prison for the rest of my life," Ray says heavily, shoulders slumped.

Yes, he's wearing down.

"Then what *did* you do, Ray?" The question comes from Mike, almost gently. "Look, we know you were up to something outside Tildy's house that night. What was it?"

"Maybe you were thinking you could get a handout from your rich girlfriend . . . only you realized then that she didn't want to be your girlfriend."

Ray glares at Quincy. "She wasn't my girlfriend."

"You seemed to think she was. 'Waltzing Matilda,' you called her." That information came courtesy of Tildy's coworker Katie.

"And we know," Mike adds, "that last Thursday wasn't the first night you were hanging around on Commonwealth Avenue."

A few of the neighbors had noticed him there before on occasion. Just sitting in his parked car at night, keeping an eye on Matilda Harrington's house.

Was he plotting her murder? Waiting for the right opportunity?

"Did you see something, Ray, that night? Something that made you angry with Matilda?"

"No, not that night."

Quincy freezes.

It was a classic slip . . .

Only, judging by the look on Ray Wilmington's drawn, pockmarked face, it wasn't a slip at all.

He's ready to talk at last.

Having borne two children—forget *that,* having lived in a sorority house filled with sexually active college girls—Brynn is familiar enough with pregnancy tests to be aware that you can get a false negative . . . but not a false positive.

Sequestered in the bathroom while Caleb is at school and Jeremy is napping, she wraps the plastic stick, with its unmistakable plus sign in the little window, in a tissue.

Several tissues.

Then she encases it in toilet paper, winding it around and around until it's securely mummified. She deposits it in the wicker wastebasket, which she carries with her to the kitchen, to add to the already-full black trash bag there.

As she ties the handles securely and spirits it out to add it to the garbage can on the deck, she's ludicrously grateful that the weekly trash pickup is tomorrow morning. They'll cart away the evidence and no one will be the wiser.

No one . . . as in Garth.

So you're not going to tell him?

No, she decides, closing the back door again and turning the knob lock and the dead bolt, and sliding the chain. She isn't going to tell him . . . yet.

Not until she has to.

Standing in the kitchen, she presses her palms against the slight swell of her stomach, beneath her belly button. She isn't showing yet; her once-taut abs long ago gave way to a permanent little rise after she carried Caleb.

But she will be showing, soon. She did almost immediately with Jeremy.

How in the world did this happen?

Because it was meant to be.

An utter twist of fate.

An accident.

But Garth might not believe her. He might think she did this deliberately.

Did you?

No! Of course not.

She's taken her birth control pills religiously every morning, even though it's been against her will for these last few months.

At least, she thinks she has.

What if she subconsciously missed a few . . . ?

No, she would have noticed. The packet is numbered by the days. On the rare occasions that she's forgotten a pill, she's figured it out promptly, the next day, and taken two.

That hasn't happened in ages, though.

Anyway, it doesn't matter.

Regardless of how or why it happened, she's pregnant.

She and Garth are going to have a third child, whether he wants it or not.

Of course he'll want it.

He might balk at first—

Might? she thinks ruefully.

Okay, he *will* balk at the news. Definitely. He'll probably be angry, accusatory toward her, even.

But once he gets used to the idea, he'll embrace it . . .

Just as Brynn already has.

Really. He will.

He *has* to.

"Dr. Saddler?"

Gathering his notes at the front of the rapidly emptying lecture hall, Garth looks up. *All* the way up, past the three open buttons on the coed's blouse. He forces himself to focus only on her face—a pretty face.

"What's up, Danielle?"

She looks pleased that he remembers her name. She should be. It's six weeks into the semester, but this is a popular course, held twice weekly in a packed lecture hall. And at this point, Garth recognizes most of his students on sight, but knows only a handful by name, mostly the intense intellectual types who sit down in front and engage themselves in active discussion.

Danielle isn't one of those, but the lithe brunette is memorable for a different reason. *Two* reasons really, and they're currently threatening to spill out of her too-tight, silky blouse.

Garth encounters one or two Danielles almost every semester: femme fatale types who engage in a subtle seduction with the professor. *This* professor, anyway.

Some of Garth's department colleagues claim that it doesn't

happen to them. Some, he's inclined to believe. Others, he suspects, are carrying on clandestine flirtations or even full-blown affairs.

"I'm not sure I understand what you were saying about the Grounded Theory Methodology," Danielle tells Garth.

"Ah, Glaser and Strauss. We'll be going over the four dying-awareness contexts in more detail at the next lecture."

"We will?"

"We will." He smiles at her. "Okay?"

"Okay." She hesitates. "This is an interesting course."

Her voice echoes a little; the lecture hall is empty now. She adjusts her backpack, slung over her shoulder, giving him an ample view of her large breasts.

"I'm glad you think so." He taps the sheaf of notes on the podium, aligning the edges. "I'll see you next week, then."

"Right." She looks disappointed.

But she goes.

He doesn't let himself watch her walk away, though he knows the view from behind is as spectacular as the full frontal.

There are things a married man just shouldn't do. Or even think about. But he'd have to be dead not to notice someone like Danielle—and not to be flattered by the way she watches him, every lecture.

Yes, he encounters at least one Danielle every semester. Sometimes she's someone he's initially overlooked; sometimes she's a blatant *Coeds Gone Wild* candidate.

And sometimes, he thinks grimly, she's a sophisticated Boston blonde whose blood is bluer than her eyes.

Yes, and now, that blood has been shed in the most horrific murder case to strike Back Bay in years.

The police reportedly do have a suspect, thank God.

But what if they start delving into Matilda Harrington's past?

What if they come knocking on Garth Saddler's door?

You wouldn't have to worry about that at all, he reminds himself, *if it weren't for what happened in June.*

Yes, there are certain things a married man just shouldn't do.

"Listen, Ray. It's time for you to tell us what you know." Deb keeps her voice as level as her gaze, so as not to jolt Wilmington when he's teetering on the brink.

"It's okay, Ray," Mike tells him, just as evenly. "We know you want to get this off your chest."

The man remains silent, chewing his lip, clearly deliberating whether to elaborate.

For his part, Quincy fights the urge to grab his skinny shoulders and shake it out of him, whatever it is. If not a confession, then some kind of revelation.

They're forced to wait for a long time, though, for a response. So long that Quincy has given up on a potential break in the case today.

Then Ray unexpectedly announces, "She had . . . someone."

"You mean Matilda Harrington," Mike clarifies, and Ray nods.

Now that we know who we're talking about, Quincy wants to say, *what are we talking about?*

"She had someone in her life? A man?" There, Deb gets it. Quincy will let her do the talking for now.

Ray is nodding.

Deb asks, "Who was he?"

Another hesitation.

Ray ignores the question, saying instead, "I saw him one night, going into her house. He had his own key."

"When was this?" From Mike.

"I don't know. A few weeks ago. Right around the time I found out about her party."

"The birthday party she didn't invite you to?" Quincy asks—a little too harshly, his impatience spurred by his furiously cramping stomach.

Dammit. Ray looks skittish.

"What was this man doing there?" Deb asks quickly. Gently.

"How should I know? All I know is he went in late and he came out when the sun was coming up."

It's pretty clear, then, Ray, what he was doing there, isn't it? Quincy almost feels sorry for the poor bastard.

"You stayed there all night," Deb asks, "just watching the house?"

Ray nods. It isn't even a sheepish nod at this point, merely resigned.

"And you don't know who this man is."

Deb isn't asking a question, per se . . . Yet Ray is nodding as if in answer to one.

"You *do* know who he is?" Quincy asks.

Wilmington shrugs.

Quincy's patience is wearing thinner than Ray Wilmington's hair. He gets in Ray's face and barks, "Tell us, dammit!"

Wilmington's slack jaw clamps shut like a clam that's just been overshadowed by a predator.

And Quincy can tell by the stubborn gleam in the suspect's eye that the moment is lost.

Dozing on the couch, Brynn hears the front door start to open, only to be caught by the thick brass chain.

Startled, she sits up on the couch and in a second, confirms that the boys are still right in front of her, on the floor, absorbed in the Disney DVD she put on for them when Caleb got home from school.

In the next second, she sees that dusk has fallen beyond the picture window, remembers Tildy's murder, and panics at the sound of someone pushing the door against the chain.

Then she hears Garth's voice. "Brynn? Open up. It's just me."

He's home early.

Today, of all days.

"Coming," she calls, standing and catching her disheveled reflection in the mirror above the couch.

She looks rumpled, pale, exhausted . . .

But not pregnant.

Garth will never know . . . unless she tells him. And she won't tell him today. Or tomorrow.

She won't tell him until she's had a chance to absorb the news herself, and figure out the easiest way to break it to him.

Easiest way?

Ha.

Least excruciating way would be more like it.

As she hurries toward the door, she remembers, with a pang, the night she told Garth she was expecting Caleb. She found out around Memorial Day but somehow managed to keep the news to herself until mid-June.

Early on a Sunday morning, she presented Garth with breakfast in bed.

"What's the occasion?" he asked groggily.

"It's Father's Day."

"But I'm not a—"

He broke off, seeing the look on her face. Then he exploded in an exhilarated frenzy of bear hugs and questions, phone calls and plans.

He was almost as excited the second time around. It was Caleb who broke that news, informing his father that, "I'm gonna be a big brudd-ah."

Brynn has a momentary lapse of joy, imagining two big brudd-ahs leaning over her shoulder to see a precious bundle cradled in her arms.

Then she realizes she forgot to insert Garth in her imaginary picture. And when she does, he's in the background, arms folded, mouth set in a straight line.

Which is ridiculous of her. He won't be that way after the baby's born. He'll love it as much as he loves his sons.

And he'll still love me, Brynn assures herself.

Of course he will. He's her husband.

She just hopes he'll believe that she didn't do this on purpose.

But you don't have to worry about that yet.

She glimpses a wedge of Garth's face through the crack in the door. "Sorry," she calls, and pushes the door closed so that she can unfasten the chain.

Opening it, she steps aside to let him in. "You're home early. Really early," she realizes, grabbing his arm and turning it so she can check his wristwatch.

"I was worried about you."

Their eyes collide.

He's not talking about the pregnancy, she reminds herself. He's thinking about her and the boys being alone in the house after what happened to Tildy. And, maybe, he's thinking about the dead bird on their countertop.

But she doubts he's thinking that it has anything to do with what happened in Boston.

He did mention, that first day, how coincidental it was that something so unnerving had happened here on the night of Tildy's death. But he said it in passing.

And he hasn't brought it up again, other than to tell Brynn at one point that he called Officer Demuth to see if the police had uncovered any leads.

Of course they haven't.

The Cedar Crest police aren't concerned with finding the culprit in a minor neighborhood prank; they have their hands full, with the Stonebridge semester in full swing and Greek rush season kicking off as well.

They did say that they had tested the blood they found on the counter, and that it had come from a cat.

"You know, you don't have to leave campus early every night to come running home to me and the boys," Brynn tells Garth, secretly glad he has. She doesn't like to be alone here after dark now, and she's dreading tomorrow, his late night.

"I know I don't have to, but I can't help it." He leans over and kisses the top of her head, brushing her hair back from her eyes. "You look worn out."

"I'm fine," she says quickly. "Just tired. I'm upset, you know . . ."

"Do you want me to stay here this weekend, so you can go to Boston for the funeral by yourself?" he offers, not for the first time.

"No," she says firmly. "I'm driving out to the Cape on Friday when Caleb gets out of school and my father and Sue will watch them Saturday. You have to go to Arizona and present your chapter at the symposium. That's important for you to do."

"It's not as important as you are."

She shrugs, smiles. "Publish or perish, right?"

"Right." Garth returns her smile, but his smile doesn't reach his eyes.

CHAPTER 14

Wake up, run to bathroom, vomit, rinse.

The vicious daily cycle has begun, and Brynn doesn't expect it to let up until after Christmas, if at all. With her first pregnancy, the nausea plagued her for the duration. With the second, it eased after the first trimester, which, according to a couple of well-meaning friends from Caleb's playgroup, was supposed to indicate that she was carrying a different gender. Of course, she wasn't.

This time, she's not even going to second-guess. She'll be thrilled with a third son or with a daughter.

What about Garth? she asks herself, as she makes her way out of the bathroom and toward the kitchen in the house where she grew up.

Garth won't be thrilled either way.

Well, at least he's not under the same roof this morning. The past few days, it's been a challenge to muffle her morning sickness.

But Garth was still clueless when he went off to Arizona yesterday, distracted as usual by his fear of flying.

"I'm just glad you aren't going to be here alone while I'm

gone," he said, giving Brynn a last tight hug before he dashed out the door.

So is she, although there are places she'd rather be than in her childhood home . . . or at the looming memorial service for an old friend.

This weekend is something to be endured, she thinks, as she steps into the kitchen and sees her stepmother. Sue is lean and outdoorsy with a perpetually ruddy complexion, her blonde hair always kept short, in an attractive cut.

In contrast, Brynn's mother was soft and curvy, with porcelain skin and black hair she wore in waves that fell to her shoulders.

And I miss her so much I feel sick, Brynn thinks now, even after all these years. She should be standing there first thing in the morning, with the sun streaming in the windows, the way she used to.

Sue is drinking from a sports bottle of water and wearing a sweat-dampened T-shirt. On the counter beside her, the coffeemaker is hissing into action.

"Good morning, Brynn." Sue is still breathless, probably from a morning run. "Did you sleep okay? It was a little chilly and I forgot to tell you there was an extra blanket on the top shelf of the hall closet."

I know there's an extra blanket on the top shelf of the closet. There's been an extra blanket on the top shelf of the hall closet much longer than you've lived here.

Brynn says only, "I was fine, thanks."

"Are the boys still asleep?"

"They must be." Caleb and Jeremy are in bunks in the upstairs dormered room that once belonged to Brynn's brothers. The house is a classic Cape: two bedrooms up and two down. The three boys were upstairs and Brynn's room was on the first floor, next door to the master bedroom.

When Sue moved in with her father, Brynn moved upstairs to get away from her, camping with her brothers until she went to college. Her girlhood quarters are still intact down here, right down to the high school photos tacked to the bulletin board. It's the one room in the house Sue hasn't dared to change.

Brynn crosses the recently installed tile floor—Mom always longed to exchange the worn linoleum for tile—and glances out the window where a pair of frilly white Priscillas once hung. Now there are only vertical blinds.

Marie Costello hated blinds, vertical, horizontal . . . all blinds, Brynn remembers as she sees the sun's promising glint on an array of golden branches, and notes that it's going to be a beautiful day.

A beautiful day for a funeral.

She turns away, toward the stove, and realizes there's no tea kettle on the back burner.

"Can I help you find something?" Sue asks, behind her.

"I was going to make some tea." *Since I can't drink coffee again until next summer,* she thinks grumpily.

"Oh, you're going to love this. Look." Sue turns a lever at the sink, and steaming water comes out of a side tap. "I just had this put in. See? Boiling water on demand."

Brynn murmurs an appropriate comment, opens the cupboard, and begins hunting through a row of boxes for something herbal: chamomile, or apple . . .

"We've got all kinds of tea in there."

"Any decaf?"

"Decaf? I don't think so . . ." Sue comes to look over her shoulder. "But, oh, try this one. It's really good. Your father doesn't like tea, but even he—"

"No, thanks." Brynn turns away from the box her stepmother proffers.

I know my father doesn't like tea. You don't have to tell me that. He's never liked tea.

She feels a gentle touch on her arm. "Honey, I'm so sorry about your friend. What a terrible, tragic thing to go through."

To her horror, Brynn is overwhelmed by a sudden impulse to cry. Because of Tildy, because of her pregnancy hormones, because of Sue's kindness, because she's the wrong person standing here offering comfort and sympathy.

It should be my mother, not you.

"Do you want me to go to the memorial service with you today?" Sue offers, her hand now weighty on Brynn's shoulder. "I hate the thought of you driving there alone and going through that ordeal by yourself."

"I won't be by myself. My friends will be there, Fiona and Cassie."

She hasn't seen either of them in over a week, nor have they spoken other than to make brief arrangements to meet in Brookline today. Brynn has thought more than once of calling each of them, not just to discuss Tildy and Rachel but to unburden her pregnancy news. But she couldn't bring herself to do it.

"Well, you'll be in good hands if you're with your sorority sisters, then," Sue says, lifting her hand from Brynn's shoulder at last.

Brynn is surprised—and, all right, touched—that Sue remembers their names and that detail about Brynn's relationship with them.

"I was never in a sorority but I always considered my friends to be my true sisters. I was closer to them than I ever was to my blood sisters," Sue adds, and Brynn's temporary spark of warmth toward her evaporates.

Right. Sue was close enough to one friend in particular that she moved right into her life the moment she was gone.

Brynn tries to imagine one of her own "sisters" doing that, should anything ever happen to her.

Nah. Workaholic Fiona would never want to deal with the kids. Cassie is embarking on her own domestic adventure with Alec. Tildy—

Oh, God. Tildy is gone.

The ugly truth hits her all over again, and with it, the fear that her own life might still be in danger.

She's been trying to convince herself that the chances of

that are remote. But she can't ignore the dead cardinal, the card . . .

Or that Tildy died on her own birthday.

If the Boston police knew what Brynn and the others know, they wouldn't be looking among Tildy's coworkers for the killer.

They'd be looking for a woman who supposedly died ten years ago.

Dressed in a black suit, Isaac stands over the bed, watching Kylah sleep.

This lying and sneaking around can't go on any longer. He's going to tell her the truth. Tonight.

After he gets back from Matilda Harrington's memorial service this morning in Boston.

He wasn't planning to go, at first. Especially when Puffy told him it's being held today, of all days. Kylah's cousin Amy is getting married this afternoon; she's in the wedding party, of course.

But he'll make it back to New York in time for the reception later. He booked a round-trip flight on the shuttle. After boarding the plane this morning, he'll be in Boston in less time than it takes him to make it across the Triborough Bridge during rush hour.

"I'm glad you're coming," Puffy told him. "Tildy was a good friend of Rachel's."

No, she wasn't. Not really.

Rachel never clicked with Matilda Harrington the way she did with her other sorority sisters. Isaac remembers Rachel mimicking her snobby airs . . . but only for him, of course. To Matilda's face—and in the presence of the other sisters—she was always her warm, upbeat self.

That's the best thing about Rachel. Having weathered her parents' bitter divorce and subsequent multiple remarriages, she learned not to make waves. She treated everyone in her life as though she was crazy about them, regardless of how she really felt inside.

That's also the worst thing about Rachel.

You could never really be sure where you stood.

It's different with someone like, say, Kylah. She wears her heart on her sleeve.

I should appreciate that about her, Isaac tells himself, *instead of always comparing her to Rachel. It isn't fair to her.*

With a twinge of guilt, he turns away from his sleeping girlfriend and makes his way through the early-morning shadows to the door.

He'll tell her tonight about Rachel.

And maybe, he thinks hopefully as he strides toward the elevator, Matilda Harrington's memorial service will be cathartic.

Maybe it will even enable him to let go at last, after ten years.

Ten years of keeping his own weighty secret . . .

And Rachel's.

Ashley Hagan likes to sleep in on weekend mornings, but her mother never lets her. When she wakes up in her own bed at home on a Saturday or Sunday morning, it's to a bleating alarm clock, same as on weekdays.

Mom doesn't believe in lazy self-indulgence.

Daddy does.

And, luckily for Ashley, she wakes, lazily, to find herself in the brand-new, almost-bedroom he built into a corner of his apartment.

"I had to make it so that the wall can come down when I move out," he explained last weekend, when he first revealed her new quarters.

"When are you moving out?" Ashley asked, momentarily alarmed.

"Probably never, so don't worry," Daddy said. "At the rate I'm going, I'll never be able to afford a condo."

"It's okay, I like this place," Ashley lied.

Well, she does like it better since he put up the new wall and bought her all new bedding and a new dresser where she can keep her things. She used to just have a drawer in his—which was fine, because Daddy doesn't have tons of clothes, like Mom does.

Ashley can hear him rattling pots and pans beyond the new partition, and something smells good: butter . . . and batter.

Pancakes!

She stretches and gets up, walking barefoot into the little kitchenette.

"Sleeping Beauty! There you are." Daddy is standing at the griddle on the stove, a spatula in one hand and a can of Red Bull in the other. He drinks one every morning, to wake up.

He has a stubbly face, his dark hair is standing straight up the way it does before his shower in the morning, and he's wearing his weekend-morning uniform: T-shirt and boxer shorts.

On the counter, beside the box of Hungry Jack mix, she sees a telltale empty plastic produce container. Peering into the mixing bowl, she sees that the creamy batter is studded with sliced red berries.

"Strawberry pancakes?" she asks excitedly.

"Your favorite. What do you feel like doing today?"

"I don't know . . . What do you want to do?" That's the great thing about Daddy. He doesn't schedule things way in advance, like Mom does. He likes to play it by ear.

"How about if we go to the movies?"

"Okay."

"Want to ask Meg and her mom to come along?"

"Yes!"

"Good. That's what we'll do, then."

Ashley smiles as she watches him heap her plate with golden-brown silver-dollar-sized pancakes, then dab them with butter and smother them in maple syrup.

Mom makes her eat boxed cereal for breakfast at home.

Unsweetened cereal, like horribly dry shredded wheat or those disgusting fiber pellets that look like cat food. She refuses to buy the good stuff like Cap'n Crunch and Lucky Charms, especially since Ashley needed a filling at her last dental checkup.

"There you go." Daddy hands the plate back to Ashley. "Dig in."

"What about you?"

"I'm making mine now. Eat those while they're hot."

Ashley perches on a stool at the breakfast bar that separates the kitchen from the living area. She has to clear a space for her plate; the counter is covered with mail and stacks of legal documents from Daddy's job.

Ashley isn't sure exactly what he does . . . He's some kind of lawyer, she thinks.

"But lawyers are rich," her friend Meg said when Ashley mentioned that once. "How come your dad isn't rich like my dad?"

Ashley has no idea, but she's glad her dad is nothing like Meg's dad, who is divorced from Meg's mom. He's snooty and he lives in a fancy house in Stockbridge with his snooty new wife and their two bratty little kids. He just had a heart attack not too long ago, from working too hard. Meg's stepmother said Meg can't spend the night there anymore because they're trying to reduce stress. Like Meg would cause extra stress compared to his bratty other kids who are there all the time.

Meg hates her stepmother, who wears clothes only from Ralph Lauren and Calvin Klein, and other expensive designers Ashley has never even heard of.

Ashley doesn't blame Meg for hating her. She herself would probably hate having a stepmother, too.

Unless it was somebody nice. Like Meg's mom, Cynthia.

"Wouldn't it be cool if we could get my mom to marry your dad?" Meg asked once. "Then we could be sisters."

Ashley agreed that it would be cool, and she and Meg spent a couple of days cooking up matchmaking plans.

They gave up, eventually. Her dad and Meg's mom are friendly, but they don't seem like they're in love. Meg's mom isn't that pretty, either. Not like Ashley's mother. So maybe that's why Daddy isn't interested in her.

Anyway, as much as Ashley would like to have Meg as a sister, if she was going to have a stepmother, she would rather have Brynn than anyone else.

Too bad Brynn is married to Mr. Saddler.

If she wasn't, Ashley would definitely try to get her to marry Daddy.

Mom probably wouldn't like that, though. Even though she hates Daddy. Something tells Ashley she wouldn't want her friend marrying him.

Especially if Ashley would rather live with Brynn than with her. Which she would.

"What are you thinking about, Ash?" Daddy asks, glancing up from the griddle.

"I'm thinking sometimes I wish I didn't live with Mom," she blurts.

Daddy immediately sets aside the spatula. "Why is that?"

"No, I . . ." Ashley shrugs. "I don't know. She's just not home that much."

This weekend, of course, Mom has a good reason to be away. One of her old friends died in Boston. Ashley doesn't know the details, but it must have been a car accident or something, because it seems like it happened unexpectedly.

Even Daddy was nice to Mom about it. He actually hugged Mom when he picked up Ashley last night.

Mom looked pretty stiff when he did it, though.

Like she didn't even want him to touch her.

Which Ashley thought was rude, because Daddy was only trying to be nice.

"Ash, do you want to come here and live with me?" Daddy asks now. "Is that what you're saying?"

Not really. Well, maybe she wants to live *somewhere* with him—not necessarily here. And maybe she wants Brynn to be her stepmother . . .

Anything you want in this life can be yours, Ashley, Mom always says. *All you have to do is be willing to work for it.*

But she's talking about careers. Not impossible fantasies.

Daddy is still watching her, waiting for an answer.

Behind him, on the stove, the griddle is starting to smoke.

"Dad!" Ashley points toward it.

He turns away, but he doesn't change the subject.

"If you want to live with me, Ashley, you can," he tells her, as he slides the tip of the spatula beneath a singed pancake and flips it. "All you have to do is say the word."

She remains silent, once again hearing her mother say, *Ashley will live with you, Pat, over my dead body.*

Fiona marvels at the irony that she's driving to Boston on this glorious October morning, while James Bingham is traveling in the opposite direction. She knows his current whereabouts because he called her as he was leaving his house in Wellesley about an hour ago, just as she was leaving hers in Cedar Crest.

At some point, she's sure, they'll pass each other on the Massachusetts Turnpike.

In fact, she's actually been keeping an eye on the oncoming traffic, hoping for a glimpse of his sleek black Mercedes.

Which is ludicrous, because there are hundreds of black Mercedes driving on the Mass Pike this morning.

And because you're a grown woman, not a high school girl. Or did you forget?

There's just something about James that makes her feel decidedly girly-giddy.

Right, a sardonic voice pipes up in her head, *that would be his power and money.*

She won't deny that those things first drew her to him, but it's beyond that now. She's falling for him, for real.

Next thing you know, you'll be calling his house and hanging up.

Rolling her eyes, she lights a cigarette and cracks the window. Then, realizing it's warm enough out there to lower it further, she does, relishing the wind in her hair.

James loves her hair.

That was how it went a step further between them than it should have, really, the other night. There they were, having a 2 AM after-dinner drink in an elegant Back Bay martini bar, and James commented that he would love to see her let her hair down for a change.

Her laugh fluid with top-shelf vodka, she protested, "I'm relaxed right now."

"I mean literally let your hair down, Fiona," he said, and reached out brazenly toward the clip at the back of her head.

In one swift move, he had it unfastened and her hair was falling down her back.

The next thing she knew, he was taking her hand and leading her out of there, and she was casting professional decorum to the wind . . .

Not a brilliant move on her part. Not just because he's her client and she can't afford to lose his account, but because he's her future. She's already decided that.

And, as she likes to tell her daughter, *Anything you want in this life can be yours. All you have to do is be willing to work for it.*

Well, she's going to work to win James Bingham.

Luckily, she nipped things in the bud before they went too far . . . that time. Next time, she might not be able to muster enough willpower to leave him and make the solitary wee-hour drive from Boston back to her own bed.

Provided there is a next time.

For now, because he's miles away and because she isn't an infatuated teenager, she should put him out of her head.

That plan lasts all of the few seconds it takes her to switch the car stereo from radio to CD and press PLAY.

The CD that comes on is the same one she was listening to as she drove home after leaving James that night, the night Tildy died.

She turns up the volume and the opening drums reverberate through her as she exhales a stream of smoke into the warm breeze.

U2; it's an old CD, a relic of her high school days. And her college days. And her life with Pat.

You'd think she would have long since given up anything associated with her ex-husband, but she doesn't know new music, doesn't have time for it. She just sticks with the tried and true.

Anyway, she still loves U2. She and Deirdre had major crushes on Bono when they were kids, arguing over who would get dibs on him if they ever crossed paths.

As if two scrawny preteens from a working-class household had a chance of hooking up with rock superstars.

But they spent a lot of time arguing about it. Fee always maintained that she should get Bono because she's a few minutes older than her twin, and Deirdre could have The Edge. Deirdre protested that she had the lead singer's name tattooed on her arm in ink.

Of course, it was from a Bic pen. But she refused to wash it off for a whole year, hiding it from their parents and going over it again whenever it started to fade.

When her twin confessed her true sexual preference years later, Fee even brought that up, unable to shed her disbelief.

Deirdre snorted. "Believe it or not, Fee, I never slept with Bono."

"But you wanted to!" Fiona clung to her flimsy "evidence" out of . . . what? Shock? Dismay? A sense of betrayal? They were supposed to share everything. Deirdre's secret was huge.

"We were, what, twelve? And even then, I knew. I just talked about Bono—and boys—because you did. I wanted to be normal, and I didn't think I was."

Coming to her senses, Fiona assured her sister that it didn't matter who she slept with—unless, of course, it was Bono.

"I get permanent dibs on him now," she reminded Deirdre with a laugh.

And the air was clear again.

Deirdre was grateful for her support, and it was the only family support she had. Mom and Dad had kicked her out, and she couldn't live with Fee in the sorority house. She crashed there for a couple of nights, but Fee had to tell her she couldn't stay. It was against house rules.

So Deirdre went from there to Europe, where she had adventures and fell in love—a few times—and even saw U2 play live, in Dublin.

"They play live over here, too," Fiona couldn't help telling her sister during that fleeting, long-distance phone call.

"I know, but . . . Have you seen them?"

No, she hadn't. That was back in the bad old days when she was stuck in a dive apartment with a new baby, flat broke, fighting nonstop with Pat.

She sat at home, wistful, resentful, as her twin sister traveled all over Europe. She brooded and she played her U2 CDs, including this one. The music helped get her through that unhappy time in her life.

Now, listening to Bono wailing "A Sort Of Homecoming," Fiona is struck anew by the lyrics, and she isn't thinking of her turbulent marital past with Pat.

See the sky, the burning rain . . .

Nor is she even thinking of James Bingham, though she certainly was when she drove home after she threw caution, and professional decorum, to the wind, that night in Boston.

She will die and live again . . .

No, as she drives to the funeral of her sorority sister, unmercifully slain on her birthday, she isn't thinking of anyone but Rachel Lorent.

Isaac waits to turn his cell phone back on until he's in the rental car and safely on his way to Brookline. Boston isn't an entirely familiar city to him; it was tricky to negotiate the network of roads leading away from Logan Airport.

But now he's on the right track, and he can relax . . . if only for a few minutes.

Or, maybe not, he thinks as he realizes there's a message from Kylah.

"I woke up, and you were gone." Her tone is unmistakably brittle. "I thought maybe you were out for a run or something, but who am I kidding? I know something's up with you, Isaac. And I'm sick of feeling like you're avoiding me . . . or lying to me, which is even worse. So don't call me until you're ready to tell the truth about whatever it is you've been up to lately. I'm not stupid."

No, she isn't stupid.

And she deserves better than this.

He dials her number—their number—without even thinking through what he's going to say.

She answers on the third ring.

"It's me. I'm in Boston."

"Boston?" she echoes. "On business?"

For once, he doesn't hesitate. "No. Not on business."

There's a pause.

"I didn't think so."

"I'm sorry, Kylah."

She's silent.

"We should probably talk . . ."

She snaps, "I've been trying to."

"I know . . . and I'm sorry."

I'm sorry. I'm sorry.

Everything else he can possibly tell her; but every single line that comes into his head about this sounds like a lousy cliché.

I can explain . . .

It's not what it looks like . . .

You have to trust me . . .

He says none of that.

Only, "I promise to make it back to New York for the wedding."

"Why would you?"

"Because you want me there . . . don't you? And because I want to be there," he adds hastily, more decisively.

But he can tell she doesn't believe him.

Understandable, since he doesn't believe him either.

He doesn't *want* to get dressed up in a tux and go to a fancy catering place out in Great Neck. He doesn't *want* to sit at a table with an eclectic assortment of strangers whose dates and spouses are also in the wedding party.

But he'll do it. For Kylah.

Because if he doesn't do it—if he doesn't start stepping up—he's going to lose her.

"If you don't make it back here for the wedding," Kylah says tearfully, "then you can go to the apartment instead, and you can pack up all your stuff. Just make sure you're gone before I get back."

"I'll be at the wedding, Kylah. I promise you."

Another pause.

Then, "Are you in love with someone else, Isaac?"

Yes. But it's not what you think. Not at all.

CHAPTER 15

The church is quintessential New England: white clapboard and stained glass, its steeple rising majestically against a backdrop of glorious peak foliage and a cloudless sky that is precisely the shade of Matilda Harrington's eyes.

The throng of press and curious onlookers is held at bay behind police barricades.

There is no funeral procession, no hearse, no casket.

According to the newspaper reports that gleefully dredged up the family's tragic past, there was none of that for Matilda's mother and brother, either, twenty-five years ago. Their bodies were incinerated in the crash; there were no remains.

Matilda's savaged corpse has yet to be released to the family. When it is, reportedly Jason Harrington will have his only daughter cremated and the ashes buried in the family plot in Brookline.

Standing beneath a dappled canopy of red maple leaves, Quincy surveys the crowd of mourners making their exit down the broad brick steps. Deb and Mike are posted nearby, doing the same thing.

First to emerge from the church, as soon as the double

doors opened, was Jason Harrington. Boston's answer to Donald Trump looked wan and ravaged, supported by his loyal friend, the celebrated Troy Allerson, by his side.

They kept moving, their faces veiled by the requisite dark shades as the press snapped photos and shouted their names. Holding Allerson's hand was his striking young wife, head bent, wiping tears from behind her own sunglasses. The three of them disappeared into a limousine that immediately drove off toward the Harrington mansion.

Now the remaining well-heeled contingent, similarly clad in dark designer clothes and sunglasses, is slowly making its way toward the line of waiting town cars stretching down the street.

The others mingle on the sidewalk in the unseasonably hot Indian summer sunshine, hugging, weeping, chatting in muted tones.

Quincy watches them carefully, wondering if Tildy's mystery lover—assuming Ray Wilmington was telling the truth—might be among them.

Her e-mail account yielded a confirmed reservation for the Glenwood Springhouse in Central Massachusetts this weekend—which explains the cryptic G.S. entry in her date book. Obviously, the letters weren't initials after all, but shorthand for her weekend getaway plans.

She had reserved the inn's Weekend Romance package, which means she probably wasn't planning on a solo escape.

Was her boyfriend planning to join her? And why was she so secretive about her relationship?

Quincy has a couple of good theories: either he was married, or dirt poor, and thus unsuitable. Or all of the above.

A sudden brisk breeze kicks up, stirring the branches overhead.

Maybe, Quincy thinks, Ray really did kill Matilda in a fit of jealousy over her secret boyfriend.

Or maybe he's a psycho stalker who killed her and then made up the secret boyfriend story.

Or maybe her secret boyfriend does exist and killed her himself, in a fit of rage.

Quincy isn't ruling out any of those scenarios—or anything else, at this stage.

A hired killer, say, if it was premeditated—and the lack of fingerprints at the scene suggests that it was.

Then again, Quincy can't help but acknowledge that a hit man would have stopped at the mortal blow to the victim's head. You're in, you're out. You don't hang around before or after to stage a scene; you don't leave anything behind.

He studies the crowd of mourners intently, zeroing in on every face for some slight but telltale anomaly.

So . . . Was it someone else?

Someone who knew her well enough to be present today?

Someone who is, at this very moment, expertly feigning grief . . . and masking guilt?

Someone who—

Quincy's thoughts break off abruptly.

He squints into the sun, then shades his eyes with his hand to be sure he's seeing what he thinks he's seeing.

Yes. Without a doubt.

And the Harrington murder case has just taken a drastic turn in an entirely new direction.

As another gust permeates the warm sunshine falling on her hair and shoulders, Cassie shivers, disproportionately chilled to the bone.

Standing here at the foot of the church steps, she can't help but feel as though someone is watching her. Someone who knows about that night ten years ago—and that Cassie's birthday is tomorrow.

Every time she thinks of it, she feels physically ill.

What if . . . ?

No. Stop. For now, anyway.

She's gone over the endless *what ifs* nonstop for over a week now.

Alec offered to join her for the memorial service this morning, as did her mother. Her fiancé's motives were undoubtedly pure, unlike her mother's, but she turned them both down unequivocally.

She did it over the phone, because that's always easier than face-to-face, and because she hasn't seen a soul in days. Alec is at the end of his rope, demanding to see her, demanding that she get some help. He says it isn't normal to react this way, even to your friend's murder.

But he doesn't know the whole story.

Barricaded in her condo for the past week, the new alarm system set and the shades drawn, she has yet to return to her pediatric residency. At this point, she doubts she'll be welcomed back with open arms.

She hasn't returned a series of increasingly curt phone calls from the staff, including Dr. Prevatt, in a few days now.

But sooner or later, she'll have to return to the land of the living. She's been telling herself she just has to get through today, and then she'll be able to function again.

Today—and tomorrow.

After that, she'll start picking up the pieces, salvaging what she can from her employment and her relationship.

"Are you okay?" Brynn asks in a low voice, standing beside her, looking surprisingly put-together in a black crepe dress and low heels.

"Sort of. Are *you* okay?" Cassie returns.

"Same as you. This is surreal."

For a moment, they watch Fiona chat with a well-dressed businessman she met while they were both sneaking a curbside smoke earlier, before the service.

Now, as Fee exchanges business cards with him, Cassie murmurs, "Some things just aren't sacred with her, are they?"

Brynn flashes a tight-lipped smile. "What, you mean networking at a funeral isn't acceptable behavior?"

"It wasn't a funeral, it was a memorial service," Fiona declares, rejoining them. "And he owns a chain of paint stores that's branching out into western Massachusetts. He's thinking of hiring a publicist, so . . ." She shrugs.

Neither Cassie nor Brynn comments.

What is there to say? Fiona will always be Fiona.

"I'm going to get going," Cassie decides, taking her car keys from her purse.

"Why don't we all go somewhere and get some lunch?" Brynn suggests. "Because we still need to talk about—"

"Shh!" Fiona cuts her off, looking around.

"I really have to get back." Cassie jangles her keys, nerves fraying.

Brynn touches her hand. "Listen, you need to be careful, Cassie. I mean it. Tomorrow is—"

"I know." She swallows hard and is surprised to hear herself blurt, "I was thinking of going someplace for a few days."

You were?

Yes, she was. She just didn't really acknowledge it until this very moment.

"You mean . . . going somewhere to hide?" Fiona asks, and Cassie nods.

"You can come home with me," Brynn offers promptly.

"No, I mean someplace where nobody would ever think to look for me. Just until this blows over."

"Maybe you should," Fiona tells her thoughtfully. "If . . . you know. If it'll make you feel safer."

Cassie shrugs, uncertain anything could make her feel safe at this point.

"Listen, if you do decide to go somewhere to wait it out, Cassie, do us a favor and call to check in. Okay?" Brynn asks.

"You know what? I'm not going to do it," she says hurriedly. "I mean, I'm sure it'll be fine. They've got a suspect."

Brynn shakes her head. "Yes, but that doesn't mean—"

"But it probably does," Fiona cuts in, her expression hidden behind black sunglasses. "We just have to think that it does because what else can we do? And don't answer that, Brynn. Going to the police isn't an option."

Sidling up to Deb, Quincy gently elbows her in the ribs and tilts his head toward the nearby group of attractive college-aged women.

"Take a look at that."

"What is it?" Following his gaze, Deb surveys the sorority girls who traveled here from the town where Matilda Harrington attended college.

It takes only an instant before her eyes widen and she curses softly.

"I've been watching everyone here, including them. How did I miss that?"

"They didn't put them on until the wind kicked up a few seconds ago," Quincy informs her, his eyes fastened on the identical sweaters a few of the girls have donned.

Sweaters that are precisely the shade of gray and red found in the scrap of fabric the killer left behind with Matilda Harrington's corpse.

"Obviously, Fee, we aren't going to see eye to eye on this," Brynn says as they watch Cassie walk away.

"Obviously not."

"So which one of us gets her way? What do we do?"

"Nothing."

Then you get your way, Brynn thinks, shaking her head and breaking eye contact with Fiona. *Because that's exactly what you want to do about this. Absolutely nothing.*

She closes her eyes momentarily, rubbing them with her

fist. Exhausted, nauseous, emotional, she wishes everything would just go away.

If only she could be home, right now, in bed, with the covers pulled over her head.

Well, she has a few more days to endure before that can even happen. Right now, she needs to convince Fiona that it's wrong to keep hiding what they know after all these years, and then she needs to drive back out to the Cape and hug her children.

A lump clogs her throat at the mere thought of the boys. When she left this morning, they were happily eating waffles with her dad and Sue, who were full of plans for the day.

Brynn looks at her watch and realizes that they've probably finished at the bowling alley by now, and have moved on to lunch at their favorite pizza place before the matinee movie they're going to.

So she doesn't have to rush to get back out—

Suddenly, a familiar face catches her eye on the far end of the crowd, where the Zeta Delta Kappa sisters are waiting to board their rented minibus back to Cedar Crest.

That man . . . she knows him.

But she can't place him.

"Look over by those red bushes, Fee. Who is that?"

Fiona glances in that direction and recognition registers on her face. "It's Puffy."

"No, I know Puffy," Brynn says impatiently, "I see her around town. But that guy she's talking to . . . who . . . ?"

Then all at once, recognition dawns . . . and with it, shock.

"What's wrong?"

"That's Rachel's stepbrother. Isaac."

"Excuse me!" Quincy touches the arm of the round-faced woman who just finished talking to a handsome younger man, and is now on the verge of climbing the steps onto the waiting bus.

"Yes?"

"Detective Quincy Hiles, B.P.D." He flashes his badge. "Can I talk to you for a minute, ma'am?"

"Did you say 'Detective'?"

He nods. "Can I ask you some questions?"

Looking startled, the woman bobs her wobbling double chins and allows him to pull her aside. The chattering girls, boarding the bus, fail to notice. Quincy keeps a peripheral eye on them as he asks the woman her name.

"It's Sarah Trovato, but nobody calls me that."

"What do they call you?"

"Puffy."

"You mean these girls?"

"I mean everybody. But yes. My girls call me Puffy."

"Your girls?"

"I'm their housemother."

"Those sweaters your girls are wearing . . . Do all of the sorority sisters have them?"

"Yes. Why?"

"Are they always the same, every year? The same colors, the same style . . . "

"Always exactly the same. Why?" she asks again, frowning.

"Can anyone off the street buy one of these sweaters?"

"Not these. They're one of a kind."

He shifts his line of questioning. "And you knew Matilda Harrington . . . ?"

Puffy's dark eyes dim. "Of course. She was one of my girls. I shouldn't say was, though . . . Once they move into the Zeta house, they're mine, even after they move out and move on. I don't have any biological children, so the girls are my children."

"And you've been regularly in touch with Matilda all these years, since she graduated? Stonebridge College, wasn't it?" Quincy asks, trying to remember the biographical specifics gleaned from the victim's family and friends.

"Stonebridge. Right. And not regularly in touch, no . . . But it's not as though she lives around the corner from the house."

"Did she ever come back to visit?"

"Not so much lately, but she used to. Matilda was the chapter president. She was always loyal to ZDK, and that group of sisters that graduated with her were tighter than ever because of what they went through together that year . . ."

"What did they go through?"

"One of the girls vanished into thin air."

Quincy looks up, stunned. "What happened to her?"

"We still don't know. She was never found. Poor Rachel. It was her birthday, too—just like it was Matilda's. It's such a strange coincidence."

A strange coincidence? Quincy thinks. *Are you freaking kidding me?*

He opens his mouth, but before he can say anything, Puffy adds, "That was her brother I was talking to just now."

Adrenaline surging, he asks sharply, "You mean that young guy who just walked away?"

"Yes. He has to catch a flight back to New York."

Quincy looks around for the man, but he's already disappeared into the crowd. "Do you know where I can get in touch with him?"

"Why?"

"So that I can speak to him."

"About Rachel?"

Quincy shrugs. "He's here today. Was he a friend of Matilda Harrington's?"

"No. But he knew her, and she was a friend of his sister's, so . . ."

Thoughts whirling with new possibilities, Quincy asks the housemother details about the decade-old Missing Persons case. He jots down information about the disappearance as the bus driver waits impatiently, parked, the engine idling.

"Puffy!" one of the girls finally calls out the window. "A bunch of us have to get back to campus for field hockey."

The housemother looks up at him. "I'm sorry. I have to go."

"All right, Ms. Trovato . . ." He looks over her contact information, making sure it's complete. "I'll be in touch."

She hesitates. "Mind if I ask why?"

"I'm investigating the murder of one of your girls." He chooses his words deliberately. "I know you and the other girls will want to do anything you can to help. Especially considering that this isn't the first time one of the Zeta sisters has had a run-in with tragedy . . ."

On her birthday.

"Wait, what are you doing?" Fiona grabs Brynn by the arm and pulls her back.

"Isaac walked away. I'm going to catch him."

"Why?"

"So we can talk to him."

"About . . . ?" Fiona's heart is pounding. She can't let Brynn do this. Everything is hanging in the balance.

James Bingham is hanging in the balance.

"We have to tell him what we suspect about Rachel," Brynn says hurriedly.

"What you suspect."

"So do you."

Fiona doesn't argue. Nor does she budge.

"Come on, Fee, maybe he knows something."

"If he does, do you honestly think he's going to tell us? After all these years? You think he's going to welcome questions about his dead stepsister?"

"Dead stepsister who might be alive."

"Stop saying that, Brynn! I swear to God . . . I don't want to hear it anymore."

"Because you're afraid it's true. So am I. And so is Cassie."

"The only thing I'm afraid of is being dragged into a scandal or worse, and that's exactly what will happen if we drag all this out to the police. It'll wind up all over the papers, on television . . ."

"Not necessarily."

"Are you kidding? Look at that." Fiona gestures at the horde of reporters and satellite news trucks surrounding the church. "Tildy's murder is huge news. That's not going to die down anytime soon. Rachel's disappearance was big news, too, ten years ago, and if the media can manage to link it to this . . ."

"So it'll be in the papers. We'll just have to deal with—"

"Are you ready to go to jail, Brynn?" Fiona cuts in, wanting to grab her and shake her. "Think about it. Are you prepared to leave your two kids and your husband to serve time in prison? Because unless you are, you need to stop talking about going to the police."

Brynn is silent for a moment.

Then she says, "I just want to talk to Isaac, then. Before he leaves. Come on."

"You're on your own," Fiona snaps, and turns toward her BMW, parked against the curb a block away. "I'm going home."

Parked in full sun in the church parking lot, the car is unbearably stuffy when Cassie climbs into it. She rolls down the driver's side window and inhales fresh air, grateful that this morning's ordeal is over at last.

Now on to the next, she thinks grimly, and shifts into REVERSE.

She spots Brynn striding purposefully toward the parking

lot and her heart sinks. Brynn is going to try to stop her, try to talk her into going out to lunch again. Or into coming home with her.

But Brynn doesn't even seem to see Cassie; she's going in the opposite direction, probably toward her own car.

I guess Fiona didn't want to hang around for lunch, either.

At the exit to the street, she tries to remember which way she came in. She has no idea.

You could always go back and ask someone for directions.

Or, you could just take your chances.

Right or left?

It's a crapshoot.

She goes left.

Isaac is halfway to his rental car in the far reaches of the church parking lot when, incredibly, he hears a voice calling his name.

A female voice.

But it isn't Rachel's.

It never is.

He turns to see Brynn Costello—Brynn Saddler, now—hurrying toward him.

She was the sweet one, he remembers. At least, that was Rachel's assessment. His stepsister filled him in on all of her friends whenever he visited her at Stonebridge.

Brynn, he recalls, is the one who had lost her mom the year before she started college, and craved the female companionship she found in the Zeta Delta Kappa house. Rachel found it ironic that she wasn't particularly close to Matilda Harrington, who was also motherless.

"She's the only one who could possibly *get* what Brynn is going through," Rachel commented once. "Too bad Tildy is about as nurturing as a rattlesnake."

Isaac saw for himself that Matilda Harrington had an edge, and he now suspects that it hadn't exactly been softened over the years.

Yes, the church was packed just now for her memorial service, but the only person who truly seemed distraught was her father. Jason Harrington's choking sobs echoed heartbreakingly over the crowded pews.

Isaac hated himself for thinking *at least you get closure*.

The Lorents never even had a memorial service for Rachel. How could they? They didn't have a body. No, they were holding out hope that Rachel was still alive, that she'd come home one day.

But where *is* home?

Isaac likes to think she might come to his apartment off Gramercy Park. He moved in the summer before she disappeared; she loved the high ceilings and the hardwood floors.

He told her she could move in with him the following summer if she wanted.

She said she'd think about it.

So he's kept it, for ten years, just in case. Just so she'll know where to find him.

Where else would she go, if she came back?

Her mother's now-vacated former brownstone on West Eighty-Third Street, or her late father's old co-op on Central Park South; perhaps even to Isaac's father's floor-through in the East Village, or her sorority house in Cedar Crest . . .

There were a lot of places Rachel might consider home.

Or maybe she considered none of them home.

Maybe that's why she never came back.

Or maybe she really is dead.

Now, watching her old friend Brynn heading his way, knowing that she's married with two children and a real home, Isaac feels a flicker of resentment.

Rachel should have what Brynn has.

Rachel should be here, hurrying toward him in the autumn sunshine.

It isn't fair.

"Isaac? I'm Brynn." She comes to a stop a few feet away. He nods. "I remember."

"I—you—are—can—" Brynn stops helplessly and shrugs. "I don't even know where to begin."

He's silent, watching her, remembering the last time they spoke. It was right after she graduated; he stopped by the sorority house to see Puffy.

"What are you doing in town?" the housemother still used to ask whenever she saw him back then.

She gave that up a long time ago. Now, she just sighs and hugs him when he turns up on the doorstep of the ZDK house, well aware that he's looking for Rachel.

Even now, after ten years. Always looking for Rachel, haunted by what she had told him in her last phone call, on her birthday.

He had already graduated from West Virginia University and was working in Manhattan. He had driven up to Cedar Crest to spend that long Memorial Day weekend retracing his lost stepsister's regular routines again, hoping to stumble across some clue he'd missed before.

The sorority house was nearly vacant that day, only a few stragglers left clearing out their belongings or waiting for their summer jobs to kick in. The upstairs was usually off-limits to outsiders, but he convinced Puffy to let him take a last look at Rachel's old room. Her things had been removed long before that, and her roommate had already moved out. The room was empty. He stood there in the hallway for a long time, looking at the bare mattress, remembering . . .

Then he heard footsteps behind him in the hall, and there was Brynn, carrying a bulging black garbage bag.

She hugged him when she saw him; asked him if there was any news.

Of course there wasn't.

They chatted awkwardly for a few minutes, then said an even more awkward good-bye.

Isaac hasn't spoken to her since.

But he knows all about her life now: the details are posted on the sorority's website, on the alumni page. He's all but committed her updated bio to memory, just as he has Rachel's other sisters. Brynn Costello Saddler: married, a stay-at-home mom to two children, lives in Cedar Crest . . .

And he's even seen her on a few occasions. He's driven to her house, wanting to stop and talk to her about Rachel, just in case there's some tiny detail they've all overlooked, something that might help him trace her.

But he's never found the nerve. Maybe he's just afraid he might slip and reveal what Rachel told him that night . . .

And he can't do that.

He swore to her that he wouldn't.

So he never stopped and talked to Brynn; not even when he saw her out in the yard pushing her kids on the swing, or sitting on the porch steps with her husband, Rachel's former Soc professor.

"I'm sorry, Isaac," Brynn says now, shaking her head. "I have so many questions for you, I think we need to go someplace to talk."

Questions.

What he needs are answers.

"Do you want to get a cup of coffee somewhere?"

He looks at his watch, shakes his head. "I can't. I have to catch the shuttle back to New York."

New York, and Kylah, and her cousin's wedding. He promised.

And he never breaks a promise.

No, you just lie, and sneak around, and—

"I really need to talk to you, Isaac," Brynn says. "It's important. It's about Rachel."

Rachel.

Of course. What else would it possibly be about?

Isaac hesitates, jabbing the toe of his polished black dress shoe against the low concrete parking barrier.

Kylah.

Rachel.

He looks up at Brynn. "Okay."

Meg and her mom, Cynthia, are waiting for Ashley and her dad in front of the movie theater. Like Ashley, Meg is wearing her jeans with the pink embroidered butterflies, just as they planned on the phone this morning.

"Ashley, I hear your dad had a surprise for you," Meg's mom says with a smile. She's usually kind of drab-looking, but Ashley notices that she's wearing mascara and lipstick today, and her brown shoulder-length hair is kind of puffy, like she curled it.

"You told them about my room, Daddy?" Ashley asks him in surprise.

"He didn't tell me," Meg protests. "What are you talking about?"

"My dad built me a bedroom in his apartment!"

"Cool. Can I sleep over sometime with you?"

Both Daddy and Meg's mom laugh.

"Sure," Daddy says. "Anytime."

Jittery with excitement at the thought of it, Ashley can't help but compare Daddy to Mom, who won't let her have a sleepover at home. She says it's too distracting for her to have kids in the house making noise overnight when she has to get up so early for work every day.

If I lived with Daddy, I could have sleepovers anytime I want.

This morning, Daddy told her to think very seriously about coming to live with him. He said that if she did, he would be able to get a bigger place, and she could go to the same school, and have visitation with Mom, just like she does with him.

Ashley realized that if she did that, she might actually end up seeing a lot more of her mom than she does now, because Mom would have to spend that time with her, and not working. She wouldn't be able to leave Ashley with a baby-sitter during her visitation . . . would she?

"Isn't the movie starting?" Meg asks, bouncing a little. "I want to make sure we have time to get popcorn and Milk Duds."

"And strawberry Twizzlers," Ashley puts in.

Daddy smiles, checks his watch and says, "I'll go get the tickets."

"Let me treat, Pat," Meg's mom says, opening her purse.

"No, Cyn, that's okay, I've got it."

Cyn?

Ashley looks at Meg, who raises her eyebrows.

Hmm. Maybe Daddy is interested in Meg's mom after all. She does look kind of pretty today. Nowhere near as pretty as Mom, though, Ashley thinks loyally. Or Brynn.

If Daddy got married again—to Meg's mom—Ashley would want to live with him for sure. Then it would be like having a real family.

What about Mom, though? She'd be all alone.

But maybe, Ashley can't help thinking, that's how she wants it.

Cassie turns right. Right again, attempting to retrace her way back to the highway, negotiating leafy side streets lined with American Dream houses.

Her cell phone rings.

Dammit. She turned it off for the church service, and absently turned it on again when she saw Fiona do the same thing earlier.

Why did I do it? I don't want to hear from anyone.

She flips the phone open to check caller ID and recognizes the number.

She hesitates, then realizes she can't avoid him forever. "Hi, Alec."

"Where are you?"

"Just leaving Boston."

"So you'll be back in, what? A couple of hours?"

She shakes her head mutely.

"Cassandra?"

"Alec, I'm not coming right back," she blurts. "I'm going away for a few days."

Silence.

Then, "What do you mean?"

"I just need to get away. To think."

"About what?"

"About what I want."

After a pause, he says grimly, "I take it you're not talking about what you want for your birthday tomorrow."

"No."

"You're talking about us, aren't you? Marrying me."

"That, and other things. I just need time to think."

"So you're going away?" he asks flatly.

"Just for a couple of days," she says, feeling her way. "Or maybe a week . . . I don't really know."

"But where—"

"Alec, please don't push me right now."

"Push you? You're telling me you're about to take off for God knows how long, to God knows where, a month before our wedding. Don't you think I have a right to ask some questions, here?"

"You have a right. And I have a right not to answer them. Good-bye, Alec."

She closes the phone with a snap and tosses it onto the seat beside her. Her heart races as she tries to focus her attention on the unfamiliar stretch of road ahead through the windshield.

I can't believe I just did that.

Now what am I supposed to do?

You can't do anything but drive. And breathe.

She gulps the welcome, almost balmy fresh air.

Where is she?

She must have missed a turn somewhere, because this area is looking unfamiliar: a series of McMansion developments rise on either side of the road, some still in various stages of construction and landscaping. The lots are dotted with signs that display the builder's contact information.

All this can be yours, they seem to scream.

Yes, if you want it.

And I don't want it.

As if to punctuate Cassie's thought, her cell phone begins to ring again.

That's it.

She's had enough.

Without pausing to see who it is—without pausing to think at all—she snatches the phone up and hurtles it with all her might out the open car window.

It disappears into a thicket of dense undergrowth alongside the road, where it can ring on indefinitely.

I should eat something, Brynn thinks as the waitress sets two menus and two glasses of ice water on the table between her and Isaac.

They're in a small café a few blocks from the church. She followed him over from there, and this is the first restaurant they came to. Rough-hewn floors, exposed brick, hanging plants, stacks of freebie papers, and a community bulletin board. It's crowded with students, yoga moms, soccer dads. Several groups are waiting to be seated, but there was a small table for two in the back, near the kitchen.

The air is heavy with the scent of raw garlic. This could

be a problem. Garlic makes Brynn sick when she's pregnant. The taste, the smell, the thought . . .

Salivating profusely—from nausea, not hunger pains—Brynn scans the menu, looking in vain for something palatable. Predictably, she finds plenty of tofu, spelt, and sprouts.

If I eat any of this, I'll throw up.

Then again, if I don't, I'm going to throw up anyway.

She orders decaf tea and white toast.

"We only have whole grain," the waitress informs her.

Of course you do.

"And would you prefer organic juniper berry or Jamaican sarsaparilla tea?"

"Do you have plain old decaf?"

"No. But these are detox teas. They're very good for you."

I'm sure they are, unless you happen to be pregnant. Brynn asks for bottled water instead.

"And you, sir?" She turns to Isaac.

"Just coffee."

"Decaf?"

"Hell, no." He grins charmingly.

His good looks aren't lost on the waitress, who flashes him a return smile before walking away.

The grin evaporates instantly. Isaac checks his watch and goes back to being silent and brooding.

This isn't how Brynn remembers him. He had visited the sorority house only a few times, but Rachel spoke of him often. Their parents were married from the time she was in seventh grade until she left for college, and she was closer to him than to any of her other siblings—whole, half, or step.

Brynn had the impression that Isaac and Rachel were kindred free spirits who shared a passion for music, art, and food.

"*Real* food," as Rachel used to say. She was a meat-and-potatoes girl, much to Puffy's delight. The sorority house-mother frequently complained that the other girls wanted to eat only salad and vegetables.

Brynn can still picture tiny, skinny Rachel sitting in the dining room at the sorority house, contentedly tucking into a double cheeseburger with the works.

Struck by an unexpected pang of grief, Brynn attempts to reconcile her fond memory with the image of a vengeful murderess. She just can't do it.

Then again . . . A traumatic experience and ten years will transform anyone, she reminds herself. If Rachel is still alive, she isn't the person she once was.

Isaac's coffee and her water arrive.

They sip in silence, and glance at each other.

Uncomfortable, Brynn tries to think of something to say as an opener. Realizing he isn't going to bail her out, Brynn settles on, "Rachel would have hated this place."

"You got that right. She'll take Arby's any day over health food like this."

Noting his use of the present tense, Brynn comments, "Personally, so will I."

They fall silent again.

Brynn takes another cautious sip of her water and wrinkles her nose. There seems to be a metallic aftertaste.

"Are you okay?" Isaac asks, watching her. "You look a little green."

"I'm just queasy from . . ." *A pregnancy hormone surge.* "From this morning. That was rough, at the church. Tildy."

He nods.

"I'm kind of surprised you came," she tells him.

"She was a friend of my sister's."

"They weren't that close, and it's been so many years since . . ."

"Since Rachel disappeared," he fills in for her when she trails off. "Yeah, I know."

He checks his watch again and says, "You said you had questions for me. What are they? Because I've got to make a flight in about eighty minutes, so . . ."

"I'm sorry. I just wondered if you ever heard anything more. About Rachel."

It sounds so lame, phrased that way.

Apparently he agrees, because his eyes darken and he returns, "No, have you?"

"Me? No! I just thought maybe your family . . ."

"I haven't talked to Elise since she got married again and moved to San Diego. That was a few years ago."

Elise is Rachel's mother, who was married to Isaac's father for a few years. Brynn met her only after Rachel vanished, when she was distraught and fragile, so she has no real way of judging her personality.

"Would she have told you if Rachel turned up?"

"Sometimes I wonder," Isaac admits with surprising candor, looking down at the table, pushing the salt shaker around with his index finger. "But then I remind myself that if Rachel came back, she probably wouldn't know where to find her mother. She might not even know that her father died. But I'm still in the same apartment I had ten years ago. It's why I keep it."

"So you don't believe she's dead, either?"

He looks up sharply.

Either.

The word just slipped out.

Brynn backpedals, feebly. "I mean, it's not that I think she's alive for sure, you know, but I've always hoped . . ."

Isaac is watching her intently, as though he's wondering if she knows something he doesn't know.

And, Brynn realizes uneasily, as though *he* knows something *she* doesn't.

Having crossed through Newton and reached Interstate 95 on its western loop around Boston, Cassie heads north. If she were going home, she'd pick up the westbound Mass Pike a few exits up. From there, it's about two and a half hours home to Danbury.

But, apparently, she isn't going home.

Alec has probably been trying to call her ever since she hung up on him, but of course, she doesn't have to listen to her phone ring . . .

Because I threw it out the window.

God, that felt good.

Her only regret is that now she can't tell Alec right away that she's made up her mind to call off the wedding next month.

She's come to realize that anything—even hurting Alec— is better than going ahead with their plans as though nothing has changed.

Everything has changed, these past few weeks. *She's* changed—on the inside, anyway.

Now you just have to find the nerve to change the outside.

Since Rachel's birthday and Tildy's death, she's spent a lot of time, too much time, looking back. In the process, she's seen her life for what it really is: testimony to someone else's dreams, first her parents', and now, Alec's.

Maybe she'd be soul-searching anyway, on the cusp of thirty.

Maybe she'd be dredging up the past, examining every misstep that led her to where she is now.

Faced with the constant, overwhelming reminder of her own mortality . . .

She simply can't go home now.

Maybe not ever.

You tried to run away already, and you couldn't go through with it, she reminds herself. *You would have gone home eventually even if you hadn't found out about Tildy that morning.*

But this time, there can be no turning back, even if she changes her mind.

Not after what happened to Tildy, and with her own birthday looming tomorrow.

Cold fingers of fear clutch at her as she boldly bypasses the exit for the Mass Pike.

She keeps a close eye on the rearview mirror to make sure she isn't being followed.

It's hard to tell.

She picks up speed, changing lanes a few times. Then, driving in the right, she impulsively veers off a Lexington exit at the last minute, without signaling, just in case . . .

But no other car follows her down the ramp.

And no other car follows her as she drives a little ways down the road, just to be sure. Satisfied she's on her own, she pulls into the first bank she sees and uses an ATM to make a maximum withdrawal from her checking account. There. That will tide her over for awhile, at least.

After consulting a road map, she follows a meandering route back up to I-95. Still, there isn't a suspicious car on the road behind her.

Back on the interstate, Cassie continues north, uncertain where she's headed.

She only knows that she isn't being followed. Without her cell phone, no one can possibly reach her; by using only cash, no one will be able to trace her.

This time, she has to get away to a place that's much farther from home.

A place where no one will ever find her.

Not her parents, not Alec . . .

Not the silent, invisible stalker whose presence seems to dog her every move.

This is, by far, the hardest part: the waiting.

Knowing that you have to get through another night, and part of another day, before you can accomplish the monumental task ahead.

Keeping up a cool demeanor, going about your business as though this was any other Saturday afternoon, making sure no one would ever in their wildest dreams guess what's going on in your head.

So far, so good.

The party supplies are tucked away; the gift-wrapped box is ready. Inside it is a special memento selected for the occasion. Cassandra won't have the chance to open it, of course, but that's all right.

She doesn't need a reminder.

She knows what she did.

Is she wondering, even now, if she's going to die tomorrow?

Does she realize that it's only fair?

That's the tricky part.

If she suspects, she might try to get away.

Go ahead, Cassie. You can run from me.

And you probably think you can hide, too.

Maybe you really can . . .

From the rest of the world . . .

But what you don't realize is that you can never hide from me.

CHAPTER 16

For Brynn, Sunday morning dawns just as the others have: with a tide of nausea that propels her straight to the bathroom.

Already weary of the routine only one week in, she brushes her teeth and wonders how she's possibly going to keep her pregnancy from Garth when she gets home.

He might not wake up in their bed every morning, but he's bound to notice her morning sickness. The walls are thin and the house is small.

The same thing is true of this one.

So she shouldn't be surprised to step out of the bathroom and find her stepmother standing there wearing her jogging clothes and a knowing expression.

Brynn's heart sinks.

"You're pregnant," Sue whispers. "I thought I heard you getting sick yesterday morning, too, but I figured you might have eaten something that disagreed with you."

Brynn considers, then dismisses, the notion of going along with that theory. She was obviously fine last night. Her father treated the whole family, including two of her brothers and their wives and kids, to dinner at a seafood place followed by a visit to Cold Stone Creamery.

Maybe she was eating from nerves—seeing Isaac really was unsettling. Or maybe she was merely eating because she was starved, and the nausea had finally worn off.

But everyone joked about the way she devoured twin lobster tails and a gigantic waffle cone heaping with Pecan and Cream Passion.

"Please don't say anything to Daddy," she tells Sue, realizing she might as well admit the truth. She'll find out sooner or later anyway. "And don't mention it to the boys, either. I haven't told anyone yet."

"Not even Garth?"

She shakes her head. "It wasn't planned. I was on the pill. I can't believe this happened . . . I never missed one." She's talking more to herself than to Sue.

But her stepmother asks, with the efficiency of the OB-GYN nurse practitioner she once was, "Have you been on antibiotics lately?"

"No, why?"

"Because they can interfere with the pill's effectiveness."

"Well, I haven't—" Brynn stops short. Oh, yes, she has.

She was on antibiotics right before school started, when she and Caleb both had strep throat.

That explains it.

"The doctor should warn people about that." She shakes her head in disbelief.

"I'm sure there are warnings in the pamphlet that comes with the pill packet. And most pharmacists print out drug interaction information when they hand over prescriptions, too."

Irked by Sue's implication that Brynn could have avoided this situation had she been paying closer attention, even if it's probably true, she says defensively, "Well, nobody bothered to give me that information."

"Well, I'm sure you're looking forward to a new baby, and Garth will be, too, when you tell him. When are you going to do that?"

None of your business, Brynn thinks, further irritated.

"Waiting for the right moment again, huh?" Sue smiles. "I remember that Father's Day when you—"

"No, it's not like that," Brynn cuts in brusquely. "I just . . . Listen, Sue, no offense, but this is really a personal matter and I definitely don't feel comfortable talking about it right now with you."

She didn't mean to put emphasis on the last word, but somehow, it comes out that way.

With *you.*

It comes out sounding as though Brynn would prefer to discuss her pregnancy with just about anyone else in the world.

Which, come to think of it, is almost true.

Yet, seeing the flicker of hurt in Sue's eyes, Brynn fends off remorse.

"Point taken. And I won't say anything to anyone until you give me the green light," Sue promises quietly. Then she adds, looking Brynn pointedly in the eye, "You might not like me, but you can trust me."

Brynn watches her stride down the hall and disappear into the kitchen.

I should probably go try to explain, she thinks guiltily.

She starts after her stepmother, with no idea what she'll say—only that she doesn't want Sue to think she doesn't like her . . .

Even if it's true?

Well, she can't deny that Sue has really stepped up for Brynn and the boys this weekend. Daddy is getting older, and tired. He eagerly took them to the basement, where they have always loved to play with Brynn's brothers' childhood train set, but he was wiped out in no time and had to take a nap. It was Sue who crawled around on the floor with the kids, and made them peanut butter sandwiches without the crusts when they were hungry before bed, and played endless rounds of Candyland so that each boy could win twice.

I don't have to like her . . . But I don't have to hurt her, ei-

ther, Brynn thinks as she steps into the kitchen to make amends.

But she's just in time to see the back door close as Sue leaves the house.

Opening her eyes on Sunday morning, Fiona finds herself facing a wall of windows looking out over a breathtaking mountain tapestry bathed in golden sunlight.

Her lips curve into a smile as she realizes exactly where she is.

Turning her head, she sees James lying beside her, tangled in the sheets, sound asleep.

She waits for the inevitable morning-after pang of regret . . .

But it doesn't come.

Everything about last night felt right.

She impulsively called him from her car as she headed back home from Boston after the funeral, thinking she should make up some professional reason to speak to him. It still hadn't come to her by the time he answered the phone, so she figured she'd wing it.

He sounded glad to hear from her.

"When are you coming back to town?" he asked.

"Right now."

"Really. What are you doing when you get here?"

"I'm not sure . . ."

"Come over."

She laughed. "Is that an order?"

"Yes, it is."

At last, she got to lay eyes on the fabled "cottage"—a three-story stone structure rambling along a majestic overlook. What a far cry from the cabin she still owns with Pat, not far from here.

"What do you think?" James asked.

That I could definitely see myself living here.

But, of course, she didn't say that.

James grilled chicken and vegetables on a grill that cost more than the sum total of every appliance in Fiona's kitchen at home. He opened a bottle of wine, a rare vintage. And he kissed her on the moonlit terrace with the lights of Cedar Crest twinkling far below.

She didn't want to leave.

Ever.

And he didn't want her to leave—at least, not last night.

Now, checking her watch—the only thing she's still wearing—Fiona realizes that her fantasy interlude is about to skid to a crashing halt.

She'll have to scramble if she's going to make it home before Pat drops off Ashley.

She considers calling to tell him she can't be there—she can say she's still hung up in Boston. He assumed she was spending the night there anyway, consoling Tildy's family or something.

She turns to look at James again.

No, she should go.

Now, before she inadvertently says or does something to ruin this budding dream-come-true.

Back in her room, Brynn climbs into bed, determined to catch a little more sleep.

But the guilt has followed her.

She doesn't want to feel bad about Sue; life would be easier if she was immune to any feelings at all for her stepmother, good or bad . . .

But lately, especially, good.

It isn't easy to maintain resentment for someone who treats Caleb and Jeremy—and, all right, Brynn's father, too—so well.

Still . . .

If my mother were standing here, instead of her, I'd be pouring my heart out about this pregnancy.

And about Rachel, even.

In fact, I would never have kept that to myself for ten years if she were around.

Ten years.

It's been even longer than that since her mother died. Is there ever going to come a day when Brynn isn't unexpectedly blindsided by pain and longing?

Maybe the grief isn't as raw as it once was, but it's still there.

She finds herself thinking of Tildy's father, so anguished as he passed up the aisle after the service yesterday, leaning heavily on Troy Allerson's arm.

People are supposed to lose their parents, painful as it is. That's the natural order of things.

But Jason Harrington will have to survive the loss of his wife and both his children.

Just as Rachel's parents—and siblings, especially her poor brother—had to survive their loss.

Seeing Isaac yesterday brought it all back: the terrible days in the immediate, frenzied aftermath of her disappearance, when searchers were roaming the area looking for her. Brynn's overwhelming guilt for hiding information that might have helped them find her . . .

Unless she didn't want to be found.

Did Isaac suspect, back then, that Brynn and the others might know more than they were telling? Is that why he kept coming back to Cedar Crest, back to the sorority house?

Could he be—?

She cuts herself off hastily, telling herself there's no way Isaac is the one who killed Tildy. What reason would he possibly have?

What if he saw what happened with Rachel?

What if he wants revenge?

Brynn burrows into the quilt as if she can stave off the cold dread stealing over her once again.

Isaac wasn't even in Cedar Crest the night his stepsister vanished. He didn't get there until the next day, just as her absence was coming to light.

How do you know that? Brynn asks herself.

Because he told me.

She isn't just frightened now, she is starting to feel nauseated again, and this time, it isn't mere morning sickness.

She remembers that she was on the porch of the sorority house with some of the other sisters when Isaac pulled up in his car. He told them he had just driven from Manhattan to see Rachel.

He was immediately upset when Puffy told him she was missing. In retrospect, more upset, perhaps, than he should have been at that early stage. At the time, Brynn was more concerned with concealing her own guilt than with Isaac's reaction, but she does remember that he wouldn't accept the housemother's theory that Rachel had just spent the night with a friend somewhere and was still hanging out.

No, Isaac seemed to sense even then that something was very wrong. And, of course, Brynn, Tildy, Cassie, and Fiona *knew* that there was.

Does he believe, even now, that Brynn knows something?

Is that why he was looking at her so intently yesterday in the café?

And what is it that he isn't telling her about Rachel?

He's hiding something, too.

She has no real evidence of that, just a vibe she sometimes gets about people. Usually people she knows well; Garth, in particular.

I swear you can read my mind, he says sometimes.

But not lately.

Before he left for Arizona, he seemed preoccupied.

Well, of course he was, Brynn tells herself. *He was wor-*

*ried about me, and upset about Tildy's murder, and the bird
on the counter, and trying to finish the research material he
was planning to present at the symposium . . .*

Who wouldn't be preoccupied?

Anyway, Garth's frame of mind won't be important until
they're back at home, where she'll have to figure out how to
deliver her pregnancy news.

Right now, she's more concerned with Isaac Halpern's
frame of mind.

Why did he show up in Cedar Crest the day after Rachel's
birthday?

He never said.

And Rachel never mentioned that he was coming. Why
not?

She was so upset that night . . . Did it have something to
do with Isaac?

"If I could tell you, I would, Brynnie. But I can't," was
Rachel's response when she asked what was wrong.

Now, Brynn would bet her life that it had something to do
with her brother . . .

And that he, like Brynn, knows more than he's willing to
tell.

"God, what time is it?"

Isaac looks up from the Sunday *Times.*

Kylah has emerged from the bedroom. Her face is smudged
with yesterday's wedding-heavy makeup; her slept-on hair is
still in a salon-sprayed bouffant. She's wearing just panties
and the gray T-shirt she pulled on after discarding her brides-
maid's gown in a heap on the floor beside the bed.

"It's early. Go back to bed."

She shakes her head and stretches. "Is there coffee?"

"Yes." He sets aside the paper and walks over to the kitchenette to pour her a cup as she leans against the door frame,
looking wan. "How do you feel?"

"Not so good."

"Champagne mixed with beer and tequila shots will do that." He hands her a steaming mug.

She looks down at it and makes a face. "Are we out of milk again?"

"No, but drink it black. It'll help."

She sips it in silence as Smoochy materializes to rub against her shins, purring.

"Are you hungry, baby?" she asks the cat.

"I already fed him."

Kylah looks up at Isaac in surprise. Then she says, "Really." As if she's pondering that unexpected development.

They both know he never bothers with the cat unless she asks him to. Now, Isaac realizes, she's thinking that he's trying to appease her. For yesterday. For taking off to Boston without explanation.

And she's right.

He managed to make it to the wedding with time to spare. Despite everything that's gone on, he somehow got caught up in the spirit of the occasion. He ate, drank, talked, and danced. He met Kylah's extended family and was sure to charm all of them, especially her eighty-five-year-old grandmother, when he asked her to dance.

He and Kylah even joked and laughed—and kissed—in the backseat of the cab home. Of course, she was drunk— too drunk to remember that she was angry with him. And Isaac was a little tipsy himself.

The evening as a whole was a welcome reprieve, the first in a long time.

But now it's back to reality. If she demands an explanation, he owes her one.

But he'll tell her only as much as he told Brynn, and nothing more.

* * *

It's cold . . .

Really cold.

Cassie snuggles deeper into her down comforter . . .

Only, she realizes, it isn't her down comforter.

As her memory of yesterday gradually returns, she remembers that she's lying beneath a shiny-stiff quilted bedspread that smells faintly of wood smoke, as though someone had huddled beneath it around a campfire on a recent, chilly night.

For the second time in as many weeks, Cassie opens her eyes on unfamiliar territory.

This time, though, she isn't shell-shocked.

She probably should be.

Hell, she should be scared out of her mind.

She's never even been to Portland or Kennebunkport before, let alone the backwoods of Maine, miles from civilization. It took her well over four hours to find her way up here; she'd have kept right on going if she hadn't passed the VA-CANCY sign right around the time she realized she was burning daylight.

It was a nerve-racking drive. And it took her a long time last night to settle into a sleep that was, in the end, surprisingly sound.

Now, as she gazes around the rustic cabin, she feels only contentment laced with relief.

I'll be okay here for awhile. I can do this. I really can.

The cabin is small: just one room, with a square window on each of the four log walls. There's a woodstove she could have used last night, and electricity. No plumbing, though; you have to go down the path to the community bathhouse to use the toilet, wash, or take a shower. A minifridge is tucked into one corner, but that's the extent of the kitchen appliances; any food preparation has to be done on the outdoor stone fireplace. She checked it out last night, beside the rushing stream just a stone's throw from the door.

Cassie plans to do some grilling there. She doesn't mind,

but if she did she'd have no choice anyway: there are no restaurants in a half-hour radius of this place. Louise, the wheelchair-bound woman who runs the camp, said there's a small grocery store in the nearest town. But it's a twenty-minute drive back down the winding road through the forest.

Cassie has a feeling she'll be heading that way pretty frequently; she paid for the entire month of October when she checked in. She used cash, of course, and entered a fake name on the register.

"You're lucky I got a last-minute cancellation," Louise said. "Otherwise, I wouldn't have a vacancy on a holiday weekend. This is the last hurrah, though. Foliage is past peak, and the camp will be emptied out by this time Monday. I hope you like peace and quiet."

"That's why I'm here."

"Then I won't bother you. You can see that it's impossible for me to get up that way these days, anyway." Louise gestured at her useless legs propped on the chair's footrest. "My housekeeping girl comes in every few days to clean the bathhouse and stock it with towels. Other than that, you probably won't see anyone around."

"That's fine."

"Well, if you get lonely, feel free to come on down here and chat or play a hand of cards with me."

"I will, if I get lonely," Cassie told her, knowing she won't.

"What are you doing up here by yourself, anyway?"

"Writing a book." She was glad she had come up with a believable story in advance. "It's due to my editor next month and I needed to get away from everything to finish it."

"How exciting! I'll make sure nobody disturbs you up there."

"Thanks."

The other cabins might still be occupied right now, but they're all so far apart and secluded that Cassie has yet to see another living soul—human, anyway. There's plenty of wildlife; she was unnerved by rustling in the undergrowth as she walked down to the bathroom last night at dusk, carrying the flashlight provided in the cabin.

"That's prime time to see a moose," Louise mentioned. "So keep your eyes open."

She'll keep her eyes open, all right.

She has to remind herself repeatedly that she's in no danger here; nobody is lurking, watching her, waiting to strike . . .

Today.

Today, she remembers, is her birthday.

She's thirty years old.

And there's no one around to wish her Happy Birthday.

But that's fine with me, she thinks staunchly.

As long as there's no one around, and no other living soul can possibly know where I am, I can be sure that I'll live to see another day.

Fiona is freshly showered and changed into a navy sheath, her hair pulled back in its usual chignon, when Pat arrives with Ashley.

"Hi, Mom!" Ashley has on a pair of jeans and a denim jacket, her hair pulled back in a straggly ponytail.

"Hi, sweetie." Fiona hugs her quickly with one arm. "Hurry up and go get ready for mass."

"Can't I go like this?"

"What do *you* think?"

Ashley sighs and gives her father a fierce hug.

"Thanks for a great weekend, Daddy! Can we do our sunrise hike next time I come?"

"We'll see."

"Sunrise hike?" Fiona asks as Ashley heads for the stairs.

"She's been wanting to see the sun come up over the mountains," he explains.

She has? I never knew that.

But then, there seems to be a lot Fiona doesn't know

about her daughter these days. That wouldn't bother her if it wasn't sometimes obvious that Pat does know those things . . . and more.

Well, that's how girls are, she tells herself. They adore their daddies and resent their mothers. Especially at this age.

Then again, Ashley isn't an adolescent yet.

But she's always been a Daddy's Girl.

And anyway, Fiona isn't a sunrise-hike kind of mom. She has other things to offer her daughter. Things Pat can't possibly give her. A sense of responsibility, financial stability, career ambition, personal style, a beautiful home, a solid work ethic . . .

"Bye, Daddy!" Ashley calls from the top of the stairs.

"Bye, sweetie."

Left alone with Pat, Fiona finds him watching her, looking concerned.

"So, how was your weekend?" she asks, to fill the awkward silence.

"We went to see that new Disney movie with the Reynoldses."

The Reynoldses.

Fiona is blank.

Of course, Pat notices. He seems to gloat a little as he clarifies, "Her friend Meg and her mom."

"I know."

"Then we played minigolf, and went out to dinner at Applebee's."

"That's nice." Fiona finds herself surprisingly envious. Not that she particularly wants to hang out with Meg's mother—she doesn't have time for that. And she likes minigolf about as much as she likes Applebee's. Still, her ex-husband shouldn't be socializing more with Ashley's friends and their parents than she does.

She makes a mental note to invite Cynthia and Meg Reynolds to lunch sometime.

"So, Fee . . . How *are* you?" Pat asks, not in a casual way.

"I'm okay." Uncomfortable under his gaze, she decides it's easier when he's not being civil to her.

"The funeral had to be hard."

"It wasn't fun. And it wasn't a funeral, it was a memorial service." Why does she find it necessary to keep clarifying that detail?

She knows why. Because she's feeling ornery.

And that's partly because she feels that way whenever she's around Pat, but, today, it's mostly because James didn't mention seeing her again when they said good-bye earlier. Nor did he protest when she told him she had to leave.

"I have to get back home anyway," he told her.

"Aren't you spending the weekend here?" she asked, disappointed that there wouldn't be another opportunity to see him in the next day or two.

"No, I've got some things to do in the office back in Boston."

It wasn't that he was rude. More like . . . disinterested, and preoccupied with whatever it is he's got to do today.

She, of all people, should be familiar with that mode. But for the first time in a long time, her current obsession isn't her work.

"Well, Ashley and I had a good weekend. I think she really liked the room I set up for her."

"Good. That's great." Fiona wonders if she should call James after church, just to thank him for the nice evening.

"Oh, I heard her sniffling a little this morning. I'm thinking it might be because of the sawdust—not that I didn't clean it up really well, but that stuff sticks in every crack for awhile. Anyway, it could be that she's coming down with a cold."

"Mmm-hmm." No, she shouldn't call James. She should let him call her.

And he will, she assures herself.

"You should get her some strawberries. Did you know they have more vitamin C than citrus fruit?"

Fiona shakes her head impatiently. "I had no idea. Well, we've got to get ready for church now, so . . . thanks."

Pat is getting on her nerves now, just as Brynn was getting on her nerves yesterday, hinting around again at going to the police.

But that's not going to happen, she assures herself, closing the door after her ex-husband.

All Fiona has to do if her friend brings it up again is mention the prospect of prison. Brynn can't bear the thought of anything coming between her and her family.

Two kids and a terrific husband—that was Brynn's description of her life in a nutshell. Fiona overheard her say it when she was catching up with one of their old sorority sisters before the funeral.

Two kids . . . But how terrific is her husband?

Fiona can't help but remember that June night at Aura in Boston, when Tildy introduced her to James. The three of them were having a nightcap at the bar when Fiona spotted Garth, of all people. It turned out he was staying there at the Seaport Hotel for an academic conference.

He'd already had a couple of beers and was more than willing to ditch his stuffy colleagues when Tildy invited him to join them.

Fiona didn't miss the silent look that passed between the two of them. Maybe, if she hadn't been so preoccupied with James at the time, she'd have nipped it in the bud right there.

"It" being whatever might have happened between Garth and Tildy after James drove Fiona back to her own hotel at Copley Plaza.

Was it a mere flirtation that wound up with both of them going their separate ways at closing time?

Or was it a repeat performance of their secret tryst that began back in college and continued—right under Brynn's nose—well into the year after graduation?

They were living together at the time. And Fee doesn't think Tildy and Garth were constantly hot and heavy. But Tildy had a thing for older men, and she could be intensely seductive. It isn't hard to see why Garth continued their on-and-off fling for awhile after meeting Brynn.

It stopped when they got married, though. Tildy confided in Fiona that Garth told her to steer clear; he was taking his vows seriously.

That was before he and Brynn had kids, though, and she went from doting wife to supermom housefrau.

Garth was probably ripe for some seductive attention by the time he ran into Tildy in Boston. Fiona doesn't know exactly what happened, though.

She keeps trying to tell herself she doesn't care.

But she does, for Brynn's sake.

She alone realized the potential implications of the investigation into Tildy's death.

If the detectives start sniffing around her past in Cedar Crest, tracking down every man she ever slept with . . . Well, the trail would eventually lead to the Saddlers' door.

Fiona knows Brynn well enough to realize what her husband's premarital infidelity—with one of her closest friends, no less—would do to her. Never mind how she would react to Garth's postmarital infidelity, if that really is the case.

I should have confronted Tildy about it while I had the chance.

Now there's a very good chance she'll never know what happened that night.

She certainly isn't about to ask Garth, and she doubts he'd tell her the truth anyway.

But she has other things to worry about right now. Things that are far more important than the true state of the Saddlers' fairy-tale marriage.

Brynn waits until noon to dial Garth's cell phone.

Yesterday morning, she made the mistake of calling him at five in the morning his time, having forgotten he was on the opposite side of the country. Pregnancy hormones again, afflicting her with temporary amnesia.

He called her back in the afternoon, as she was driving back to the Cape after lunch with Isaac.

"How horrible was it?" he asked.

"Pretty horrible," she admitted around a sudden lump in her throat, missing him desperately.

He's so far away, she realized. And she was acknowledging not just the hundreds of miles, but the monumental secrets—hers—that lay between them.

Weighted by guilt, she filled Garth in as briefly as she could about the church service, then told him she couldn't stay on the phone because she was behind the wheel.

They haven't talked since.

She's about to hang up now when Garth answers sleepily.

"There you are! Did I wake you?"

He yawns. "No, I was up."

Brynn laughs. "No, you weren't. Sorry. But I wanted to hear your voice."

"Well, I don't mind hearing yours, either. In fact, I wish today were tomorrow and I were headed home."

"Me, too. How did you do yesterday with your presentation?"

"You know. The usual. Everyone listened politely and asked pertinent questions, but all they really wanted to do was present their own material. How are the boys?"

"Still in bed. They're worn out. Late night last night."

"Did you have fun?"

It's Brynn's turn to say, "You know. The usual."

"What are you doing today?"

"More of the same, I'm sure."

"Are you okay? You sound wiped out."

She hesitates, wishing she could tell him the truth about what's going on with her. All of it.

But she can't tell him any of it, so she assures him that she's fine, just tired.

"Me, too. I can't wait until we're home again, and everything's back to normal," Garth says.

Back to normal.

So easy for him to say.

If he had any idea . . .

But, of course, he has no way of knowing that for the Saddler household, *normal* is a long way off.

Isaac doesn't recognize the number in his cell phone's caller ID window.

He answers it anyway, standing on the street, on his way to the deli for sandwiches. Kylah said she needed carbs.

"Mr. Halpern?" an unfamiliar voice asks.

"Yes?"

"This is Detective Hiles of the Boston Police Department."

Isaac's heart lurches into his throat, rendering him momentarily mute.

"I'm investigating Matilda Harrington's death and I'd like to speak to you as soon as possible."

"To me?" Isaac has recovered his voice—or someone else's, judging by the uncharacteristically high pitch. He clears his throat in an attempt to lower it. "Why do you need to talk to me?"

"Routine."

"I really didn't know her well. I was there more because she was a friend of my sister's, years ago."

"That's fine. This is just routine," the detective repeats. "We're talking to everyone who's had any contact with her."

"But I haven't. Not in years, and even then . . ."

"It's just routine." The detective emphasizes the word yet again. "We're touching base with everyone who was at the memorial service yesterday. I'll be in New York tomorrow. What time is good for you?"

* * *

Cassie never should have waited until late afternoon to try and find her way back to that grocery. Especially on a Sunday.

The place was closed by the time she arrived. A couple of teenagers on skateboards in the parking lot told her how to get to a larger market, but either they gave her the wrong directions, or she took a wrong turn.

Hopelessly lost, she drove in circles, finally deciding to forego food in favor of making it back to the cabin before dark.

That didn't happen; she had traveled farther than she thought, in unfamiliar territory.

Now, at last, she's made it back.

She parks at the designated spot about a hundred yards down the path from her cabin, cuts the headlights, and immediately wishes she'd thought to bring the flashlight.

Wow. It's pitch-black out here.

Never in her life has she experienced such complete darkness. There's no moon tonight; the dense canopy of trees would probably obstruct the light even if there was.

Her heart is pounding as she begins to pick her way over the rutted path.

Again, she hears an unnerving rustling in the bushes.

Again, she reminds herself that it's just a moose.

But then, Louise did say the best time to see a moose was in the hour before dusk . . . not two hours after.

Are moose—or is it *mooses?*—nocturnal creatures?

It doesn't matter, surely plenty of other animals are.

Still, the closer she gets to her safe haven, the cabin, the more incongruously uneasy she feels.

You're fine, she assures herself.

Nobody even knows where you are.

She reaches into her pocket to find the key to the cabin. The lock is a joke, really. It's an old-fashioned one, with an old-fashioned key—the kind hotels stopped using years ago because they aren't secure.

Cassie inserts the key in the lock, thinking of her alarm system and series of dead bolts back home.

But none of that is necessary up here, she reminds herself as she opens the door and steps into the cabin, which is even darker than the inky night beyond the threshold.

She's safe here.

No one knows where she is.

There's no way anyone could—

"Happy birthday, dear Cassie," a voice sings, close to her ear.

Then she hears the click of a lighter, and the darkness is pierced with an eerie glow.

In that one, terrifying instant, Cassie takes it all in.

The cake.

The candles.

The decorations.

The face . . .

She opens her mouth, but a hand roughly closes over it, stifling what would have been Cassandra Ashford's dread-drenched last words.

What are you *doing here?*

She recognized me.

That's obvious. Even in the dim light, even in this god-forsaken spot where she would never expect to see a familiar face . . .

Let alone mine.

And as much as I'd like to look her in the eye and tell her exactly what she did to me . . . and what I plan to do to her . . .

She's struggling, instinctively raking her fingers at her captor, fingernails acting as weapons.

This isn't good; she's fighting and clawing like a panther, leaving telltale marks that may be hard to conceal.

No, this isn't good at all; there can be no delay.

If she manages to wriggle free, there might not be another living soul nearby to help her, but there will be plenty of places to hide out here in the wilderness.

A person can get lost for days, weeks, months, even. Just wandering around in the middle of nowhere, unable—no, *unwilling*—to be found.

Right.

That can't be allowed to happen now.

I've found her, and I'm not letting her go. All I have to do is drag her a little closer, suppress those hands of hers, and get a good angle on her throat . . .

"Happy Birthday, dear Caaaa—"

Arms pinned but legs still flailing, she lands a well-placed kick.

But, unlike Matilda Harrington, she fails to succeed in freeing herself. No, she succeeds only in interrupting the song. But just for an instant.

"—ssie . . . Happy Birthday to yoooouuuu."

There.

The singing has been completed.

Check.

Next task: incapacitate the birthday girl so that the party can go on uninterrupted.

Not easily accomplished with all this violent writhing, but not impossible, either.

All you need to do is get hold of her hair with your left hand . . .

There. Grab a fistful of cornrows, tug as hard as you can . . .

Cassandra Ashford's head is abruptly jerked backward; her long, graceful neck arches tantalizingly near.

Now, raise the knife with your right hand, steady, steady, good . . .

Oh, this is good.

No time, however, to relish the sight of the blade glinting

in the candlelight, or the sound of a strangled scream that strains to escape her about-to-be-severed vocal chords.

Just do it.

Now.

The knife descends methodically as if of its own accord, splitting a thin layer of supple mocha-colored skin, slicing into flesh.

Blood begins to spurt; Cassie thrashes, gurgles.

The knife rises, strikes again, hacking vocal cords, windpipe, hitting bone . . .

Ah. Good. The birthday girl has been swiftly silenced, has gone limp in the arms that hold her. Warm, sticky blood drenches the hands that still clutch her hair and the knife, pouring over everything, draining from her lifeless body.

"There. That wasn't so bad, was it?"

A soft chuckle disturbs the morbid silence inside the cabin as a chorus of crickets go on chirping, uninterrupted, beyond its walls.

Cassandra Ashford is dragged over to the seat of honor and propped there. It isn't an easy task; she keeps toppling forward, nearly hitting the beautiful cake.

Then again, it isn't so beautiful anymore. An army of bugs has already invaded the white frosting and the message, first in icing, done by the bakery: Happy Birthday—then in blood, painstakingly accomplished back at home: DEAR CASSIE.

In no time, the bugs will undoubtedly make their way from the sugary cake to feed on the corpse beside it. There's no telling when Cassie's body will be discovered . . .

And that's good.

The longer she stays hidden away up here, the better.

Fiona and Brynn will have no inkling that another of their sisters has paid for the sin they committed together . . .

But they must sense, even now, that their own days are numbered.

And if by chance they don't . . . I'll be sure to let them know.

CHAPTER 17

"Morning, Daddy." Brynn bends low over the kitchen table to kiss her father's stubbly cheek. In the process, she is assailed by an overpowering whiff of the contents of the full plate before him.

Scrambled eggs fried in butter and onions . . . His favorite breakfast.

Brynn, whose stomach was emptied in an early-morning bout with nausea, finds herself swallowing a tide of saliva.

Eggs . . . butter . . . onions . . .

Bleh.

She looks away, battling queasiness, and catches Sue watching her from the sink, where she's washing out the frying pan.

"How about some toast, Brynn?" Sue offers knowingly. "It's all made."

She wants to say no thanks, but if she doesn't get something bland into her stomach, she's going to find herself dry-heaving over the toilet.

She sits across from her father and nibbles a piece of toast, willing the nausea to abate.

"I was thinking we could ride over to Chatham today to

visit your brother and show the boys some lighthouses," he suggests around a mouthful of egg.

"Joe, don't talk with your mouth full." Sue slides into the chair beside him, clasping a fresh cup of coffee.

He's always talked with his mouth full, Brynn wants to shout at her. *My mother gave up on trying to get him to stop. She used to laugh about it. So leave him alone!*

Instead, ignoring Sue—as does her father—she says, "That sounds great, but we can't go to Chatham today, Daddy. We have to get back home."

"Not until later."

"No, it's a holiday. There's going to be a ton of traffic leaving the Cape. I don't want to sit in it."

"But you haven't even seen your brother yet."

He's talking about Joey Jr., the oldest of the Costello boys, who lives just north of Chatham with his wife and three kids. He couldn't make the Saturday-night dinner, unlike her other two brothers, Charlie and Al, who live right here in town.

"We'll be back in a few weeks for Thanksgiving," she reminds her father. "I'll get to see Joey then."

"That's more than a few weeks. It's the end of November."

"Joe, cut it out. She's got a long drive alone with two little kids. Let her go early if she wants to. More toast, Brynn?"

She shakes her head at Sue's question, forcing down the sodden wad in her mouth.

"What's the big rush?" her father persists. "What time is the Professor coming home from that fancy meeting?"

The Professor. Her father gets a kick out of calling Garth that. Never out of respect, and never to his face.

Fancy meeting?

Yeah, Garth would love to hear his academic symposium thus described. Brynn finds herself already dreading the return visit for Thanksgiving.

"He's landing late this afternoon."

"So stay here with me awhile longer, baby girl." Her father reaches out to lightly pinch her cheek. "I don't get to see you enough anymore."

"Well, you could come visit us," Brynn suggests, noticing that there's more gray than black in her father's hair now. "We'd love it if you would."

He brushes her off, as always. "I don't know. It's a long drive. We'll get there when we can."

Brynn can feel Sue's sympathetic eyes on her, but she refuses to meet her gaze.

I wish she didn't know, Brynn finds herself thinking. *Of all the people in my life, why does she have to be the one who knows about the baby?*

It's not that she's afraid Sue will tell.

No, it just bothers Brynn that the one person with whom there's no love lost now knows the one thing she doesn't want anyone to know.

No, she immediately amends, *not the* one *thing.*

Far better that *this* secret has been spilled than the other one.

After all, her pregnancy will eventually have to be shared anyway.

Eventually, Garth will get used to the idea. He loves her; he'll love the baby.

But if he found out that she's been keeping this information about Rachel from him—from Rachel's family, from the authorities—for all these years . . .

Well, chances are, he wouldn't be so understanding.

Fiona is right, Brynn realizes with sudden clarity, imagining how her life would come tumbling down around her if they went to the authorities now.

I can't get caught up in something like that . . .

Detectives, lawyers, reporters. A public scandal, an investigation, a trial? Prison?

She has two children to raise and another on the way. What would Garth do if she was found guilty of a crime and had to serve time? He'd be left alone with the kids, not to mention that his reputation on campus might be severely damaged—guilt by association. He might lose his job.

Would he possibly stand by her? Forgive her?

Is he capable of that kind of unconditional love?

Unconditional love—that's what you get from a mother. Not necessarily from your spouse.

Brynn no longer has that person in her life. Someone who would staunchly support her if the whole world was against her. Someone who would step into her shoes and care for her children if she couldn't.

Yes, Fee is right. Why didn't I realize it before? We can't tell. No matter what.

"This isn't easy for me." Isaac forces himself to look directly at Kylah, seated beside him on the couch.

She shrugs, still wearing the carefully noncombatant expression she had donned when he woke her a few minutes ago and told her they have to talk.

"Now?" she asked, trying to burrow into her pillow.

"Now," he said.

He just spent a sleepless night thinking about his upcoming meeting with that detective, and he's well aware that his past might be on the verge of exploding into the present. He'd better prepare Kylah.

"I know you think I'm involved with someone else," he begins awkwardly.

She doesn't respond, verbally or physically.

"And I understand why you might think that."

"Because you are?"

"No. I'm not. I'm not cheating on you. That's not why I've been . . ."

He can't bring himself to say it.

She, however, can: "Lying to me?"

Isaac winces, wants to protest, but how can he? That's precisely what he's been doing.

"I'm sorry."

"You keep saying that. But you never say anything else."

"I know, and—" He bites back another *I'm sorry*.

He can't delay this any longer.

"I had a younger sister," he tells her abruptly.

Surprise alights in Kylah's widened eyes. She knows only about his older sister, Carolyn, who lives near his mother in North Carolina.

"She was a stepsister," he clarifies. "I never told you about her, because . . . Well, it's really hard for me." He takes a deep breath, lets it out shakily.

Kylah is silent. Waiting.

"Her name was Rachel."

Was.

"She died?"

"She disappeared. Ten years ago."

Kylah touches his arm. "Oh, my God. What happened?"

Struggling for emotional detachment, he briefly describes it in a couple of concise sentences that sound almost like a lead paragraph from one of the many decade-old newspaper articles.

Kylah shakes her head, trying to digest it. "Do you think somebody kidnapped her and killed her?"

He winces.

"I'm sorry," she says immediately. "I know how painful that had to be for you."

He nods.

Kylah falls silent. He can see the wheels turning.

Then she asks tentatively, "Ten years ago—Wasn't your dad married to Maggie?"

Maggie, of course, is his current stepmother, who is childless. Kylah hasn't met her, but she knows about her— and that his father was married twice before.

"Yes, he was married to Maggie then, but Rachel and I were still close."

"So—not to be . . . I mean, what does any of this have to do with your lying to me and sneaking around? And why didn't you tell me about her?"

Because I've tried that. With Lindsey, and with other girl-friends who came before her. In the end, every relationship I have falls apart because of Rachel. In the end, I get accused of being obsessed by another woman . . .

And you are, he reminds himself. Just not in the way they might think.

"I didn't tell you because I was trying to put it behind me," he tells Kylah. "And I really did, for awhile . . . But then, in September, when the anniversary rolled around again, I couldn't help it. It happens every year at this time. Sometimes in between, too. But every September, no matter how I tell myself to stay away, I have to go back up there, to Cedar Crest."

"Looking for clues?"

He nods.

Yes, he's looking for clues . . .

And looking for her.

Thinking maybe Rachel will decide her birthday is a good time for her to come back to life, so to speak.

"Do you think she might still be alive?" Kylah asks, as if she's read his mind. "Maybe she just took off and didn't want to be found."

"I don't know. Maybe."

"But, then again, she had to know what it would do to everyone she left behind. Why would anyone do something like that to their family and friends?"

Why, indeed.

"I have no idea," Isaac tells her.

Lying again.

But this is it.

This is as far as he's willing to go.

The rest of it is his alone. His, and Rachel's.

* * *

"Are you really going to work today?" Ashley grumbles from her leg-dangling perch on the counter as Fiona takes one last sip of her still-hot coffee, standing at the kitchen sink. "It's a national holiday. No one is working today."

"Plenty of people are working today. Doctors, soldiers, firemen—"

"Yeah, but they *have* to work. You don't."

"Yes, I do." Fiona dumps the remainder of her coffee down the drain and rinses the sink. "I have to support us."

Ashley says nothing.

Fiona turns away, knowing she wouldn't *have* to work this Monday holiday if she hadn't shirked both Saturday and Sunday.

Now she's fallen hopelessly behind, and it means spending all day today at the office, playing catch-up.

Which, Ashley's disappointment aside, is fine with her, really. She's used to it, and, anyway, it's not as though there's something better to do. James is back in Boston. She was hoping he'd call her last night, but he never did.

She's been trying to convince herself that he's just busy. That he isn't avoiding her now that they spent the night together.

But something tells her she may have gone too far and scared him off: the ultimate cliché.

The doorbell rings; that's the sitter.

Fiona was lucky to find one on short notice. At twelve, Andrea Carson is young to stay with Ashley for such a long day, but her older sister had plans. Anyway, it's not as though Fiona is leaving her with an infant.

"Make sure you eat some breakfast, Ash," Fiona says, picking up her satchel and quickly opening the top to make sure she has the files she needs.

"Can me and Andrea make pancakes?"

"No."

"Why not?"

Fiona bristles at her tone. "Cut it out, Ash, you know I don't like whining. And stop kicking your heels against the cupboards, you'll nick them."

"With bare feet?"

"Stop."

Ashley stops. "Why can't we make pancakes?"

Still whiny, but . . .

Choose your battles, Fiona reminds herself, as she so often did during the divorce.

"For one thing, because Andrea is just a kid and I don't want you two cooking when I'm not home. It's dangerous."

"If she's just a kid, why is she babysitting me?"

Ignoring that comment, Fiona continues, "For another thing, because pancakes aren't good for you. They're too sweet, and you've already had a cavity. Have cereal."

"I'm sick of cereal. I want pancakes."

Fiona looks up sharply from the file folder in her hand. It isn't like her daughter to make waves like this.

"What's wrong with you today, Ashley?"

"Nothing." Ashley idly toys with the handle of a knife sticking out from the Henckels set in the butcher block holder.

"Careful, Ashley, those knives are sharp." *And expensive,* Fiona wants to add, watching her daughter run a fingernail along the handle and hoping it doesn't leave a scratch mark.

"I'm not touching the blade. Just the handle."

"Leave it alone."

Ashley lifts her hand from the knife and scowls.

The doorbell rings again.

Fiona shrugs; she gives Ashley a kiss on the cheek and a quick squeeze. "Tonight when I get home, we'll get pizza and watch a movie. Okay?"

"What time will that be?"

"I don't know . . . around seven?"

"With you, Mom, that means nine. And it's a school night. You won't let me stay up that late."

"Tonight, I will." She pauses in the kitchen doorway. "How's that?"

"Good, I guess," Ashley says, and at least she's smiling when she looks up.

Fiona slings her bag over her shoulder and strides away to open the door.

Andrea Carson is one of those girls who will probably never take advantage of her potential—physical or otherwise. She's about fifteen pounds overweight, with acne and stringy hair. All of which can be remedied. In fact, every time Fiona sees her, she thinks, *If she were my daughter* . . .

But she isn't.

And Fiona's got enough on her plate without offering a makeover to the neighborhood ugly duckling.

"Hi, Mrs. Hagan."

Fiona's skin crawls at the name, but she doesn't bother to correct the girl. She's told her, how many times now, that she prefers to be called *Ms. Fitzgerald,* but it never sinks in.

"How are you today, Andrea?" She aims her key remote toward the BMW and hears it beep as she unlocks the doors.

"I'm good."

"So I'll be at the office, call me if you need—what is that?" she breaks off to ask, seeing that Andrea is holding out a package toward her.

"I don't know. It was propped against your door. It's for you, see?"

"I see," Fiona murmurs, staring at the block letters that read FIONA.

Quincy Hiles has never liked New York City.

Maybe that's because it's unfamiliar turf; he doesn't know his way around the vast network of streets, bridges, and tunnels.

Or maybe it's simply because this is the home of his hometown baseball team's archrivals.

Yeah, that's it. And maybe it's lame, but he can't help it. As a fan, he takes the sport almost as seriously as he did when he was playing it.

Routed off the New England Thruway by an accident, Quincy is riddled by unpleasant memories as he drives past Yankee Stadium with Connelly in the passenger's seat.

He finds himself telling Mike about the time, back when he was first married, that he and Bev spent a long weekend in New York and went to a ball game at Yankee Stadium.

Quincy wore a Red Sox cap—and came out feeling lucky to be alive. The Yankees weren't even playing the Sox that day; they were hosting the Blue Jays. But that didn't matter. Mercilessly heckling fans welcomed the telltale red *B* on Quincy's blue cap about as warmly as . . .

Well, as warmly as Fenway Park would have welcomed an intertwined white *NY* on a navy one.

Of course Quincy kept that cap on his head, no matter how much his wife begged him to take it off so they could enjoy the game in peace.

"No wonder she dumped you." Mike shakes his head. "You're a stubborn S.O.B., you know that?"

"Yeah, I know that. Comes in handy on the job."

But not in a marriage.

Now that he's on the verge of putting his career behind him, too, he wonders if he's ready to maybe start dating again. It's been years since his first feeble attempts after the divorce. He quickly concluded there was no room in his life for both women and work, so he chose work.

Maybe in retirement, though, he'll go back to women.

By the time they've reached midtown Manhattan, ninety traffic-snarled minutes later, his IBS is acting up. Not just because he's in Yankee territory, or thinking about dating again, but because of overall job stress.

And he's yawning so much he'd kill for a cup of coffee, but of course it's taboo.

He hasn't slept much the last few nights. Insomnia sets in whenever he's embroiled in a case like this.

Once, when Quincy's daughter Sondra was about ten, the two of them spent a rainy beach-vacation day working on a puzzle they found in their rented condo. No matter how hard they tried, they couldn't put it together. Finally, they realized that an entire cluster of key pieces was missing—and that someone had dumped stray pieces from a similar puzzle into the box.

Quincy can't help but feel that this case is like that. He was in the process of solving one puzzle when pieces of another started popping up.

In terms of the original questions surrounding Matilda Harrington's death, they still haven't been able to corroborate Ray Wilmington's story about her secret romance.

And Wilmington still isn't talking. It doesn't help that his mother keeps going on and on about the shame he's brought to her, and that he lost his job in the wake of all this. For him, that was apparently the final straw. It's as if some switch in his brain has cut off any willingness to communicate on any level. Of course, the detectives have him under constant surveillance, and they keep bringing him in for questioning, but no one is making any headway with Wilmington's monosyllabic answers.

Quincy's gut tells him that that whole angle is a dead end, though. Why would Wilmington—or some secret boyfriend, married or dirt poor or not—leave a scrap of sorority sweater at the crime scene?

He probably wouldn't.

That piece of evidence was left to taunt the police, to send some kind of message—a message that seems to be somehow tied to Matilda's sorority-girl past.

Yes, Quincy is stumped, despite having spent yesterday with Deb at the Zeta Delta Kappa house learning as much as they could about Matilda Harrington's college years, and

Rachel Lorent's disappearance. The housemother was as helpful as she could be, but she doesn't have any answers.

She did provide the names of several of Matilda Harrington's close friends from her sorority days: Brynn Saddler, Fiona Fitzgerald, and Cassandra Ashford.

Quincy couldn't reach any of them by telephone last night and opted not to leave messages. He'll try them again.

Meanwhile, he and Mike are going to talk to Isaac Halpern, who agreed to meet him this morning. Quincy said they were contacting everyone who attended Matilda Harrington's memorial service, and Halpern seemed to take the interview request pretty much in stride.

Walking into the relatively quiet diner on East Twenty-Second Street with Mike, Quincy immediately recognizes Halpern. He's sitting alone in a booth toward the back, nursing a cup of coffee.

"You guys didn't drive all the way down to New York just to talk to me, did you?" he asks after the detectives have been seated, dutifully shown him their badges, and ordered: coffee for Mike, herbal tea for Quincy.

"It's routine," he assures Halpern, thinking that with his dark good looks and natural charisma, he doesn't seem like the kind of person who might have anything to do with a grisly murder.

But then, Quincy reminds himself, neither did the notorious Scott Peterson, or Ted Bundy, or countless other depraved killers who had everyone around them fooled.

True, only the slimmest fraction of psychopaths are cold-blooded murderers, but those who are can expertly pass themselves off as loving husbands, caring fathers, loyal sons . . . and, yes, concerned brothers.

"Tell us about your sister," he urges Isaac.

"My sister? I thought we were going to talk about Matilda Harrington. Not that I know much about her, like I said."

"She was friends with your sister, though," Mike points out.

"Right."

"Have you been in touch with her since Rachel disappeared?"

"Her, personally? No."

Quincy tilts his head skeptically. "But you came to her funeral anyway."

"Because I've been in touch with Puffy, and because . . ." Isaac looks him in the eye with surprising fortitude. "Because I'm still looking for Rachel, okay? And anyone or anything connected to her is of interest to me."

"Why?"

"My sister was a tiny little thing who never hurt anybody. She disappeared—*on her birthday*—when she was living in the Zeta sorority house. Ten years later, a Zeta girl is killed—on her birthday. Do you think that's a coincidence?"

No, Quincy thinks, as beside him, Mike shrugs. *I sure as hell don't.*

"Tell us about your sister, Isaac," Connelly suggests, leaning back.

"What do you want to know?"

"Everything."

Isaac Halpern begins to talk.

By the time he's finished, the detectives know a lot about Rachel Lorent.

But not as much as you do, Quincy thinks, watching the younger man glumly sip his coffee. *You're not telling us everything. Not by a long shot.*

Brynn is momentarily disappointed to see that Garth's car isn't in the driveway when she pulls in at eleven thirty Monday morning.

But, of course, she knew it wouldn't be.

When she packed up the kids and left her father's house early this morning, she was well aware that Garth's flight wouldn't be landing until late afternoon.

Brynn told her father and Sue she wanted to beat the holiday weekend traffic off the Cape, which is true.

But it's not the only reason she made a hasty retreat. *You didn't want to spend part of yet another day with Sue sneaking those curious little looks at you . . . and your belly.*

But now that she's here without Garth, long hours stretching ahead in an empty house, she wishes she had waited a little longer.

Mostly because she misses him, and not . . .

Not because she's scared.

Yes, you are. Admit it.

All right, she *is* scared.

Even in broad daylight, with all those dead bolts.

Being back here in Cedar Crest is bringing back the nightmarish feeling that somebody is hiding in the shadows. Somebody who knows her darkest secret.

"I'm thirsty," Caleb announces, climbing out of the car as she unbuckles a snoozing Jeremy from his booster seat.

She snaps back into mommy mode, welcoming the intrusion. "All right, we'll go in and get you some juice."

"Apple?"

"If we have it." Brynn kisses her younger son's head. "Hey, come on, little guy, wake up."

Jeremy opens his eyes sleepily and closes them again.

Smiling, she brushes pretzel crumbs off the backseat and gathers tossed sippy cups, crumpled napkins, and the ziplock bags Sue had filled with dry cereal for the boys to snack on.

"Come on, Jeremy." Brynn gently tries again, this time nudging him out of his seat.

"Tired," he complains, rubbing his eyes.

"I hear ya. I wouldn't mind a nap myself right now."

But she really should get the kids back outdoors as soon as she unloads the car. It's a beautiful autumn morning. Birds call from red and gold boughs overhead and the Chases' leaf blower is humming in the background.

Maybe she'll take the boys to the park. There won't be many more days like this before another dismal mountain winter blows in.

"Mommy! What's this?"

She looks up to see Caleb holding up a rectangular package wrapped in brown paper.

"Where was it?"

"By the door. It says B-R-Y-N-N—hey, that's your name!" he announces, pleased with himself. "I read it, Mom!"

"Great job!"

But there's a tremble in her voice.

Which is absurd, really . . . because it's just a package.

You must have ordered something and forgotten about it.

So there's absolutely no reason for goose bumps.

Yet there they are, on her forearms, and each pale hair there standing on high alert.

She looks over her shoulder. The sidewalk and the street behind her are deserted.

Stop this. It's crazy. Everything is fine. The sun is shining and the neighbors are around and you're on familiar territory.

Yes. Just like her kitchen was familiar territory, in broad daylight, when she discovered that dead cardinal.

Brynn closes the car door with her hip and leads Jeremy toward the house with one anxious hand, holding the backseat clutter in the other.

"Let's see the label, Caleb," she says when she reaches the steps.

"There's no label. See?" He tilts the package toward her and she sees that her name is scrawled in black marker.

No answer at Brynn's house, still.

This time, Fiona leaves a message, talking in a low voice from the upstairs extension though Ashley and the babysitter are two stories below, playing Yahtzee in the basement.

"Brynn, it's me. You have to call me the second you get home. It's really important." She hesitates, wanting to say more, but she doesn't dare. What if Garth gets the message first?

After hanging up, Fiona paces across her bedroom again. Stopping in front of the window, she lifts a corner of the shade and peeks out onto the street.

She half-expects to find a figure standing right there on the sidewalk, watching her.

But she sees no one other than a couple of neighborhood kids playing hopscotch halfway down the block.

That doesn't mean someone isn't concealed in the shadows of a hedge or parked car, keeping an eye on her house.

Fiona shudders, drops the shade, and dials Cassie's number. Again.

She probably isn't home yet either, but—

"Hello?"

Greeted by an unfamiliar baritone, Fiona hesitates before asking, "Is Cassie there?"

"No. Who is this?"

"Who is this?" she counters, heart pounding.

"Her fiancé. Alec."

"Oh." Fiona sinks to the edge of the bed in relief, feeling slightly foolish.

What were you expecting? Did you think he'd say, "This is the crazed psycho who killed your friend Tildy, and now I've come for Cassie, too"?

"Who is this?" he asks again.

"I'm sorry, it's her friend Fiona."

"From the sorority."

"Right."

"You were with her yesterday in Boston, then?"

"Yes," Fiona says, then immediately wishes she hadn't.

"Where the hell is she?" Alec demands.

"You mean . . . She never came home from Boston?"

"No. She told me she was going away for awhile, but that's not like her, and—do you have any idea where she might be?"

"No," Fiona says slowly, "I don't."

And, frankly, right now, considering what I just found on my doorstep, I hope nobody else does, either.

"Ouch."

That cut, the deepest one just beneath the right eye, really smarts.

Who would have guessed that Cassandra Ashford, who, through the years gave in to everyone's will but her own, would have fought so violently?

Not that I expected her to curl up and die for me, but still . . .

These scratches are going to take awhile to heal. A thick layer of makeup covers them somewhat, but it doesn't look natural.

It would be a good idea to lay low for a few days, at least.

All things considered, though, Cassandra Ashford was another success.

True, she was supposed to die at home, just as Tildy did.

But this was better. Much better.

Her being tucked away up in Maine, miles from civilization, has bought some time. It throws everyone off for a bit. Maintains the element of surprise.

So, thank you for running scared, Cassie. I didn't think you had it in you to shake things up that way.

Chances are, nobody's going to find her for awhile. Those cabins don't have housekeeping services. Hers is one of the most secluded, and there won't be many people around there after today, anyway.

Plus, she paid rent for the rest of October. The receipt was on a table in the cabin, made out to a Marsha Johnson.

Marsha . . .

No doubt a sly tribute to Marshmallow, her beloved horse.

Marshmallow is also the password for her online e-mail account. That wasn't hard to guess. Trial and error, and . . . bingo! You're logged in.

Ah, Cassie. You should have galloped away on horseback. If you had, I might not have found you.

Because, of course, you can't plant a homing device on an animal without some groomer eventually finding it.

Poor Cassie. She had no way of ever guessing that the surprise party invitation wasn't the only thing left behind on her car that day at Glenwood Springhouse.

Now, to further delay the identification of her body whenever it is found, her car has been moved to a remote part of the camp, the homing device removed.

There was some satisfaction in watching the car go sailing over the edge of a ravine, landing in a crumpled heap in the dense woods at the bottom.

And, yes, I left it there, Cassie.

You know why? Because it's just a heap of metal . . . not a person, for God's sake.

Funny, how the decade-old ache hasn't subsided a bit now that yet another so-called sister has paid for what she did.

If anything, it's grown more intense; the need for vengeance more urgent than ever before.

But, once again, there's nothing to do but settle in and wait.

Quincy Hiles is in the passenger's seat for a change, with Mike at the wheel as they sit in late-afternoon holiday weekend traffic on the Mass Pike.

He's mulling over their provocative conversation with Isaac when his phone rings.

It's Deb Jackson.

"Where are you?"

Greeted with only that brusque question, Quincy provides an equally brusque answer. "On the road."

"Listen, something just happened with Wilmington."

"What happened?"

"We went over there to bring him in for more questioning . . ."

"Yeah." That's nothing new; they've been on him relentlessly, determined to get him to crack.

"So his mother said he was still in bed."

"Yeah."

"What's going on?" Mike asks, eavesdropping on Quincy's end of the conversation.

Quincy holds up his index finger as Deb goes on, "We told her to go wake him up. She went up there and the next thing we know, there's a hysterical scream."

"What happened?"

"Wilmington's dead, Quincy. He slit his wrists."

Quincy emits a shocked expletive.

"What?" Mike asks. "What the hell happened?"

"That's not all," Deb goes on breathlessly in Quincy's ear. "He left a note. And you're not gonna believe this . . ."

"What are we going to do?" Brynn asks, elbows propped on the kitchen table, forehead buried in her hands.

"I don't know." Fee is uncharacteristically desolate, staring into space, cell phone in hand. "I just wish Cassie would return our calls."

"I know." She pauses, trying to phrase her next words.

"What if," she says carefully, "we went to the police—wait, don't interrupt," she adds when Fiona opens her mouth, "and we didn't tell them anything about what happened with Rachel? What if we just told them what's going on now, and that somebody is obviously threatening us, and let the police take it from there?"

"How long do you think it's going to take them to figure out that what's going on now has something to do with something that happened in the past? Specifically, when we were in college?"

Brynn shakes her head. Fiona is right. She just keeps sending it around and around her thought processes, hoping to come up with some new spin on things.

But no matter how you look at it, there's no way they can go to the police without incriminating themselves. If not right away, then eventually.

"Hang in there, Brynn." Fiona gives her hand a pat.

"If Cassie would just call us back . . . You did leave her a message on her cell phone voice mail, right?"

"Three."

"I swear, I really can't take much more of this . . . And Garth is going to be home in a couple of hours, and I don't know how I'm going to keep this from—"

"Just calm down, will you?" Fiona almost sounds like her take-charge self again.

Almost. But her green eyes are tinged with uncharacteristic trepidation.

"Cassie said she was going to take off, remember?" Fee goes on. "And she told Alec the same thing."

"That doesn't mean she's safe."

"No, but we both know there's no reason for us to start panicking until we know for sure something's happened to—"

"Stop!" Brynn holds up a hand to cut her off. "Don't even say it, Fee. I can't stand it."

"I'm sorry." Fiona takes a cigarette from her pack, toying with it for a moment before holding it up and asking Brynn hopefully, "Can I—?"

"God, no." The mere thought of smoke turns her stomach.

Fiona puts away the cigarette.

They fall silent again, listening to Caleb and Jeremy laughing together as they build a Lego city in the living room.

Brynn hugs herself, still quaking from her latest bathroom bout with nausea. This time, it has nothing at all to do with her pregnancy and everything to do with what she found inside the parcel left by her front door.

There was an identical one at Fee's door.

Both packages contained framed copies of their sorority composite picture from ten years ago.

Four smiling faces are circled in thick black marker: Brynn's, Fiona's, Cassie's, and Tildy's.

And both Cassie's and Tildy's are crossed out with an ominous, blood-red *X*.

"He was about to blackmail her to get the cash he needed to save his mother's house."

Deb is talking about Ray Wilmington and Matilda Harrington.

"He admitted that in his suicide note?" Quincy tilts the phone out from his ear so that Mike can hear, too.

"He sure as hell did admit it. And you know why?"

"Why, what?"

"Why he could blackmail her?"

Quincy hates guessing games. "Cut the crap and tell me, Jackson."

"You're not going to believe this," Deb says again, obviously sitting on something that's going to blow the case wide-open, and relishing Quincy's suspense.

"Try me."

"Because not only did he find out that Matilda Harrington was sneaking around with a married man—"

Bingo, Quincy thinks.

"—but because of who that married man happens to be."

"Wilmington knew who he was, then?"

"*Everyone* knows who he is."

Deb pauses.

If Quincy was in a room with her, he'd be tempted to collar her and shake her right about now.

"Who is he, Jackson?"

Deb announces almost gleefully, "The holier-than-thou Republican governor who's supposed to be running for president; the one with the wife and triplets. Troy Allerson."

PART IV

HAPPY BIRTHDAY,
DEAR FIONA

CHAPTER 18

Amazing, Brynn can't help but think as the month wears on, how daily life can whisk you along like a moving sidewalk.

Regardless of where your head and heart are, regardless of almost constant apprehension, you just keep moving forward physically, propelled through each day from dawn to dusk with almost disconcerting normalcy.

It's been over a week now since she got home from the Cape.

Over a week since both she and Fiona received that bone-chillingly altered composite sorority picture.

At least they've both heard from Cassie since they said good-bye to her that Saturday in Boston, when she said she was thinking of going into hiding.

Apparently, that's what she's done.

She's sent a couple of reassuring e-mails to Brynn and Fiona:

> *Hi, guys, just wanted to let you know I'm safe. Let me know that you are, too.—Cassie*

*Me again. Still hanging in there. Hoping to come
home soon.—Cassie*

*Just checking in. Hope you guys are okay. Miss
you.—Cassie*

Brynn wrote back every time, telling Cassie that she and
Fiona are fine.

But Tildy . . .

Tildy is gone.

Every time she thinks about what happened to her, Brynn
wants to scream, cry, faint, vomit.

But, miraculously, she doesn't do any of those things . . .

Well, except vomit. Mostly in the mornings.

Garth has yet to catch on, though. For him, things seem to
be status quo.

His flight was delayed several hours on Monday night because of a mechanical failure. There was trouble with one of
the engines before takeoff; he called from the plane to say it
was being repaired. Predictably, he was a nervous wreck—
too nervous, at least, to note any tension in Brynn's voice.

By the time he got home late that night, she was asleep.
She was dimly aware of him leaning over to kiss her, whispering, "I'm home," but she was too exhausted to fully
wake up.

Nor did he stir when she woke to find him sleeping beside
her in their bed—just before she ran to the bathroom.

The past week the Saddlers have resumed their usual routine: Garth coming and going from campus; Brynn carting
the boys around, doing the housework, making meals.

All the while, she can think of little but that ominous picture she hid behind stacked sweaters on the top shelf in her
closet.

But she can't do anything about it.

Unless she wants to risk upsetting the already precarious
balance of her life.

And she doesn't dare. Not right now, anyway.

So, like Fiona, she's come to realize that there's simply nothing the two of them can do now.

Nothing but wait.

Feeling, every second, as though they're playing out their lives in the crosshairs of an invisible rifle scope.

"That's it. Emily . . . You're fired."

"What?"

"You heard me." Seated at her desk, Fiona waves her hand at the girl. "Get your stuff and go."

"But—"

"You're fired," she repeats.

"Who are you supposed to be, Donald Trump?" Emily protests, her intended sarcasm largely overshadowed by blatant dismay. "You can't fire me for one little mistake. That's not f—"

"I can, I did, and I'll mail your last paycheck. Get moving."

Emily hovers in the doorway of Fiona's office another split second before she turns and scurries away. Moments later, Fiona hears her close the outer door.

"Good riddance," she mutters, and lights a cigarette with a shaking hand. Screw the no-smoking rule.

She realizes Emily left behind her open can of Diet Pepsi on Fiona's side table, where she set it—without using a coaster, of course.

I doubt she'll be back for it.

I doubt she'd even come back for her paycheck if I don't mail it.

Maybe I shouldn't.

Fiona inhales a stream of smoke—and with it, all right, maybe a bit of remorse. But it doesn't last for long.

She'll send Emily her paycheck, but she won't feel bad about firing her. This has been a long time coming.

And it wasn't about just one little mistake, as Emily claimed. She's made plenty.

But this one, in particular, is unforgivable.

Emily forgot to send out an important client document. She took it with her to Mail Boxes Etc., and lost it somewhere along the way. Then she apparently forgot all about it.

"What do you mean, you *forgot?*" Fiona demanded of Emily, who shrugged.

Fiona was already having a bad day before this happened. A bad week, really.

All right, perhaps the worst week she's ever had in her life.

What with that creepy picture showing up on her doorstep, Cassie still in hiding but sending e-mails, Brynn calling her every five minutes, skittish and apparently just making sure Fiona is still alive, and her own birthday looming just days away . . .

And then there's James.

He hasn't returned her calls in the last few days.

He had an assistant return them . . . as though he assumed she might be calling him about something business-related.

Of course, she had to pretend that she was.

She even tried e-mailing him, yesterday—a simple *Hi, what's up?*—but there's been no reply.

So, yes, she's been in a foul mood.

And, yes, Emily was on the receiving end of the inevitable fallout just now.

But she deserves it. She screwed up.

And now I'm going to have to deal with an irate client, and a million stupid, mindless administrative details Emily should have been taking care of.

She doesn't need any of that. Especially not now.

The phone rings.

Speak of the devil, she thinks dismally. It's probably her client.

The phone rings again.

It takes Fiona another moment to remember that she has to pick it up herself.

"Fiona Fitzgerald Public Relations."

"Hey, it's me," her twin sister says. "I've had three messages from you in, like, three days. What's up?"

"Where the heck have you been and why don't you get a real phone?"

"I've been here, and this *is* a real phone."

"Then why don't you return calls?"

"Because you keep asking me if I'm coming up there for our birthday this weekend, and I'm still not sure what I want to do."

"Well, it's not like it's months away, so, obviously, you aren't coming."

"Not necessarily. I've been toying around with it."

"Is it that Antoinette doesn't want you to come up? Because you're both welcome."

"No, she actually thinks I should come. And she can't, herself, but she doesn't care about that."

"So do you want me to buy you a ticket?" Fiona offers, and takes a deep drag off her cigarette, trying to calm her nerves.

"No, I can get my own ticket."

"It'll cost you a fortune."

"Haven't you ever heard of last-minute ticket deals?"

"So get one."

"I will . . . if I decide to come."

"Dee"—the childhood nickname spills from her lips and her sister doesn't protest—"please come."

"I might."

"But you might not. Where's Antoinette? Put her on the line."

"Why?"

"Because I'm going to tell her to bring you to an airport and put you on a plane."

"She doesn't follow orders, and, anyway, she's not here right now. Listen, Fee, if I can get there, I will. I even still have the key to your house, so maybe you'll come home from work and I'll be there to surprise you. Okay?"

Fiona hesitates. *No. That's not good enough. I need you. Now.*

That's what she wants to tell her twin.

Instead, she says just, "Okay, try hard," and hears her voice crack.

Terrific, she's on the verge of tears.

"Fee? Are you all right?"

"I'm fine." She sinks the remains of her cigarette in Emily's Diet Pepsi can. "Call me when you know what you're doing."

As she hangs up, Fiona hears a muffled movement in the next room.

Someone is there.

For over a week now, Quincy has been trying to figure out where that piece of an old sorority sweater fits into the Harrington case.

The fact is, it fits in about as well as Governor Troy Allerson would fit in working a factory assembly line.

If it wasn't for that scrap of gray and red wool—which lab tests proved were embedded with microscopic particles of soil and vegetation ordinarily found at a much higher elevation—Quincy would be feeling a lot better about Allerson as a potential suspect.

No, he doesn't doubt what Ray Wilmington revealed in his rambling note, which was primarily an apology to his mother for the shame he had brought her.

Sprinkled in with ad nauseam *Please forgive me*'s and *I never meant to hurt you*'s was that believable revelation about Matilda's clandestine relationship with her godfather.

There's not a doubt in Quincy's jaded mind that a man like Allerson, whose esteemed and promising political career is built entirely on his wholesome family-man image, would kill in order to protect that image.

So maybe he jilted Matilda and she threatened to go to his wife. Or the press.

More likely, maybe Ray Wilmington made that threat, as he claimed.

Blackmail.

That was why Ray was hanging around that night in front of the victim's house.

He confessed that he was planning to extort money from her in exchange for keeping quiet about her affair with Allerson. When he saw that she was inebriated—a fact corroborated by the coroner's office—he left without confronting her.

Or so he claimed in his letter.

He also claimed that he never approached Allerson at all.

Quincy's team is doing its best to gather evidence of the high-profile politician's involvement with Matilda Harrington. But so far, they're having a hell of a time. Allerson covered his tracks remarkably well.

Not just the affair, but the murder as well, if he really was behind it.

Citing routine procedure, Mike and Deb questioned him yesterday, to no avail. They even came right out and asked him, point-blank, about an affair. They said he went pale, but kept his composure, and admitted nothing.

Wilmington didn't come right out in his letter and accuse Allerson of the murder. He didn't even write that he saw him there the night of the murder.

But did he?

They'll never know.

Quincy can't help but acknowledge that a guy like Allerson pays people to cook for him, clean for him, shop for him, and probably to buff his toenails. He wouldn't choose to get blood—even if it is blue blood, like his own—all over that fancy wardrobe of his. Not if he could help it.

Did he hire someone to do it for him? The lack of prints

at the scene would indicate premeditation and, perhaps, professionalism.

But the overkill element would seem to indicate a crime of passion. Or is the demonstration of passion deliberate, intended to cover up the real motive?

And what about the bizarre calling card left at the scene? None of it fits together.

And it's giving Quincy one hell of a perpetual stomachache.

For a moment, Fiona sits, absolutely frozen, her thoughts whirling immediately to Tildy's murder.

What if . . . ?

Suddenly, she finds herself more outraged than afraid.

She takes her jewel-handled letter opener from her desk and clutches it in her hand like a weapon.

Then, holding her breath, her pulse roaring in her own ears, she sneaks over to the door and pulls it open a crack.

Emily is back, furtively going through the top drawer of the desk . . . which happens to be where Fiona keeps the petty cash.

"What are you doing?" she asks sharply, and the girl jumps and presses a hand to the base of her throat.

"You scared me."

"Ditto." Fiona tosses the letter opener back on her desk. "I thought you left."

"I did, but . . ." She trails off.

"What are you doing?" Fiona repeats.

"Just looking for that package. I thought if I could find it—I really need this job."

"Forget it. You're done. I have a copy of it that I can print out and send again, and I wouldn't give you your job back even if I thought you really were looking for the original."

Emily's eyes flare. "Are you calling me a liar?"

Fiona shrugs.

Emily slams the drawer closed so hard the framed photo of Ashley on its surface tips over. "Fine, I'm out of here."

"Wait." Fiona reaches around the corner into her office, then extends the can of Diet Pepsi. "This is yours."

Emily storms silently out the door, carrying the can.

Watching her go, Fiona finds herself smiling for the first time all day.

The ringing telephone startles Brynn from a sound sleep, and it takes her a moment to get her bearings.

Oh. Right. It's the middle of the afternoon, and she's taking a nap on the couch while Jeremy takes one in his bed.

The cordless phone is on the coffee table; she set it there after she hung up with Garth right after lunch. He said he'll be home late tonight . . . again.

He's been working full speed ahead on his book, fueled, apparently, by his experience at the symposium. He's spent every weeknight and most of this past weekend at the campus library.

Snatching up the phone before the ringing can wake Jeremy, Brynn is surprised—and dismayed—to hear Fiona's voice.

"What's wrong?" she asks immediately. Fee rarely calls her; it's usually the other way around. Especially during a workday.

"I have an offer for you."

Brynn relaxes her grip on the phone a bit. So it isn't bad news. Thank goodness.

"What kind of offer?"

"How would you like to earn some cash?"

"How?" Maybe Fiona needs her to stuff envelopes again. Brynn did that for her last year, from home, and earned enough to replace the broken bedroom television.

"I need a new assistant. I just fired Emily."

"Oh . . . Fee, I can't come to work for you."

"Why not?"

"Because I have Jeremy." *And another child on the way.*

"You can put him in day care. The woman I used for Ashley is still—"

"Fee, stop, I can't put him in day care."

"Why not?" Fiona answers her own question. "It's not that you can't, it's that you won't."

"You're right. I won't. I'm a stay-at-home mom, Fee. That means I stay at home."

"But you guys are pinched for cash. You've said it yourself. How about if you just help me out temporarily, until I can hire someone full time?"

"I can't. I'm sorry."

"Fine. I just thought I'd try to help you out, but . . ."

No, you didn't. You thought I'd help you *out.*

"Thanks anyway," Brynn tells her. "Good luck finding someone."

Fiona hangs up without saying another word.

If Cassandra Ashford's corpse has been found by now, it hasn't been identified yet.

That's going to be an interesting challenge for the investigators when they can't immediately find her wallet, her car—her fingers, or her teeth, either.

It was worth the extra time to painstakingly pull them out and pocket them, rendering Missing Persons' dental records useless. And cutting off her hands to eliminate her fingerprints took no time at all.

It *was* a challenge to dispose of the teeth and hands, but they're well hidden, buried a good foot beneath the earth, several yards into fairly remote underbrush off a highway somewhere in central Massachusetts. The wallet was tossed into a strip-mall Dumpster, the identification removed, and burned.

So when somebody finally does check that cabin, and finds a decomposing corpse—wearing a pointy party hat, of course, and surrounded by birthday party trappings—it won't immediately be clear that it belongs to Cassandra Ashford of Danbury, Connecticut. She herself made sure of that, having used cash and a pseudonym to maintain her anonymity.

So she was running for her life, obviously. Which is why her family has yet to even report her missing. She probably told them she was going away for awhile.

Nobody is looking for her.

Some hapless soul will have to stumble across her by accident.

Eventually, of course, the gory details will wind up in some police database, as well, perhaps, as in the press, and a connection will be made to Matilda Harrington's murder.

But for now, as far as the authorities know, that was an isolated incident.

Which means not only are the police probably not looking for Cassandra Ashford . . .

But they aren't looking for me, either.

Not yet, anyway.

Now what? Fiona wonders, lighting a new cigarette from the one in her hand.

She really thought Brynn would jump at the chance to get out of the house, where, as far as Fiona can tell, she's spent her days cooped up and paranoid.

Plus, she can probably use some extra money, especially with Christmas coming.

Never mind the fact that I'm left in a lurch without an assistant and I really need her, Fiona thinks, stubbing out the original cigarette and inhaling the new one.

Who else is there?

Deirdre.

Maybe she should just come right out and ask her sister

for help, instead of beating around the bush, inviting her to come up for their birthday as if everything is just fine.

Yes, she should have asked Deirdre for help, and she should have told her what's going on. She should have admitted that she needs her . . .

Because I'm alone. And I'm scared. And I have no one else.

She dials her sister's cell phone.

It rings several times and goes into voice mail.

"Dammit," Fiona mutters, and shakes her head. She hangs up rather than leave a message she knows will go unanswered for several days, and tries a new tactic.

Clutching her cigarette between her lips, she flips through her Rolodex to find her sister's girlfriend's number.

Antoinette answers on the second ring.

"Hi, it's Fiona!"

There's a brief pause.

"Fiona? What's going on?" Antoinette asks in her lilting island patois.

"I'm just looking for my sister and I know she doesn't answer her phone so I hoped you'd answer yours and put her on."

"I would if I could, but I can't," Antoinette tells her. "She's gone."

"Gone?"

"We broke up, and Deirdre moved out over a month ago. I have no idea where she went."

I can't keep doing this, Garth tells himself as he peeks into the boys' room, bathed in the golden glow of a Sponge-Bob night-light. His sons are both sound asleep.

Of course they are.

It's five in the morning.

Garth closes the door quietly and tiptoes down the hall,

past the master bedroom where Brynn, too, was deep in slumber when he looked in on her a moment ago.

This is nothing new, this creeping around his own house in the dead of night. But lately, it feels wrong.

He has to start coming home at a reasonable hour again so that he can see his children, eat with them, tuck them into bed. He has to start being a better father. And, yes, a better husband.

In the den, he settles into his recliner with a newspaper and a mug of herbal tea. He's feeling too keyed up to sleep, but maybe if he reads, and sips—

Somewhere in the house, a door creaks.

Footsteps scurry.

Another door closes.

One of the boys? Garth bolts from his chair and makes a beeline for the hall, where he sees a crack of light beneath the closed bathroom door.

Relieved, he pulls it open, expecting to see Caleb trying to avert one of his infrequent bed-wetting episodes.

But there's Brynn, kneeling on the floor in front of the toilet, throwing up.

"Hey," Garth says gently, and touches her hair. "You've got that stomach bug? It's going around on campus."

She says nothing, and continues retching.

When she's finished, she stands, looking wan, and rinses her mouth at the sink.

"I hope the boys don't catch it." Garth takes a towel that's dangling from the broken-off towel bar's protruding prong and hands it to her.

Brynn takes it from him and wipes her face and hands, saying, "Yeah, so do I."

Fiona reaches over to turn off her alarm clock the minute before it's set to go off.

She often wakes before it does, but this morning is different.

It's different because she didn't wake up; she hasn't slept at all.

Paranoia—fueled by Tildy's murder and Cassie's disappearing act—has taken over now.

Fiona has spent the last eight hours coming to terms with the fact that she's entirely alone. James hasn't called her. Emily is gone, and Brynn won't step in to help, and her business is too much to manage single-handedly. Especially now. And Deirdre . . .

God, even her twin sister has lied to her and fallen off the face of the earth.

That, of course, was the final blow. Deirdre is a grown woman; she has a right not to answer her phone or return calls. But why didn't she at least confide in Fiona about the breakup?

According to Antoinette, Deirdre was probably afraid to admit to Fiona that their relationship didn't make it.

"That's because she was always proud that she had succeeded in the only place where you had failed. She said you were good at everything. You had everything she didn't: a college degree, a great kid, money, a thriving business right there in your hometown where everyone respects you. Deirdre always said she could never live up to all that."

Antoinette's words stung. It never occurred to Fiona that her sister had an inferiority complex—and that she could hide it so well for all these years.

For Fiona, it's as if the invisible cord that joined her to her twin has suddenly snapped, and she's been catapulted into an alternate universe where nothing is familiar.

And danger is lurking at every turn.

Maybe she's wrong about that.

But Fiona can't afford to take any chances.

Because if she doesn't do something drastic . . .

If she just continues to go about her daily business from now until Sunday . . .

She might not live to see Monday.

She knows what she has to do.

And she knows that there are only two people she can possibly ask for help.

One is Brynn. She'll agree to help. With this, anyway. Fee can count on her.

As for the other . . .

Fiona can only cross her fingers and hope she won't be rebuffed.

She picks up her purse and makes sure she has several quarters for the pay phone down the block. She isn't even going to risk making a call from here.

Maybe it's paranoia, but she can't help feeling like the walls have eyes and ears.

You should have told him.

The refrain has been running through Brynn's head all day.

This morning, when Garth caught her being sick in the bathroom, would have been the perfect opportunity to break the news of her pregnancy.

She actually thought for a moment that it was so obviously morning sickness, he would *have* to figure it out.

But no, not Garth. He cluelessly assumed it was a stomach bug, thus letting her off the hook.

You still could have told him.

You should *have told him.*

And she will.

Yes, over the coming weekend, provided he doesn't spend every minute of it in the campus library again.

At the moment, her primary concern is returning a call to Fiona. There was a message from her just now, when Brynn returned from Stop & Shop with a carload of groceries and Jeremy, who is hungry for lunch.

"Brynn, it's Fee, just give me a call as soon as you can." Fiona paused for a moment, then added, *"Don't worry, this isn't about working for me, and it isn't about Cassie or anything like that."*

Brynn is grateful for that reassuring addendum. Still, she won't delay calling Fee back. She hasn't spoken to her since yesterday, when Fee all but hung up on her when she turned down the job offer.

Brynn dials her office number. The groceries can wait in the car for a few more minutes, and Jeremy can temporarily occupy himself with a plastic tub full of cars and trucks on the living room floor.

"Fiona Fitzgerald Public Relations, Fiona speaking."

So she hasn't found a temporary receptionist yet. "Hey, it's Brynn. What's going on?"

There's a pause.

"I'll call you back in a few minutes, okay?"

"Okay."

Puzzled, Brynn hangs up and waits.

Almost a full five minutes, wondering with increasing anxiety if she should forget about Fee and go get the groceries.

Then the phone rings, and the caller ID number is unfamiliar.

She hesitates before picking up.

It's Fiona.

"Where are you?"

"On a pay phone."

"Why?"

"Just listen, and don't say anything specific in case someone is listening on your end."

"Nobody's here but Jeremy," Brynn says, but her voice is hushed and she looks around uneasily just the same.

"Brynn, I need a favor."

Of course you do.

"As long as it's not about my working there—"

"I already told you it isn't. I have to go away for a few days."

"On business?"

"Brynn—my birthday is Sunday."

Oh. Of course.

It isn't that Brynn hasn't been aware that every passing day brings Fiona's milestone ominously closer. She just assumed, because Fee hasn't brought it up, that she isn't worried about it.

But clearly, she is. And in the face of her friend's unprecedented vulnerability, Brynn is left feeling as though she herself is precariously clinging to the sheer face of a massive rock wall, and one of her sturdy iron toeholds has just been plucked out from under her.

"What do you need, Fee? Whatever it is . . . You know I'm here."

"I need two things. One is absolute secrecy. You can't tell another living soul that I'm going away."

"I won't."

"I mean it, Brynn. Not Garth. Not your kids. Not my kid."

"You're not telling Ashley?"

"I'm not telling *anyone*. This is her weekend with Pat. He picks her up from school today and he doesn't bring her back until Sunday."

"Sunday is your birthday."

"That's where you come in, Brynn." Fiona lets out a deep breath.

She's a nervous wreck, Brynn realizes, and her own anxiety kicks up another notch.

"I need you to be at my place, waiting, when Pat drops off Ashley Sunday morning at eleven. Make sure you have the boys with you—Ashley will jump at the chance to spend time with them. Just bring her home with you and keep her there for me, until you hear from me. Bring her to school Monday, and keep doing it until I'm back."

"But—"

"Brynn, I can't take any chances; I'm laying low until my birthday is long gone."

"Where—"

"Shh, please, don't say anything. Just in case. And I can't tell you where I'm going, Brynn. I'm not telling anyone."

Maybe she's just going up to her cabin in the mountains, Brynn thinks. Few people even know she has it, and those who do wouldn't expect to find her there.

"I knew I could count on you," Fiona is saying.

"But . . . What am I supposed to tell Ashley?" she whispers. "And Pat?"

"Just say that something came up and I asked you to take care of Ash for the day."

"What if Pat gives me a hard time?"

"He won't. He's a great guy when he's dealing with everyone but me."

That's true. Brynn can't imagine affable Pat standing in her way, especially when he sees Ashley's affection for Caleb and Jeremy.

"Fee, I'm worried about you."

Her friend is silent for a moment.

Then she says, her voice laced with stark fear, "So am I."

CHAPTER 19

It's getting worse.

The morning sickness.

Yesterday, it lasted well into the afternoon. Now it's kicked in, violently, before the sun has even come up.

Then again, it *is* officially morning.

As in four forty-three, Brynn notes, glancing at the illuminated digital clock as she climbs back into her empty bed following a particularly vicious vomit session in the bathroom.

She tried to keep the noise down in there, but it was hard. She half-expected Garth to come knocking on the door to check on her, but he didn't.

He must be sound asleep in his chair in the other room.

Or maybe he isn't even home yet.

He spent last night at the library again, working on his book. When he left, she jokingly complained that she's beginning to feel like a single mother.

Garth didn't crack a smile. He only said, absently, "Sorry, I've got to get this done," and then he left.

Just as well. The less time they spend together, the easier it is to conceal all that she's hiding from Garth right now.

She's content to let him spend his time on campus while she stays home alone with the boys. Caleb and Jeremy don't notice her brooding, or jumping at every unexpected sound, or turning green every time she opens the fridge and smells Thursday night's leftover Chinese food.

Brynn rolls over and yawns. The alarm won't be going off for at least—

Wait a minute. It won't be going off at all. Today is Sunday.

Good. She can go back to sleep.

Then, suddenly, Brynn remembers what else today is.

Fiona's birthday.

Opening her eyes, Fiona senses it's early.

How early?

There's no clock nearby; she has no idea.

She gets up and slips over to the window to peek between the wooden slats of the blinds.

The sun is coming up, painting the eastern horizon in glowing pinks and golds with the promise of a beautiful day.

And I'll be here to see it, she thinks with a sleepy, satisfied yawn, before lying down again. *But not until later . . .*

It's been years since she's slept this well.

Maybe that's because, for once, she's not worrying about her business, or her schedule, or even her daughter.

Right now, she's not even worrying about falling victim to whoever has been stalking her with mementos of the past, and her association with Rachel.

I finally feel safe, she thinks as she drifts off again.

Ahhh, good. She's sound asleep.

On the couch, surprisingly.

Not in bed, where you'd expect her to be at this hour.

No, she's dozing in the living room, half-sitting up, still

fully dressed . . . almost as though she's been waiting for someone.

But not for me.

It's tempting to wake her, just for the final satisfaction of letting her see who's in charge now.

Tempting . . . but far too risky.

Fiona Fitzgerald will undoubtedly go down fighting, given the chance.

But I can't afford to give it to her.

This old Tudor is solidly built; not a floorboard creaks as footsteps, muffled by the luxurious designer rug, swiftly cross the room.

Fiona's impudent features are unexpectedly sedate in slumber. How deceptively benign she seems now.

But she isn't.

Nobody knows better than I do that she's about as benign as a rabid bear.

And, like a rabid bear that has destroyed an innocent victim, she has to be put down before she can do any more harm.

The knife was taken just now from its place of honor in her own kitchen, plucked from a butcher block stand on her counter top. It's a Henckels chef's knife—which probably costs more than a month of Ashley's private school tuition— ironic, since Fiona doesn't even cook.

Doubly, and delightfully, ironic that the knife will be put to good use anyway.

The blade is held, clenched in two hands, for a long, breathtaking moment, poised high in the air above the sleeping woman on the couch.

This time, there's no inclination to linger, to savor.

This time, there's only an urgent desire to accomplish the task that has been repeatedly envisioned through the years.

Envisioned so many times that when the knife is brought down in one tremendous, sweeping arc, it strikes its target with admirable precision.

Bull's-eye!

The well-honed blade sinks into her heart as if catapulted by Cupid's bow itself.

Her body convulses reflexively as a red stain spreads across her shirt, and her eyelids flutter for a moment, but her eyes never open.

"Look at me, you bitch! Look at me!"

Who said that?

I did.

The words were hurtled unexpectedly, almost seeming to come from somebody else's lips, but there's nobody else in the room.

Nobody other than Fiona, dying swiftly, silently, on her own designer couch, without knowing why it has to be this way.

Without realizing that she's no longer in control of anything at all . . .

No, I am.

And I want her to know that.

"Look at me! Open your eyes, dammit! Look at me!"

But she doesn't open her eyes, not even when she's violently grabbed by the shoulders and shaken.

She's gone.

She doesn't know.

She'll never know.

Her body is hurtled to the floor like a rag doll, kicked hard, with little satisfaction. The hilt is pulled, with some effort, from deep in her chest.

The blade gouges into one of her eye sockets and then the other, brutally twisting, turning, digging.

Seeing the bloody pulp oozing in its wake brings some pleasure . . . but not nearly enough.

I wanted her to see.

I wanted her to be afraid.

I wanted her to know.

But it's too late for any of that.

Like the others, Fiona Fitzgerald has paid the ultimate price for what she did.

Unlike the others, she didn't suffer enough. She didn't experience those exquisite moments of sheer, helpless terror, when you know you're going to die, and there's not a thing you can do about it.

But there's one more sister whose grim fate still awaits. She'll just have to make up for this unsatisfying experience.

A hard shoe swings back and jabs Fiona's crumpled form with another hard kick.

Don't worry. By the time I'm through with Brynn, she'll have suffered enough for both of you.

Oh . . .

I almost forgot.

What kind of birthday party would it be without the song?

"Happy Birthday to you . . . Happy Birthday to you . . . Happy Birthday, dear Fiona . . . Happy Birthday to you."

"Garth . . . Do you have a minute?"

He looks up from the rake he was about to lift from its nail on the wall of the backyard shed.

Brynn is standing in the doorway wearing her typical daily uniform: jeans, sneakers, and a sweatshirt, her hair pulled back in a ponytail.

But she looks more haggard than usual, Garth notices. In fact, she has ever since she suffered that bout with the stomach flu.

At least he and the kids didn't get it. That would be the last thing he needs right now, facing a towering stack of essay tests to grade in addition to everything else he has to get done around here today, especially in the yard.

At least Brynn hasn't been bugging him about the broken towel bar in the bathroom anymore, but he's aware that it's there. Just as he's aware that the fallen leaves are ankle-deep on their property and blowing into the neighbors' frequently raked and blown lawns.

If he hadn't been aware of that fact on his own, he would be now. He was confronted on the driveway yesterday by meticulous homeowner Andrew Chase.

"I'll get to it tomorrow," Garth promised.

"It would be better if you got to it today. There's going to be a lot of wind tonight."

Garth tried to appease him by saying he'd do his best, but that he was on his way to the campus library.

"On a Saturday night?" the neighbor asked dubiously.

"You sound just like my wife," Garth cracked, and didn't get a return smile.

Now, seeing Brynn looking so glum, and obviously needing to talk, Garth sighs and removes his hands from the rake.

"What's up?" He does his best to sound patient and keep his mind off the waiting leaves and essay tests.

"I have to tell you something, and you might not be thrilled about it."

Uh-oh.

"Why will I not be thrilled?"

"Because I know sometimes having the kids around is distracting for you, and one more . . ."

"One more?" His heart stops.

"Fiona asked if Ashley could stay here for a couple of days. And I said yes—without checking with you. And I have to pick her up in an hour, so . . . I mean, it's not like you even have a choice."

Relieved, Garth shrugs. "Is that all?"

"So it's okay with you?"

"Yeah, sure. Why not." He pulls the rake off the wall, and adds with a laugh as she turns back toward the house, "You looked so upset that I thought you were going to say you were pregnant or something."

* * *

"I think this sunrise hike was the best thing we ever did," Ashley tells her father contentedly, watching him load the remains of their picnic breakfast into the back of his Jeep alongside her flowered duffel and backpack.

"I agree. Although it would have been even better if you had seen the actual sunrise," he says with a laugh.

"Next time I'll go to bed earlier," Ashley promises.

"You were in bed by nine."

"I'll go to bed at seven thirty so I won't sleep through the sunrise."

She was just so tired and it was so dark when Daddy woke her up this morning for their hike. She barely remembers getting dressed and into the Jeep.

"Come on, Ash, wake up," he kept saying. He even gave her a few sips of his Red Bull. But as they drove up into the mountains, she kept falling back asleep anyway.

She awakened to find herself in the front seat of the Jeep, parked on a majestic overlook. The sun was already well above the horizon, shining brightly on the brilliant foliage.

"It's about time, Sleepyhead," Daddy said with a laugh.

Then they hiked up to the waterfall, and ate the strawberry muffins Daddy had made last night, and they drank more Red Bull.

"Don't tell your mother," Daddy warned her, and of course Ashley promised not to.

Now, as they climb into the Jeep for the trip back down the mountain, he looks over at her. "So you had fun."

"Yup."

"Did you think any more about what we talked about before?"

She knows what he means, but she asks, "What do you mean?"

"Coming to live with me?"

"Oh. Yeah, I've thought about it . . ."

"And?"

"And I want to, but . . . What about Mom? Will she even let me?"

"If you tell the judge that you want to live with me, that's what will happen."

Judge.

So they would have to go to court over it.

"Do I have to decide right now?" she asks her father.

"No, sweetie, you don't. And you don't have to decide anything at all, if you want to keep things the way they are. I just want to make sure you're happy."

"I know."

The thing is . . . She's not happy with the way things are.

She just doesn't know if she's brave enough to do what it would take to change them.

"Okay, guys, got everything?" Brynn asks her sons as they step out the front door.

They're on their way over to Fiona's, where she promised to intercept Pat with Ashley. You'd think it was going to be a ten-hour, rather than ten-minute, round trip, judging by all the stuff the boys are bringing.

Caleb has a Step Into Reading book and a snack. Jeremy has a snack, two red Matchbox cars, and his favorite blanket.

"Wait! I forgot my lucky hat!" Caleb is poised to run back inside, but Brynn stops him with a hand on his shoulder.

"Why don't you leave that here?"

"Why don't you leave *them* here?" Garth suggests, coming around from the side yard, rake in hand.

"That's all right, you're busy."

"It's okay, you can leave them."

"Nah, I'll take them with me."

"Why? They can help me with the leaves."

"All they'll want to do is jump in them and make a mess. We'll be right back. Ashley will be glad to see them." *And I promised Fiona I'd bring them, dammit, so stop making this more difficult than it has to be.*

"Okay, see you soon." Garth shrugs and goes back to his raking.

As Brynn straps the boys into the car, she watches him out of the corner of her eye, remembering what he had said earlier.

I thought you were going to say you were pregnant or something.

She should have just told him about the baby then and there. Didn't he give her the perfect opening?

Well, not *perfect*.

There is no perfect opening. She's been trying to come up with one all weekend, to no avail.

As she drives the network of familiar streets, Caleb reads haltingly aloud from his book, pausing every so often whenever he gets stuck.

Each time it happens, Brynn prompts him with the correct word.

And each time she does that, Caleb says, "But how do you know without looking?"

"Magical Mommy powers," is her standard reply, and he accepts it more readily, and delightedly, than he would a complicated explanation about idiom and verb conjugation in the English language.

Now they've arrived at Fiona's house, ten minutes early—but none too soon.

To her surprise, Fiona's silver BMW is in the driveway.

Pat's Jeep pulls in directly behind Brynn. Seeing her, he waves.

She waves back, wondering if Fee is home after all.

"I'll be right back, boys." Brynn gets out.

So does Pat. He catches Brynn in a heartfelt bear hug.

"Hey! It's so good to see you."

"It's good to see you, too, Pat," she says, meaning it, and feeling a little guilty.

Sorry, Fee, she thinks dutifully. But she can't help it; she's always liked jovial, laid-back Pat. He was a part of her life for all the years he was part of Fiona's—and then, with the divorce, he just melted away.

"Brynn!" Ashley squeals, coming around the Jeep. "I thought that was you! What are you doing here?"

Before she can answer, Ashley goes on, "Guess what? Me and my dad had a sunrise hike and picnic in the mountains this morning."

"Um, sunrise?" Pat cocks an eyebrow at his daughter.

Ashley laughs. "Well, I slept through the actual sunrise. Hey, are the boys with you?"

At Brynn's nod, she hurries past, quickly opening the back door to see Caleb and Jeremy.

"So how are things going?" Brynn asks Pat.

"You know . . . Things could be better. I miss Ashley like crazy."

"I can't even imagine," she finds herself saying sympathetically.

Sometimes she wishes Fee had just had that second baby and settled into family life. Then the Hagans and the Saddlers could have hung around together: hikes, barbecues, playdates, amusement park outings . . .

"Whoa . . . Are those your guys?"

She follows his gaze and smiles. "Yup, those are my guys."

Pat releases her and sticks his head into the backseat, grinning as Caleb and Jeremy return his hearty greeting.

"God, Brynnie," he says, turning back to her, "they're beautiful. And I can't believe you have two kids that big."

"You, too! Look at Ashley!"

"Yeah, she's growing up fast." He pauses to flash a warm

smile in his daughter's direction. "So what are you doing here? Visiting Fee?"

That he still calls Fiona by her old nickname strikes Brynn unexpectedly. To hear Fiona talk about him, all he ever calls her, behind her back and to her face, are four- and five-letter names.

Of course, Brynn knows there are two sides to every divorce story.

She just sees so little of Pat that it's easy to fall into Fiona's bitter mindset where he's concerned.

"Brynn?" Pat seems to be waiting for something.

Oh! She never answered his question about what she's doing here.

Here goes, she thinks reluctantly, wishing Fiona hadn't put her up to this. She looks up at the house, wondering again if Fee is here.

But if she was, she'd probably be out here by now.

No, she's gone, and wherever she went, she didn't take her car.

"I'm supposed to pick up Ashley," Brynn informs Pat.

"Why?"

"Fiona asked me to. Something came up, and she couldn't be here, so she asked me to get her."

"What came up?"

"I don't know." *I'm a terrible liar,* Brynn realizes, seeing a glint in Pat's eyes.

"I bet I do."

"You do?"

"It's her birthday," he says. "I bet she decided to take off somewhere with her new boyfriend, right?"

"What new boyfriend?"

"Ashley told me you said she had a date."

Brynn stammers, "I—no, I—when was that?"

"Never mind, Brynn. You don't have to cover for her. It's okay. She can date. I won't ask you anything else, other than, when is she supposed to come back? Tonight? Late? Is Ashley spending the night with you?"

Seeing Brynn hesitate, he shakes his head in disapproval. "Never mind. Gotcha. Hey, Ash!"

His daughter pokes her head out of the backseat, where the boys are giggling gleefully. "Yeah, Daddy?"

"You need to run in and get yourself some pajamas to wear tonight and something for school tomorrow. You're staying at Brynn's."

Brynn expects a protest, but Ashley's face lights up. "I am? Where's Mom?"

Pat lets Brynn answer that, darn him.

"Your mom had to take care of some business, Ashley, so she thought you might enjoy staying with us."

"I definitely would," she says, hiding an enormous yawn behind her hand.

"And she'll definitely conk out early for you tonight," Pat tells Brynn, chuckling. "She likes to sleep in on weekends so I had to drag her out of bed in the dark and practically carry her out to the car for the hike."

"Well, she obviously thought it was worth the lost sleep, right, Ashley?"

"Right!"

"Okay, so go get your stuff, Ash," Pat says, handing her the backpack. "You've got your key, right?"

"I'll go in with her if you stay here with my kids," Brynn says hurriedly, knowing Ashley might need enough clothes for more than just one night and day. But she doesn't want to let on about that to Pat. It would only give him more ammunition against Fee.

Let her explain her impromptu absence to her ex-husband— however long it ends up being—when she gets back.

"Sure, I'll watch your guys," Pat says amiably. "I've got some great tricks to teach them."

"Not that disgusting sound you used to make with your arm?" Brynn laughs.

"That, and I've accumulated some new ones through the years." He makes a beeline for the backseat.

Brynn follows Ashley up the steps and watches her fish a key out of her bag.

Ashley opens the door and holds it for Brynn.

"Ladies first."

"You're a lady too," Brynn protests, grinning.

"I'm a kid. You're the lady."

Brynn is smiling as she crosses the threshold.

It will be her last smile for a long, long time.

Later—much later, when the shock waves and horror have stopped screaming through her brain and coherent thought has resumed—she'll be thankful that it was she, and not Ashley, who walked into the house first.

She'll be thankful that it was she, and not Fiona's own child, who laid eyes on the hideous tableau that awaited in the dining room, immediately visible through the archway from the front entrance.

She takes it all in somehow in a stark, appalling moment that seems to last an eternity.

The room is decorated for a birthday party: pink streamers, balloons, a cake. It has white frosting and pale pink icing that reads Happy Birthday and, clumsily spelled out in darker icing: DEAR FIONA.

Someone appears to be sitting at the table.

It can't be . . .

No, dear God.

It isn't . . .

But, God help her, God help all of them, it must be.

The evidence is a telltale swath of auburn hair falling from beneath a pointy paper party hat that appears to defy gravity, tilted so that it seems as though it's going to topple off.

Fiona's face is gone. Where her features should be, there is only a sickening mass of blood-blackened flesh.

Don't scream, Brynn warns herself frantically as the

gruesome sight washes over her like an icy wave. *You'll scare Ashley. You'll scare the boys.*

Don't scream . . .

But she can't help it.

Her mouth opens and a piercing screech escapes as she backs away in horror from her best friend's butchered carcass.

Years from now, the memory will—with luck—be as deliciously vivid as it is right now.

Something like that can sustain a person for life, long after other things have fallen away. Things like youth, good health, money . . .

None of those things last.

No, all you really have, in the end, is your memory . . . if that.

I'll sure as hell fight to keep mine intact.

What a shame it would be to forget the pleasure of gauging out Fiona Fitzgerald's green eyes with that ridiculously expensive knife she purchased herself.

Then again . . . What a shame she didn't know that it was put to good use. What a shame she didn't see me, didn't hear me sing to her.

Oh, well.

The important thing is that the penultimate task has been accomplished.

She's gone. She can't hurt me, or anyone else, ever again.

Now only Brynn Saddler is left.

But it won't be long until she, too, gets what she deserves.

Then it will finally be over, after ten years.

And for me, a new chapter can begin at last.

CHAPTER 20

Quincy Hiles spends most Sunday mornings with his mother and his youngest sister, Wanda, and her family, all of whom still live together in his childhood home.

Today has begun as all the other Sundays do: first, a rousing church service, to be followed by a home-cooked meal in the kitchen. Mama has prepared all his favorites: fried chicken, mashed potatoes with cream gravy, greens with bacon, rolls and butter.

He'll pay for it later, he's sure. With his stomach acting up the way it's been lately, Quincy shouldn't be eating any of this stuff. But as he sits at the table, watching his mother open the oven to swap the batch of piping hot rolls with a freshly assembled apple pie, his mouth is watering.

Devorah tilts the cookie sheet and the rolls tumble into a waiting basket lined with a blue and white gingham cloth napkin. She sets it in the center of the table, where loaded platters wait to fill the circle of empty plates around the table.

"Michelle, you say grace today," she instructs the younger of Quincy's two nieces, who, at fifteen, is taller than he is, and wants to be a model.

"Lord, we thank you for—"

Michelle breaks off as Quincy's cell phone rings.

"Turn that thing off," his mother instructs him. "Michelle, go ahead."

As his niece resumes, he pulls his phone from his pocket, silences the ringer, and holds it on his lap to examine the caller ID window.

Mike Connelly.

Good thing Michelle's prayer is short and sweet, as always.

"Amen," Quincy says hurriedly and excuses himself to answer the call, striding with his phone to the next room as he says, "Hiles here, what's up?"

"Either Allerson gets around, or we've got ourselves a genuine serial killer on our hands."

"What?"

"One of Matilda Harrington's sorority sisters just turned up dead in Cedar Crest . . . exactly the same MO."

"How 'exactly the same'?"

"Exactly exactly the same. Somebody threw Fiona Fitzgerald a nice little party for her thirtieth birthday—which is today."

With a muttered curse that would inflame Devorah Hiles if she could hear it from the next room, Quincy is already grabbing his keys and jacket, his mother's fried chicken and apple pie forgotten.

"Here, honey, drink this."

Ashley looks up to see a female police officer holding out a plastic cup of water. She shakes her head, feeling her father's protective arm tighten around her.

Daddy is sitting in the chair beside hers; they're in a small room at police headquarters, where they were taken in a squad car.

Brynn, Caleb, and Jeremy were driven in a second car.

Garth came to get the boys so he could take them over to a neighbor's house, and then he's supposed to come here.

"Drink the water, Ash," Daddy says gently, taking the cup from the police officer and closing Ashley's fingers around it.

She takes a sip.

It's warm and it tastes yucky, she thinks idly.

Then, just as idly, *Mom's dead.*

But neither thought sinks in. It's as though her brain has been injected with Novocain. She's aware of potentially excruciating thoughts jabbing at her, but she feels nothing, just like in the dentist's chair when she had her tooth drilled.

Ashley sips more water, and she nods when her father asks her worriedly if she's okay, and she wonders when her mother is going to come get her, and then she remembers that she isn't.

Ever.

You should be crying, Ashley keeps telling herself. Her eyes are strangely dry.

But Brynn, who just disappeared behind a closed door with two detectives, has been crying—sometimes hysterically—ever since she let out that blood-curdling scream back at home.

Then she immediately shoved Ashley outside again through the open front door before she could glimpse whatever was in the house.

At that point, Brynn was so incoherent that Daddy didn't even understand what she was trying to say. He kept shouting, *"What? What is it?"* as he ran past Brynn and Ashley, and then he screamed, too.

That was the most horrible sound Ashley has ever heard in her life. A man's scream. The unnatural, violent sound sent chills through her. "She's dead!" Brynn was shrieking, over and over.

She's talking about Mom, Ashley realized. Mom must be dead.

Inside the house.

"Did she have a heart attack?" she had asked Daddy and Brynn at one point. She was thinking of Meg's father, who works hard at a stressful job, but not as hard as Mom does.

Nobody works as hard as Mom does.

Worked, she thought dully. And, *did.*

Neither her father nor Brynn answered her question about the heart attack, but Ashley overheard two of the cops talking. At first she thought they had said "prince," but then she realized it was "prints." As in fingerprints.

Even Ashley knows that you don't look for fingerprints when someone dies unless you think somebody killed them.

Who would want to kill her mother?

"Was it a robber?" she asks her father now, then notices that her thigh is wet, a dark stain spreading across her jeans. Oh. Her hand is shaking so badly that she's spilling water all over herself.

"What, Ash?"

"Did a robber break in and kill Mom?"

Daddy blinks. "What?"

She repeats the question.

It takes him a second to answer, "I don't know."

He's upset about Mom. Maybe he's thinking that they never should have gotten divorced. Maybe he thinks that if they were still married, this wouldn't have happened, because he could have protected her.

"What is Brynn telling the police in there?" She gestures at the closed door.

"I have no idea."

"Do they think she knows who killed Mom?"

Daddy just shakes his head without looking at her, and his mouth is a straight, tight line.

I walked into the house. I turned my head . . .
And I saw her.

"Let's go over this again, Mrs. Saddler."

Dazed, seated in the interrogation room, Brynn nods. She watches through tear-blurred eyes as one of the two Cedar Crest detectives glances over the pages of notes he just took.

I saw her; I saw Fee . . . Oh, Fee . . .

Oh, my God . . .

"You say your friend told you she was going away for a few days," says the more vocal detective, a balding, middle-aged man, "but that she never said where, or why . . ."

Yes, she did say why, but I didn't tell you.

I have to tell you. You need to know the whole truth.

Coherent thoughts are breaking through the haze of grief and shock more frequently now, trailing a fresh stream of guilt.

Yes, they need to know. But not yet. Not without Garth. She has to tell her husband first, so that he can hear it from her privately.

The brief contact with him, when he showed up here, was so comforting. She doesn't even know who called him; she was too hysterical to do it herself.

But suddenly, he was there, holding her tight, telling her he loved her, saying he'd get the boys.

The boys. Poor boys.

Why did I have to insist on bringing them over there with me?

Because Fee had asked her to, so that Ashley would jump at the chance to go home with her.

If only she hadn't listened to Fee.

If only she'd left them at home with Garth, as he had wanted her to do . . .

The boys started crying when they heard her panicked screams, and she was in no condition to comfort them. She vaguely remembers one of the cops in the back of the car with them, talking to them until Garth arrived.

He promised he'd drop Caleb and Jeremy at Maggie's and come right down here.

So where is he?

Maybe he's already back, waiting out there with Pat and Ashley, unaware that Brynn needs him desperately. Now. Right this second.

"Do you know if—" She breaks off, realizing she just spoke right over the detective, still recapping his notes. "I'm sorry. I didn't—"

"No, it's all right. What did you want to know?"

"Is my husband here?"

The balding, middle-aged detective looks at the other balding, middle-aged detective, who promptly says, "I'll go check," and steps out of the room.

The first detective resumes. "Ms. Fitzgerald asked you to pick up her daughter today when her ex-husband returned her after a weekend visit, but she didn't tell him in advance that she was leaving town."

Brynn shakes her head, fishing in her pocket for another tissue. The clump in her hand is sodden.

Oh, Fiona . . .

An audible sob escapes her.

The detective waits for it to subside, then goes on. "So you believe she didn't tell him because they didn't get along and she thought he would be upset with her."

She sniffles. "I didn't say that exactly . . . but, yes. I guess that's why."

As the detective continues recapping their conversation, Brynn wipes her streaming eyes and manages to comment appropriately, only half-listening.

Her thoughts are on Fiona.

On what happened to her.

Brynn can't stop reliving it.

I walked into the house. I turned my head . . .

And I saw her.

And I screamed.

As she screamed, she turned to flee, and there was Ashley.

Brynn shoved her, hard, instinctively trying to protect her.

Oh, God. Poor Ashley.

Poor Fee . . .

"So you were at the victim's home to pick up her child . . ."

"Yes."

I walked into the house. I turned my head . . .

And I saw her.

What was Fiona doing there, at home? She wasn't supposed to be there.

Did she lie to Brynn about going away? But why would she?

Did she stay at home and throw herself a birthday party that was interrupted by the killer?

How else to explain the cake, the hat, the wrapped gift in her hands, as though someone had just handed it to her in the instant before she was murdered.

Unless the killer put it there . . . afterward.

And maybe—she grips the arms of the chair to stay steady as a tide of terror washes over her—the killer also set up the "party."

"Are you all right, Mrs. Saddler?"

She shakes her head. "I'm just . . . I feel a little bit . . ."

"Faint?" The detective is standing over her chair, concerned. Kind.

He won't be, she tells herself, *when he finds out that I know more than I'm telling.*

"Let me get you some water."

She nods. Closes her eyes.

I walked into the house. I turned my head . . .

And I saw her.

"Brynn?"

Garth is here. In the room. He kneels by her chair and takes her into his arms. She can feel his stubbly beard against her temple, can smell the leather of his jacket.

"Garth—" She's clinging to him, crying again. Huge, heaving, shuddering sobs. "I need to talk to you alone."

* * *

The lower-reservoir jogging path through Central Park is crowded at this hour on a sunny October Sunday, but Isaac pays little attention to the others.

His thoughts are consumed not just by what happened ten years ago, but by all that has transpired in the past few weeks.

Three times, Isaac was tempted to spill the whole story. First to Brynn, then to Kylah, then to Detective Hiles.

All of it . . . including the secret Rachel confessed to him when he called to wish her Happy Birthday just hours before she disappeared.

Three times, he refrained.

But he keeps going over and over it in his head. The memory of that day, Rachel's twentieth birthday, is as fresh as the conversation he had this morning with Kylah over an article in the Sunday *Times*.

Sitting in his new midtown office that day ten years ago, he sang "Happy Birthday" to Rachel the minute she answered the phone.

The other end of the line was silent when he finished . . . until she suddenly burst into tears.

He figured she was just a little emotional because, as she put it, he was the only person in her life who always remembered her birthday. Even her flaky mother had been known to forget.

So, to lighten the mood, Isaac teased, "Wow, I figured my voice might be a little flat, but I didn't realize it was that bad."

She didn't laugh. "I have to tell you something, but you can't tell anyone, Isaac."

"All right."

"No, I mean you have to swear you won't tell. Do you swear to God?"

"I swear to God." He clutched the phone, wondering what it could be only briefly before the likely answer came to him.

He figured she was dropping out of school—she had threatened to do that a few times over the years. She wanted to go to Europe and study music, or hang out in the East Village and compose songs, or . . .

She had a hundred different plans.

Some even involved him—"Let's join the Peace Corps together," or "Why don't we open a great burger joint somewhere?"

None of those plans, however, involved the bombshell she was about to drop.

"Is there anything else?" Garth asks, looking at his wife. *Really* looking at her, feeling as though he's seeing her for the first time in years.

Feeling as though he's seeing a total stranger.

Brynn's bloodshot eyes are sunken into raw, red craters. Her face is blotchy, her ponytail bedraggled, sweatshirt cuffs damp as though she used them to wipe her nose.

"Anything else?" she echoes. "What do you mean?"

"I mean, is there anything else you need to tell me while we're alone in here?"

For the first time since he got here, her eyes flash a sign of life. "No," she says curtly. "That's everything."

Garth rakes a hand through his hair. "How could you not have said anything about this for all these years?"

"Because it wasn't up to me. I swore that I wouldn't."

"Some silly sorority oath? You can't be serious, Brynn. Somebody's life was hanging in the balance. Your friend's life."

"You don't understand. I didn't think that it was at the time. I thought she was dead. By the time we realized she—or her body—wasn't in the woods anymore, it was too late to say anything. We had already pretended we didn't know anything about it."

"So you just decided to go on pretending. Even to me."

She nods, still looking him in the eye, her chin lifted—but quavering slightly. "It was all we could do, Garth."

"You could have gone to the cops at some point."

"At which point? And if I had gone, it would have incriminated my friends, too."

"Even if not the cops, then . . . You could have told me," he says through a clenched jaw, shaking his head.

"I couldn't tell you."

"Because of the oath. I know."

"No, not just that. Because . . . I was afraid of how you'd react."

With an ache in his gut, he says, "You should have told me anyway."

"It would have been different, maybe, if you weren't right here, in this world. If you were someone I had met in some other place, someone who had never heard of Rachel Lorent. But you knew her, you taught her in class, you searched for her. How could I tell you?"

"How could you *not* tell me?" he returns, shaking his head.

But he knows how. He knows all about shameful secrets; about caustic guilt and consternation that eat away at you, making it difficult to look your spouse in the eye when you think she might somehow read your thoughts; making it impossible to sleep at night.

With her. Without her.

"I'm sorry, Garth."

Yes. She is. Profound remorse is vividly etched on her face.

"I know."

I'm sorry too, Brynn. So, so sorry.

There's a knock on the door.

"Whatever happens, I'll stand by you," Garth says hurriedly. "I promise, Brynn. I love you."

"I love you, too," she chokes out.

Garth bends over and squeezes her fiercely, wishing he could hold on as tight to life as they knew it.

Because he can feel it slipping away.

Then another knock on the door, and one of the detectives pokes his head in.

"Excuse me, folks, but there's someone here who needs to speak to you."

The door opens wider and a tall, bearded African-American man strides past the detective and flashes his badge. "Sergeant Quincy Hiles. I'm with the Boston P.D."

"I'm pregnant, Isaac."

Those words have haunted him for ten years.

Even now, they reverberate through his body with every pounding footfall as he moves faster still along the path.

No longer is he jogging—he's running now, full speed ahead, sprinting past everyone else on the path . . . trying to escape.

But he never can.

"I'm pregnant, Isaac."

Rachel choked it out through tears, and, at first, he wasn't even sure he heard her right.

But then she repeated it—I'm pregnant—loudly and clearly.

An unspoken question—his, of course, the logical one to ask—hung silently between them for a long moment.

Finally, he found his voice.

"What are you going to do, Rach?" That, of course, wasn't the question.

But it was a good one.

Her answer was prompt . . . But he could hear the uncertainty in her voice. "Have it. Raise it."

"Where? How?"

"I don't know . . . But I'm definitely going to have this

baby. Even if I have to drop out of school. Which I will have to do, because how else can I do this? And, of course, my parents are going to freak out if I'm a single mom without a college degree."

"Maybe not."

"Yes, they will."

She was right.

They would. For two people who went through marriages faster than they did checkbooks, Rachel's parents were surprisingly conservative, and they were very big on academics and education.

"Maybe I'll just take off," she said wistfully.

"Take off? You can't do that. You mean . . . like, just go?"

"Yes. I can have the baby somewhere far away . . . on my own—"

"Alone?"

She didn't reply to that.

Instead, she said, "I need you, Isaac. I'm scared, and I don't know what to do. Please . . . Can you come up here tomorrow?"

Of course he said yes.

Then she said, "Hang on a second," and he heard her talking to someone on the other end of the line.

She came back on and said, "Um, I have to go. Someone needs to use the phone."

Someone always needed to use the phone in a houseful of sorority girls in the days before cell phones were ubiquitous.

So that was the end of his final conversation with Rachel.

At the time, he figured his big question—the crucial one—could wait until he could hear the answer in person.

But, of course, she disappeared before he could get up there to ask: *Am I the baby's father?*

* * *

For the second time today, the familiar, shameful details spew from Brynn's lips, propelled by a decade's worth of pent-up angst.

Brynn can't help but feel like a bottle of champagne kept tightly corked for ten years, then violently shaken and abruptly released.

The Boston detective and his partner, a pretty blonde, sit and listen. They nod and occasionally ask questions. Still staunchly beside her, Garth keeps his arm tightly around her shoulders.

But she isn't leaning on him.

Somehow, she's sitting straight and tall. It's almost as if, in purging herself of the guilty burden, she's made room for some long-suppressed inner core of fortitude to expand.

Only when she's told them everything she possibly can—right up to and including Fiona's furtive plan to leave town for her birthday—does she finally sag against Garth's arm and the back of the chair, utterly spent.

Quincy Hiles rubs his beard thoughtfully. "Is there anything else, Mrs. Saddler?"

"No, sir. There's nothing else."

Nothing other than the fact that I'm pregnant, and my husband doesn't know. But I think I've spilled enough secrets for one day.

"I have a question."

Brynn looks at Garth in surprise. He avoids her gaze.

"Yes, Mr. Saddler?"

"Did my wife commit a crime ten years ago when she left her friend's body in the woods?"

"No." That unequivocal answer from Hiles catches Brynn off guard.

"Are you sure?" she asks.

"Yes. And you didn't even technically commit a crime if you thought your friend was alive, as long as you didn't push her over the edge."

"Isn't there a Good Samaritan law or something?"

For the first time, Quincy bares a smile. "In Massachusetts? You mean, like on that last episode of *Seinfeld?* People ask me all the time, and that's how I know the answer off the top of my head. It's against the law to harm another person, but the law doesn't require you to *help* another person."

Tears fill Brynn's eyes once again. But this time, sheer relief mixes with her grief over her lost friends.

If only they had known . . .

Maybe Tildy and Fiona would still be alive.

CHAPTER 21

Fiona's shaken parents opted to break with tradition and avoid a wake or funeral home visitation.

Her funeral itself is held at Saint Vincent's Church on a blustery October morning that feels more like late November. The sky hangs low and black over Cedar Crest, spitting sheets of horizontal rain on the throng of mourners huddled beneath useless umbrellas.

The press has been swarming ever since Fiona's murder was linked to Matilda Harrington's, and of course Rachel's disappearance has been dredged up all over again amid much public speculation that she, too, fell victim to the same fate ten years ago.

The authorities haven't released the details surrounding either murder scene, but the media has created sensational headlines just the same:

THE SORORITY SISTER MURDERS. THE BIRTHDAY-GIRL KILLER.

Detectives Quincy Hiles, Mike Connelly, and Deb Jackson have all but taken up permanent residence in Cedar Crest. With Ray Wilmington dead and the apparent sorority connection, Troy Allerson has been back-burnered as a potential suspect. Particularly since he was on a well-documented Washington trip when Fiona Fitzgerald was murdered in Cedar Crest.

Apparently, his affair with Matilda Harrington was an unfortunate coincidence—and one that is destined to stay hidden, at least for the time being.

Cassie Ashford's apparent disappearance has yet to materialize in the press or be publicly linked to the murders of her sorority sisters. Mike and Deb spoke to her fiancé, her parents, and her brother, all of whom remain convinced she had cold feet about her upcoming wedding and ran off. They all cited several e-mails they received well beyond the day of her birthday as evidence of her well-being.

Maybe they're right.

Quincy doubts it. Anyone can send e-mail if they can get into someone's account. And it's next to impossible to trace at this level, though he's got someone on that.

For now, unless Cassie—or her body, or at least a trail of evidence—turns up, there's nothing he can do for her or her family.

Quincy despises that feeling of helplessness. It keeps him up nights. After too many of those, absorbed in the case, he's gone back to drinking coffee. But it's killing him; he can feel it eating away at his guts. Literally.

Saint Vincent's is packed to standing room only. In the front pew on one side of the altar are Fiona Fitzgerald's parents, drawn and stoic. It's no secret around town that there's been no love lost between them and their daughter.

Make that *daughters*. Fiona's identical twin, Deirdre, also estranged from their parents, sits in the front pew on the opposite side of the altar. Throughout the service she keeps a steadying arm around her niece, Ashley, whose pitiful sobs echo through the church whenever the organ falls silent. Fiona's ex-husband, Pat, flanks Ashley's other side, with Brynn and Garth Saddler seated a row behind.

She's a wreck, Brynn Saddler—and predictably so.
Because she's lost her best friend . . .
And because she's afraid she's next.

The public doesn't realize that, though. Nobody other than those involved in the investigation has been privy to the tale Brynn revealed about Rachel that night ten years ago. To them, the murders are somewhat random; any Zeta Delta Kappa sister, or even any woman celebrating a thirtieth birthday, might be a potential victim.

No one is aware of the chilling fact that is obvious to Quincy's team: that the killer is picking off a finite group, one by one.

And Brynn Saddler's turn is coming.

Quincy's got her under police guard 24/7.

He also posted a couple of uniforms over at the Zeta house at the request of the shaken housemother.

He's certain the sorority house security is superfluous, but there was no arguing with Mama Bear Puffy Trovato. Anyway, if the killer is in their midst, watching the progress of the investigation, it's best to keep the focus as broad as possible.

Brynn Saddler's security detail is probably just as superfluous at this point.

For another couple of days, anyway.

"Don't you think it's a little too coincidental that all four of these girls have October birthdays?" Deb asked on the heels of Fiona's death.

Yes, he did . . . until he learned that they had become friends, as freshmen, *because* of their mutual October birthdays.

"That's how we were grouped in the dorm," Brynn told him, wearing a sad, faraway smile. "Rachel was on the September hall, but she said she liked us better."

Rachel.

The press might have written her off as another victim of the Birthday-Girl Killer, but Quincy Hiles isn't convinced. Not by a long shot.

He can't help but think about that scrap of sorority sweater left at the scene of Tildy's murder. And about the thick lock of curly dark hair that was inside the wrapped gift box found in Fiona Fitzgerald's hands.

Hair that was tied with thin lengths of both red and gray satin ribbon, and appears to be very similar to Rachel Lorent's color and texture.

Forensics is testing it, using DNA samples provided by Rachel's mother in California. Having long since given up hope of seeing her daughter again, she assumed her blood was needed so that her daughter's remains can potentially be identified.

She was not told that the investigators believe her daughter might very well still be alive.

As far as Quincy's concerned, with no body ever found, there's no evidence to the contrary.

And if Rachel Lorent is still alive . . .

Well, Quincy has a feeling she'll be making another appearance in just a few days.

On the twenty-ninth: Brynn Saddler's birthday.

And this time, I'll be waiting for her.

Isaac deposits a stack of non-jazz CDs on the table and picks up a flattened cardboard box from a stack at his feet.

There's no way in hell that he was going to attend Fiona Fitzgerald's funeral. He made that mistake once before, and opened the door to a police investigation of his past.

He's no closer to uncovering the truth about Rachel after all that, and he's succeeded in further complicating his relationship with Kylah.

With a deft movement, he transforms the box to three dimensions and closes the flaps.

She's pulled away emotionally ever since he told her about his missing sister. She's here, in his life, in his bed, same as always, but she's detaching herself from him. He can feel it.

Maybe she senses that there's more to the story than he'd shared.

Maybe she even senses that Isaac was in love with Rachel; that if Rachel walked back into his life right now, he'd drop everything to be with her.

Everything—and everyone.

Kylah included.

He'll never be able to lay the past to rest.

Not like this, always wondering if she's out there some-where . . . perhaps with his child.

He picks up a roll of packing tape and runs it along the closed cardboard flaps a few times, reinforcing the seam. Then he begins transferring the stacks of books and CDs from the table to the box.

Kylah left this morning for Chicago on business. She won't be back until after the weekend. By then, he'll have all his stuff moved back into his apartment.

He'll be here, though, waiting for her, when she gets home. Just as she made him promise.

Isaac never breaks a promise.

That's why he rarely makes them.

The postfuneral reception in the church hall is a long-standing tradition at Saint Vincent's. Brynn is surprised that Fiona's parents went along with it, though. It can't be easy for them to stand there in the corner beneath a flag and a mounted crucifix and greet the hundreds of mourners—many of whom saw more of their daughter than they did in recent years.

"Do you want to go over there to see them?" Garth asks, handing her a white foam cup of coffee and keeping one for himself.

"In a minute." Brynn watches Fiona's father shake hands with the dashing James Bingham, one of Fee's more recent clients. He was responsible for the towering, voluminous spray of red roses that loomed above the altar in church, dwarfing a similar one, far smaller in scale, that came from the Zeta Delta Kappa girls.

A gray-haired woman hurries past, head down, going toward the door. Recognizing her, Brynn reaches out to touch her black-clad arm.

She jumps as though she's been branded and whirls around. "Oh. Brynn."

"Hi, Sharon. I just—" Brynn's voice breaks. She reaches out to give Fiona's former assistant a hug. She seems stiff in Brynn's embrace; nothing like her old self. "I'm glad you're here. You remember my husband, Garth?"

Sharon nods, seemingly at a loss for words.

"It's good to see you, Sharon." Garth shakes her hand gently. "Not under these circumstances, though."

"No."

The three of them look at each other for another awkward moment. Brynn tries to think of something to say to the woman, who, for these last few years was more of a mother, really, to Fiona than her own mother was.

She settles on, "She really missed you, after you left. She couldn't find a replacement worth one fraction of what you were to her. She even asked me to come work for her after she fired her last assistant." She offers a strained laugh.

Sharon matches it. "I missed her, too," she says, looking around almost skittishly. "I just . . . I'm sorry, but I have to go. I wanted to pay my respects, but I need to get back on the road."

."All right. Take care of yourself."

"She seems different," Garth comments as they watch Sharon scurry toward the door as though she can't wait to escape.

"She's devastated. Like everyone else. No one will be the same after this."

Brynn swallows a lump of grief-laced nausea as she looks at the coffee, knowing she's not going to drink it. The smell alone is making her even sicker than she already felt. She'll hang on to the cup for a bit, then set it down when Garth isn't looking.

"Maybe we should call home and check on the boys," she suggests. "Do you have your cell phone?"

"I do, but I'm sure they're fine. You know they're in good hands."

Her father and Sue are here in town. They came right away, without having to be asked, and will be staying through to-morrow morning.

Having them around the last few days has been a mixed blessing. They've kept the boys occupied and shielded them from the horror of their Auntie Fee's death. But Brynn keeps catching her stepmother watching her knowingly, making her all too aware that she has yet to tell Garth about the baby.

Several times these last few days, she's come close to spilling it.

But she can't bring herself to do it. Not in the midst of all this sorrow.

And not with this unsettling new strain between them. It isn't that he's pulled away physically. On the contrary, he's spent a lot of time at home, most of it just looking at Brynn. It's almost as though he wants to say something but can't bring himself to do it. She'll be going about her business, feel the weight of his gaze, and find him staring.

Is he going to tell her that he wants to leave her?

Instinctively, she doesn't think so.

He's even been spending nights in their bed again, not just to make love but holding her close all night the way he used to when they were first married, before the boys.

But Garth's presence in the master bedroom isn't necessarily meaningful. It's probably just because her father and Sue are out in the living room, sleeping on the air mattress they brought.

Maybe Garth is waiting for things to die down before he tells her that he can't stay married to a woman who has kept something so darkly significant from him for all these years.

Or maybe he's just terrified that something is going to happen to me.

I know I am.

Her husband's voice startles her out of her grim reverie.

"You know, I swear, every time I catch sight of her, I get chills."

Brynn looks up to see Garth staring at Fiona's twin sister, Deirdre, who is sitting with Ashley on the steps to the right of the stage. They aren't talking, just sitting together bleakly, Deirdre chewing on what looks like a wooden coffee stirrer.

Pat is nearby, conversing quietly with a couple of lawyers from the firm where he works as a paralegal. He keeps shooting worried, sidewise glances toward his daughter, though.

Ashley isn't doing so well. She's been staying at Pat's apartment. He told Brynn she's been crying incessantly, and waking up screaming every night. Nightmares are to be expected after what the poor child has been through. Pat is looking into getting Ashley into therapy. He's also talking about moving into a bigger place with her.

"Would you live in Fee's house?" Brynn asked him, thinking of how much that notion would have bothered her friend.

But Pat shook his head. "Ashley doesn't ever want to go back there after what happened, and I don't blame her."

Nor does Brynn. After what she herself witnessed under that roof, she can't imagine ever crossing the threshold again without picturing Fiona's desecrated corpse.

"Come on," Brynn tells Garth now, eager to rid herself of the haunting, grisly image. "Let's go over and see Ashley. I want to talk to Deirdre. I haven't really had a chance to yet."

She merely gave Fee's twin sister a sobbing hug when

they first saw each other at church. Sitting behind Deirdre during the mass, Brynn, like Garth, was repeatedly struck by the haunting resemblance to her dead friend.

Now, as Deirdre looks up when she and Garth approach, Brynn finds herself cloaked in goose bumps.

It's almost as though Fiona has come back to life.

The facial features are the same, though Deirdre's hair is worn loose, hanging down her back, as opposed to Fiona's always-constrained chignon. She's wearing a flowing black dress that would never have a place in the tailored wardrobe her sister favored. And she's got a coffee stirrer in her hand, not a cigarette—though she's holding it like one.

The starkest difference, though, is the absence of Fee's omnipresent crackling nervous energy.

Deirdre is positively bereft, her body almost limp as Brynn gives her another hug.

"How are you holding up?" Stupid question, Brynn thinks immediately, and one with an obvious answer.

She hates herself for resorting to common funeral fodder, but she can't help it. She, too, is utterly depleted.

First Tildy, and now Fiona. It's too much.

And then there's Cassie. Brynn e-mailed her the terrible news, though she figures that unless Cassie is on a remote island somewhere without access to television, radio, or newspapers, she's already heard.

There's been no reply.

The silence is ominous.

Brynn is beginning to wonder if she's the only one—of the five girls who were up at the Prom that night—who is still alive.

But she's well aware that the clock is still ticking.

Deirdre is saying sadly, "I was telling Ashley earlier that her mother and I used to jump off this stage when we were kids, holding umbrellas, pretending we were Mary Poppins. It was our favorite movie."

"I've never seen it. But Aunt Deirdre is going to get it for me and we're going to watch it."

"That sounds like fun." Brynn musters a smile for Ashley, and notices that Garth has stepped away to greet one of the other professors from Stonebridge.

It's the first time he's left her side all day, but he's keeping a watchful eye on her even now.

"I still can't believe it," Deirdre is saying, shaking her head and unwrapping a stick of gum. "What a shock."

"Where are you staying while you're in town, Deirdre? With your parents?"

"Are you kidding?" She folds the gum into her mouth. "At a hotel."

"Have you spoken to them?"

"They tried. I just . . . I can't." She shrugs, clearly guarded in front of Ashley. She rakes a hand through her hair and shakes her head at Brynn, as though wishing she could say more.

"Which hotel are you staying in?" Brynn asks Deirdre, even as she's suddenly struck by a thought so preposterous she tries to push it right back out of her head.

"Up at Cedar Ridge Inn."

"Why don't we get together and catch up?" Brynn suggests. "Maybe I'll come up and see you there later."

"That would be so good, Brynn. I have so many questions about what's been going on."

Brynn's heart is pounding.

"Where are you staying again?" she asks Deirdre.

"At Cedar Ridge Inn. It's up on Tower Hill Road."

"Is that the road that branches off of Mountainview?"

"No, that's on the opposite side of town." Deirdre looks slightly piqued at Brynn's confusion.

Still holding her coffee in one hand and her black clutch purse in the other, Brynn asks helplessly, "Can you just write down the directions for me?"

Deirdre looks at her for a long moment. "You know what? How about if I just come over to your place later instead? I don't want to hang around at that hotel anymore than I have to."

She knows, Brynn realizes, and the icy, awful truth slithers in and seems to coil around her torso, squeezing the breath out of her. *She knows what I'm thinking.*

And that means that I'm right.

PART V

HAPPY BIRTHDAY, DEAR BRYNN

CHAPTER 22

"Hello there, Mrs. Saddler. Beautiful day to be outside, isn't it?" Arnie gestures at the bright sun in a piercing late-October sky. "Waiting for the school bus?"

"How'd you guess?" Brynn rises from the front steps on liquid legs and walks halfway down the sidewalk to greet the smiling mailman.

Jeremy, kicking his way through a heap of dry leaves on the lawn, yells, "Happy Halloween!"

"Not yet, sweetie. But only three more days," Brynn tells him.

"'Only'? When you're a kid, three days is an eternity." Arnie flips through his satchel.

Yes, and when you're an adult, every precious moment can seem all too fleeting.

Especially when you're living in sheer dread as the days fall away on the calendar.

"Looks like you've got a stack of cards today, Mrs. Saddler." Arnie hands over several bright-colored envelopes. "Is it your birthday or something?"

"Tomorrow." She manages to keep her voice steady and a smile pinned to her face.

"Well, Happy Birthday. Got any special plans?"

"I'm going up to my friend Fiona's cabin in the mountains," she tells him. Loudly. Mindful not just of the police officer concealed around the corner of her house, keeping an eye on her and Jeremy, but also of old Mr. Chase standing in his front yard next door, trimming his shrubs.

"Fiona Fitzgerald?" Arnie shakes his head. "That was such a shame, what happened to that poor woman. I knew you were friends, but I didn't want to say anything to upset you. I'm really sorry for your loss," he adds awkwardly.

"Thank you." She can't meet his gaze.

"Have the police figured out who did it yet?" Arnie asks.

"No, not yet."

"I bet you're shaken up."

"Yes. That's why I'm going to get away tomorrow."

"I don't blame you."

Brynn can sense the wheels turning in his head. She imagines him later, back at the post office, sorting mail or whatever it is that the carriers do when they finish their routes. He'll gossip about Fiona's murder, because that's what everyone in town has been doing for days, and he'll recount what Brynn just told him.

She hopes.

And Mr. Chase over there across his leafless lawn, pretending to be engrossed in his precision shrubbery, will do the same thing later inside, with his wife. Sheila Chase is a notorious gossip . . . And her social calendar is full every night. When she goes off to play bridge or whatever she has scheduled for tonight, she'll mention Brynn's birthday plans to leave town.

And she's going to stay in her dead friend's cabin, can you imagine?

But Sheila Chase and Arnie the mailman certainly don't have an exclusive on that tidbit. Brynn has been talking about it for a couple of days now, telling anyone she sees. Caleb's teacher, Mrs. Shimp, Thelma the supermarket checker, Barney the gas station attendant.

With any luck, her birthday plans will make their way to the right pair of ears. Just in case they don't, she'll be leaving a note for Garth right there on the kitchen table.

He, of course, is aware of what's going on.

And he doesn't like it one bit.

In fact, when Detective Quincy first proposed that she help to bait a trap for the killer, Garth flat-out vetoed the plan, and Brynn did, too. But she came around pretty quickly when she realized that it might be the only way for the police to apprehend someone and put an end to this caged hell she's been living in.

"Why not just do it right here at home?" she asked Detective Quincy.

"Because that's too obvious. Nobody would ever believe that you'd sit here at home alone on your birthday after what happened to your friends. You'll be expected to run away, like Cassie did, and Fiona wanted to do."

At the mention of Fiona's name, Brynn had to fight to maintain eye contact with the detective.

She hasn't breathed a word of her suspicion to anyone—not even Garth.

And it isn't her place to reveal this secret.

She'll leave that to its keeper.

Garth finds Brynn standing in the doorway of the boys' room, watching them sleep.

She gasps when he puts his hands on her shoulders.

"Sorry," she presses her palm against her chest, "I'm just jumpy tonight."

Of course she is.

So is Garth.

Not just because of the dangerous responsibility that lies before her tomorrow, but because of the one he faces tonight.

Right now.

"Come on." He quietly pulls the boys' door closed. "Let's go to bed."

"You're coming, too?" she asks in surprise. He's gone back to his old nocturnal habits since Fiona's funeral.

"Don't you want me to?"

"Yes," she says quickly. "That would be good. I don't want to sleep alone tonight."

Together, they go into the master bedroom. Garth closes the door and Brynn reaches for her nightgown on the hook behind it.

"Wait." He touches her arm. "I need to talk to you."

"About tomorrow," she says heavily. "I know, and, yes, I'm scared out of my mind, but you know that I have to do—"

"Not about tomorrow, Brynn," he cuts in.

They've been over that enough times. She keeps insisting that going along with Quincy Hiles's plan is her only option, and Garth finally pretended to agree. He's going to drive the boys out to stay with her father and Sue first thing in the morning.

"If it's not about tomorrow, then what is it about?"

"Sit down, Brynn."

"What's wrong?"

What isn't wrong? he thinks, leading her over to the bed. They both sit, on the edge of the mattress, angled toward each other.

"Garth?"

I don't want to do this.

It doesn't matter. You have to.

He takes a deep breath. Exhales.

Begins. "You know how you kept that secret from me for all these years? About Rachel?"

A shadow crosses her eyes before she closes them. "Yes."

"I had one, too."

Her eyelids fly open. "One . . . what? You mean . . . a secret?"

He nods.

"What?" The word is barely audible, tainted with dread.

"Tildy . . . She was . . . She and I were . . ."

She and I.

At that phrase, Brynn seems to instantly comprehend what he's trying to say. He can see the realization sweep through her. With it comes disbelief . . . then pure anguish.

"You had an affair with her?"

"*No*. Not an affair. You and I weren't married when it happened."

"So it was before we met?" Now she's relieved.

He forces himself to admit, "No. Not before we met. I mean, it was going on before we met, but . . . It didn't end when we did."

He wants to turn away from the stark pain on her face, but he won't let himself.

"But . . ." She pauses, swallows hard, tries again. "But you said that was against your rules."

"It was different with her. She wasn't somebody I wanted to . . . be with."

"But you were."

"Not the way I wanted to be with you, the way I *was* with you. When I met you, I knew you were different. I knew you were someone I wouldn't want to let go—and, my God, Brynn, that scared the hell out of me."

"So you cheated on me."

"No! Not when we were married."

"It's still cheating. It was still me. Still us."

Don't say that. This is hard enough.

"It didn't happen very many times. I was stupid."

"Yes," Brynn's tone is brittle as black ice, "you were. I can't believe you would—"

"It happened a long time ago, Brynn." He chooses his next words carefully. "Almost *ten years ago*."

Ten years ago.

Just like Rachel.

She closes her mouth, swallowing whatever she was poised to say next.

"I swear to you that it never happened after we were married. I never broke our wedding vows."

"I don't know if I can believe that," she says, as though she's reading his mind.

"You have to. It's true."

"How can I trust you?"

"You always could. Since we've been married. Tildy even tried, once, to—you know. In Boston last summer, she—"

"You saw her in Boston?"

"We ran into each other. Fiona was there, too, and—"

"She didn't tell me? And you didn't tell me?"

"I couldn't. I was afraid to. I was afraid you'd think something happened."

"Why would I think that? Why would I suspect that my husband would ever cheat on me with my friend?" She shakes her head and swallows audibly. "I can't believe I was so damned stupid. And blind. And that the three of you kept this from me. Especially Fee. Especially *you*."

"Nothing happened," he repeats. "Tildy tried. But nothing happened. I didn't kiss her, I didn't touch her. I love you, Brynn. I would never jeopardize our marriage."

She says nothing.

"Look," he says, reaching toward her, "let's—"

"Don't touch me." She moves back. "And don't sleep in here tonight."

"But—"

"You never do anyway. And now I guess I know why."

"That isn't true. And it isn't fair."

"Fair? Don't even say the word *fair* after what you—"

"You kept something from me, too," he cuts in icily. "Remember? And I forgave you."

"That was different."

"Not at all. You had your secret. I had mine. Now it's all out in the open."

"I wish it wasn't." She's crying now. "I wish you had never told me."

So do I, Garth thinks grimly, as he leaves the room.

"That was such a good movie." Ashley leans her head on her aunt's shoulder as they watch the closing credits of *Mary Poppins.*

They're in the small parlor at Cedar Ridge Inn, where Aunt Dee is staying.

Aunt Dee—that's what she asked Ashley to call her. "Dee was your mother's nickname for me when we were kids," she said, her eyes flooded with tears. "When I grew up, I decided I hated it . . . but not anymore. Now I miss it. And her."

There's a DVD player and television here, so Aunt Dee rented *Mary Poppins* and invited Ashley to spend the night.

She figured Daddy wouldn't be crazy about that idea, especially on a school night, but Aunt Dee talked him into it somehow.

Maybe she pointed out that she'll be leaving soon, to go back to her own life. She hasn't said anything yet about exactly when that will happen, but Ashley knows she can't stay forever.

She only fervently wishes it, every chance she gets.

"I can't believe you've never seen this movie before, Ashley. Especially since your mother always loved it so much. She knew every word to every song, and she used to go around singing them all day long. It drove everyone crazy."

"No way! I can't even imagine that."

"Oh, your mother drove people crazy all the time," Aunt Dee says with a chuckle.

"No, I believe *that.* She drives a lot of people crazy now, too. Especially me." Ashley hesitates. "I mean, she *did.* But anyway . . . I just can't imagine her singing."

"She doesn't sing?"

"Never. Not around me, anyway. She hardly even talks to

me. I mean, *talked* to me. Not unless she was telling me what to do."

Aunt Dee doesn't say anything to that. She's probably thinking Ashley shouldn't be saying anything bad about her mother.

And you shouldn't, she tells herself guiltily.

"She was a great mom," she says aloud, to make up for that. "I loved her so much."

"Really?" Aunt Dee seems happy to hear that. "Tell me some stuff you loved about her."

"Well, she was really good at her job. She built a business from scratch. Not just anyone can do something like that. It takes a lot of hard work and dedication."

"You sound just like her."

"That's 'cause she used to tell me that all the time. She said I could make anything happen, if I worked hard enough."

"That's true. What else was great about her? As a mom, I mean."

"Um . . . Well, she was really good at telling me stuff about how I should look. You know, about standing up straight, and keeping my hair around my face, and which clothes to wear. Not to eat sweets because of my cavities. Stuff like that."

Aunt Dee nods. "What else?"

Ashley thinks about it.

"Ashley?" Aunt Dee prods after a minute.

"There were just a lot of good things about her," she says with a shrug, looking down at her hands twisting around each other in her lap.

Aunt Dee puts a hand under her chin and forces her to turn her head and look at her. "I know she wasn't the perfect mom, Ashley. And so did she."

"No, she—"

"You don't have to pretend she was. I know she wishes she had spent more time with you."

To Ashley's surprise, Aunt Dee is starting to cry.

"Did Mom really say that?"

Aunt Dee hesitates before she nods, and Ashley shakes her head.

"She didn't say it. You made that up."

"It was how she felt, whether or not she ever actually said it to me, or to you, Ashley."

"I don't think it was. She didn't seem like she wished she could spend more time with me. And even if she wanted to . . ."

Cut it out, Ashley tells herself sternly. *You can't say that.*

"Even if she wanted to spend more time with you, what?"

Ashley blurts, "I wouldn't really have wanted to spend more time with her. She made me nervous sometimes because I felt like I wasn't good enough."

"At what?"

"At anything. And sometimes I used to wish . . ." She trails off.

No, that's too horrible. Don't you dare say it.

"What did you wish, Ashley?"

It sounds like Aunt Dee is holding her breath, waiting for an answer. Ashley doesn't dare look up at her, afraid she'll be able to read the terrible thought in Ashley's mind.

"I can't tell you."

"Why not?"

"Because it's really bad."

"You can tell me anything."

"Not this."

"I promise I won't tell anyone. And sometimes I wish really, really bad things, too."

"You do?"

Aunt Dee nods.

Ashley takes a deep breath. "Sometimes I used to wish something would happen to my mother, so that I could have a new mom," she says in a rush, then collapses against her aunt in a rush of tears and guilt.

Aunt Dee holds her close and strokes her hair, exactly the way a mother does . . .

Exactly the way Ashley always wistfully longed for her own mother to hold her.

But she never did.

And now she never will.

Brynn saw Fiona's mountain retreat once before, when the two of them were driving around in a realtor's Mercedes SUV looking at houses for Fee to buy.

Nestled on a wooded lot along a steep, winding road, the three-bedroom log cabin has painted green shutters, a pair of dormered windows, and a porch with wooden rocking chairs.

Brynn thought it was infinitely charming that warm spring afternoon, in dappled sunlight.

This frosty autumn morning, shrouded in cobwebs of heavy mountain mist, the cabin has a foreboding air.

Seven lonely miles from Cedar Crest, out of the nearest cell phone tower's range, Brynn feels completely isolated from the rest of the world.

But you aren't. Not really.

She should be reassured, aware that a couple of armed officers lurk just out of sight in the woods.

Instead, the palpably eerie sensation of being watched only makes her more apprehensive. Even the two dormered windows loom like hooded eyes as she walks slowly up the path from the car, tucking her keys into the back pocket of her jeans.

It's going to be okay.

At least, that's what Garth had the nerve to say this morning, when they faced each other in the kitchen after a sleepless night.

He didn't look any more convinced than she felt.

Even if *this* turns out okay . . . they might not be, together. How is she supposed to ever look him in the eye again, knowing about him and Tildy?

But he did forgive you for what you did so long ago, a

small voice reminds her. *Are you really unwilling to forgive him for something he did back then?*

It isn't just about that, though. It's that he never told her. That he and Tildy and, yes, even Fee, shared this sordid little secret behind her back.

Then again, now that the initial shock and humiliation have worn off a bit . . .

No. You can't just forgive him for something like this. It was wrong.

Hugging and kissing her sons good-bye before Garth drove them out to the Cape was the hardest thing she ever had to do.

The second hardest was to sit there while her husband told her he slept with one of her best friends.

Yes, it happened years ago.

No, they weren't married.

It could have been worse.

Still, it's pretty bad.

They didn't acknowledge it this morning before Garth left. They didn't say much of anything at all.

The boys were smiling happily as Garth drove off with them. Left alone in the doorway, she was crying.

Her father and Sue think Garth is taking Brynn away for her birthday, and were happy to keep the boys for a few days.

If they had any idea about what's really going on . . .

But, of course, they don't.

Garth will turn around and drive right back to Cedar Crest, where he'll keep a low profile as the day wears on. Quincy instructed him to go to police headquarters. If all goes as planned, Brynn will be reunited with her husband there . . .

Right after Fee and Tildy's killer comes after her as well, and is apprehended.

Brynn is utterly overwhelmed every time she allows herself to think about what Garth told her. It's been so distracting that she still can barely grasp the monumental day—and perhaps night—that lie ahead.

She tries not to think about it as she plods up the cabin's wooden steps, but she can't help feeling as though she's walking the plank to certain doom.

The wind kicks up to rustle dry leaves and creak branches in the trees overhead. A crow lifts from its perch with a fluttering of wings and a haunting caw that echoes into the foreboding sky.

Brynn bends to lift a corner of the brown straw Welcome mat, looking for the key Fiona said is always here.

It isn't.

She has a momentary flare of hope that they can call off this whole dangerous charade—

Oh. Here's the key, on the far side of the mat.

And they can't call it off. This is the only way to catch her. *Rachel*.

Brynn still can't reconcile the memory of her fun-loving old friend with the murderous fiend who slaughtered Fiona and Tildy. Maybe when she fell, her brain was damaged . . .

And she was transformed into a serial killer?

But how? Why?

Rage. Fury. That's Quincy's theory, and it makes sense.

Rachel was betrayed by her friends who abandoned her to die.

Now she wants revenge.

Ashley stares at the familiar two-story yellow-brick building from the passenger's seat of Aunt Dee's rental car.

She has to do this sooner or later, she knows. She just wishes it was later.

Then again, it's late enough. School started two hours ago, but she was so reluctant to go that Aunt Dee took her out for breakfast—strawberry pancakes. They lingered over their meal, talking about everything imaginable.

"Do you want me to come in with you?" Aunt Dee asks now, resting a hand on her shoulder.

Ashley shakes her head. It will be hard enough to go in there alone, late, with everyone staring at her. She can just imagine how they would gape if she walked in with someone who looks like the ghost of her dead mother.

"Your dad said he'll pick you up after school," Aunt Dee tells her, and Ashley nods bleakly. She knows that; she talked to Daddy, too, when he called the inn first thing this morning.

"I miss you, baby girl," he told Ashley. "Are you all right?"

She told him she was fine.

Then she put Aunt Dee back on the phone, and she figured Daddy must be asking her whether Ashley had had any nightmares, because Aunt Dee said, "No, not at all. She slept right through the night like a baby."

"Just keep your chin up, Ashley," Aunt Dee tells her now, softly, and squeezes her shoulder gently. "You'll get through this day. You can get through anything, if you put your mind to it."

Ashley jerks her head around sharply, half-expecting to see her mother sitting there.

No. It's Aunt Dee, wearing a bright-colored patchwork poncho Mom would never wear, her long hair hanging loose down her back.

"What's the matter, Ashley?"

"Nothing. You just . . . You sounded like her. And . . . It made me miss her. Kind of more than I even thought I would."

Aunt Dee smiles sadly and touches her cheek.

Then, spine steeled and head held high, Ashley marches into school, thinking that her mother would be proud of her.

The cabin's wooden, glass-paned door creaks loudly as Brynn pushes it open.

She hesitates on the threshold, trying not to think about it. *I walked into the house. I turned my head . . .*

And I saw her.

Even now, after so many days have gone by and she's had a chance to absorb the horror of that day, the intense, vivid memory catches her off guard.

Will that happen now, to me? Am I going to be slaughtered like that?

No.

Because the cabin isn't empty. Last night, Quincy installed a third officer someplace inside, ready to rush to Brynn's aid with the others, gun drawn.

She can feel his hidden presence as she reaches inside the door and flips on the light.

I don't want to go in.

But she has to; her anxiety and pregnancy-stimulated bladder, if nothing else, demands that she move forward.

Stepping into the cabin at last, she looks around the deserted great room: rustic furniture, woven area rugs, stone fireplace.

Once, she thought it was welcoming. Today, as she forces herself to close and lock the door behind her, it feels like a tomb.

She sets her overnight bag on the floor.

Outside, in the distance, she hears a rumble of thunder.

Yes. It's supposed to rain.

She listens for it but hears nothing.

Nothing at all.

But someone is here, in the cabin with her, waiting.

Not for the rain.

She can almost hear the steady breathing in time with her hollow-sounding footsteps across the timber floor.

Yes, someone is here—It's the cop, she reminds herself. *You're perfectly safe.*

She makes her way toward the second-floor bathroom, flipping on lamps as she goes, to banish the early-morning shadows. Nobody said she had to sit here in the dark, waiting for the attack.

She goes to the bathroom quickly, her uneasiness building, instinctively feeling driven to get back downstairs. Somehow, it seems safer there.

As she turns to flush the toilet, she sees a faint pink smear on the white paper in the bowl, and her heart stops.

Blood.

She's spotting.

Oh, God. Oh, God, no.

Panic swells into her throat. She frantically unfurls another length of tissue, swipes it between her legs, and inspects it.

Yes. She's bleeding.

Not much.

Not yet, anyway.

She has to get out of here. She has to get to a doctor.

As she hurries back down the hall toward the stairs, hearing the first droplets falling on the roof overhead, she breaks Quincy's cardinal rule.

"Hello? Officer?" Her voice echoes through the house. "I need help. Please . . ."

The detective had repeatedly cautioned her not to acknowledge the protective presence. *You never know whether the culprit is in earshot, Mrs. Saddler, and you don't want to scare her off.*

Her, Quincy said. As in *Rachel.*

Brynn promised she'd keep quiet.

But she didn't know then that her unborn baby's life would be in more immediate jeopardy than theirs together.

The hidden cop doesn't respond.

"Please," Brynn calls desperately, clinging to the railing as she heads down the steep flight back to the first floor. "Please, help me. I'm bleeding."

At the foot of the stairs, she stops short, spotting something out of the corner of her eye.

Something she didn't notice on her way up.

Something that sends ice flowing through her veins and drops her mouth open, poised to—

No.

Don't scream.

She closes her mouth . . .

Why?

Because you're afraid no one will hear?

Or because you're afraid someone might?

Heart racing, she stares mutely at the floor just in front of the closet door beneath the stairs, where an ominous dark stain taints the pine plank floor.

Ashley looked so small and defenseless as she walked away alone, into the familiar yellow-brick school building. She was trying so hard to be brave, but her shoulders were shaking.

She has more guts than you ever gave her credit for.

Maybe more guts than you have yourself.

She brakes at the STOP sign a block from Saint Vincent's, then resumes driving, careful to stay within the posted school zone limit. All she needs now is to be pulled over.

No, that can't happen.

There's something she has to do.

It came up incidentally, as she and Ashley ate their pancakes and chatted over breakfast at that diner.

Ashley caught a glimpse of her thick silver bracelet falling from beneath her sleeve, and mentioned that her mother always liked to wear gold jewelry.

"She only had one silver thing in her jewelry box," Ashley said. "A really pretty bracelet that was like a link of rosebuds."

"How do you know about that?"

"I saw it once when I was snooping around, trying on some of her stuff," Ashley admitted with a guilty expression. "But then I heard my mother coming so I put it back and got out of there."

"I'm sure she wouldn't have minded. All girls try on their

mom's jewelry. Your mother and I always did, when we were young. My father used to buy her costume jewelry for every occasion, and she never wore any of it. She just let it pile up in her jewelry box."

"Well, I think my father must have given the silver bracelet to her, and she never wore it, but she kept it. I used to think it meant she still loved him and they were going to get back together again, but now I don't know."

"Oh, Ash . . ." She shook her head. "Your father didn't give it to her. That was her sorority bracelet."

"No, I don't think so, Aunt Dee. I'm pretty sure it was a Ralph Lauren bracelet, from my dad."

"Why do you think that?"

Ashley told her.

And the ugly germ of an idea sparked in her brain.

It can't be . . .

No. There's no way.

Ashley must be mistaken.

But there's only one way to know for sure.

Brynn's heart is pounding as she stares at the dark splotch on the floor.

It almost looks as though something seeped under the door.

Something.

Blood.

No. You're being ridiculous.

The spot is dry, soaked into the wood; she can see that without touching it. It's probably just an exceptionally large knot in the pine.

Or perhaps whoever finished the floor splashed paint there, or dark-colored stain.

Or it's blood.

"Officer," Brynn calls again, taking a step back from the closet door, her voice tremulous. "Please . . . Where are you?"

But her invisible protector remains stubbornly silent; the only sound is the rain pattering on the porch roof, pinging into the metal gutters.

I can't do this.

Brynn presses a trembling hand against her lower stomach.

She doesn't care about Quincy's trap, or the police catching the killer, or having to live with the consequences if they don't.

At this moment, all she cares about is her baby.

The damned cop isn't answering her pleas, and she can't even use her cell phone to call for help.

I have to get out of here. I have to get to a doctor.

She abruptly turns to flee—and screams.

Unmistakably outlined in the door's glass pane is the figure of someone looming on the porch, watching her.

Parked in the deserted lot of a bait-and-tackle shop that's been boarded up for winter, Quincy stares at the crackling two-way radio in his hand and bites out a curse.

"Still no response up there. Something's wrong," he tells Connelly, standing just outside the car in the rain, training a pair of binoculars on the mountainside in a futile effort to see something.

"What do you want to do, then? Go up?"

"I don't know." Quincy's stomach burns as this morning's acrid coffee mingles with his growing uneasiness about Brynn Saddler.

For a long moment, Quincy stares through the windshield, gazing up at the forested incline now mostly obscured by low-hanging clouds and wisps of mist.

Somewhere up there, he believes, an unwitting Brynn Saddler is vulnerable and unprotected.

But if you and Connelly go barreling up there, and everything is fine, and it's just a communications problem because of the terrain or the weather or whatever—

Then he'll have tipped his hand.

And enable Rachel Lorent, if she's lurking nearby, to escape.

But if you don't get your ass up there right now and check things out . . .

Brynn trusted him. He can't let anything happen to her.

Quincy jerks his head toward the mountain in a decisive nod. "Let's go."

"Who's there?" a voice demands, as the key turns in the lock.

But it isn't Rachel's voice, Brynn realizes.

No, it's a man's.

A cop . . . It might be one of the cops. It must be. Because a stalking serial killer wouldn't be asking who's in here; he would know.

Nonetheless Brynn instinctively backs away in dread, both hands splayed against her abdomen as if to shield her unborn child.

"Brynn?"

The door opens . . .

And she recognizes his voice in the split second before she sees him.

Patrick Hagan.

Thank God.

Her knees sag in relief as they stare at each other.

Pat is wearing a red and black checked wool jacket, jeans, boots. His hair is sprinkled with droplets of rain. He blinks at her in confusion.

"I thought that was your car," he says, shaking his head like a wet puppy and rubbing a hand through his damp hair. "What are you doing here?"

"Fee said I could use the cabin whenever I wanted," is her lame reply.

She watches a frown begin to cross Pat's face, only to be chased away by a flash of remembrance.

He forgot she was dead, Brynn realizes.

For a second there, Pat was obviously annoyed with his ex-wife's open invitation to their shared property.

Now, however, he's shrugging and offering a slightly sheepish grin.

"I'm glad you took her up on it, then," he says graciously. "I'm the only one who ever comes up here—it's kind of nice to have some company for a change. Hey, I brought donuts."

She realizes he's holding a white paper bag in one hand, a take-out cup of coffee in the other.

Brynn shakes her head, still trying to reconcile her relief at the ordinariness of Pat's intrusion with the stark terror of the last few minutes.

"Are you sure? I've got glazed and—"

"Pat, listen, I need you to help me. This isn't going to make any sense at all, but . . ."

"Are you okay, Brynn?"

"No." Her voice breaks. "I'm not okay. I have to get out of here."

"What's wrong?"

"I'm pregnant . . . and I'm bleeding."

His jaw drops and he starts toward her. "Sit down. I'll get you some—"

"No, Pat, I can't stay here. We can't stay here. There's something . . ." She gestures helplessly at the floor in front of the closet door. "Do you see that stain? What is it? Paint or something? Has it always been there?"

She watches his gaze drop to the floor, sees him frown. "No, I don't know what that is."

He strides toward the door, jerks it open, and stiffens.

"What is it?" Brynn asks, somehow knowing that her worst suspicion has just been confirmed.

It was blood.

Pat turns away and she sees his stunned expression.

With a muttered oath he grabs her arm, pulling her toward the door. "We have to get the hell out of here, Brynn. Come on."

"Is it . . . Is someone . . . in there?" she manages to whimper as she allows Pat to propel her across the porch, down the steps through the rain to his Jeep.

"Hell, yes." Pat is breathing hard, his hand clenched almost painfully on her upper arm. "We've got to get the hell out of here before—"

He doesn't finish the sentence, opening the door and practically tossing her into the passenger's seat, looking over his shoulder at the cabin as though someone is going to come after them.

Brynn follows his apprehensive gaze. The porch is empty.

Then she shifts her eyes toward the woods where, she now senses, Quincy's men lie among the wet, fallen leaves like the discarded prey of a still-circling vulture.

Ashley forgot her backpack in Aunt Dee's car.

She probably should have said something when they came out of the restaurant after breakfast and Aunt Dee casually tossed it from the floor of the front seat into the backseat.

Mom never would have done that. She would have known Ashley would forget it if she couldn't see it.

Out of sight, out of mind.

Oh, well, she thinks, heading toward the cafeteria. Sister Mary Joseph gave her money so she'll be able to buy lunch, and the other teachers told her not to worry about not having her folders, notes, or textbooks.

Everyone is being so nice to Ashley today.

They feel sorry for me, she knows, and wonders how long it's going to last.

Will anyone ever treat her like a regular person again?

All this coddling kindness is making her miss her mother all the more.

What Ashley wouldn't give to hear her say, "Pull your hair forward a little, Ash. And stand up straight."

But, she keeps reminding herself, she'll never hear Mom's voice again.

Pat speeds away from the cabin as though they're being chased, keeping one eye on the rearview mirror. The tires catapult gravel along the sides of the road; the wipers beat a steady rhythm on the windshield to keep the downpour at bay.

Huddled in the passenger's seat, still reeling, still clutching her stomach, Brynn realizes she left her purse behind. And no way is she going back for it.

"Do you have a phone?" she asks Pat, who shakes his head.

Dammit. Hers was in her purse.

"We have to stop somewhere and call Quincy."

"Who?"

"The police," she clarifies. "That person . . . the one in the closet . . . He was a cop."

"What?" Pat shakes his head. "No, he wasn't."

"How do you know?"

"He wasn't wearing a uniform."

"He wouldn't have been. He was undercover, there to protect me." She shifts her weight in the seat and wonders if she's still spotting.

"What are you talking about, Brynn?" Pat takes a hard curve too quickly; the tires make a high-pitched squealing sound on the wet pavement as, cursing, he swerves to avoid an oncoming car.

"That guy is flying," he mutters, shaking his head. "What were you saying, Brynn?"

"I'll explain everything later. Just drive," she murmurs, still trembling, and not just from the close call on the curve. "Don't stop anywhere; we'll call when we get to town."

Nodding grimly, Pat presses the gas pedal a little harder, putting more and more distance between them and the cabin.

Sinking onto the cabin's steps, Quincy buries his head in his hands as Connelly tersely radios for backup.

The young cop lying face down on the closet floor had his throat slit so forcefully he was almost decapitated.

The same thing happened to the two who were concealed in the woods. Large footprints in the mud showed that somebody crept up on each of them and attacked from behind before they knew what hit them; no sign of a struggle. Their necks were probably sliced open before they could make a sound.

The security detail he promised Brynn Saddler was wiped out just like that: one, two, three. Gone.

And so is Brynn herself.

Quincy was certain they would find her body. Her car is parked right here; her purse is in the cabin. But there is no Brynn, mutilated and wearing a pink party hat. No cake, no party decorations, no gift box.

Thank God.

Still . . .

Quincy is certain she's not safe and sound. No, she wouldn't wander off without her purse—without her *car*. She must be here somewhere.

With Rachel.

Or . . .

Suddenly, he remembers the Jeep that came barreling recklessly around that curve before, on the way up here. Somebody was hell-bent to get down the mountain.

Back to Cedar Crest.

And those footprints in the woods . . .

They were made by boots—not necessarily a man's, but still too big for a woman affectionately described by her brother as "a tiny little thing."

Quincy stares unseeingly at the oppressive forest surrounding the cabin, his stomach burning as he realizes that, for the first time in a long career, his gut instinct might have been wrong.

"Wait, where are you going?" Brynn asks Pat as he turns down Tamarack Lane.

"I'm taking you home." He glances at her, touching the brakes to slow the Jeep. "No?"

She shakes her head. "I need to get to a doctor, or the hospital."

"I thought you wanted to call the police."

"I do. All right," she decides swiftly, "We'll stop at my house, I'll call them, I'll call my doctor, and . . ."

And I have to call Garth. What happened last night doesn't matter anymore.

I need him to know about the baby . . .

Before I lose it.

I need him with me. No matter what he did ten years ago. He's right. It doesn't matter.

And he forgave me, so I can forgive—

Pat reaches out and pats her clenched hand. "It's going to be okay. Hang in there, all right?"

She nods, wondering what she would have done if he hadn't come along.

You would have gotten out of there anyway. You were on your way . . .

Or would someone have emerged to stop her?

Was the killer there, concealed, ready to strike?

Probably.

And Pat's unexpected presence saved her life . . .

For now.

We gave Rachel a chance to get away. Now I'll always wonder where she is . . . and when she's coming back for me.

But she can't think about that now. She hugs her midsection as Pat pulls into the driveway, parks the car, and hurries around through the rain to open her door for her.

He helps her down with a steadying grip on her arm and escorts her toward the door, still glancing over either shoulder. She looks, too, and is reassured to see that they weren't followed.

"Come on, Brynn."

They splash through the rain to the front door. Glad she had her keys in her back pocket, rather than left in her purse back at the cabin, Brynn opens the dead bolts and steps into the familiar dry warmth of home.

Pat closes the door behind them.

"Lock it," Brynn commands, "the dead bolts, too."

"We're not even sticking around," he protests. Then, seeing the look on her face, he obliges.

"I'll call the police," she says, and starts for the phone in the kitchen.

In the doorway, she stops short.

And screams.

Using Ashley's keys from her backpack, and trying one key after another, she manages to unlock the door on the third try.

She steps swiftly and silently over the threshold into the dim interior, all but certain the place is deserted.

But if it isn't . . .

Then I'm dead.

This time, for real.

Or maybe not. He'll hurt her only if her growing suspicion about him proves to be correct.

If she's wrong, and he's harmless . . .

Then I'm safe for now.

And so is Brynn.

She moves quickly through the room to the end table beside the couch, and pulls open the drawer, remembering what Ashley told her earlier.

"I was looking for a pencil and when I opened the drawer, I saw it."

The silver rose sorority bracelet.

It was in a white box, on a square of cotton. Ashley confessed guiltily that she opened it and snuck a quick peek; her father was in the shower.

"I figured he must have bought my mom another one because she liked the first one so much, since she kept it."

No, Ashley. He didn't buy the first one for your mother.

He didn't buy the second one, either—for her, or anyone else.

And it isn't Ralph Lauren.

Ashley thought it was, she said, because of the silver letter charms hanging from it: *R.L.*

Rachel Lorent.

That bracelet was on Rachel's wrist the night she disappeared.

So what is it doing in Pat's apartment?

It isn't, she realizes, staring into a drawer that's empty, aside from a couple of pencils and an old issue of *TV Guide*.

It isn't here at all.

Ashley must have been imagining things.

She slowly closes the drawer and walks back to the door, before thinking better of it.

No.

God, no, please . . .

For an endless moment, Brynn is rooted to the floor, staring at the shocking sight that lies before her.

Even in the dim light, she can see that her kitchen has been transformed as if for a child's birthday party: crepe paper, balloons, paper place settings.

Just as Fiona's dining room was.

In the center of the table is a cake, spiked with unlit candles. It reads Happy Birthday in expertly scrolled pink icing, and, in darker lettering, DEAR BRYNN.

Just like Fiona's cake.

She's here.

The realization doesn't strike Brynn like a lightning bolt; no, it painstakingly makes its way into her consciousness, seeping slowly like a pool of blood from beneath a closet door.

She's here, and she's going to kill Pat . . .

Then she's going to kill me.

My baby. Her arms cross over her stomach. No.

And Caleb, and Jeremy, and Garth . . .

They're going to be left alone . . .

Just like we were, when Mommy died.

History is destined to repeat itself. Brynn's children will grow up as she did, longing for maternal love snatched away far too soon. They're younger, far younger, than Brynn was when she lost her mother.

I can't let it happen.

I have to get away.

She begins to spin on her heel—then freezes at the telltale sound of a match being struck, and a flickering, eerie light permeates the room.

It's not as bad as Ashley feared . . . being back at school.

Not even on a gloomy day like this.

In fact, she almost welcomes the familiar glare of overhead light banishing the gray behind the tall windows, the hiss of steam heat, the smell of wet wool, and, here in the crowded cafeteria, of hot dogs.

She can almost pretend that her life beyond the walls of Saint Vincent's School is the same as it always was. She can almost imagine that her mother is at work in her office a few blocks away.

"Where do you want to sit?" Meg asks as they hesitate with their plastic lunch trays, surveying the rows of tables.

Ashley can feel people looking up to stare at her, nudging each other, whispering.

Look, there she is. The girl whose mother was killed.

"I don't care," she tells Meg under her breath, "let's just find a spot, fast."

They carry their trays to the vacant end of a table by the window and sit down.

"So my mom said you're going to live with your dad for good now," Meg says.

"How does your mom know?"

"She talks to him a lot, I think."

"Really?" Ashley dully recalls how Daddy called Meg's mom "Cyn" that day at the movies.

"Maybe they'll fall in love and get married after all," Meg says.

Ashley contemplates that for a moment. That prospect doesn't hold the same allure it once did. She doesn't want a stepmother. Or a new mother.

She only wants her own mother back.

She swallows hard over a lump in her throat and blinks away tears as she unwraps her straw.

"Your dad told my mom he wants to move into a better place, though."

Ashley nods, jabbing her straw into her carton of chocolate milk.

Daddy told her that, too.

"He wants to go someplace where you can have your own room—a real room. And maybe even a pet."

"Really?" Ashley looks up. That might be kind of cool.

Then she remembers something, and shakes her head.

"What's wrong?" Meg asks.

"I don't want a pet."

"Why not?"

"Because I would be really upset if it ran away or something."

"It won't," says Meg, who has two dogs and a cat.

"It might."

Ashley can't help but think about poor Mrs. Josephson, who lives upstairs from Daddy. Her cat ran away a few weeks ago, and she's still looking for her. She sounds so sad whenever Ashley hears her standing at the door, calling for her lost cat.

"Here, kitty kitty . . . Come here, Agatha . . ."

"What are you doing?" Brynn asks in dread as Pat's hand—the one that isn't holding a lit match—once again closes around her arm. Hard.

But this time, she doesn't mistake the iron grip as protective. This time, she sees it for what it is: a vise from which now there is no escape.

Pat.

Pat is the one.

Not Rachel.

"But . . . why?" she chokes out.

Ignoring the question, he drags her across the floor to the table. There, he holds the lit match to each of the three candles as it burns perilously close to his fingers.

"One for every decade," he says calmly, impervious to the fire singing his skin. Sickened, she can smell it burning.

"Why are you doing this?" Brynn whispers.

"I think you know by now." He waves the match to extinguish it.

She shakes her head mutely, struggling in his grasp, knowing it's futile to attempt escape.

Her only hope is to keep him talking. "But I *don't* know, Pat," she says desperately. Truthfully. "I don't know why."

For the first time, she spots the gift-wrapped box on the

table. The pink paper matches the one on the box she glimpsed that day in Fiona's dining room, gripped in a pair of waxen, lifeless hands.

"Please . . . I just want to have my baby. Please don't do this."

Pat goes absolutely still for a moment, as if something just unexpectedly permeated his consciousness.

Has he suddenly come to his senses?

She dares to look at him, and sees that his dark eyes are unmistakably glittering with madness and hate.

Hearing Kylah's key turn in the lock, Isaac hurriedly lifts Smoochy off his lap and sets the purring cat gently on the floor.

"*Now* you decide to like me," he mutters, shaking his head as the cat rubs against his ankles. Brushing cat hair from his jeans, he turns toward the door as Kylah steps inside.

"Hey," she says, looking surprised to see him. Pleasantly surprised. "You're here."

"I promised I would be when you got back."

"I know. I just . . ."

She didn't think he'd keep his promise.

Wearily, she sets her purse on the floor, closes the door, and looks around. "Your stuff is gone."

It didn't take her long to figure that out.

Surprising, since there wasn't much around here that belonged to him. He never fully moved in, so it didn't take him long to fully move out. Just his papers, and some books and CDs, computer equipment, and clothes.

Now it's all back in his apartment fifteen blocks away.

"You're leaving," she says heavily, not moving, just looking at him. "I thought you'd be gone before I got here, actually. I didn't expect you to stick around and say good-bye."

Expect?

Does that mean she thought this would happen—him leaving? That she's considered how it was likely to happen?

An unexpected swell of contrition laps at his soul.

"I wouldn't just run out on you, Kylah. Is that what you thought?"

She looks him in the eye and nods.

"My stuff is gone. I'm not. Not really."

What are you doing? You were going. You were outta here.

"Just because I don't want to live together right now doesn't mean it's over," he hears himself say. "I just need some space."

Her blue eyes roll toward the ceiling and she sighs.

"I know it's a cliché. But I don't want this to be over; I just—I should never have moved in so soon. But I still do want us to be together, I want to work on—"

"I don't," Kylah reaches back abruptly and jerks the door open again.

"You want me to leave? For good?"

Her resolute nod slams him hard.

That's what you had in mind, remember? You didn't want to work on your relationship with her, you wanted it to be over, so you could focus on . . .

Rachel.

It always comes down to that.

No other relationship in his life can replace the one he had with her . . .

Because it never ended.

It only ebbed, like the tide, and he's been waiting for it to sweep in again.

"I'd tell you to come back when and if you ever find Rachel," Kylah says, arms folded, "but you know what? I'm not so sure she's even what you're looking for."

*   *   *

A search of Pat's small apartment doesn't yield the silver sorority bracelet, or much of anything else . . .

Until she gets to the locked file cabinet.

It's a cheap metal one, the kind you can buy in an office-supply warehouse store. The kind whose flimsy lock can be easily picked with a bobby pin, a trick she learned back in her days at Saint Vincent's. It was the only way to keep track of what the nuns were writing in your files—and, on occasion, to change certain details you don't necessarily want on your permanent record.

She's reaching up to pluck a bobby pin from her hair before she remembers there isn't one.

Dee doesn't wear her hair in a chignon like her twin sister, Fiona. No, Dee's hair is long and loose . . .

And it's driving me absolutely crazy.

Not as crazy, though, as having given up smoking cold turkey. But maybe it won't be much longer.

In the kitchenette, she rummages around, looking for something to use. In the process, she comes across a prescription bottle of sleeping capsules tucked in the back of a drawer. An unfamiliar name, Esther Josephson, is on the label. Did he steal them? And why would he need sleeping pills? That lazy S.O.B. never had any trouble sleeping.

She pockets the bottle and continues her search until she's assembled a corn cob holder, a paper clip, a metal skewer, and assorted other potential picks.

The corn cob holder doesn't work; the prongs are too short.

The paper clip does, though.

The drawer slides open.

She begins rifling through the files inside, not quite sure what she's looking for . . .

Until she finds it.

* * *

"I wanted my baby, too, Brynn."

"What are you talking about?" she asks Pat, trying to keep her voice from giving way to shrill hysteria. "You have your baby. Ashley is—"

"No! My other baby."

"I don't know what you—"

He cuts in impatiently, "With Rachel."

Rachel?

Rachel was . . . *pregnant?*

That was her secret, Brynn realizes. That was why she was so distraught. And no wonder.

"You were there that night," she breathes, remembering the snapping twig in the forest, the sensation of being watched. "Why?"

"To talk to Rachel."

Keep him distracted, Brynn tells herself, and asks, "What did you have to talk to her about?"

"I needed to say I was sorry."

"For what?"

"For what I said."

Miraculously, she's sustaining a conversation. And every second, she's trying wildly to figure out a way to save herself, and her baby.

"What did you say?"

"I said . . ."

She's startled by the choked emotion in his voice, but she does her best not to react. She can't jar him out of the past, because then he'll remember what he means to do now, in the present.

"I said . . . something terrible . . . But I loved Fee, and I knew if she ever found out about me and Rachel . . . because it was just once. I gave her a ride from the Rat, and—"

Brynn is shaking her head in disbelief. Rachel slept with Pat? Rachel was carrying Pat's child?

"Why did I say it?" he asks plaintively. "I told her to get rid of it. Our own child," he whispers, tortured.

And in that instant, Brynn can only imagine how Rachel must have felt.

How she herself would feel if someone told her to get rid of the tiny life that's taken hold in her own womb.

"Rachel was such a live wire, she was livid. She threatened to tell Fiona, and she took off. I let her go, but the more I thought about it . . . Well, I ended up going over to the sorority house to find Rachel and tell her I didn't mean it."

No, Brynn thinks, watching him. *You did mean it, and of course it made Rachel angry. You were afraid she was going to tell Fee, so you came after her, to do God only knows what, to stop her from talking.*

"You saw us leaving the house, and followed us up to the Prom, didn't you, Pat? You saw her fall."

He nods. "After you left, I went down there. She was dead."

Like Tildy said.

"So I carried her away," Pat goes on in a monotone. "I buried her way up in the woods. I didn't want her to be found. I was afraid . . ."

Afraid that if her body ever turned up, her pregnancy would have been revealed. And connected to him. And Fiona would have found out.

Now the pieces are falling into place.

Oh, God.

"It all would have been okay, Brynn, if Fee had just loved me the way I loved her. But she robbed me. She stole my baby."

"No, Pat, Fee gave you Ashley."

"She destroyed my babies," Pat roars.

"You mean the one Rachel was carrying? But Rachel fell, Pat. You said yourself she was dead when you—"

"She was . . . but maybe the baby wasn't yet. If the four

of you had gotten help right away, the baby might have survived."

Yes, the baby he had told Rachel to destroy, Brynn thinks
incredulously. He's making no sense. He's insane. And he's
going to kill her, too, like he did the others.

"Pat, you can't blame us for your baby's death."

"Babies' deaths."

"What are you talking about?"

"Don't pretend you don't know."

"But I don't."

"Shut up. Sit." The arm jerks her roughly, forces her
down into a pulled-out chair. "I'm going to sing to you."

"But—"

"Shut up!"

She clamps her jaw shut, seeing the mad gleam in Pat's
dark eyes as he begins to sing "Happy Birthday."

"Can you at least stay for a cup of coffee?" Brynn's stepmother asks Garth as his sons go with their grandfather to
play with the train set in the basement. "It'll be ready in two
minutes."

On edge, Garth tells her, "I really need to get back." But
he eyes the countertop, where fragrant coffee is hissing into
the filter and dripping steadily into the glass carafe.

He hasn't slept well in . . .

Years, he thinks ruefully, and rubs his raw eyes. But these
last few weeks have been worse than ever. And last night was
the most brutal of all.

But he and Brynn can get through this together. Now that
everything is out in the open, they'll work on mutual forgiveness. Garth figures that every marriage has rough spots—
especially when the kids are little and money is tight.

But this, too, shall pass, he's been telling himself. They
love each other. That, he never doubts. He's loved Brynn

from that first night. He was a fool to keep things going with Tildy on the side. His only excuse is that he was young and brash and scared to death of commitment.

But I made one. And when I took those vows with Brynn, I meant them. I never broke them. I never will.

Yes, Tildy came on to him that night in Boston. And, yes, he might have been tempted—for a few seconds. But there was no way he would risk hurting, or losing, his wife.

Tildy seemed to understand. She'd always had an easy-come, easy-go attitude where he was concerned, anyway.

"Go home to your wife," she said somewhat wistfully, "and give her a hug. She's luckier than she realizes."

We both are, Garth thought at the time.

And still does.

Someday the kids will be more self-sufficient. And, someday, hopefully sooner than later, they'll have an additional cash flow. He's been killing himself to try and get—

"You look like you could use a jolt of caffeine," Sue comments, and Garth opens his eyes to see her watching him. "I'll give you a go-cup if you want to take one with you. I don't want you falling asleep on the road."

Right. He felt dangerously drowsy on the drive over. Thank goodness for the jumbo bag of M&Ms he bought when he stopped for gas, and for Caleb haltingly reading aloud from the backseat, needing prompting with a difficult word every couple of lines.

Eventually he stopped reading and started complaining about an upset stomach, but they made it here without his getting sick.

"So . . ." Sue takes a plastic insulated coffee mug from the cupboard and holds it up to him with a questioning look.

"Thanks," Garth tells Sue. "That would be good."

She nods and sets it on the counter beside the coffee-maker.

"How's Brynn feeling?"

"She's hanging in there."

"That's good." Sue is wearing a strange expression, as though she expects him to say something else.

Garth shrugs. "You know, she's been through hell lately, so she's definitely seen better days, but . . ."

"I'm glad you're doing something for her birthday. She needs—"

"Sue!" Brynn's father calls urgently from the basement.

She hurries down the steps with Garth on her heels. They find Caleb standing in a pool of vomit.

"I told you I felt carsick," he says accusingly to Garth, who looks around for something to use to clean his son and the floor.

"And I told you that you probably shouldn't have been eating all those M&Ms and reading."

"But Mommy throws up all the time," Caleb points out as Sue lifts him out of the pool of vomit, "and she doesn't eat M&Ms and she hardly ever reads anymore."

"Yeah, well, Mommy—" Garth stops short, remembering something. "What do you mean, Mommy throws up all the time?"

"She does. Every day."

"Every day? When does Mommy throw up?"

"Before breakfast and school."

Garth shifts his gaze thoughtfully away from his son and finds himself locking gazes with Sue. In her eyes, he unexpectedly finds the answer to a question he didn't even realize he was asking.

She stares for a long time at the medical record in her hand; an exact duplicate of one she keeps in her file cabinet at home.

It's locked, of course.

About as securely as Pat's file cabinet was, she acknowledges grimly.

So he knew . . . for how long?

When did he find out Fiona had been pregnant with their second child?

And that she terminated the pregnancy just before she told him she wanted a divorce . . .

It was a mistake. Not the divorce. The abortion. It was the worst mistake of her life.

She just didn't realize that until these past few days.

Only when she was able to step outside of her own life could she really see it clearly.

Fiona Fitzgerald had always believed she had everything that mattered, and she was right about that.

Just wrong about those things being her business, her status, her connections.

When the end came, none of that mattered.

Seeing the grief in Ashley's eyes awakened something deep inside of her. Some maternal instinct she had never even realized she possessed . . .

Until it was too late.

Or is it?

She can continue to live this life, a remorseful coward hiding in plain sight.

Or she can find the courage to reclaim her own, live with the consequences—and try to change. Try to become the kind of parent whose daughter won't hesitate when asked again, one day, what she loved about her mother.

She sits for a long time, mulling it over, wondering if she has what it takes.

Then, with a trembling hand, she reaches for the phone and dials.

"Cedar Crest police."

She hesitates.

Then, closing her eyes and focusing on Ashley's face, she says clearly, "My name is Fiona Fitzgerald."

* * *

"Happy Birthday, dear Bry-ynn . . ."

Never before did Brynn realize how inherently mournful the melody is. Especially the way he's singing it, a cappella, his voice low and eerily close to her ear as he stands behind her chair.

She can see his reflection in the kitchen window across the room; can see the silver glint of the knife he's holding poised at his side.

As soon as he's done singing, he's going to use it.

Garth will walk into this house and see what she saw when she walked into Fiona's. He'll be a widower, her boys will be motherless, her unborn child will be buried with her.

No!

Rage boils up inside of Brynn.

"Happy Birthday to—"

She jerks to her feet without warning, slamming her head up and back with all her might.

Her skull makes painful contact and she hears a grunt behind her as Pat, caught off guard, falls backward.

The knife drops from his hand and she lunges for it.

But he's faster than she is, it's closer to him.

His hand is already closing around the handle; it's too late for her to grab it. Her only chance to save herself now is to run.

She scoots forward, crawling under the table, kicking a chair into his path as she gets to her feet. But he's right behind her, leaping on her with a snarl, dragging her back. He has a brawny arm around her shoulders now, his other hand yanking her hair hard so that her throat arches back.

There's no escape now.

She sees the metallic flash as he wields his weapon overhead, then swoops it toward her helplessly arching neck.

She's going to die.

She's going to leave Garth, and . . .

Oh, dear God, my babies, is her last despondent thought . . .

Before the blast of gunfire erupts out of nowhere.

*   *   *

I'm not so sure she's even what you're looking for.

Kylah's words haunt Isaac as he walks slowly uptown toward the oddly empty apartment he thought would feel like home if Rachel ever walked through the door.

That's never going to happen.

Rachel is gone.

Whether she's dead or has run away; whether she had his baby or was ever expecting it in the first place . . .

She's gone.

Isaac stops at the wide crosstown intersection at Fourteenth Street, staring at the red DON'T WALK sign on the opposite curb.

Rachel is never coming back, not the way she was.

She isn't going to stroll back into his life someday and complete it.

No, that—making it complete—is up to him.

So maybe, he thinks, looking over his shoulder, it's time to let go.

Maybe . . .

The light has changed; a white WALK signal beckons.

Isaac hesitates.

Then he turns and retraces his steps, all the way back to Kylah's.

Pacing the porch of the cabin, Quincy watches flashbulbs popping like grounded lightning bolts amid the trees beyond the length of yellow crime scene tape. He pauses to sip from a bottle of cold water one of the investigators handed him, as another set of tires crunch along the gravel lane.

Probably the medical examiner's car, he thinks, and idly turns his head to see if he's right.

Wrong.

Wrong again, he thinks bitterly. *Your gut instinct is on one hell of a roll, Hiles.*

It's another squad car; the place is swarming with them.

Then he sees Deb Jackson waving at him from the passenger's seat of this one. She's out of the car before it stops.

Quincy holds his breath, bracing himself for bad news.

"She's alive," Deb calls.

He sags against the porch rail.

Brynn. Brynn is alive.

Thank God.

Thank *God*.

He lets out a deep breath he didn't even realize he'd been holding.

"What happened?" he asks Deb when she's reached his side.

"The cops found the Jeep you described in the driveway at the Saddlers' house and ran the plate. They traced it to Patrick Hagan—"

"Fiona Fitzgerald's ex?"

Deb nods vigorously. "She had just called to report that he—"

"Wait, who called?" Quincy asks, confused.

"Fiona. Long story short, she's alive."

"Jesus. 'Long story short'?" He snorts. "Are you kidding me? What happened?"

"Do you really want me to get into the details now?" At his look, she elaborates, "Her twin was the one who was killed—she had shown up at Fitzgerald's place to surprise her for their birthday and Hagan mistook her for her sister."

Quincy's mind is racing. "So it was Hagan? We never even looked his way."

"Why would we? Classic psychopath, from what I can tell. The guy oozed charm—and he manipulated the hell out of everyone who crossed his path."

"So Fiona Fitzgerald is alive?" Quincy reiterates, stuck on that. "You're sure?"

"Positive. And so is Brynn. Our guys surrounded the house, got up to the back deck of her house, saw what was going on, and shot Hagan through the kitchen window. He's in critical, but they think he'll pull through so we'll at least get some answers."

Quincy nods, for now, his concern on the real victim here. "So Brynn is fine, then?"

Deb hesitates.

His stomach turns over. "You don't look so sure."

"Hagan didn't hurt her, but . . . Quincy, she was pregnant."

"Was?" He curses under his breath. Had he known about that—

"They took her to the hospital," Deb tells him. "I think she's in trouble."

"Brynn . . . Are you awake?"

No.

She's asleep.

And she wants to stay that way. It can't be morning yet. She's so exhausted . . .

"Brynn, come on, wake up."

She opens her eyes reluctantly and sees Garth. "Just a few more—"

Wait a minute.

She isn't at home in bed, and it isn't morning, it's—

Fragments flash back into her mind: the cabin, Pat, the knife, the *knife* . . .

"The baby!" she wails, trying to sit up, realizing she's in a hospital bed, hooked up to an IV. A blinding pain in her head stops her and she sinks back against the pillow with an anguished sob.

"It's okay," Garth leans in to stroke her cheek with the back of his hand. "You were spotting, the doctor said, probably from stress—but you're still pregnant."

Still pregnant.

Garth knows.

He knows, and . . .

He's smiling at her.

"Are you sure the baby is—"

"They did a sonogram. You were probably too out of it from the concussion to remember, but they got a strong heartbeat. The baby is fine. And you will be, too. *We* will be fine."

She realizes what he means and, in a flood of relief, that he's right.

"It was an accident, Garth. The baby. I swear I didn't—"

"I know."

"You do?"

"It doesn't matter how it happened." He shrugs. "I had no idea how much I wanted this baby until I found out it might not make it. I've never prayed so hard in my life."

"How did you find out?"

He hesitates. "The police told me. I called from the Cape to make sure you were still okay up at that cabin, and they told me what had happened, and that you had been taken to the hospital."

"Garth, it wasn't Rachel," she says, needing him to know. "It was—"

"Hagan. Shh, I know. Don't even think about him right now. It's over."

She closes her eyes, trying to shut out the image of Pat's menacing face.

No, think of something else. Something pleasant.

"What about the boys?" she asks, smiling faintly. "How are they?"

"They're fine. They're with your father and Sue, probably eating junk and playing Candyland."

Brynn manages a weary smile. "That's good. I have so much to tell you, Garth."

"I have some things to tell you, too. But there'll be plenty of time for talking later. And for visitors, too. There's someone waiting to see you."

Yes, she thinks, closing her eyes contentedly.

There will be plenty of time for everything.

After all that worrying about how he was going to react . . .

He's still here.

And he wants this baby as much as she does.

Brynn drifts off into a pleasant dream in which Fiona is alive again, holding her hand and telling her that everything's going to be okay from now on.

EPILOGUE

"Happy Birthday to you . . . Happy Birthday to you . . . Happy Birthday, dear Brynn . . . Happy Birthday to you."

The song ends with a chorus of cheers, and Jeremy urging, "Make a wish before you blow them out, Mommy!"

Brynn nods, looking at the concentric circles of flickering candles on the bakery cake. There are thirty-two. One for every year of her life, plus an extra for luck.

Luck.

She's had more than her share of that in her life.

More than her share of wishes come true, as well.

But there's always room for another.

She closes her eyes and makes one.

Then she opens her eyes and blows out the candles with as much breath as she can muster.

Standing on either side of her, Jeremy and Caleb puff their cheeks and exhale noisily.

"We got them all, Mom!" Caleb announces. "Your wish is going to come true!"

"Say cheese, guys," Sue calls from the opposite side of the table where she's standing beside Brynn's father, aiming a camera at them.

Brynn pulls her sons close and smiles as her stepmother clicks and the bulb flashes.

"One more. Garth, get in there with Marie."

Brynn turns to see her husband stepping in with their five-month-old daughter proudly held in the crook of his arm.

Little Marie looks strikingly like her daddy. People say that all the time. But Brynn knows he would dote on her regardless of that. By the time she was born last May, you would think the whole pregnancy had been his idea. It seems so very long ago that Brynn worried he might leave her over it. Long ago, and ludicrous.

We've come a long way since then, she thinks, watching Sue take aim through the camera lens. *All of us.*

This milestone year taught Brynn how to let go. How to move on. And, most importantly, how to forgive—not just Garth, but Sue. And Fee. Even Tildy.

But not Patrick Hagan.

Perhaps she can forgive him for what he did to her, but not for the lives he took.

Ashley's might have been destroyed completely, if not for the twist of fate that saved her mother.

That weekend, Fiona had been picked up by Sharon and whisked to the safety of her home near Albany, where she planned to lay low until it was safe to return.

Tragically, her sister Deirdre, getting over the breakup with her girlfriend, had come to surprise her for their birthday and let herself into the house.

It was she, and not Fee, who was killed that night. Brynn realized it at the funeral when she saw Fiona trying to mask her left-handedness and when her hair fell back into its natural part on the right.

Fiona was understandably stunned when she heard the news of her own death—and devastated that her beloved sister had died in her place.

"I had to pretend I was Deirdre," she told Brynn tearfully

when they were reunited at the hospital. "I had no choice; it was the only way I could stay alive for Ashley."

Ashley.

Brynn turns her head and spots her, absently toying with a paper cup filled with Pepsi.

Fiona's daughter has suffered through this past year of loss, but the child psychiatrist she's been seeing believes she'll come through it relatively intact. It's just going to take a lot of time to work through the euphoria of having her mother seemingly come back to life, the grief for her lost aunt—and a whole gamut of emotion for her father.

There was never any question that Pat loved his daughter. But that love was tainted by festering fury over what might have been. He even jeopardized Ashley's safety to carry out his plans. He confessed to drugging her with a stolen prescription sedative before bed on the night he intended to murder her mother, and waking her on the pretext of taking her on a sunrise hike. He got her to take more of the tranquilizer by lacing a beverage can that supposedly contained Red Bull. Chillingly, she was unconscious in the Jeep, parked in an empty lot around the corner from her own home while her father was inside attacking Deirdre Fitzgerald.

In Pat's twisted mind, it was justified.

Everything about his life had been a failure: his law career, his marriage, his finances. The only redeeming thing he had was Ashley. But as time went on and he reflected on the past, he came to believe that he should have had three children, not one. That he had been cheated.

When he stumbled across the evidence that his ex-wife had terminated a second pregnancy, it was too much for him. He descended into a private world of hatred and delusion, consumed by the need to punish not just Fiona, but the other three girls who had been there the night pregnant Rachel fell to her death.

Poor Rachel.

When Brynn was finally able to piece it all together with Isaac, she learned that in the summer before Rachel's death, her troubled friend had been involved not just with Pat, but with her stepbrother as well.

Isaac said she had suffered terrible guilt over their clandestine relationship. They weren't blood siblings, but in Rachel's mind, he was her brother, and it was wrong.

"I never felt that way, though," he confessed. "I was crazy in love with her. To me, it felt right."

Finding out she was pregnant by either him or Pat was too much for Rachel to bear. She must have been drinking so much in an effort to numb her pain that night, or perhaps she was hoping to miscarry the baby.

Some questions will never be answered.

Others have been, thanks to forensics.

Pat led the authorities to the spot where he buried Rachel that terrible night, deep in the forest above Cedar Crest. From what was left of her determined that she had died when she fell from the rock, and she was, indeed, pregnant . . . with Isaac's child.

Her stepbrother took that news perhaps a little harder than he took the confirmation of her death. He told Brynn that in his heart, he had already come to realize she was gone. Still, it was upsetting to learn that he hadn't just lost Rachel, but his child as well.

"I'll learn to live with that, too, though," he said optimistically, and Brynn agreed.

You can learn to live with just about anything.

Isaac sent Brynn a birthday card yesterday. It was postmarked in Hawaii, where he's vacationing with his girlfriend, Kylah.

I know this might be a tough birthday for you, he wrote, *but stay strong and count your blessings.*

Quincy Hiles sent a card, too. His came from Florida, where he lives now. A man of few words, he merely signed his name. But Brynn was touched nonetheless by the gesture.

She still speaks to the retired detective from time to time. He likes to call and check in with her and Fiona, grateful that they, at least, escaped with their lives.

Unlike Deirdre.

Tildy.

And Cassie.

She was discovered, dead, somewhere up in Maine. Brynn didn't ask for details, but she assumes Pat staged a birthday party scenario for her as well, because Quincy did mention that he left behind a wrapped gift box.

In it was Rachel's driver's license, which he had pulled from her pocket the night she died. He had left Fiona a lock of Rachel's hair, and Tildy a piece of the sorority sweater Rachel had been wearing.

In the gift box he intended for Brynn was a silver sorority bracelet that bore the initials *R.L.*

Rachel's bracelet.

Fee said Ashley had told her she had seen it in Pat's apartment. She thought it must be a Ralph Lauren bracelet because of the initials, but Fee immediately knew what they meant.

It wasn't easy for Fiona to accept the horrific truth about her ex-husband. But her quick thinking saved Brynn's life.

"And you saved mine," she says, often—to Ashley.

She's speaking figuratively, of course.

Ashley's candid conversation with her mother—whom she believed was her Aunt Dee—was Fiona's sobering wake-up call.

She, more than anyone, has changed in this past year. She quit smoking. She moved to a smaller house in Brynn's neighborhood. She's hired two PR associates to help with the workload, and Sharon came back to work for her, saying Fee needs her more than her daughter does.

Landing new clients—or a rich new husband like James Bingham—is no longer the focus of Fiona's life.

Ashley is.

Fee isn't the perfect mom, but she's trying. She takes Ashley to the mall and the movies, and they even went on a mother-daughter Girl Scout campout with Ashley's friend Meg and her mom, Cynthia.

"I didn't think I'd like her," Fee told Brynn. "Especially after I found out that she was involved with Pat. But she's a victim, like everyone else was."

It turns out Pat convinced an unwitting Cynthia to take Ashley off his hands the weekend he killed Tildy—and then he pretended, to Fiona, to be angry about it.

"He had us all fooled," Fee said. "Even me. I knew he was a sick, twisted bastard, but I never realized to what extent."

How could any of them have suspected a monster lurked behind the affable, familiar face that was part of their everyday lives?

Brynn believed for a long time that she would never trust anyone ever again.

But she was wrong.

Feeling a hand on her shoulder, she turns to see Garth.

"Somebody's hungry," he says, tilting their fussing daughter into her mother's instantly outstretched arms.

Nuzzling Marie's soft black baby hair against her cheek, Brynn croons, "It's all right, little one. I'll feed you now."

"I'll dish out the cake, then," Fiona offers as Ashley and the boys pull out the extinguished candles and lick the frosting from their wax tips. "Do you have dishes?"

"Right there." Brynn indicates the stack of paper party plates beside the cake.

Fiona glances at the plates. Then her gaze meets Brynn's.

I know what she's thinking, because I'm thinking the same thing.

Brynn shakes her head slightly.

No, Fee. We can't let every birthday party remind us of what he did to your sister, to our friends.

We have to let go. Move on. Try to forget, if not forgive.

Fee smiles sadly at her, then nods, picking up the plates. "Who wants cake?"

Sitting in a quiet corner, Brynn nurses her baby daughter, contentedly watching as the others gather around the table to devour their cake and ice cream.

Stay strong and count your blessings.

Isaac's advice was sound, and well heeded.

"If she's done eating, I'll take her now."

Brynn looks up to see Garth standing over her as she finishes burping the baby on her shoulder.

"Oh, it's okay," she says. "I like to hold her."

"But if you're holding her, you can't open this." He extends a wrapped gift.

Her heart skips a beat.

No. Don't think about that, she warns herself again. *Let go.*

Pushing Pat, and his horrible gift-wrapped calling cards, from her mind, Brynn exchanges little Marie for the package in her husband's hands.

Hers tremble as she rips away the paper.

She finds herself holding . . .

"A book?" she asks, turning it over. "What is it?"

The title is *Dead and Buried: American Postmortem Rituals*.

Puzzled, she looks at Garth. He gestures at the book again. She looks down, wondering if she missed something.

Is he somehow trying to help her get over what happened to—

Oh! All at once, she sees the author's name emblazoned on the hardcover.

"Garth Saddler," she reads, and looks up in astonishment. "Oh, my God!"

He grins, then nods, looking quite pleased with himself.

"It's your book! You sold it?"

"I sold it. Not for a fortune . . . But it will be enough to keep Marie in diapers and the boys in peanut butter sandwiches for awhile." He smiles and pulls her close with the arm that isn't holding the baby. "And my publisher wants a proposal for another one."

"But . . . When did all this happen?"

"I sent it out to a couple of publishers last fall, right before your birthday. Before . . . everything. I wanted it to be a surprise."

"And it sold. How did you manage to keep this a secret?"

"It wasn't easy. But I figured you wouldn't mind if I kept this one, just until your birthday. I thought it would be the perfect present for the girl who has everything."

She laughs. "It is. I'm so happy for you, Garth. This is your dream."

"No," he kisses the top of her head, and gestures at the baby snuggled in his arms and the room filled with family and friends, "*this* is my dream."

"Mine, too."

Yes, thinks the girl who has everything, *sometimes dreams—and birthday wishes—really do come true.*

Thrilling Suspense from
Wendy Corsi Staub

__**All the Way Home**   0-7860-1092-4 $6.99US/$8.99CAN

__**The Last to Know**   0-7860-1196-3 $6.99US/$8.99CAN

__**Fade to Black**   0-7860-1488-1 $6.99US/$9.99CAN

__**In the Blink of an Eye**   0-7860-1423-7 $6.99US/$9.99CAN

__**She Loves Me Not**   0-7860-1768-6 $4.99US/$6.99CAN

__**Dearly Beloved**   0-7860-1489-X $6.99US/$9.99CAN

__**Kiss Her Goodbye**   0-7860-1641-8 $6.99US/$9.99CAN

__**Lullaby and Goodnight**   0-7860-1642-6 $6.99US/$9.99CAN

__**The Final Victim**   0-8217-7971-0 $6.99US/$9.99CAN

Available Wherever Books Are Sold!

Visit our website at **www.kensingtonbooks.com**

More Thrilling Suspense From
Your Favorite Thriller Authors